The End

The End

ISBN: 978-1-7384158-0-9

vannerpress@mail.com

The Vanner Press
'...because we are all travellers...'

Dandelion, dandelion, please tell to me,

Who is my lover, and what will he be?

'He will ride a fine horse and be gentle of face,

He will bow when you meet, he will kiss you with grace.'

Will he carry me far from the pastures and fields?

From dark frosty mornings and rough spinning wheels?

'You will cross the great sea where the hungry gulls cry,

To the land that lies under the end of the sky.'

ENGLAND

'Oh come all you tradesmen who travel along,
I'm asking you now where the work has all gone,
Long time I've been travelling and I cannot find none.
(Traditional)

1.
Uckington, Gloucestershire
Tuesday, January 17th, 1860

My sister is going to die today; don't ask me how I know, I just do.

Even the sun seems like it's about to cry, as if it's picking itself up after a fall, rising slowly with grazed and gritty hands and bloody knees; clambering above the edge of the world and bleeding orange all over this crunchy white grass - but it ain't going to melt it.

The sun don't want to be here this time of year according to Mother, so it just comes up a little bit, not much higher than Mary Magdalene's tower, then it turns from blush to jaundice for a few short hours before hurrying off to where it's still young; Africa or India, toasting the natives and filling the skies with brightly coloured birds and the scents of flowers with long clever names.

But today it looks specially sad.

We have known Mary Ann was going to die since before Christmas. She don't speak and is very thin. She's nearly seventeen but lighter than me and I'm only ten and three quarters.

3

Mary Ann had a baby called James who is one and a half now and living with Uncle Michael because there is no room for him in our cottage and Mary Ann can't look after him with no fat on her bones, let alone milk in her breasts.

Father spent an hour last evening burning most of a candle to mend this bucket but there's still a little dribble of milk seeping through the join in the wood just below the iron band; it ain't dribbling as quickly as it was but it still means no dawdling on the way back from Gorse Farm.

Do you know that cold can burn you? It sounds daft, but it can. It can burn you and make your skin go red and make your fingers drop off and it hurts to breathe and your lips go numb and you're afraid to wipe the snot off your nose in case you wipe your nose right off too!

Grandfather William said that happened to a man from Coombe Hill, right off in his hand his nose came - and it was all black... like Joseph Rudd's big toe probably. His wife cut that off with a red-hot bill hook to stop his foot going manky and she got the one next to it too which wasn't manky at all. That must have hurt mind you - wonder what they did with it? Burnt it or buried it most like. I don't s'pose a toe is worth a funeral.

The milk in the bucket might be steaming now but it's cooling fast. Not as fast as me; my feet feel like they are turning into solid lumps of ice even though they are wrapped in wool to pad out the difference between their size and the size of my boots. I got these off Emily, there's a fair bit of wear in them.

Emily can afford new boots now she is employed. She works for Mr Turze the undertaker cleaning the stables and helping the groom. She gets five shillings and sixpence a week - six shillings if she works on a Sunday morning which Father says is very fair and generous for a young woman of sixteen. Old Mr Turze is kind to her too. He gave her a Welsh wool shawl on New Year's Day and an extra two shillings.

He never so much as lays a finger on any of his staff and when his best horse was ill, he stayed up all night with it, talking to it and stroking it. Mother says anyone who treats animals cruelly insults Jesus and cannot be a good person. Father kills sheep sometimes if they are sick or lame but that's to put them out of their misery and he's always sorry, not only because it causes the Agent to be angry but because he really feels for them.

We don't like the Agent, but he speaks for the Master and we live in the Master's property and it's the Master who puts the food on our table in exchange for Father's shepherding. Mother has said there was to be no mention of the Agent in our home, so sometimes when Emily and I are out on an errand we'll make sure nobody can hear us and we'll shout, 'Albert Porritt is a bloody fat fox turd!' Or 'The Agent is an ugly red-faced pig.'

We got into trouble when my younger sister Esther was with us; we were shouting off as we went down Lowdilow Lane and when we got home Esther said, 'The Agent can go to Hell and bugger him all the way there!' Lucky it was Father who heard her, and he sat us all down and gave us a talking to.

Mother would have given us the ladle - and no supper, she was out feeding the chickens though. She usually hears things before Father as she has weak eyes, so the ears must make up for it. She can't make us out one from another sometimes, she waits for us to speak afore calling us by name.

We live in a cottage, The Shepherd's Cottage, sometimes called Old Gorse Barn or The Bullingham's Cottage - that's us, The Bullinghams.

There is another Bullingham's cottage, called Ivy Cottage, up on Tewkesbury Road, just this side of the churn table where that little boy got snatched by tinkers, that's where my Uncle Michael lives with Auntie Mary and my cousins, Eliza, Harriet and Richard.

Our cottage is on the road to Elmstone Hardwicke in the corner of Monk's Field which don't flood much. It is a nice cottage with a big room on the ground level and a little room leading off it with an open range which is where the cooking and the laundry gets done. Part of the big room is curtained off and that's where Mother and Father sleep with my brothers William who's five and Walter who's three - although Walter cries a lot with colic at the moment so it's a wonder any of them get any sleep.

Up the ladder is the top room and that's where I sleep with Emily, Esther and Mary Ann who is going to die today. I am not going to cry but I think Esther will. She has a tender soul according to Grandfather William who once saw a priest cut in half by chain shot in Spain and the legs kept on running.

The kitchen-laundry room is where Grandfather William sleeps. Father's Father has been living with us since last year when Granny Sabina died. She was beautiful, and he loved her ever such a lot. He tells us he is a hundred and thirty-six, but Father says he is eighty-one. When Grandfather William was young, he fought against Napoleon; he has a medal in a small tin along with the musket ball that killed his father-in-law's donkey. His hands look as though they are made from leather, but his eyes and ears are still good. He has a white beard - Father's beard is still mostly black but there are white bits around his ears.

This latch on the gate between Gorse Field and Monk's Field is always stiff and it takes both hands to lift it over the gate post. I've got to wrap my hands in the corner of my shawl to do this today as everything is covered in thick frost. It takes a high leg and a kick or two to loosen it but eventually it flicks over, and the gate creaks open for me to pass through into a ploughed field where my ankles turn this way and that over the rutted hard-frozen mud.

Mother was laying a fire afore dawn and there is smoke coming from the chimney now. I'm going to put the bucket down a minute if I can find a flat bit and blow on my hands one last time. Hark at them big black crows croaking; they're in that line of skeleton trees behind the cottage where the sun's catching them. The smoke from our chimney is going straight up so probably no snow today; that's good news for Father.

In we go, followed as usual by a troupe of chickens, and we'll put the bucket down in the stone porch.

'MILK!' (It hurts my throat to shout like that in the cold).

Who's in and who's out? Father has already left for the fields with his dogs, Jones and Evans; Emily has left for her three-mile walk to work (I think she should take up Mr Turze's offer of a room over the stable although we would miss her of an evening) Esther is rubbing sleep from her eyes, wrapped in her blanket, she don't want to leave wherever it is her dreams has taken her and return to this frozen world of school and chores. The two boys are still in the Land of Nod. Grandfather William is using the privy in the back garden, singing quietly as he does so.

'Ellen?'

Here's Mother, climbing down the ladder from where she has been checking on Mary Ann. Mother is older than Father by about five years, but it seems more than that with her grey hair swept back in a hastily tied bun. She is small, like me and squints a lot, trying to focus her weak eyes to see a little more of the world than God meant her to. There are eyeglasses of course but we can't afford them - and anyway Mother has said she wouldn't wear them even if we could as they would make her look old and infirm. Father told her he would love her no matter what she looked like.

A pan of milk is soon on the stove, heating up for porridge. Mother is hovering over Esther, clothes draped over an arm, hurrying her up to get dressed for school.

And here's Grandfather William, blowing on his hands and shivering.

'Be that porridge a 'coming Sarah my lovely?'

I love his voice, it's deep and rumbly and tumbly - like I reckon God would sound if he could speak for himself.

Mother peers closely into the pan, pouring oatmeal into the simmering milk and stirring.

'It'll be done when it's done, sit yourself down - Ellen, have you got your writing book?'

'Yes Mother.'

The End of the Sky

You can still see the price in the front of my writing book, three ha'pence. What you can't see in here though is yesterday's exercise which I was supposed to have done as homework. Instead, we sang the evening away, me and my sisters and Grandfather William - and now there were going to be questions to answer from Mrs Brooke.

We had been entertaining father as he mended the bucket while Mother was spinning to knit a new shawl for Esther. We sang the wassail we had been taught for Christmas just gone, then 'Little Sir Hugh' and then Grandfather William's favourite, 'Whatever You Do To My Old Ewe, I'll Do the Same To Ee!' which even made Mother laugh when he joined in, pulling faces as he sang.

School is good. There's them that says, 'What's the point of learning about things you ain't never going to see?' But I love learning - especially geography and different countries; reading and writing too, I'm second best in class just behind Robin Berry but he gets extra help because his father is a bookkeeper and sits down in a warm office all day so when he comes home, he ain't too tired to read to Robin and his sister.

Robin is twelve and thinks he is handsome, but he is not. His ears stick out too much and his one eye is browner than the other and when he smiles, he looks like the chimpanzee in Mrs Brooke's book about African animals. He smiles at me in school and in church sometimes and when he does, I stick my tongue out at him. Esther says we are in love really, but that is most definitely not true!

Even with a belly-full of porridge I ain't no warmer. I am trying to think of excuses to tell Mrs Brooke but all the way to school Esther is at my side yabbering away without stopping for breath!

'I hope it's not history, I don't care for history and I think kings and queens are stupid... Amos says he drinks cider at home. There's a crack in my slate, I'm going to see if I can change with Joan Greenlea, Mrs Brooke likes her, so she will give her a new slate...'

For a few seconds there is silence, just the sound of our footsteps, the occasional rough 'Caw' from the trees on the side of the lane and the bleating of distant sheep somewhere across the fields behind the approaching village. Esther has put her shawl over her head and is sniffing. She is going to go down with a chill which no doubt she will pass to the boys and everyone else. She frowns.

'Do you think Mary Ann will be alive when we get home?'

I don't, but I say, 'That's not something for you to be worrying yourself about; what will be, will be.'

'Do you think God is punishing her because she had a baby without a father?'

There is a bonfire burning in the churchyard and just around the corner is the house of Mrs Brooke with our schoolroom in it.

My voice sounds tired like mother's does sometimes, 'You can't have a baby without a father - you can have one without a husband but she's not being punished, she's just poorly. Anyway, Grandfather William says even if everybody stopped sinning today, God would still take a century to catch up.'

10

Robin Berry and his sister Charlotte are waiting in the schoolhouse doorway. He smiles at me and winks as we pass by, (I told you about those ears, didn't I? You can see the light through them!) I just ignore him, but Esther manages to say, 'He really likes you,' loud enough for him to hear.

As we file in and sit - sixteen of us this morning out of eighteen - there comes a stroke of luck. It is not Mrs Brooke who enters from the house but her daughter Ruth.

School costs a penny per week per pupil but Esther and I do not have to pay, likewise Amos Carpenter or the Ludmore children, (two boys and their little sister, Laura who was born with only one hand). Mrs Brooke's husband, Major Brooke, set aside a sum of money for educating the poor; he is a good man. He is in India serving in Queen Victoria's army. Mrs Brooke went out there with him but had to come home as she could not suffer the climate (it is terribly hot). Grandfather William says it is so hot in Spain that if you go out without your head covered your hair will catch fire! I'm not sure I could live anywhere as hot as that, but on winter days like these, summer is a pleasant memory.

'.... and that left Cesare Borgia free to follow the career he had always dreamed of - Ellen Bullingham will now tell us what that career was...'

That's buggered it! The sound of my name brings me back into a world where I appear to be the centre of attention. I had been watching the man in the graveyard, he was piling more frost-covered branches on to his fire

11

and pressing them closer to the flames with a gaitered boot, sending sparks swirling into the cold air.

Now Robin Berry's odd-coloured eyes are twinkling at me as he sits sideways in his chair looking over his shoulder and Miss Ruth stands expectantly at the head of the class, arms folded, a pretty brooch at her throat, her blouse mustard-coloured and a fold-over grey skirt fastened at her tiny waist.

She is small like Mother, blue eyes and chestnut hair all done up in a bun.

Small she may be but she's filling the world now and I don't know who on earth Chays... Barger...is.

She raises one eyebrow in expectation and taps a foot on the flagstone floor, watching as my mouth opened and closed silently like a trout; I must have frowned, Robin Berry turns back to the front and raises a hand.

To my relief Miss Ruth turns her attention to him; he lowers his hand and gives an account of the cardinal and son of a pope who became a soldier. Behind Miss Ruth a coal fire is glowing in the grate; the classroom is warm and more than one of us is getting heavy eyelids as the day wears on.

School is supposed to last until two o' clock but Miss Ruth lets us all out at just after one. It is no surprise to see Robin Berry waiting in the porch as Esther and I pass through into the pale afternoon sunshine. Despite the frostiness of morning there is a gentle hint of warmth now, but it won't last. As soon as that sun dips below the hedges the fearsome winter cold will be back to turn the world hard and white again.

'I reckon I saved your bacon in there, Miss Bullingham,' (If I should ever meet a real-life chimpanzee, I shall call it Robin and I'll bet it will answer). He gets a glance in reply quite in keeping with the season as we pass silently by. He calls to my back.

'I was trying to help - I did it because I like you.'

I try to walk on, but Esther stands square in front of me, glee-faced, preventing my escape. I turn; Robin is smiling now as opposed to grinning. I manage a curt reply.

'Well, thank you I'm sure.'

'That's alright,' he saunters down the path towards us. 'Truth is, you're better than me at writing and spelling and reading, but I've probably got a better memory for people and dates and that sort of thing. Umm.... that's a nice shawl.'

It's not really a nice shawl, it was Emily's old shawl which she had given to me after Mr Turze's New Year gift, it's a bit threadbare and the colours have faded. Mother said she would help me make a new one as soon as she had finished Esther's, whose shawl was even more tired than mine.

'Charlotte is walking home with Emma Swindon; may I walk up the lane with you as far as Chestnut Corner?'

'Of course, you may,' Esther answers in a silly 'lords and ladies' voice and receives a frosty glance from me for her trouble.

'Well, it's a free country, I'm sure,' I stare into the middle distance to underline my disinterest and my eyes are caught by the still-smouldering fire in the churchyard where a few magpies and blackbirds were enjoying an unexpected feed on tiny creatures awakened too soon by the warming of the soil. I quickened my pace; Robin keeps up, smiling as if he is constipated.

'I see there are new tea rooms on the corner of Clarence Street and The Parade.'

'Really? How interesting.' I tried to sound as disinterested as possible.

'Rather fine pastries, so I'm told.' He spoke to the sky before gazing this way and that in the manner of a squire walking his estate.

'Is it true you've got a harpsichord in your house?' Esther rudely interrupts. Robin is now walking with his hands in his breeches pockets which Father always says is bad manners for a gentleman when in the presence of a lady. He takes one out to straighten his cap. Perhaps he suddenly realised how ungentlemanly he has been because he takes out his other hand and links them behind his back as we walk.

'Umm, not exactly, my uncle is an elder of St Mary's Church and they have the loan of a harpsichord, which belongs to Lady Whitley, while the organ is under repair. Charlotte is learning her scales on it; you are most welcome to come and try it out if Uncle permits.

We walk side by side along the lane with Esther a few paces behind smirking broadly every time I turn around to check on her. Robin stares ahead, then down at his feet as he walks in a measured gait.

Now he is telling me how, very soon, there will be a scientific way of predicting what the weather is going to be days ahead. Father and Grandfather can already do that, and they are rarely wrong. This new science method will probably be for townsfolk who know a lot but understand little.

The lane divides ahead. A large and ancient horse chestnut tree stands at the junction in the corner of Murder Meadow. Our lane lies to the right, travelling along the edge of the meadow and skirting Monk's Field, passing our cottage on its way to Hardwicke while Robin Berry's route takes him on the left path down Dog Bark Lane.

'Well then... thank you for your company,' he smiles an actor's smile which is a shame as his own is much better. I am getting used to his face now and you don't notice the ears so much after a while. He holds out a hand...

After a pause and a harsh prod in the back from Esther I take it, expecting a formal handshake but instead, before I can withdraw my hand, he bows and kisses it. Straightening, he doffs his cap, grins and strides off on his path home. Esther is hopping on the spot with excitement.

'You're blushing!' She is squealing like a startled piglet.

'I am most certainly not!' I spin away and walk too quickly, feeling my face turning into a plum as rising blood drives away the icy breath of January Jack.

Mary Ann died in the night. Esther was sent downstairs to sleep with the boys while Mother came up to dress my sister and prepare her for the undertaker. Mother never came up at night unless called, she must have known. Perhaps Mary Ann's spirit said goodbye to her before leaving as some are said to do.

Mother has gone back downstairs now to see to the awakening of the house and I still must fetch the milk, but first there is a moment to sit in the silence of this room we shared to watch my sister sleeping in peace.

It is surprising the sense of emptiness left behind when a spirit leaves - but there is more than one soul here. There is a mouse hole in the corner, you can't see it in the shadows but when the sun shines in the morning it shows the little gap between the dark stones. She is only a little mouse, but a tireless one, scurrying in and out searching for her next meal and praying to her mouse god to put something edible in her path. Like all of us, trying so hard to stay alive.

We are fortunate that our family has a relationship with Mr Turze the undertaker. Mary Ann will not go into a pauper's grave, unmarked and disrespected. Mr Turze will see she goes in a proper wooden box with a Christian burial. Probably Emily will work off the bill a little at a time out of her wages.

How still the dead are. Mother has dressed Mary Ann in a clean cotton nightdress and combed her lovely light-brown hair; she is laid on her back with her arms over the blanket; so still. I feel a single tear escape and creep down my cheek, squeezing my eyes shut causes a few more to dribble around my chin and drip off. I bite my hand to stifle sobs; the last thing Mother needs now is more distress.

Mary Ann's little pale oval dolly face almost has a smile on it... she always had such pretty eyes, blue like mine but closed now. I'm tempted to lift an eyelid to see if they still look blue and alive, but I shan't be disrespectful; her body belongs to the next world now.

When she was fit and well, she used to sing and hold my hands and swing me round and round and when she stopped, we would both be so dizzy, staggering about sending the chickens scurrying and trying not to fall over... and we would laugh.

She was going to marry the Prince of Wales and live in a house with deer in the grounds and ride in a carriage and all her daughters would go to the Ladies College and learn to talk like titled folk.

She is not suffering anymore; Father has gone to tell Uncle Michael who is caring for baby James with Auntie Mary; Emily has already set off for work because she has to speak to Mr Turze. I will say a prayer for Mary Ann now; it won't be a church prayer because they are all written for someone else and our vicar, The Rev Byron, sometimes reads them as if he is not really thinking about the words. Here is mine....

'Please God let Mary Ann into Heaven, she was kind and would have been a good mother...'

'ELLEN - MILK!'

Mother sounds tired as she calls up the ladder.

'COMING MOTHER! ...

'... We all loved Mary Ann, God - and I know you will too when you get to know her. She has suffered enough, Amen.'

2.
St George's Street, Cheltenham,
Monday, April 15th, 1861

I cried last night; burying my face in the bolster so no
one could hear me. I still feel like crying now, but
I'm not going to. There are eight people and two dogs
living in in our cottage and no matter how hard
everybody tries, there is not enough of anything - food,
space or money.

Emily works and contributes three shillings a week
to the household. Mother spins and knits, cooks and
cleans while Grandfather William tends our allotment of
land. Esther, William and Walter are still too young to
contribute but at twelve it is reasonable to expect me to
carry a share of the burden. Going out to
work like Emily does and returning each night would
have been the most desirable but such employment for
young ladies is rare.

Instead, I am sent be a servant at an inn in town and
live on the premises; Uncle Michael is on speaking terms
with the landlord, a Mr Wells. The pay is four shillings a
week but there is a shared room, and all my food will
be provided. The prospect is heart-breaking; no longer
attending Mrs Brooke's classroom with Esther and my

friends; no longer sharing the warmth of my family's presence in the evenings. The need for it is understandable, but it still seems so unfair.

Grandfather once warned me never to enter an inn if the sign had a bullet hole in it. The sign hanging outside The Noah's Ark Inn on St George's Street appeared to have no holes but was certainly in need of repainting. The chains holding it to the bracket were rusting; the words were still clear, but the picture was so faded as to be hardly visible at all. I think it was supposed to be an ark on a stormy sea.

It probably wasn't showing its best face under a sky that hung like a soaked grey woollen blanket dripping down chill and drizzle into the murk of a reluctant dawn; the narrow street and high buildings on either side further reduced what little light managed to struggle to the ground.

Across the way, a man older than Father but younger than Grandfather was shuffling, hands in pockets and head down, not bothering to step around the puddles but splashing through them; a tired coat was tied around his sparse waist with a length of rope and for want of a hat there was a headscarf knotted under his chin with most of the knot hidden inside a straggly grey beard. The woman following him was lame and struggling to keep pace, she called on him in a piping Irish voice to wait or slow down, but he seemed to be cosseted in his own world.

From a second-floor window next door to the Inn a head appeared, then disappeared before a cloth was shaken out, discarding fowl bones which fell in a scatter to the earth. A pair of fat black crows swooped noisily on to them and as I turned to knock on the Inn door, it swung open.

The woman standing in the doorway resembled a hawk in clothing; sharp and predatory, she looked down from the high step as if deciding whether I was edible. She had blue eyes and auburn hair pinned back in a bun and wore a crisp white smock over a blue dress with shoes designed for function rather than beauty. And she could raise one eyebrow in a way I have never succeeded in mastering.

From the interior drifted an odour that was to become unforgettable - the smell of an early morning inn - stale drink, tobacco smoke, smouldering embers from the fireplace and cooking range and the lingering scents of the patrons, of their places of work, the tannery, the killing floor of the slaughterhouse, stables, forges and woodworking shops. The woman studied me, expressionless. Feeling it was probably my place to break the silence I gave the slightest of curtsies.

'Good morning, my name is Ellen Bullingham.'

The Hawk Lady spun on her heels and called over a shoulder, 'This way.'

Pulling my new shawl tighter and picking up the bag containing the rest of my clothes and a few treasures, my books - and some bread and dripping in case they did not feed me on my first day - I walked into the gloom across floors sticky with spilt ale and cider. In the half-light I could make out tables, chairs and benches scattered this way and that; many covered with the spoil of the previous day's activities.

Covering one table was a set of scattered playing cards, a dagger-like knife and a hat so weather-beaten as to be barely recognisable as a headpiece; while at another, a small bunch of bluebells, wilting for want of water, lay discarded. She spoke over her shoulder.

'Wait here.'

We stopped before a door and the woman passed through. I did not want to put my bag down on the dirty floor so taking it in two hands I leaned back for balance. The door opened admitting a man who defied all my preconceptions of what an innkeeper should look like. Mrs Brookes had acquainted us with Charles Dickens' work in class and I was expecting a landlord much along the lines of a rough, cold-eyed cut-throat, cudgel in hand ready to beat his drunken customers into obedience. But Mr Thomas Wells was slight, neat and immaculately dressed.

He wore a Harris Tweed waistcoat, which matched his trousers, over a high-collared starched white shirt and necktie. His hair was parted in the middle and well-oiled, which however failed to tame the natural curliness. His moustache was neatly clipped and waxed, and he smelled of bathing soap. He would not have looked out of place in the offices of a bank or counting house. He smiled as he spoke which soothed a lot of the butterflies that had plagued me since setting out.

'Miss Bullingham? I'm Mr Wells, I am acquainted with your Uncle Michael and he tells me you're not afraid of a bit of hard work, is that correct?'

I curtsied, almost stumbling due to the weight of my bag, 'Yes Sir, thank you for considering me for employment Sir.'

'Yes... well Mrs Bolt will show you to your room, you can leave your... belongings in there and come straight back down and we'll find you something to do.'

The woman who had opened the door reappeared, unspeaking but with a beckon of her head she indicated me to follow her. We climbed stairs, many stairs, one flight... two... along a corridor of drably painted walls to a heavy door; she turned the knob and leaned her weight into the door, it opened with a creak. Inside was a bed covered in a plain and cheerless quilt, a small table and chair and a rough wooden wardrobe with one door missing. The room contained nothing else except a window that it seemed had not been cleaned since God's dog was a puppy. It overlooked the street, the grimy glass sandwiched between a pair of curtains of the same dark brown as the walls, the floor was a desert of bare wooden planks.

'This is your room,' She raised an eyebrow again as if inviting me to comment before continuing. 'The servant's room is actually in the basement, but it suffers from damp and so Mr Wells felt you would be more comfortable here.'

I curtsied again, 'Thank you, it's very nice, err... there is just one bed, I was told I was to share a room?'

Mrs Bolt frowned, 'Not my understanding, Mr Wells did not mention hiring another servant. There are others on this floor you will encounter, they are all paying lodgers. The chamber pot can be emptied at the far end of the corridor, the door is clearly marked 'Ablutions' - you can read I take it?'

'Oh yes, very well thank you.'

'Good, well then, yes, Ablutions - you can wash yourself in there too - but don't take too long, it is a shared facility.'

'I understand, thank you. Please tell me, how would you wish me to address you? And how should I address the Master?'

'You may call me Mrs Bolt, I am the cook here and the kitchen is my domain - and Mr Wells is your employer, not your master.' For the first time, she smiles and holds out a hand, I take it gently, returning her smile and we shake. She removes a hair pin, tightens her bun and replaces it,

'Mr Wells was a soldier in Crimea, and he says that after a man has been a soldier, he will look on no-one as his master. If you work hard, you'll find him a good employer - and a fair one. Tuck your things away and come back downstairs. I have breakfasts to prepare but Mr Wells will show you what is what.'

She left and I took my few clothes out of the bag and placed them in the wardrobe but somehow I couldn't bring myself to unpack my books, there were two, the Dickens volume from Mrs Brooke and The Three Musketeers by Dumas translated from French by William Barrow - a present from Robin Berry, it has a note written on the flyleaf, 'To Mademoiselle Ellen Bullingham with deep and sincere affection from your admirer, Robin Berry;' He had received a kiss on the cheek in return for his heartfelt kindness. It must have cost him a pretty penny, I was aware his family were better-off than mine, but it was still a generous gift and one which my dear Father could never have afforded to buy for me.

I told myself that as long as my books remain within my bag then I am not unpacked, and this is not my home. Strangely, it was the bag itself more than the books that stirred my homesickness. Father had made it out of a sack; it had carrying handles and a lace-up top. 'This will serve you well,' he had smiled, and I had felt loved and warmed by the closeness of family. My home, my beloved home, which lies along the Tewkesbury Road, out into the lanes, across fields hanging subdued under morning mists. It was where my heart remained. The milk would have been fetched by now and Mother would be hurrying Esther off to school. Grandfather would be... No! There was no time for this; duty called.

Going back down the staircases, I tied my hair back more securely in a ponytail, smoothed down my dress and over-apron and took a deep breath. The act of stepping out into the bar area, despite the gloom and the mess, was uplifting. There was the front door and through that, the road home. What would my family's reaction be to an unexpected return? Mr Wells appears from behind me.

'All settled in?'

'Yes Sir.'

'Good, splendid - well we open for business in two hours and so it's all loaders to the guns. Mrs Bolt will be cooking breakfast for the lodgers who will be eating it in the guest room. But now it's cleaning, beginning with these tables, then the floor. Come along, I'll show you where all you will need is to be found.'

I am accustomed to work, but not as much as I did on that first morning in the Noah's Ark. Tables to scrub, ale pots, plates, glasses and cups to be washed, dried and shelved ready for the next opening. The floor was mopped, dry-mopped then mopped again, the bar was polished, and I even cleaned the insides of the windows. Finally, I put the small bunch of rescued bluebells in a glass of water and placed them on the end of the bar closest to the window, so they would get some sunlight. As I did so Mr Wells appeared, looked around, beamed at me and said, 'Jolly well-done Ellen, yes, splendid.' And then he opened the doors....

I had, of course, helped Mother at mealtimes by laying the table and bringing out the food to the family as they took their places; but they were family, we knew each other and all our ways. Approaching a table of complete strangers whose manners and tempers are unknown is something that needs to be learned and at first can be frightening. Mr Wells could carry a tray of drinks in one hand and two meals in the other, swaying this way and that between patrons and furniture without spilling a drop. My journeys to and from the bar and kitchen out to the patrons were fraught with perils and were taken slowly and carefully.

It did not help that I was little higher than the belly button of most standing customers and if they did not look down to see me, I was going to get knocked over; so, it was up to me to do the dodging and avoiding and it's a quickly learned lesson that a smile and a light curtsey on delivery make up for slowness - or the shaking that sometimes results in spillage. I carried a cloth to quickly wipe away the results of my inexperience.

The daytime session passed without me buggering anything up too much and at three o' clock the doors were closed for clearing, washing up and preparing for the evening session. This also allowed me an hour's rest to eat and - most welcoming of all, to sit down. There was no need to resort to my bread and dripping as a delicious hot meal of stew was provided, but the food brought from home would be dispatched at bedtime so as not to waste it.

After eating it was back to my cleaning duties; the doors were pegged open allowing the draymen to roll in fresh barrels of ale and cider. I saw through the doors one of them delivering a nasty blow with his whip to the poor horse standing in the drizzle, just for taking a few steps forward. I dare not say anything, but I gave the man a scowl which could have frightened a Frenchie at a thousand yards. He paused to return my glare but must have thought I was not worth a cuff around the ear. Had he done so I would have maintained my scowl in a defiant silence.

There are those who believe animals are here merely to serve us and feed us and there are others who weigh the souls of beasts and find them as substantial as those of humans. Grandfather William once said, 'A horse is not a machine, it is a strong and strangely-shaped man or woman and deserves the same respect.' Mother would nestle a chicken in her lap, stroking it and murmuring softly as she tickled its comb. It never felt the twist and pull - and before it realised any better, it was flying on angel wings like the free bird of the air it had always dreamed of being, with Mother's soft voice still purring in its head.

The End of the Sky

Mrs Bolt lived just a few doors away from the Noah's Ark. She never seemed to be rushed even though she was rarely at rest. She would shout from the kitchen, 'Stew... Mr Webster!' then, remembering that the serving girl was new and had no idea who Mr Webster might be... 'Stew, yellow coat, black hair next to fireplace.' At the same time, I had to be attentive to Mr Wells or Edgar the barman calling from the bar, 'Drinks, party of four, just left of the window.'

I was kept so busy that it grew dark outside unnoticed and with it came the realisation that this was really where I was going to spend the night. I took a deep breath, promising to ponder on this and come to terms with it the next time a chance presents itself. Weaving through the forest of bodies I place a mug of cider on a patron's table as directed. I turn to depart, engrossed in my situation only to be pulled up short as a rough hand gripped my wrist like a spring trap. I was pulled backwards and another hand, belonging to the same assailant, gripped my neck. It hurt; leaving me confused and unsure of whether to attempt to tug myself free or call out to Mr Wells.

Granny Sabina used to say that every face is a book which tells the story of the journey of the soul behind it. 'Look into the eyes of a stranger...' she would tell us, '...and you may not learn who they are - but you will know what they are and where they have been.' To look into the eyes of the man holding my neck was to peer into a world where no flower had ever bloomed, or bird had sung. Eyes too light to be brown and too dark to be yellow, they were hypnotic, autumnal - and utterly still.

In a face accustomed to reflecting compassion, such as Father's or Grandfather's, such eyes may have been rare and beautiful, but in that face - sharp-edged, predatory and hostile, they were terrifying. I saw in that face not a single scrap of pity. Rev Byron often preached about 'Emissaries of Satan' and this appeared to be my first encounter with someone who, to my unworldly eyes, had arrived fresh from Hell. The voice at my side came as a tremendous relief.

'Good evening, Mr Drew, is everything well?'

The man slowly turned his baleful gaze on to Mr Wells who is smiling at my side. My neck was released but the firm grip on my arm remained.

'This careless little sowlet spills half my drink and goes to walk off without a by or leave!'

Mr Drew's hold on my wrist finally slackened allowing me to pull my arm free, I rubbed the area where the outline of his grip was still prominent. His gaze flashed back to me for a second, causing me to look away; a group of nearby customers turned briefly in our direction before snapping quickly back to safer matters.

'I'm afraid she is new; this is her first day - allow me to replace your drink with my compliments.'

Mr Drew picked up the pot, drained it and pushed it across the table toward Mr Wells, his eyes never once left my employer. Mr Wells gave the briefest of smiles and turned to me.

'Ellen, would you be so good as to fetch a fresh pot of cider for Mr Drew here - and please don't spill any.'

I curtsied and turned to walk off on my errand, but Mr Wells places a hand gently on my shoulder; '...and for his part, Mr Drew will I'm sure agree never to manhandle a member of my staff again, isn't that right, Mr Drew?'

Mr Drew's stare grew from menacing to murderous; he uncoiled himself from his seat and rose like a cobra about to strike. The briefest flicker of fear passed across Mr Wells' face, but he stood his ground. I was too paralysed with fright to move a fingertip. Mr Drew's voice was ice.

'If any other jubbin' innkeeper spoke to me like that I'd...'

Mr Wells interrupted; his voice as untroubled as a dawn millpond '... No other innkeeper is going to speak to you like that because you are barred from their premises. The Noah's Ark offers the only welcome in Cheltenham for you Mr Drew,' the landlord's smile never wavered.

Mr Drew grinned; and it was a grin completely without warmth or mirth which, if anything, made him appear even more evil. He closed the distance between himself and Mr Wells to almost nothing.

'You have seed what I have seed, you have bin where I have bin - and you knows what I can do,' he hissed. The bar room became a tomb, still and silent, tankards and cutlery hovered in mid-air.

'I have indeed shared many of your experiences, Mr Drew,' Mr Wells smiled calmly, '... and that's why there is such a warm welcome for you here in the Noah's Ark..' he turned to look down at me, '...Mr Drew's drink now Ellen if you please.' I left like an unleashed hare-hound, still shaking from the experience and wondering how, it would be possible in such a state to deliver an unspilt drink back to Mr Drew's table.

29

While the pot of cider was being poured by Edgar the barman - a dour and uncommunicative plump man of middle age with a warty nose and eyes that appeared permanently half-closed - I turned to see Mr Drew seated again and Mr Wells has crossed to another table to conversing with two younger gentlemen and a lady whom Mother would have referred to as wearing 'More paint than petticoats.'

I served Mr Drew without further incident, placing his drink unspilt and giving a slight curtsey before leaving. He sat, face down, elbows on the table staring at his hands, not acknowledging me at all, much to my relief. I returned to what was described as my waiting station, a spot equally distant between bar and kitchen door. Mr Wells approached me and gently took my elbow, guiding me into the quiet of the private corridor that led to the stairs and upper levels.

'Are you feeling well? Is your arm alright?' He appeared genuinely concerned.

'Yes Sir, thank you Sir, just a little startled is all.'

'Yes, well I'm sorry you had to endure that. I should have noticed who that drink was for and served him myself. You have just had the dubious pleasure of meeting John Drew - known to all in these parts as Adder - Adder Drew.' Mr Wells sat on the bottom stair and patted the space next to him, inviting me to sit; he took out a pipe and carefully worked a plug of tobacco into the bowl just as Grandfather William did on the occasions when we could afford it. Mr Wells lit his pipe with a friction match and continued; '...I served in Crimea you know, North Gloucestershire Regiment of Foot, although I got to ride much of the time as I was temporarily attached to a cavalry unit d'you see - terrible place, terrible.

'Anyway, they say war changes a man - I disagree with that, I say war brings out of a man what was already in there and paints it on a bigger canvas. When John Drew was a boy his father used to beat him black and blue, used to beat his mother as well. He had a little sister and when she was... about your age I suppose, her father took to... well... let me say that beating would probably have been better.

'It's said she threatened to go to the constable and her Father choked her. John witnessed this and his Father was set to kill him too, but the lad dodged the drunk and then pushed him down the stairs, killing him. His mother was in no fit state to care for John, so the boy was taken and put in the workhouse where he not only got as many beatings as he had taken from his father but... I'm afraid some of what his poor sister had endured as well.'

It dawned on me what Mr Wells was referring to. It was one thing to be courted by the gentlemanly Robin Berry, but even in the most innocent of liaisons there was always the realisation that the wooing and winning was a means to an end; as Mother said, 'It's only a short walk from hand-holding to haystacks.' However, there is a class of men to whom even this short walk is too much for their patience to endure. We sat, enveloped in the smoke from Mr Wells' pipe, a scent I have always found comforting; besides, my legs and feet were grateful for the rest. He continued.

'Now all this was still inside John Drew when he took Queen Victoria's shilling and in Crimea, he found a way to pay back the world for what it had dealt out. Most soldiers, if they have to kill at all, do so out of fear - kill or be killed - d'you see? But there are a few who do it out of hate and pleasure, John Drew was now one of these. Of course, as long as those he killed were enemies nobody in authority minded but it became clear that, to Infantryman Drew, it was the killing that mattered and the brutal ways in which he did it.

In the end even his own comrades - hardened soldiers who had seen it all - avoided him and he became an outcast. It is said that on the voyage home not a soul shared a single word with him, he stepped off that ship as alone as a man can be into a world he saw as a jungle and where he would always be an outsider. Now then...'

Mr Wells stood and I wearily did the same, feeling some sort of response to his story is in order and would not be considered too forward. 'Thank you for explaining to me Sir, My Grandmother used to say, "Hate and anger are the scars of wounds we cannot see, so we must not be quick to judge."

Mr Wells smiled, he looked tired too; 'Your Grandmother was clearly very wise. Now then, I think you have done enough for a first day, so you may retire if you so wish and if you pass the kitchen on the way, please give my compliments to Mrs Bolt and tell her you have come for your supper.'

It would be wrong of me to say my room was too warm because that would imply the fault lay in the surroundings. In fact, the room was just warmer than the bedroom at home. The window rattled in its frame as rain and wind battered it, but the heat of fires and ranges from the rooms below warmed the wood beneath my feet and made the air thick and close.

There was still the occasional shout and peal of laughter from the distant barroom and these blended with the shouts of passers-by and the hoof beats of the shod heavy workhorses. Supper had been mutton and potatoes, filling and most welcome. Tired... lonely... undress... nightclothes...

Mr Wells seemed a kind and courteous man, Uncle Michael and Father would never have entrusted me to anyone of dubious character. But there were others in this new world - as Grandfather William had warned there would be.

Climb into bed... blanket under chin... surprisingly comfortable...

Mr Wells did not permit unaccompanied ladies in the bar room, but there were a few ladies in there tonight who seemed to be accompanied by different gentlemen as the evening had worn on. There were loud and boisterous men who got louder with each drink; there were quiet groups of men who sat, heads together, as if conspiring some adventure or questionable undertaking. There were prosperous men who ate in one meal as much food as eight of us back home would have had and there were those with barely a penny, as thin as scythes, who nevertheless spent what they had on drink instead of food or footwear. And then there was Adder Drew.

A chill swept over me even though it was warmer that it ever was at home. The only other unpleasant man who came to mind from my life's encounters was Albert Porritt, the Master's agent and while he is rude and a bully he is not terrifyingly evil in the way that Adder Drew is.

Porritt is just interested in money as all his class are and as long as we pay our rent, he leaves us alone, but Adder Drew?

What would it take to make him leave someone alone? Probably nothing less than the satisfying of his appetite for cruelty! Following this train of thought could lead to nightmares, especially after a heavier than accustomed supper and so I close my eyes and ponder on the many delightful presents; pet monkeys, jewels and brightly coloured parrots, that Robin Berry will bring me back from his first African expedition.

Tomorrow I will feed my tired dripping sandwiches to the drayman's horse.

It was only an errand to collect bread, but it was a delight to get out of the Inn and into the air of an early Cheltenham morning. My journey took me on to High Street and up to the Arcade Market and Sandwell's Bakery. The walk carried me quite close to the premises of Mr Turze the Undertaker where Emily works but it is unlikely she would have arrived by this time of a morning; besides, it is certain Mr Wells knows precisely how long the bread collection should take.

Accompanied by a four-wheeled trolley with an iron handle and waterproof waxed-canvas cover attached in the event of rain, the trundle down St George's Street took no time at all. Yesterday's storms had cleared and the sun rose in a sky dotted here and there with white fluffy clouds making it look like a child's painting.

There was a queue at the bakery and in front of me a lad a year or two my senior held the handle of a trolley that appeared to be a larger version of mine.

'Morning,' he blinked and squinted, raising a hand to shield bright blue eyes from the rising sun behind us. He held out a hand (there seems to be a lot of hand-shaking in town) 'Richard Price - Carters Yard. Bread for the men's dinner you see; they pay me to make it and I do a heavenly stew - although of course self-praise is no recommendation.'

I took his hand, 'Ellen Bullingham - Noah's Ark Inn.'

'Ah, you'll be alright there,' he smiled, and we inched forward as another customer left the queue, 'Mrs Bolt's your cook isn't it? She does a damn good dinner and all; there'll soon be some meat on you mind.'

The boy had a Welsh accent, a version of which Father often used when talking to his border collies, Jones and Evans to make them feel at home. Accents are beautiful - except the ones the gentry use which make them sound like neighing mares.

Granny Sabina's accent (which still lives in my head) was warm, musical and exotic; Grandfather William's speech is full of old words that people twenty miles away would not know; it is an echo from a time before steam where only horses and the power of the wind carried men far from home - and the lucky ones back again.

Richard Price had reached the front of the queue and his trolley was being filled with warm loaves by an unsmiling and preoccupied man in a white apron and tall white floppy hat. With trolley full the boy turned and grinned; 'See you,' he winked and headed off with his cargo, allowing me to pull my trolley into the space he had vacated. White Hat Man gave me the briefest of glances and turned away. I said 'Noah's Ark if you please' to his back, but it was clear that after a couple of visits he now recognised me.

Without a word he dragged a wooden crate from nearby and began transferring its contents to my trolley. From somewhere outside the bakery gate came the sound of a woman singing; the dawn air was full not only of the smell of fresh bread but also smoke, steam and hundreds of indistinguishable scents from vegetable and fruit stalls where wares from far afield, unheard of when Mother and Father were my age, now sit side by side with local produce.

Despite having been raised in a home where it was almost impossible to have space to oneself, the sensation of being in the midst of scores of people felt uncomfortable. For those raised in towns or, even more so, great cities, it must seem normal and they in turn would have found my childhood strange and alarming. Rev Byron says all mankind are one family under God, but to me family means familiarity - knowing each other's ways - being aware of each other's likes and dislikes, noises and habits. It was a strange thing to suddenly realise that being in a crowd made me feel lonely for the first time in my life.

3.
Cheltenham
Thursday, September 10th, 1862

It is not very often that a mere serving girl becomes the cause for gossip throughout much of the locality; but according to Mr Wells the evening of Monday, September 7th, 1862 will go down in the history of the Noah's Ark for an event so shocking it is a surprise (according to Edgar the barman and Mrs Bolt) that it did not appear in the Chronicle!

Adder Drew is a poacher. Everyone knows it, but the duty constable and bailiffs let him alone. It is only small game - rabbits and the occasional pheasant mostly - and the landowners take the view that while he is stalking their fields no other poacher would be setting foot there because, however much they were tempted by an illicit supper, they would rather chew tree bark than cross Adder Drew's path in a lonely place.

Before heading out of town he would typically call in for a few pots of cider. Mostly he would abide by the house rules and leave his gun behind the bar as our sporting clientele do, but if he was not planning to stay long, he would lean his gun against his table as he drank; alone, always alone. We had not exchanged words since our encounter on my first night and it had become second nature to me to take extra care with his pots.

Monday evening was a busy one, there had been a race meeting and the bar was a throng of hee-hawing, red-faced racegoers and their weaselly attendants. Someone threw a damp log on the fire and that, along with a blow-back on a windy evening caused a temporary smoke cloud which sent patrons coughing to the door and window. A particularly tall stranger banged his head on the door to the ablutions and needed a bandage but in other ways it was a regular night. It was while passing the only table in the bar where someone sat alone that my trailing foot caught the stock of a gun sending it clattering to the floor.

Adder's eyes snapped up and bore into me like twin brands. I was carrying two full pots and began to shake so much that the ale in them trembled down the sides. I felt the colour draining from me and as he placed his hands flat on the table as if to rise, I actually thought I was going to faint. His lips bared over surprisingly healthy-looking teeth and the malevolence spread outward like a winter wind, freezing first the adjoining tables and then those more distant as realisation of the event circulated through some unspoken instinct like the scent of an unseen wolf in a busy pasture.

Let me try and tell you how that moment felt.

Even though ghosts have never held any fear for me there was one time, at the age of eight or nine when I was sent on solitary errand to Uncle Michael's; the visit was much longer than planned, causing me to walk back home in darkness. The lane was as familiar to me as my own reflection, it was a night when a full moon played hide and seek with fast-moving clouds helping to light my way and a cool wind shook the hedges.

It would have been an uneventful walk but for the fact that a few evenings previous Emily had read out an account from a newspaper of a demonic black dog that supposedly roamed country lanes and lonely places. As a result, every crack of twig, rattle of branch and rush of wind behind me was taken as evidence of the beast's presence. The story had stated that to look into its glowing coal-red eyes was to die of fright.

It was too terrifying a prospect to glance behind and with that came the increasing conviction that at my shoulder was the sound of its great padding steps, panting and even the smell of its warm breath. Increasing my pace only increased my anxiety, finally forcing me into a blind run that lasted like what seemed like forever before I screamed breathless into the cottage, almost leaping into Father's lap as he sat dozing by the fire. There followed much hugging and soothing and an edict from Father that such stories were strictly banned in future.

But there had been no demon dog, just the demons in my mind, soothed away by the comforting embrace of family. Adder Drew, by contrast, was altogether too real. The bar was now virtually silent. Mr Wells was nowhere to be seen and neither Edgar the barman nor any of the customers showed the slightest inclination to stand between me and this devil-made-flesh. In the leftover smoke of the blowback, he stood and was in every way Satan incarnate presiding over his demonic kingdom of fire and brimstone. In anticipation of the terrible fate awaiting me my shaking increased and I began to cry; silently at first and then in great gulping sobs, the pots in

39

my hand were no more than half-full now but I could not move to put them down, finding myself frozen in this terminal moment.

Then the strangest thing occurred. Adder's gaze never left me, but his entire face transformed and in the place of fury came in quick succession, confusion, surprise and finally something approaching compassion. He reached out a hand toward me.

'Hoy... don't cry wench; hoy there, don't cry... here come on... sit...'

It was not a voice used to softness, he spoke as someone who had once heard compassion in another and was using himself for the first time; he pointed to the empty chair at his table, beckoning.

'Come on... sit... that's a girl....'

Without thinking, I sat, as did he; I put down the now half-empty pots on his table and wiped my eyes, still very much unsure of whether this was the Noah's Ark or a lion's den. He leaned down and picked up his gun, giving it a cursory examination before resting it once again against his table. There was a low muttering around us now. Mr Wells had arrived back from wherever an errand had taken him somewhere upstairs and he was observing the situation from the waiting station, as transfixed as everyone by the sight of me - or anyone - actually sharing a table with Adder Drew. Encouraged both by the Landlord's presence and by the fact that, had Adder wanted to tear me limb from limb he could have done it by now, a small and croaking voice managed to find its way out from somewhere inside me.

'I am very sorry for my clumsiness Sir.'

'Aye, well,' he peered down the barrel of his gun, 'No harm done by the looks of things, they don't make these buggers anymore see.'

That was the most words anyone in the Inn had ever heard him say in one sentence, but it was only a curtain-raiser for what was to come. He gave me a sideways glance as he took out a filthy rag and began polishing the stock of the weapon which, unlike its owner, appeared to be clean and well cared for.

Adder wore what appeared to be his only attire; a calf-length dark hide coat over a homespun shirt and brown baggy breeches tucked into scuffed brown boots, his felt hat sat on the tabletop allowing long unkempt corn coloured hair to frame his face and drape over his shoulders. He sported long and uncultivated sideburns turning to grey along with the lengthy stubble of one who shaves only on high days and holidays.

'You don't want to go a-cryin' wench; it lets folk know they can hurt ye and the world'll hurt ye enough when you'm grown.... See, now this weapon be older than you - it be prob'ly older than me even.' He rested it across the tabletop allowing me to get a detailed look at it while blinking away the last of the tears.

'It's a Brown Bess isn't it Sir?'

Adder looked up surprised; even with the anger and hostility gone from his face it was still a countenance that commanded a horrid fascination.

'Good God, aye; so it is. How comes a scrap of a wench like 'ee knows that?'

'My Grandfather used one to fight Napoleon and he's got a book about how to look after them.... If I might be so bold Sir, I wouldn't have thought it was the best

41

weapon for hunting at night...' (I paused for breath) '...it would be hard to half cock and charge with powder in the pitch dark and even harder to see your game.'

I had his full attention again but on this occasion his face was at first impossible to read; one golden eyebrow was raised, and those unnerving eyes were glittering with a bewildering light. His shoulders began to shake.

And then he laughed.

Had any other denizen of the Noah's Ark broke into a laugh it would have been commonplace and unremarkable but for Adder Drew to laugh was akin to hearing a cat bark or a chicken whistle. It was a loud and rattling laugh as if a door that had not been opened for an age was creaking back into life. It stopped all other sound in the Inn, jaws dropped, patrons looked at each other to confirm their sanity.

'Aye by God... aye... you're right Wench; it'd be jubbin' hard to bag a bun with this long bastard, wouldn't it?'

He pushed a hand into one of his coat pockets, pulling out a couple of snares and tossing them on to the table, 'Here's what I get's dinner with... Bess here is just to frighten the bailiffs!'

He leaned forward conspiratorially, beckoning me to do likewise. With our heads just inches apart I could smell hedgerows and autumn mist around the edge of the cider - and I could see the demons dancing in his eyes.

'Truth is, it ain't even loaded... can't get lead for balls or a mould to make 'em; every time I goes round the blacksmith on Hewletts Road the swine hides and sends his lad out to say he's indisposed....' Adder grinned evilly,

'If I didn't know better, I'd say the vazey bugger was frightened of me!'

My laugh was a blend of delayed relief, continued nervousness and the discovery that this man who my mind had converted from blackguard to Beelzebub actually had a sense of humour; Adder half-smiled and nodded.

'There, that's more like it, that's a pretty little face you got and all the more so for smiling.... little girls faces should never have tears on 'em - or little boys for that matter.' His voice flattened, trailing off into a growl as if a spell had been broken.

'I'll have another pot when you'm ready wench.'

Standing, I smoothed down my apron and the room became familiar again. I picked up the tray with the half-full pots.

'Right away Sir.'

The walk back to the bar was occupied with me wondering whether what just took place had been some sort of dream or vision. I was, however, persuaded of its reality on passing Mr Wells - who had never sworn in my company. As I waited for Edgar to refill Adder's pot there came the astonished mutter from the landlord behind me.

'I'll be well and truly buggered!'

It was about fifteen or twenty minutes later that Adder stood to leave, gathering up his gun, shouldering a battered grey bag and pulling on his hat. He usually departed anonymously seemingly possessing the ability to vanish unnoticed from a room but on this occasion his exit coincided with me passing by his table to pick up his empty pot. On reaching for it his hand took mine, gently, not like the first time he had gripped me. He raised my arm; staring at the ground he addressed the busy bar.

'You lot!'

He had not spoken loudly but his tone of voice was enough to paralyse the room.

Once again, the clientele developed rubber necks in an attempt to look while feigning disinterest. The silence could have been carved into slices.

Adder looked up and around, his gaze dripping contempt. Mr Wells was approaching from the waiting area, but his rescue was to prove unnecessary.

'Whatsoever anyone does to this wench... they does the same to me!'

His words carried enough chill to form icicles in every mind present; even a pair of dogs belonging to a fat man smoking a churchwarden pipe slunk under the table to take sanctuary behind their master's legs and it would not have been a surprise to discover spiders abandoning the centres of their webs in the rush for dark nooks and crannies. Adder Drew walked out of the dumbstruck Noah's Ark without a backward glance and his footprints made no sound.

A week later, Mr Wells sacked Edgar the barman for stealing money from the till and for helping himself to drinks. As a result, we were acquainting a new barman with knowledge of where everything was - he is a well-spoken gentleman from Charlton Kings called Gerald who apparently speaks Latin. If the Romans return, we will be the most welcoming hostelry in town.

Gerald is tall and slim; he wears braces and a bow tie and has a moustache that could be described as 'frisky' which matches a fine head of white wavy hair; he smokes a churchwarden pipe when not in the process of filling pots and glasses. He once worked in a large hotel in London and travelled to Paris and Venice in his youth. One of his first acts was to compliment me on the little vases of wildflowers I had placed on the end on his bar and in the window. He knew all of their names - not just their proper names but the long Latin ones too.

I knew that the next time Robin visited he would find our new barman fascinating and would ply him with questions about his travels. Robin had promised to call in sometime this week after college if his studies allowed; but it was not he who was first through the door that evening.

Richard Price entered and sat at the small table beneath the window, almost concealed by the heavy green curtain. Normally he would stand at the bar hoping to catch the eye of Mrs Bolt when the kitchen door opened as she occasionally let him have some surplus vegetables or bread that would not keep.

He had his own kitchen now in the Carters Yard and fed not only the Yard's employees but several regular passers-by, including many desperately poor children from what people called The Rookery - a collection of over-populated hovels in a desperate state of repair full of immigrant Irish as well as penniless locals. Many inns would not welcome the Irish - even when they had the money to buy drinks, but Mr Wells had served with soldiers of many nationalities and faiths in Crimea and would tolerate no blind judgements.

The hungry children, with brown sticks for arms and eyes far too large, would congregate on the corner near the Carter's Yard waiting for Richard to beckon them across. They would not dare approach before the signal for fear of being chased by the owner's dogs which they had heard ate children. Richard would then fill their pathetic cans and wooden bowls with stew and, if he had some, a chunk of bread. They would jostle and barge for position, their bare feet squelching in the churned-up mud and manure, wiping their noses on ragged sleeves.

Beggars were banned from finer areas of the town and were in danger of a beating or incarceration should they be seen in the vicinity of the Spas, Montpellier or most anywhere on the other side of the Chelt River. Some, once their faces had become too well known to the constabulary, would lurk in the areas around the railway station and goods yards to try and get on a train to Birmingham, Bristol, Gloucester or somewhere where rumour had it that there was the possibility of work, charity or shelter.

I have decided Richard Price is a good man, a little intense and with a whiff of danger about him but essentially more angel than devil. As I caught his eye, he beckoned in a manner both anxious and furtive. Weaving between tables and chairs, almost all of which were vacant that early in the evening, I reached his side and offered a smile; he was drumming his fingers and tapping his foot, looking around furtively like a mouse unsure of the baited trap.

'Ellen, I'll have a pint of Black and... listen... can you do me a rather large favour?'

'Of course...' my silence and raised eyebrows coaxed him out of his reticence.

'It's just that... should anyone ask, could you say that I've been here for the past couple of hours... maybe helping you out or something?'

I frowned, 'I suppose so - but why?'

He ignored my question, continuing; '...and could you possibly put this in a safe place until I leave?'

He handed over a rolled up small sack which I took from him as he offered a relieved smile, 'Thank you - you're a good friend.'

With eyebrows still raised I headed off to get his drink and to deposit the mysterious and weighty bundle in the cupboard under the serving hatch, arriving back at his table with a pint of Black at precisely the moment that Mr Mossley the Constable entered and after a quick look around spotted Richard at his table and joined us; hovering over the sitting youth and switching his considerable weight from one leg to the other.

Richard Mossley is a wheelwright, and he was wearing his working clothes, a stained grey woollen jacket, knotted scarf (despite the fact that it was scorching outside) and thick woollen trousers with a patch in the backside made out of a sack upon which the word 'Meal' was visible. He was also sporting a Thomas and William Bowler hat a size too big for him which only his ears were holding up. Pinned to his jacket was a metal badge stating, 'Gloucestershire Constabulary' which his brother who worked in a forge had made for him - and upon which both the words 'Gloucestershire' and 'Constabulary' were spelt wrongly.

Tilting back his hat and scratching a chin in need of a visit from a razor he squinted in the relatively dim light of the Noah's Ark bar.

'Mr Price?'

'Yes indeed,' Richard smiled, 'Can I help you Constable?'

Tucking his thumbs into his belt and rocking self-importantly back and forth the constable grinned apishly at the sitting youth as I hovered nearby going through the motions of polishing the next table.

'P'raps you can, yes... p'raps you can indeed... It appears that a quantity of gunpowder has been removed from the premises of a certain Mr Pigeon of Hungerford Street which is, of course, not more than a short walk from where we find ourselves here. Mrs Pigeon states that she observed a youth, answering a description that made me think of you, leaving the yard at the rear of the premises and it is fortunate that I was in the process of passing by at the time. Now, lo and behold, here you are in the very same part of town!'

Richard frowned and rubbed his chin. 'Yes, I see what you mean, but I'm afraid it could not have been me; you see, I was brought up a strict Methodist and I would go straight to Hell if I stole anything.' He smiled beatifically up at the constable whose piggy eyes glittered with a growing malevolence. I felt my stomach turn over at the revelation of what was probably in the sack Richard had given me to hide. A misplaced spark from Gerald's pipe and the Noah's Ark and everything in it could be blown to St Peter's Gates. I scowled in Richard's direction, but his attention was still on the constable who curled up a lip to show front teeth the colour of burnt pancakes.

'Yes, well in my time I've had 'em all in my cells, Methodists, Baptists, Catholics, Jews, Mohammedans...

and... well, perhaps you could tell me where you have been for the last hour?'

Constable Mossley was a wheelwright not a detective. In his law enforcement role, he was little more than a blunt instrument, a cudgel unable to see beyond the two dimensions of crime and consequence and never into the context of cause. Richard turned to me, grinning, but my scowl was still in place and so he quickly switched his attention back to the constable; 'Right here, enjoying a refreshing drink or two after a hard morning feeding hungry carters and several unfortunates down on their luck. Isn't that right Ellen?'

The constable looked at me as a pig might look at a trough of sugar beet. Had he done so at the start of my career I might have withered under such an interrogative stare but since then I had endured the undivided attention of some of Cheltenham's most intimidating 'lookers' and so I simply nodded and confirmed Richard's statement.

'Yes, well in the abstinence of any proof I will have to let the matter rest for now but should such a thing as a witness come forward you and I will be conversating again.' The constable gave a cursory doff of his bowler in my direction, turned gracelessly on his heel and left.

'Lucky his proof was abstinent, eh?' Richard cackled and downed half of his drink in a single gulp before grinning up at me with a frothy top lip.

'Are you mad?' I was still furious with him - let alone the danger, if Mr Wells had seen me carrying the package there could have been a few uncomfortable questions. 'Are you trying to blow us all up?'

'No, not you Ellen, never you - but me and the lads are thinking of sending a threshing machine to whatever Hell such demonic, job-stealing inventions are destined for. Don't worry, there's not enough gunpowder in the package to blow the Noah's Ark up, maybe rattle a few tables though. Do me another favour will you, stick your head out the door and tell me if the bobby has gone.'

By now I was eager to get Richard and his disturbing package as far away as possible and so I went to the door, opened it and looked up and down St George's Street. All was quiet looking down towards Swindon Road, in the other direction carriages were at a standstill on High Street due to an overturned cart and I could see Constable Mossley stooped over a pile of strewn merchandise. Returning indoors I retrieved Richard's parcel, now handling it was if it were a new-born baby. Passing it over to him, he tucked it carelessly under his arm.

'He's under a cart on High Street, head down to Swindon Road, you'll be alright then.' My voice was clearly full of urgency as a looked fleetingly at the adjoining door fearful that Mr Wells or Mrs Bolt would appear at any moment.

'You're a good friend Ellen,' Richard beamed, his eyes full of danger and devilment; to my surprise he kissed me on the top of the head before skipping quickly away, pausing at the door long enough for a wink and farewell grin.

It was almost a month before I saw him in the Noah's Ark again. He entered with his usual band of friends and sat at the window table. The table had been occupied a few seconds before by a plump man with a collapsible telescope tucked into his coat pocket - a racegoer judging by his appearance. He had left to visit the gentlemen's' cloakroom discovering on his return that the table had been commandeered. Seven young men were squeezed around it, deep in conversation so, shrugging, he moved to another vacant seat on a table of similarly suited and booted turf supporters.

Richard caught sight of me on approaching their table to take their order; he rose to his feet, towering over me as most people in the Noah's Ark did, and to my embarrassment placed an arm around me, sharing a grin full of puck and peril with all present.

'Ah-ha, here she is lads - careful what you say mind you... she tells lies to bobbies, this one!'

I lifted his arm off and scowled at him.

'What can I get you... gentlemen?' I enquired, the last word dripping with a sarcasm that would have earned me a remonstration from Mr Wells had he overheard.

'Aww, please don't tell me you're still cross,' Richard sat, 'It would only have been a little bang and we're ever so grateful - hey, want to come with us and see an event that Guy Fawkes would have been proud of?'

'No thank you,' despite myself I was stifling a smile, 'Now then what can I get you?'

Richard and his companions ordered and a few minutes later I was back at their table with seven pots of beer and cider. Standing again, Richard took his pot from the tray as I rested it on a table crowded with hats, pipes and what looked like a bayonet in a sheath.

'Introductions lads, this is Ellen Bullingham - a good and loyal friend, daughter of a hard-working shepherd and a true lass-of-the-land,' the assembly nodded and - having been put on the spot - I felt it only polite to offer a slight curtsey and a Mona Lisa smile of acknowledgement in return. 'Ellen, here we have a band merrier than that of Robin Hood himself... say hello to Tad Mitchell, Adam Mitchell, Will Danton, Enoch Johnsey, Tom Coombes and Abel Isgrove.'

There followed a muttered chorus of 'Evenings' and 'How d'you dos' and a 'Please to meet you I'm sure' from me in return. A single empty chair stood between one of the men and the heavy curtain, for a moment I thought Richard was going to invite me to occupy it, but a call came from Gerald at the bar with another order to deliver.

The gathering of youths had three refills before leaving en-masse. Richard and one of the others, whose name I am afraid I had not committed to memory, waved on departure.

Mr Wells asked me to work on Sunday morning as he was entertaining a special party on Sunday afternoon and required the bar area as clean and neat as an officer's mess. He had paid a boy - a runner, to go out to Uckington to inform my family that I would be home later so as not to cause them undue worry and for my extra services I was to be paid two shillings and would receive the following Wednesday off, which I agreed was more than generous.

Mr Wells had always proved a kind and fair man, there had never been a cross word between us. He was well known and respected in and about Town and seemed as permanent a fixture as the stone gargoyle's head by the fireplace that had allegedly stood on the corner of a

52

building near to this spot since the time of King John. Therefore, his announcement on closing the doors that evening came as a complete surprise. He sat himself at the small table close to the fireplace where the embers lay dying at evening's end for want of coal and from the collected ash beneath. Gerald had left to walk home a few minutes earlier, his pipe puffing as he headed out on to St George's Street like a two-legged railway train. Mrs Bolt had departed more than an hour before.

'Ellen, I would like you to sit down here for a moment, I have something to tell you.'

I have always frowned when faced with unexpected news, it is something Father has persistently tried to get me to stop doing but I cannot seem to help it. I felt myself frowning as I sat, twiddling a loose cord on my damp apron, pausing to brush a wayward strand of hair back behind an ear and staring fixedly at the tiny flames.

'I have to tell you that at the end of next month I shall be leaving the Noah's Ark for a new position in Birmingham. There will be a new hotelier here and I have been informed he will not be seeking to employ a servant.'

My surprise must have been evident; suddenly the future was like one of the maps in Robin Berry's atlas across which was written 'Terra Incognita;' My naive expectation had been to remain in service at the Noah's Ark until a husband came along but instead there was now the immediate need to seek new employment. At thirteen, it was unreasonable in such challenging times to expect my family to clothe and feed me. Mr Wells smiled kindly; I must have appeared close to tears; he placed a hand on my shoulder.

'I have a business acquaintance who provides catering at the racecourse in Andoversford and upon enquiring it appears she might be in need of an experienced young woman. Should you be successful - and I shall of course provide a splendid reference - you would have good and gainful employment and there may be opportunities to gain further experience. And you may be assured - Miss Doplin will surprise and delight you.'

The End of the Sky

4.
Andoversford, Gloucestershire, England
Tuesday, May 1st, 1866

Miss Dorothy Doplin came from Birmingham as a
teenager, her father had been the renowned blacksmith,
John 'Dark Jack' Doplin, who could allegedly throw a
carthorse shoe over a church spire and lift a yearling clear
off the ground on his back. He had died after being
kicked in the head by a Belgian racehorse while in the
process of shoeing it. Dorothy's mother had died in
childbirth and she had been left to care for a twelve-year-
old brother. She had retained ownership of her father's
forge, renting it to another smith for a while before selling
it to buy a tearoom on the site of the racecourse and now
her little establishment was, everyone concurred, an oasis
of gentility in the sometimes raucous and belligerent
world of fun-seeking race goers and their retinues.

Her brother had long since left home to join the navy
and her current staffing requirements had been made
necessary due to her renting an adjoining building which
she planned to convert and open as a bar room and
dining establishment.

All this I had learned from Mr Wells prior to leaving
for my appointment. He had met Dark Jack in Crimea
where the man's skill and strength became legendary. It

was said he once shod the horse of Lord Raglan himself and, following the Charge of the Light Brigade, Captain Morgan had him smelt down the horseshoes of his mount Sir Briggs to fashion a commemorative paperweight in the shape of a horse's hoof - which he did with such craftsmanship that the noble officer gave him five guineas.

Mr Wells had told me much about Miss Doplin and also told her a little about me, but he had neglected to give any indication of her appearance; and so, approaching the tea rooms I was alert for any sighting of a woman likely to be my prospective new employer.

The tearoom looked like nothing of the sort being more akin to a barn when viewed from the outside and it was only the metal sign fixed to the featureless brick wall stating, 'The Doplin Tea Rooms' and an advertisement for 'Dainty cakes and pastries you will want to linger over,' that indicated the building's current use.

Around the side of the building there was a half-glass door where a sign on a string stated, 'Closed'. Seeing through the lace curtain a woman within, I knocked the kind of knock that strives to be heard without being intrusive. There was no response and so I turned the brass knob and found the door unlocked. The woman looked up from menu that had until then occupied her attention, I was about to address her when she beat me to it.

'Miss Bullington?'

'Bullingham, Ma'am, Ellen Bullingham,' I politely corrected.

'Dolly Doplin', she held out a translucent and delicate hand, I took it as I would have an achingly thin china cup.

It was surprisingly warm, and a further novelty was to look a potential employer in the eye instead of the midriff. She wore a black dress fastened in an overlap to the neck with what appeared to be black onyx buttons. Her travelling hat suggested she had just arrived; it was small brimmed like a riding hat and with a delicate veil, also in black, that stopped at the eyebrows, revealing grey eyes in which laughter regularly danced. Her hair, what I could see of it, appeared to be similar in colour to my own, a light brown verging towards auburn like the coat of a harvest mouse. From what Mr Wells had told me of her history she would have been about thirty, but her face suggested she was closer to twenty-five.

'Thomas tells me you are well accustomed to serving and waiting and that you are no stranger to the hundred and one things that need to be done to make an inn tick like a well-oiled clock?'

'Yes Ma'am, I have learned a lot in my time working for Thom... Mr Wells at the Noah's Ark.' I must have appeared road-weary and dishevelled after my two-hour trudge. She frowned; 'Oh my Dear, forgive me my manners, you have walked such a long way.' Pulling out a chair from the nearest table she invited me to sit which I did with regrettably little delicacy. She sat too and called over a shoulder.

'Edith!'

Almost immediately a woman in her middle age in a waitress dress that appeared a shade too tight for her substantial girth appeared from behind us.

'Be so good as to bring a pot of tea for two, would you?' Miss Doplin asked, getting a slight curtsey and the smile of a toad from the woman as she turned on a heel and departed.

Miss Doplin looked so delicate that a slight breeze might make her dance in the air like an errant leaf, and so feminine that I felt gauche and carthorsey in her company. She rested one hand on top of the other as she made herself comfortable and it was hard to equate the butterfly before me with the tales I had heard of the mighty Dark Jack Doplin who fathered her.

We sat next to a dead fireplace in which coal and clinkers had been placed over sticks and paper in readiness for the next time the tearoom was to open. There was no smell of the ash or ale, stale smoke or boiling vegetables that had been part of the tapestry of the Noah's Ark. For the best part of an hour Miss Doplin regaled me with a history of her establishment, herself and her plans for the new enterprise. She was, as one would expect, very knowledgeable about the equestrian world; I hoped she was not seeking someone who shared that particular enthusiasm. I had never sat on the back of a horse while in command of it and had no desire to change that state of affairs.

I do not know precisely what Mr Wells had told the lady opposite me but, even though I had said little throughout, I was offered a position - and a very responsible one too. Miss Doplin had been thrown into the adult world of commerce and self-sufficiency when just eighteen months older than me and it must have left her with a faith at just how much potential can be packed into a small frame. She tested my reading and writing and got me to add up five different sums of money in my head. Finally, she asked me how I would deal with clientele whose restraint had been chased out of their brains by too much drink. For some time, this had not been a problem for me as it was common knowledge in the Noah's Ark that anyone trying to tweak the whiskers of this little Uckington rabbit would find they had the lupine Adder Drew by the tail. I did not believe, however, that Adder Drew visited Andoversford to take tea very often and so, remembering the advice of Mr Wells, I told her that diplomacy delivered in a firm voice was the best weapon which seemed to please her.

The new enterprise had rooms above it, one of which would be mine and I would be in charge of opening the doors, ordering and maintaining the stock, securing the takings and locking up at night. And for this I would receive the sum of fourteen shillings a week plus my meals and lodging.

'May the fourteenth it is then.'

Miss Doplin stood and held out a hand, I stood too and took it with a curtsey.

'... and there is no need to curtsey - furthermore, my name is Dolly, and you are Ellen, agreed?'

I liked her already.

'Agreed,' I smiled.

The clouds were clearing promising a fine evening. Tea and the rare treat of pastries, plus the long sit down and restorative powers of good news would, I was sure, propel me back to the Noah's Ark before it became dark. A young man whose face was vaguely familiar leaned against a stock fence on the road out of the racecourse.

He was in no more than shirtsleeves beneath a brown leather waistcoat despite a chill wind that had sprung up from the north. Long black hair hung over his shoulders and a clay pipe drooped lazily from the corner of his mouth causing a smile to appear lopsided. He touched the brim of his hat as I passed, and I nodded politely in return.

'Afternoon, Lass-o'-the-Land', he called at my back as I headed on my way. I paused, considered turning but decided against it - and then walked on.

'That will be enough, Ellen.'

Mr Wells placed a light hand on my arm, stalling me on my way to the kitchen with a pile of plates and cutlery for washing. He took them from me; 'I will take these; now you - off with that apron and be seated at the table under the window if you please.'

My usual countenance when confused must have manifested itself because he added, '... and you won't be needing the frown this evening.' I immediately wiped it off and tried to smile but I think it made me look constipated.

It was six pm and there were four hours of my day's work still to go with tables to be waited and drinks on the bar to be delivered. Mr Wells deposited the plates at the serving hatch and with a busy wave of his hand herded me to the table, holding out a chair for me under the eye of a trio of nearby gentlemen who had rented rooms for the weekend whilst taking the waters. I tried to sit in a ladylike manner, a small, tired figure in a tired and faded blue dress, scuffed brown boots and a yellow strip of what had once been Esther's nightdress tying back my hair in a pony's tail. I wondered if I had been guilty of some misdemeanour on my last ever day, but Mr Wells had not looked or sounded displeased. He hovered over me, towel on one arm and notebook poised.

'Now...might I recommend the lamb shank Miss? It comes with pan-roasted potatoes - locally grown; parsnips, carrots and Mrs Bolt's celebrated mint gravy - and to compliment the meal perhaps a Gloucestershire cider as an aperitif and a modest glass of wine served alongside would be most agreeable.'

He was smiling widely at my obvious confusion; looking across the room to the bar there was Gerald leaning on his counter, pipe in mouth, holding up a bottle of wine and grinning in my direction. 'Well?' Mr Wells, still smiling, prompted my response.

All day long I had been haunted by a melancholy; my chores and duties had been routine and yet there was the pervading sense that I was doing everything for the last time and seeing familiar things never to be seen again; the table with the dark brown knot at the edge that always snags the duster as you wipe it, the brass knob on the serving hatch that had been so dull until properly polished, the large and threadbare creaking chair by the fire usually occupied by Mr Porter the night-watchman who came in every night for his supper which he called 'breakfast' and the many familiar sights and sounds and creaks and squeaks that this old stager of a building made.

I was looking forward to my new position at Andoversford, but this Inn had been my life for the past two and a half years, I had done so much growing up here and it was going to be painful to say goodbye to familiar friends, workmates and regular guests - and now my master, my employer, was preparing to wait upon me - a serving girl - in a lovely act of unnecessary kindness. I tried really hard to hold back tears that had been probing against my defences all day long, but I failed and cried in great sobs like a silly eight-year-old.

'There, there, come on young lady, 'Mr Wells spoke velvety and encouragingly with the voice one uses when a ewe needs one more push to get the lamb out.

'... It may be a while before you are on the receiving end of some fine service again so make the most of it my dear.' He beckoned Gerald over who arrived with a glass of cider.

'So then... lamb shank?'

I found a smile, wrestling for equilibrium in this unaccustomed role.

'Yes, please Mr Wells.'

He smiled in return, spun efficiently on his heel and headed for the kitchen. Gerald grinned down at me and headed back to his bar, patting me reassuringly on the shoulder as he departed.

It occurred to me, not for the first time, how little I knew about my employer. He was a private man who, according to Mrs Bolt, was parent to two daughters and so clearly had once had a woman in his life but where were they? It was a closed book and I had never mustered the courage or the impertinence to ask. But he certainly knew how to run an inn.

The meal was, as he described it on serving, a dish '*par excellence*' and for someone who had been anticipating a fifteen-minute break with a bowl of bone stew on the lap in the corner of the kitchen it was manna from Heaven; delicious and all the more delightful for the fine cutlery and crockery which I had washed countless times but never used before.

The End of the Sky

I ate, savouring every bite unhurriedly while paying scant attention to the tables around me. The cider was refreshing and the wine - a first experience - seemed exotic and left behind it a warm glow of wellbeing which cast the familiar surroundings of the Noah's Ark bar room in a new role as somewhere palatial and full of good humour.

When a gentleman seated nearby raised his wineglass to me and called out, 'Your very good health Miss,' I laughed gaily and, raising my own glass, responded with, 'You too, good Sir.'

It's hard to say whether it was the unaccustomed wine, emotion, a particularly hearty meal or a combination of all three but I was suddenly so tired. There was a roaring fire in the grate and the air was heavy and warm in the bar room. I looked at my hands, they were dishwashingly clean, small like Mother's and with a black nail on the middle finger of my right hand where it had been caught in the heavy oven door a week before. Mr Wells had collected my plate and cutlery and I had declined the apple pudding as there was nowhere inside me to put it. Instead, at my employer's insistence, I sat and rested away my final hours of servitude at the Noah's Ark thinking of the many days and nights I had spent in this room, all the strange characters, the peculiar, ungodly but often hilarious songs and the transient people from far and wide with their odd ways of speaking.

As I studied my hands a small object fell on to the table - a flattened dull metal disc about the size of a half crown punched with a hole and tied on to a leather thong. Looking up to see where it had arrived from brought me eye to eye with Adder Drew.

'Present for ye - parting gift.'

He sat in the chair opposite mine, resting his Brown Bess against the curtain, causing the drape to open a little giving a view of the flickering gas light at the junction of St George's Street and High Street. As he tilted back his hat, I picked up the object to study it more closely. It was a flat and almost round piece of lead; the one side was blank but on the other an inscription had been stamped or impressed. 'Psalm 91:11'.

'It's made out of a lead shot - cove in Crimea used to do them; it's got some Bible thing wrote on it. I don't know what it is, I asked the parson in the army and he told me there was no point in me knowing because I was beyond saving. I often thought about going in a church and asking a vicar but if I walked in a house of God my feet would burst into flames.' He chuckled harshly and mirthlessly. I held the object, moved by the simple generosity of the gesture and the knowledge that for Adder Drew any act of sensitivity was a deeply uncomfortable experience.

'Are you sure, Mr Drew? I am very grateful for it, but it must be special to you if you have had it for so long?'

'Ain't nothing to me now and you've got a hell of a lot longer road to travel than I have.' He took out a clay pipe and began filling it. Reaching behind he lifted a candle from a table occupied by two locals who wisely said nothing, he lit his pipe and replaced their candle.

Can... can I get you a pot of cider?' I began to rise.

'Sit down, I ain't stopping - just came to say goodbye is all. You take care of yourself out at that racecourse - you'll meet some black hearts behind white shirts I can promise; so, make certain you watch the buggers like a hawk.'

'I promise I'll...' but Adder Drew hadn't finished.

'.... remember - them as wears diamonds didn't do the digging to get at 'em and you can spot an honest man by the holes in his shoes...'

I nodded politely but kept silent; not wanting to interrupt what was probably the longest speech he had ever made.

'... and drink lowers your defences, right? Now I got me lots of defences so I can afford to lower some of 'em but you ain't got none - couple o' glasses of that wine and your drawers will be off and some Rupert'll be riding you like a charger; you understand what I'm sayin'?'

It's funny how his face didn't frighten me anymore - even when he was looking as menacing as he did when delivering his cautions. I felt the tears coming again.

'I shall miss you.'

He paused, clearly baffled by a display of affection, 'Shut up you daft wench, close your eyes and count to five; open 'em on four and I'll skin you like a weasel.'

I did as he said without questioning; as I closed them, I felt the leather thong dropping about my neck; four.... five; I opened my eyes and Adder Drew was gone. I held the lead disc, rubbing it between thumb and forefinger as I pondered on the many and mysterious forms in which goodness can manifest itself. There followed the consoling thought that I would inevitably encounter him somewhere out in the fields around Uckington or Elmstone Hardwicke at that time of day when only the horizon is light, the sky is full of stars and a mist hangs above the fields so that you cannot see your feet and you stumble over molehills. Gerald the barkeeper was a well-read man and saved me the job of looking up Psalm 91:11.

'For he will command his angels concerning you to guard you in all your ways.'

No one who met Adder Drew would mistake him for an angel but he had guarded me in my time at the Noah's Ark and now I hoped an angel would not only guard me - but him too for there are a lot of people whose feet do not catch fire when they enter a church but who are foolish to think that an hour of false contrition a week will save them on judgement day; and likewise there are those who do not worship on the pews but who nevertheless live according to what Grandfather calls 'The true lessons of the Lord.'

5.
Andoversford, Gloucestershire, England
Friday, May 18th, 1866

A filly was being put through its paces as I watched from racecourse edge. I had taken a break from stocking shelves with bottles to catch some spring air and surprisingly warm sunshine. The bar and dining room would be opening for business in a little more than two weeks and there was much to organise. Stock was arriving daily as well as some very nice tables and chairs which Dolly had bought at auction in Gloucester.

'Oh, there was a woman in our town, and in our town did dwell....'

The young man approached, singing loudly, propping a leg against the racetrack fence before leaning on it, tanned arms drooping over the top bar. He had a short clay smouldered in the corner of his mouth, a breeze whipped away the smoke and caused his long black hair to dance, restrained only by a felt hat which had been pulled down over his forehead; tilting it back revealing dark eyes, almost black, squinting as he peered after the now distant racehorse. Removing the pipe, he turned and grinned at me, revealing a gold canine glittering among surprisingly white teeth.

67

'What a joy it is to see a happy filly on a spring day!'

I returned his smile in what I hoped was a reserved and polite way. He had studied me now for a length of time that was approaching rudeness and so I looked away.

'Bit of a change out here from being stuck in the old Noah's Ark eh?'

Now I looked to him again, frowning; it was slowly dawning on me where I had seen him before:

'You're one of Richard Price's friends?'

He held out a hand, rings on the two middle fingers, 'Enoch Johnsey - and you're Ellen if my memory is as good as my singing voice.'

I took the proffered hand, it was surprisingly warm and not as rough as I would have expected a workman's hand to be, 'I am, pleased to meet you - again; do you work here at the racecourse?'

'Only if someone's watching, otherwise I loaf around like the gentleman of leisure I was surely born to be. I'm a stable lad at present - most of 'em dream of being jockeys but I'm too tall, anyways I'm going to be a famous balladeer or failing that, prime minister.'

'I see...' I found myself returning his smile with an involuntary one of my own. I needed to get back to work but it is always advisable to make as many acquaintances as possible in a new environment and so I humoured him, '... and have you written many ballads?'

'Oh aye - quite a few; well, I say written - writing ain't my strongest skill but I does a sort of code - my own kind of writing that aids my remembering - a bit like Egyptian horo... hirey...'

'Hieroglyphics?' I offered.

'Aye, that's it, I draws simple pictures of things and they then mean what the words are - like a cross is 'church' of 'chapel', a 'heart' means love of course and I know a fair bit of proper writing, so I gets by.' And I can speak in many tongues!' He spread his arms wide as if addressing a congregation before laughing at my confusion.

'Well,' I smiled again in a way I hoped didn't look too patronising, '... that must be very useful around here, you must teach me sometime - and now, not being a lady of leisure, I must get on with my work.' He swept off his hat and bowed, chuckling before turning away in the direction of the stables while I headed for the Bar.

In the two weeks that followed, Dolly and I rose each day, worked until bedtime, slept and then rose again but two small ladies with their sleeves rolled up aided by some willing hands saw to it that Dolly's Dining Room was prepared to open for business on schedule. It may not have been momentous news that would shake the world, but we were proud of our efforts. Enoch had proved himself a good helping hand, I do not know what his employer would have made of it had he not been abroad buying horses, but it seems his lad spent more time amongst the flying dusters and rattling bottles of the diner than he did in the stables.

Having worked the past two weekends I was, with Dolly's consent, taking Monday and Tuesday off to spend some time at home before the opening of the Dining Room. Mother was laying the table for a Monday lunch of bread and cheese and some porridge left over from breakfast which was rubbery enough to pass for a bread pudding now but was a favourite of Grandfather's.

'I will have to go and wake Grandfather from his nap or he'll...' Mother's sentence was interrupted by the sudden barking of Evans and Jones followed almost immediately by a forthright and frame-rattling knock on our door. Father rose from his seat by the hearth and opened it.

The presence of Agent Porritt would have been unwelcome enough had he been alone but when accompanied by the expressionless Bailiff Haynes the sense of foreboding fell on us like a January fog. My stomach flipped over, Mother took my arm and pulled me toward the kitchen where Grandfather was asleep in his cot seemingly undisturbed by the noise. We stood behind the door.

I have never known anyone to whom the adjective 'reptilian' was more appropriate. Mark Haynes, the circuit bailiff could remain as motionless as a mannequin, his blink being the only evidence of life within. He represented a small but malevolent presence as cold and white as skimmed whey and with a waxwork's basilisk face in which toad eyes floated behind half-closed lids. He was a man avoided by all but his masters - the titled and monied, secure and unassailable. He was also one of the very few people the normally accommodating Mr Wells never welcomed in the Noah's Ark.

Father's voice was calm with an undercurrent of surprise.

'Yes?'

I peered around the kitchen door to witness Agent Porritt tucking his thumbs self-importantly into the pockets of his waistcoat.

'Ah, Bullingham - I take it you know who this gentleman is?'

Father tucked his own thumbs into his belt.

'I do.'

There was age and tiredness in his voice, perhaps resignation, but his stance perpetuated the falsehood that this visit was of little consequence.

'Mr Bullingham...' Bailiff Haynes' voice was chipped, economic and devoid of emotion; even in an empty church I believe it would have been echoless. He took out a small notebook and opened it, '...On Friday last, a man and a youth from Cleeve Hill, while acting together came into possession of three sheep - two yearling ewes and a juvenile ram. These sheep belonged to your master, but these fellows did not purchase them from your master - or from your master's agent here, Mr Porritt.'

At my side Mother gripped my arm tightly and I felt her dread as if it were the Angel of Death itself who hovered above our home. She closed her eyes tightly, squeezing out involuntary tears that trickled around her nose into the corners of her mouth.

'Three sheep eh?' The puzzlement in Father's voice was forced - and clearly so.

'Three sheep,' Bailiff Haynes repeated, '...and do you know who these gentlemen say they purchased them from...?'

Father remained silent.

'...They say they purchased them from you, Mr Bullingham and the animals were then passed through

71

the gate at the corner of Monk's Field and driven by these men down the lane and through Swilgate Field. They were apprehended by Mr Porritt here in the company of your Master - who then notified me. I took the pair to Constable Mossley who locked them up. They have signed a confession but have insisted they believed you had the lawful authority to sell them the animals, being their legal owner.'

'It's all news to me - they must have mistaken me for another.' Father's tone gave away the falsehood; he had never been good at untruths.

'They damn well called you by name, Bullingham!' Agent Porritt took off his bowler, smacked it against his leg and replaced it firmly on his head.

Bailiff Haynes blinked lazily, his tongue peeking between his teeth. 'Now my duty is to call Constable Mossley, have you arrested and taken to a cell, but Mr Porritt here has persuaded your Master that there may have been some kind of misunderstanding, in that he told you earlier that day that you could, and I quote...' (He squinted officiously at his book) '...have those sheep to take down to the home field; meaning, of course, that he wished them moved, but you somehow interpreted that instruction to mean that he was passing ownership of the animals to you – is that the case?'

To my surprise Agent Porritt and taken a step backward and was now out of sight of Bailiff Haynes and in that position, he nodded, wide-eyed, to Father indicating that agreement would be advisable. Father, as shocked as I, nevertheless caught on quickly.

'Err, aye, that's the right of it.'

'I see...,' in his pause Bailiff Haynes managed to convey both distaste and disbelief but, with a sigh like that of a hunter watching a grouse take flight while his gun barrel still smoked, he simply shrugged, '...then the matter can be satisfactorily concluded with a payment for the sheep to Agent Porritt here.

'Payment?' Father frowned as someone whose relief had been proved premature and Mother's grip on my arm, which had slackened, closed tightly again.

'Five pounds Bullingham.' Agent Porritt extended a hand.

This time Mother gasped aloud as Father's shock became starkly apparent; both hands flew to his head, glossing back his greying hair and pulling the lines from his forehead.

'I ain't never seen five pounds in all my born days!' was all Father managed to say in the voice of one who has just seen the dead walk.

'Five pounds, Mr Bullingham - today is Monday, you'll have five pounds in Mr Porritt's hand by Friday or spend as many years breaking stones or treading the mill.'

The pair turned and departed without a further word.

> *'Sneeze on Monday, you sneeze for danger,*
> *Sneeze on Tuesday, you kiss a stranger,*
> *Sneeze on Wednesday, you sneeze for a letter,*
> *Sneeze on Thursday for something better,*
> *Sneeze on Friday, you'll sneeze for sorrow,*
> *Sneeze on Saturday, your sweetheart tomorrow,*
> *Sneeze on a Sunday your safety seek,*
> *For the devil will have you the rest of the week!'*

I had sneezed on Monday when danger came to our door, I had sneezed too on Tuesday, but no stranger had kissed me. Today I have received no letter despite doing little but sneezing and wheezing as a summer cold does its best to add to my woes on what should be a day of excitement. Dolly's Dining Room opens this morning and looking around it I can think of nothing that could have been done that has not been done.

It is hard to think of work and my responsibilities here when in less that forty-eight short hours Father, my dear Father, will be taken from all he loves and thrown into a cell away from any human kindness and hope. He has been near for all of my life and none of us can bear the thought of him not being at the heart of his family. Worst of all, we are suffering for Mother, how can she bear to face each morning knowing the love of her life is breaking rocks or treading a mill pointlessly day after day without a word of kindness or a smile and how can she lie alone each night without the comforting presence of her soul mate by her side?

Agent Porritt and Bailiff Haynes are servants of the Devil and although I have been preached at often enough that vengeance is the province of the Lord, I hope one or both of them meets Adder Drew one dark night and that he does his worst!

Dolly has employed a cook to work with me in the Dining Room; she is only nineteen but very big and strong for her age and she certainly seems to know her way around a kitchen. Her name is Ruth Fletcher, and she appears quite at home among the smoke of ovens firing up, crackling sticks and singing coal as they conspired to drive away the odour of carbolic that had made the little establishment in my charge smell like a chemist's shop these last few days.

I have not mentioned my family's predicament to Dolly beyond saying that Father faces problems that require my attention on Friday. Fortunately, my new employer is generous and not overly inquisitive; she has given me that day off as it is likely to be quiet here anyway - with Thursday and Saturday being the only race days this week. And it is the fact of racing being here tomorrow that has given me an idea that might yet save the day.

A talk with Enoch the stable lad has enlightened me about wagering and it works like this... Supposing a horse is not likely to win a race and the bookmaker decides it has a one in ten chance of crossing the line before all the other horses, then the 'odds' of it winning are ten to one. So, however much is wagered on it, should it win, is returned tenfold. I plan to choose a horse tomorrow with odds of ten to one and place ten shillings of my savings on it. Should it then win I will have five pounds and Father will be safe. Of course, there is a chance I will lose my money, but I am confident Enoch will point me in the right direction as he seems to know one horse from another - or so he claims. He also paid me a compliment, stating he had assumed we were the same age; (he is twenty and he looked surprised when I enlightened him to the fact that I was just seventeen.)

I did not have to seek out Enoch as he was the first customer through the doors the following morning, seeking what he described as 'two breakfasts on one plate'. He need not have worried; I had not yet found time to talk to Ruth and so he received probably the most generous breakfast he had ever encountered. I approached him just as he had conceded defeat and slumped back in his chair with a third of the plate undevoured.

'May I seek some advice?'

I had waited until he finished eating and was drinking coffee with the same expression - somewhere between pain and surprise that Father used when tasting anything hot.

'Of course, ask and ye shall receive!' He waved a hand expansively and attempted to adopt an expression of patriarchal sagacity, adding 'I am a mine of information!'

'Well, I want to place a wager on a horse, but I need some assistance in selecting one; they all look pretty much the same to me, but I understand race goers can tell by signs and mannerisms which animal is a good prospect.'

'You... want to bet on a horse?'

To his credit he did not sound mocking but incredulous; without invitation I sat at his table as another pair of hungry breakfasters entered. Ruth had spotted them, however and was advancing to take their orders.

'I ... that is... yes. I want to place a small wager to raise some money.'

He shook his head in between slurps of coffee, 'Betting on horses ain't the way to make money - unless you're a bookmaker.'

'Even so, I believe with some expert guidance I may have a chance, so can you offer me any advice?'

He fixed me with a strange and old-fashioned look, then his eyes lit up and I am not sure whether it was angels or demons I saw dancing in them.

'You want Creeping Jane, so famous she's had songs written about her.' He chuckled.

'I need odds of ten to one,'

Enoch shook his head, smiling but his confidence had emboldened me, I was determined to take this chance. I thanked him, heading into the kitchen to warn Ruth of my short absence.

The man before me in the queue wore a long green coat that looked both warm and expensive. The tails were spattered with mud as were his brown calf boots; in his tall hat he was a giant, whose shadow cut a long hole out of the early sun, dwarfing my tiny shadow which lay crooked on the grassy bank at the side of the track. He held banknotes which he thumbed through as if they were no more than receipts or shopping lists, there must have been ten at least, five-pound notes, any one of which would...

There was no point thinking what Mother called fluffy cloud thoughts. Green Coat Man reached the front of the queue and casually handed over two of his five-pound notes – at least four months of dawn-to-dusk hard toil for a working man - and he spoke in one of those voices that sent children into mills and men to their deaths under foreign suns before sauntered off, silver-tipped stick tucked under an arm as he studied his betting slip.

The bookmaker looked down at me over an expanse of brown waistcoat, blue eyes twinkling porcine in a flushed face framed by rust red whiskers.

'Yes Miss?'

This was my last chance to back away, mumble an apology and keep my hard-earned ten shillings for the rainy days that were sure to come with such an uncertain winter ahead. But then, what if Creeping Jane were to win as Enoch had assured me she would? How would I feel knowing that due to my lack of courage Father was going to face years of incarceration?

'I would like to place a bet on a horse if you please,' I stopped myself from curtseying, recalling that I was a paying customer.

'Would you indeed?' The bookmaker grinned, thick lips pursed and nostrils flaring in anticipation of exercising a wit he probably did not possess. 'And what is the horse's name and in what race is the creature running?'

I frowned; 'I am not sure of the race, but she's called Creeping Jane and I would like odds of ten to one if you please.'

It was the man behind me in the queue who laughed first, loudly and rudely, turning to the man behind him and passing on a few words causing him in turn to share in the mirth. The bookmaker remained silent but his whole frame was shaking, his face and chin became a mass of wobbles, tears forming in the corners of his squeezed eyes; he snorted and made a noise like a dog being sick before managing to force out a few coherent words.

'I'll tell you what young Miss...' he was shifting his weight from fat leg to fat leg, '...if you want to bet on Creeping Jane, I'll give you a hundred to one, not ten to one, how about that?'

His statement set off not only the pair behind me but the rest of the queue as well and also a group of men, including Green Coat Man, standing nearby. I must have looked as confused as I felt because the bookmaker suddenly sniffed, tilted back his bowler and leaned down to me, his voice now soft leaves where it had recently been briar.

'Listen my darling, someone has been having you on... pulling your leg, you know...' He tugged on an ear, '... there ain't no horse called Creeping Jane, leastways there was one once, so they reckon, 'bout a hundred year ago, but folks say it now to mean a horse that seemingly ain't got a chance - but then surprises 'em all and wins by a distance...'

I frowned and fought back tears of anger and embarrassment, the bookmaker's smile was kindly and seemed to have been dragged into the light from the darkness of deep memory,

'Ain't a bloke here as wouldn't like a few quid on a Creeping Jane - but if I was you, I'd marry a fortune or work for it c'os you ain't going to find one anywhere near a racetrack - and it might not be my place to say it, but shame - bloody shame, on whoever made a monkey of a pretty little thing like you.'

It was hard to walk away with dignity, but I remembered a poem Mrs Brooke had told us once about an army sergeant who had his foot shot off by a savage during the Indian Mutiny and still managed not to cry out and demoralise his men. I stared straight ahead, my face, I knew, was still glowing but the shame was slowly giving way to a deep and all-consuming anger the like of which I had never felt before.

It was anger at the sheer injustice of the threat hanging over my family who are, by no means saints or angels but who are nevertheless good souls who would not turn

79

away a hungry waif or pass by suffering without stopping to help. And it was anger at appearing a complete fool of in front of strangers who I might depend on for my livelihood.

But it was, at that moment, mostly anger at betrayal by someone I had thought a budding friend who had used me cruelly for amusement.

6.
Wednesday, June 6th, 1866
Andoversford, Gloucestershire, England

'Bloody bastarding bugger!'

I surprised myself with my own vehemence; my voice sounded strange, as if it were not my own. Had I really said that aloud? Yes, a boy of around ten carrying a bucket of horse manure and a small shovel was looking at me open-mouthed and when I met his gaze, he dropped the bucket, turned and scurried away. I thought absently that Esther would have been proud of me, she was already and expert swearer and often forgot herself at home, earning herself frequent admonishments from Mother and Father and stifled laughs from Grandfather.

I was almost at the door of the Dining Room where duties awaited but I could not work with this rage in me, besides breakfasts were over and lunches would not be served until noon and so I turned and headed for the stables.

It was warm in the stables despite a crisp morning outside; the block adjoined the smithy from where came the sound of metal hammering on metal. The unmistakable smell of tortured iron combining with the scent of manured straw gave an essence of the very heartbeat of the motion and industry that had kept man a step ahead of all God's other creations for thousands of years.

Horses were being rubbed down and groomed by various shirt-sleeved lads; each, it seemed, competing with his brothers for the prize of best turned-out mount. A tall black man in fine livery was holding the reins of a magnificent racehorse as ebony as himself, he was whispering in the beast's ear and stroking a mane that trailed through his fingers like midnight silk.

I found Enoch in a side stall seemingly repairing a stirrup. I stopped as he looked up, he smiled in recognition, but it died on his face, frozen out of existence by the look of fury and naked hatred I sent in his direction. He frowned as if puzzled.

'Something wrong?' He paused in his work to study me, feigning a concern that might have fooled me yesterday but today seemed part of the mockery he clearly revelled in.

'Creeping Jane,' I hissed, shaking in an effort to control my fury.

'What?' He persisted in feigning innocence.

'Creeping Bloody Jane!' I shouted, causing a pair of faces to peer curiously around the side of the stall, disappearing just as quickly.

'What about Creeping Bloody Jane?'

Was he genuinely that insensitive or had I misjudged a simpleton? He stood, wiping his hands on his breeches and reaching for his felt hat hanging from a post, pulling it on as he closed the gap between us. I was struggling not to cry; I would not give this oaf the satisfaction of seeing how much he had upset me with his boorish humour.

'I have just made myself look a complete fool because I trusted you and thought you a friend - or have you forgotten your advice about horse racing? Eh? Perhaps that's it, it was of no importance to you - just small diversion to lighten your day?'

He took his hat back off and swept his long hair off his face. Then the look of confusion was slowly replaced by a dawning realisation that, to my further annoyance, conveyed more humour than remorse.

'You... didn't actually... try to place a bet on ...'

'On Creeping Jane - yes I bloody well did! And now I look an idiot and... and you have no idea the damage your joke has done.'

He had been about to laugh but I could hold it in no longer and the true weight of my worry over Father overwhelmed my restraint and I fell into huge sobs; I buried my face in my hands and turned to half-walk half-run away from the stables - and Andoversford and everywhere. I just wanted my family around me, I wanted to hug Father. I wanted to go home.

I heard his urgent footsteps behind me padding through a floor of damp straw as I approached the stable door, then I felt him take my arm. I tugged angrily to shake off his grip, but he persisted. I shook him off again and the footsteps stopped as I bustled away.

'Ellen... wait; hey! Come on, wait...'

I marched on, sucking in breath between sobs, out through the door and into the sunlight hastily brushing any trace of distress from my face and composing myself. I had assumed Enoch had given up his hopeless attempt at renewed ingratiation but suddenly there he was at my side, and this time his look of concern appeared genuine, mixed as it was with a hint of shock.

'Stop a moment, Ellen, please...'

Despite my resolve, I found myself slowing and then stopping but I still could not bring myself to look at him.

'I'm sorry - very sorry... I... I didn't realise you were taking what I said as Gospel - I was trying to tell you not to bet unless you know a dead cert - and there ain't many as does I can promise you. Have you got the bums after you or something?'

'The what?' I knew my voice sounded flat, I was still staring at nothing but there was a dawning realisation that I might have been, in part at least, responsible for the situation between us.

'The bums... debt collectors... joobs; is that why you needed the money all of an urgency?'

I had no reason to trust him but there was something in his demeanour that reminded me of Grandfather - a wisdom or otherworldliness, hard to define but nevertheless as tangible as the scent of a flower in that it was both there and yet impossible to point to.

I told him the whole story while we sat at a table in the dining room drinking coffee. He was sewing a stirrup strap in his lap but listening to every word, interrupting with the occasional utterance of 'Joob' or 'Bastard' at the mention of Bailiff Haynes.

I finished my tale with a sigh. Enoch put down his repaired stirrup, brushed back his hair and stared at a place far beyond the walls of the Dining Room. 'My Granddad on Mother's side, Granddad Banse, was a wise man, I'll tell you all about him one day and all the things he could do; now he had a saying that he was fond of churning out whenever something was going arse over head...'

I suddenly realised Enoch had his hand over mine on the table; it had seemed so natural I had completely failed to notice it before. He raised his other hand, pointing a finger to the sky, his voice taking on an octogenarian and decidedly evangelical quiver, '... Deshshel worlds 'bout every turn!' Which means, there's a thousand worlds around every corner - which in turn means don't worry about what might happen because it ain't happened yet and very possibly might not.'

I sniffed, 'There may be a thousand worlds around my family's corner but in every one of them Bailiff Haynes and Agent Porritt are lurking like fat poisonous slugs.' An involuntary shiver raised Enoch's hand off mine and his arm folded around my shoulder, giving a comforting squeeze. He smiled; 'Granddad Banse also said, 'Yekka buliasa nashti beshes pe done grastende!' No elaboration was forthcoming, so I frowned at him quizzically. He grinned, 'Romany - You can't ride two horses with only one arse! Not sure what he meant but he only ever said it after a good bellyful of nettle wine.' I surprised myself by laughing for the first time that day but still counted the moments until the evening stage could take me home for my family's last night together in God knows how long.

It was a truly splendid evening meal; potatoes, sprouts, turnip and mutton followed by rock cakes and cream; and Father ate it like it was his last, breaking his own rule about talking at the table by joking and swapping anecdotes with Grandfather throughout. William and Walter were old enough to understand this was a special occasion. We were all going to temporary homes until we could be back together again; it was going to be an adventure. Mother, steadfast, brave and inscrutable served second helpings where required, assisted by Esther who wore her Sunday dress for the occasion; how beautiful she was turning out, two years younger but already a shade taller than me.

We talked about the unseasonably warm weather, Mrs Brooke's recent illness from which she was thankfully making a full recovery, Rev Byron's escaping goat and a hundred and one other small things that gave us pause from staring into the abyss that lay open before us. The boys were rubbing their eyes, fighting sleep on such a strange evening and Father allowed them a little longer before packing them off behind the curtain.

Grandfather produced a jug of cider and he and Father took a mug each. Esther suggested a song as Mother stood to feed the fire with a log or two. Then a knock rattled the door.

'If they've come a day early, I'll do bloody murder on 'em,' Grandfather growled as Father stood, took a deep breath and fixed his face in defiance. He opened the door.

It was quite dark outside and in the dim flicker of Father's window lamp it was possible to see little other than the outline of the tall figure in a felt hat standing a few paces back from the threshold and when it removed the hat and spoke it remained anonymous - except to me.

'Good evening Sir, sorry to call at such an hour but it has taken a while to find the right house. I was wondering if I might have a word with Ellen if she should be awake?'

As Father moved the candle closer to the visitor to get a better look the first thing to reflect the light was a glint from a gold tooth in a wide smile.

'Oh aye? And who might be calling on her?' Father's voice dripped suspicion.

Before there was time for an answer I was at Father's side, sharing his puzzlement.

'It's all right Father, we are acquainted; this man works at the racetrack.'

'Enoch Johnsey Sir,' the figure's smile widened, he gave a slight bow as he stood in Father's gaze, hands behind back, trying and failing to appear nonchalant.

'Well... you had better be coming inside then,' Father stood aside as Enoch entered. He was wearing a rather fine looking dark brown riding coat over a clean shirt and waistcoat - and shining boots. He offered a short bow to Mother and Esther and winked cheekily in the direction of Walter and William whose drowsy but curious faces had appeared around the curtain. Finally, he turned to me; fishing in a pocket of his breeches he produced a drawstring purse and offered it up.

'I thought I'd better deliver this for you as I was in Town anyway.'

I took it gingerly from him, frowning and confused both by his presence in my home and the curiosity of his apparent reason for visiting. Squeezing the purse suggested the presence of coins within. Enoch coughed discreetly behind a hand.

'It's your winnings; I didn't want to carry it around with me too long, there's some dusky coves about the track and what with you being off work until Saturday...'

'Winnings?' Mother's question had a sharp edge.

'Gambling on horse races?' Father's question by contrast was like a storm front moving in. He directed it first at me then at Enoch who in the meantime had raised a coy giggle from Esther with a wink and a grin. Father's growing disapproval of our caller was palpable as he took in the shoulder-length black hair, gold tooth and - if any further confirmation of the youth's waywardness were necessary - he was wearing a gold ring in his ear. I was about to deny all knowledge of gambling or ill-gotten 'winnings' when Enoch responded, suddenly appearing crestfallen in the manner of a minister whose attempts to save a fallen woman had failed as she drifted back to a life of sin.

'Much against my advice Sir; I warned her quite forcefully about the folly of gambling. I said that only bookmakers and owners profited from it - is that not what I said Ellen?'

That at least was true, and I found myself nodding. I loosened the purse strings and turned it upside down dropping four sovereigns and four crowns - five pounds exactly, into my hand. Stunned, I looked to Enoch for an explanation, he offered a beatific smile. 'Creeping Jane eh? Who would have believed it? Ten to one!'

At the mention of the horse's name Grandfather burst into laughter that ended with a coughing fit and Mother patting his back. It seemed to break a roomful of tension. On showing Father the money, his whole demeanour changed as if an evangelical presence had torn a demon from his back. He smiled widely and the sun shone again in our home. Esther was not long in being infected by the mood, hugging Mother who had yet to see the coins but who nevertheless understood she was in the presence of salvation. Esther enlightened her, 'It's five pounds Mother, five whole pounds!' Father took Mother up in a hug and it was only when I turned to seek out Enoch that I realised he had slipped away.

He had almost reached the end of our path to the lane and was about to untie a horse from the ash tree next to our gate. He paused as he saw me approaching in the dim light from our window. I reached him and was in an instant at a loss for what to say. How do you thank someone who has, by some means beyond you, come to the rescue of the thing you love most in the entire world?

He too, unusually for him, seemed to be tongue-tied. Clutching the lapel of his coat I reached up and kissed him on the cheek, there would be time for questions and formal thanks when I returned to work on Saturday. I smiled, hoping he could see it in the dark before turning to head back to the house from where laughter was still leaking. He caught my arm, halted my retreat.

'Well, that one was worth about a shilling...'

Lifting me up he gave me my first ever big proper kiss, full on the lips and it seemed to go on for minutes. I wondered when it would stop, then I hoped it wouldn't, my arms were around his neck as though they had a life of their own and when, through the necessity of breathing, we finally paused he whispered.

'You seem taller in the dark.'

'That's because you are holding me off the ground,' I replied.

He chuckled as he lowered me gently, 'See you on Saturday, Lass of the Land.'

I watched in the dark as his horse clopped away up the lane towards the Tewkesbury Road until I could see him no more and only then did I turn for the house to join in the celebrations. Halfway up the path I paused, screwed up my eyes and sneezed... on a Thursday... for something better.

7.
Cheltenham, England
August 28th, 1867

Throughout that unforgettable summer Enoch and I walked out together in Cheltenham and rode two to a horse around the lanes of Uckington as he seemed to find his way to our cottage almost every day.

Dolly's little enterprise did not survive the storms that swept through the world of trade and commerce in England that year and so I found myself once again under the same roof as my parents. I earned a little money delivering fruit and vegetables from Cheltenham market to customers about town.

Enoch and I went visiting to Abel Isgrove and his young wife in Little Bayshill Terrace and to Mr and Mrs Bolt formerly of the Noah's Ark where we enjoyed a delightful afternoon tea. I discovered Enoch could be really charming and had clearly been brought up to have the most impeccable manners.

One rebellious and mercurial October day, Enoch dismounted in the shade of a horse chestnut tree somewhere along a lane near Bishop's Cleeve. He helped me down.

'Why are we stopping here, we are due at Mother's for tea and…'

He raised a finger, a smile quite unlike a normal Enoch smile, passed across his face, if I had blinked, I would have missed it. He knelt, picking from the dancing grass a horse chestnut husk, prising it apart, he took out the glistening brown nut.

'Do you want a game of conkers?' I asked, recalling a Robin Berry lecture on the new pastime he had discovered in Oxford.

'Ain't never heard of that,' Enoch replied handing the nut up to me, but if you carries one of these in your pocket, you'll never have piles or rheumatism, don't eat them mind, they're poisonous. And don't give them to horses neither, they're called horse chestnuts, but they don't do horses a lot of good.'

'Is that why we've stopped here, so you could tell me how to avoid rheumatism?'

'No,' he grinned, 'I stopped here to ask you if you wouldn't mind marrying me, but when I knelt down to say it proper, I saw that horse chestnut and it sort of distracted me.'

He took advantage of the fact that I was shocked speechless to continue.

'Well… that's that anyway, so …seeing as I'm kneeling now, will you marry me or not?'

'S'pose I might as well.'

I tried to remain nonchalant, but I laughed with delight and spoiled it.

The End of the Sky

However, before any announcement and the seeking of permissions, I had a rather less comfortable liaison to navigate.

Robin Berry had written to inform me he was home for a half-term recess and that he would be pleased to call on me for a few hours about the Town. And call he did, in a fine suit, a new bowler hat and even a cane, looking every inch the city gentleman. He had grown taller in the short time we had been apart and clearly impressed Mother who had made no secret of the fact she would prefer a potential doctor to a stable hand as a son in law - especially a stable hand with a 'Touch of the lanes' about him.

And so, Robin and I walked up Swindon Road into Town; we spent a long time looking in a shop window where a display of mechanical toys and automatons caught the attention of a group of ragged young children from The Rookery who jabbered in indecipherable tongues clearly enraptured by the unattainable treasures within. Little tin soldiers shouldered arms and saluted, a tin lady and gentleman dressed in ballroom attire waltzed around each other while a merry-go-round carried painted horses in a dance about a maypole with a tiny flag of England at the top.

I felt Robin's hand slip into mine and the pain of what I knew I had to do lay in me like lead. I loved him but, I now knew, it was a platonic love, a sibling love. He was a dear friend and the very thought of causing him pain was a heavy fall of snow upon my soul. We walked on, arriving at a little cake shop where we had once shared afternoon tea. I stopped; 'Let's go in here.'

Robin held back the chair as I sat, he took the opposite seat at an intimate round table covered in a pink cloth. A small vase of wooden flowers sat between us. He picked up the menu, frowning at it as if it were an unfamiliar textbook; 'Hmmm, you go first...' He passed it to me, I looked at it without reading.

'Actually, I'm not that hungry.... it's...'

He frowned, 'I say, not going down with something are you? You've been a bit off all day.' He took my wrist between thumb and fingertips, simultaneously consulting his pocket watch.

'Pulse is a bit fast; stick your tongue out old girl.'

I pulled my arm away, a little too roughly causing his frown to deepen. I instantly regretted my brusqueness and wrapped my admonishment in velvet before delivery, 'I'm not going to poke my tongue out while sitting in a cake shop - next you'll be asking me to ... to strip down to my bloomers or something.'

He actually blushed and my affection for him grew; this could not endure any longer; 'Robin, listen, I have something to tell you.' He rubbed an earlobe and seemed suddenly unsure of where to look.

'Have you really? Oh dear.'

I took a deep breath, 'I have met someone; a young man I have become quite fond of.'

His face became unreadable, drumming his fingers on the tablecloth he picked up the menu and gave it no more than a fleeting glance before replacing it; then he took out his pocket watch and replaced it without consulting it. An over-ornate wall clock in the Swiss style chopped time into small pieces with deep tocks while across the room two expensively dressed ladies spoke in sotto voices and touched each other's arms to emphasise the gravity of their words.

'I see' Robin spoke to the tabletop.

There was little I could add; 'I'm sorry, I really am... but I thought...'

'Well,' he announced breezily, 'I'm having a jam scone - how about you?'

Was he really unconcerned? Had I possibly misread him all of this time? I had six or seven letters written to me from Oxford, the last just two weeks before, in which he had spoken at length about the city, his studies, college life and even the hornbeam tree he could see from his window. He had stated in every letter just how much he missed my company and had inevitably signed off with, *'My deepest and most profound affection - your eternal admirer, Robin Berry Esq.'*

He called a waitress and ordered scones and tea. We spoke of my family and his, the market for produce, steam engines, great paintings, Shakespeare, maladies of the mind and the moons of Jupiter. I began to believe my announcement had been set aside as an insignificance but as we rose to leave, he helped me into my coat he surprised me with;

'Local chap, is he? Your young man?'

Momentarily wrong-footed I rallied and attempted to load my reply with diplomatic nonchalance, 'Oh... yes... Colesbourne,'

Robin nodded, 'Lovely little place, nice gardens, near the source of the Thames you know.'

I paused as we reached the door, 'You are Robin, and always will be, my dear, dear friend and I hope you feel the same?'

'Umm, oh yes, of course my dear Ellen, gosh... yes; you don't shake me off that easily old girl.' He smiled, his eyes did not.

We took the Tewkesbury stage as far as Uckington; he kissed my hand at our gate before raising his hat and walking briskly off down the lane. I watched until the turn in the path took him out of sight. He did not look back.

Nature is to the laws of man what an Atlantic storm is to a candle. Grandfather saw it first, he may not always tell you the day of the week, but he could tell you the time of year as accurately as any migrating bird or birthing ewe - and he could tell from the light in a lass's eye, from her voice or even from the way she looked out of her own world into the larger one, whether or not her innocence had taken flight.

Enoch took me in a carriage to meet his family in Colesbourne. The Johnsons lived in a small cottage next to a stream surrounded by rolling fields and in sight of the Church of St James. The little house appeared in need of repair from outside, but the interior was as fine as any I had seen, the living room being smaller than our room but cosy and with framed embroideries on the walls. A small, black one-eyed dog had rushed out to greet us, wagging first his tail and then his whole body at the sight of Enoch. It followed us in through a door so low Enoch was forced to duck as we entered into the family's main room.

Enoch's father and mine could have been brothers; both being dark, bearded and tall. Edward Johnsey, however, exuded an air of severity; he was dressed in a black frock coat, high collar, cufflinks and gaiters. He had

Enoch's dark eyes, longer than average hair greying at the temples and he moved with the grace of a prize fighter. His manners appeared rehearsed and his courtesies flawless, but they seemed reserved and stiff. Enoch assured me his father was no stranger to levity but there was little evidence of it on that first encounter.

Enoch's mother, Mary had the most striking eyes, cornflower blue in the sunlight of the front cottage garden but heliotrope under lamp or candlelight. She spoke with an Irish accent, slowly and deliberately pronouncing each word as if it were a priceless gift. She and Enoch's sister, Susan - two years his junior but a year my senior and unmistakeably his sibling - served a dinner of chicken broth and delicious soda bread. We ate unspeaking, the only sounds coming from outside where the family hens gossiped like judgemental chapelgoers. Mrs Johnsey eventually broke the silence.

'So... Ellen, Enoch tells me he first met you when you worked at an inn in Cheltenham?'

Mr Johnson looked at his wife rather than at me when he spoke, his voice deep and biblical with a lyrical brogue less pronounced than Mary's mingled with the familiar burr of rural Gloucestershire,

'...An inn... a drinking establishment?'

It sounded more of an accusation than a question, but it nevertheless begged a courteous answer, 'Yes Sir, The Noah's Ark, St George's Street - are you familiar with it?'

Enoch looked suddenly pained as his father finally turned his attention to me, 'I do not drink alcohol; this is a house of abstinence; although I believe my son has fallen into the arms of the sirens of insensibility on more than one occasion.'

While Enoch stared at the ceiling, I took a deep breath. Two years earlier I would have been frozen into silence but there were few viewpoints I had not encountered in my time at The Noah's Ark. I mustered my sweetest smile, 'Indeed Sir, but they also served wholesome local meals and what I am told was the finest tea to come out of India.'

It might have been my imagination but I'm sure the briefest of smiles passed across the patriarch's face before he once again returned his attention to the meal. Mary Johnson did smile, to herself, before rising to help Susan clear the table; I rose to help too but was politely reminded that I was a guest.

With dinner finished we sat in chairs around a cosy hearth and when the little dog came wagging in from the direction of the kitchen and leapt into the lap of Enoch's father it seemed to transform the man. Sternness and rigidity were at once replaced by smiles, deep laughter and mutual affection and I saw for the first time the soul behind the mask.

It broke a spell with Mrs Johnson and Susan now also seemingly free from the shackles of convention and everyone began chattering at once. Susan left when a friend called for her; then Mr and Mrs Johnson went visiting - and then Enoch bolted the door, took my hand and I followed him unprotestingly up a narrow wooden staircase and along a low corridor to his room; and when we came back down some considerable time later I found myself wondering whether it was indeed a loving God or merely jealous priests who frowned on such a joyous thing, for surely to disapprove of such an act of love was to also to frown upon flowers, music, good food or the million other natural wonders and blessings of creation. No matter how pious and evangelical the preacher, he could not stop a single flower from blooming when nature told it the time was right.

And when I went home, Grandfather knew.

8.
Cheltenham, England
Sunday, June 20th, 1869

The day hardly dawned at all. When the sun rose above the horizon it did so behind a thick shield of ominous clouds, it didn't even shake next door's cockerel out of dreamland, it was gone six o' clock before he managed a rusty crow. At seven o'clock we still had the lamp lit in the living room so that Esther and Ann could fuss and fart about with my hair, never being satisfied with the end result. Finally, we decided to take all the adornments and ties off and just part it in the middle, letting it hang down with just a wildflower tiara to set it off.

Father had sneezed while lighting his pipe and a small spark of hot ash had landed on the sleeve of my cream cardigan leaving a small brown mark. Mother could not see it of course and so we all agreed not to mention it as she would have burst into flames herself.

Emily, Samuel and William were coming in on a carriage from Deerhurst, picking us up on the way and I hoped and prayed the full and sagging sky would retain its load until the Bullinghams arrived safely at the Chapel.

'It's as black as the Earl of Hell's waistcoat out there!' Esther came in through the yard door inelegantly adjusting her dress and still carrying a hairbrush, 'It's going to pi... pour down,' she deftly changed direction in mid-sentence on spotting Mother in her chair.

'Aye, well, the sooner you all get there, the better then.' Father sat in his own chair, picking up his copy of the Looker-On and stretching his legs until his feet almost reached the hearth.

Father had sat me down last night before bed and explained why he could not give me away. While he was happy to bless our union, being asked to enter a house of prayer that, to him, did not pay appropriate reverence to the Almighty, was pushing it a bit too far. He would be honouring us with his presence at the little wedding party in The Royal Oak after the ceremony.

The duty of 'Giving me away' has therefore fallen to my brother, Walter, who at just thirteen looks quite the gentleman-about-town in a suit bought almost new from Mrs Arthur whose son had outgrown it having only worn it twice. Esther is to be my chief bridesmaid and official witness along with George, Enoch's uncle. (Enoch's parents share my own parent's antipathy for Baptists and so will also be joining us later.)

I had feared that Enoch's father would have shunned the wedding party too; being as he is averse to the demon drink and excess levity but while Mr Johnson Senior shuns alcohol he does, according to Enoch, occasionally put things in his pipe which makes him laugh and relax. He gets this magical smoking mixture during rare visits from his brother-in-law Edgar Banse who works at the dock in Avonmouth and who once brought a pet monkey home. It escaped and lived wild around Colesbourne for a whole summer surviving on apples and nuts. And, so the story goes, it piddled on a fine lady who was visiting the Elwes family at Colesbourne Park as she passed under a tree in which it was hiding. Her husband was so incensed he fired his pistol into the tree but missed the monkey. The shot did, however, bring down a passing swan which landed in a punt.

The horse and wedding carriage arrived - it was really the Deerhurst blacksmith cart, but it is surprising what several determined and skilful pairs of hands can accomplish with a few wooden benches, commandeered bed sheets and bunches of colourful flowers.

Brother William burst in with all the urgency of a soldier, entreating us to get a move on. He was in a brown suit, rather too thick for summer wear but on a subdued day like today he would probably get away with it. He also wore a bowler hat made for a head one size larger. At almost fifteen he looked quite the young man, tall and with the gait and demeanour of Father.

Mother placed her hands on my cheeks, her eyes restless behind cruel clouded lens but what might have been a mask of tragedy was converted by a smile into a face that refused to acknowledge misfortune as a master.

'You've always worked hard my lovely... good little lass, you are.'

I placed my hands over hers, her smile remained but the eyes frowned.

'The next time we meet you'll be Mrs Johnsey.' A chill ran through me at the sudden realisation of the enormity of this day. Mother whispered as if divulging a well-kept secret accessible only to married women, 'Now the real work begins, aye and worries too, but if you take good care of your lad and he takes good care of you there ain't nothing to be afraid of in this whole wide world.'

Emily and Samuel were waiting in the carriage as Esther, Walter, and I squeezed inside. The journey to the chapel was likely to take about half an hour and although this was to be one of the great turning points of my life, I appeared to be the calmest of the sisters, Emily and Esther hardly came up for breath throughout the journey, Samuel engaged Walter in some smithy talk about the differences between Welsh and Staffordshire Iron and I, like Mrs Beeton in a kitchen full of servants, simply let them all get on with it.

My clothes and belongings were packed; many of my things had already been transported to Enoch's.... to *our* ...house in Little Bayshill Terrace and I would soon be exchanging one roof for another yet again - this time along with my name and status. Miraculously, through a gap in the blackest of the clouds a bright blue eye of sky appeared casting a shaft of light ahead of us and grounding somewhere in the centre of town much like an illustration I had seen of the Magi being guided to the stable. There came another break, then another from the west promising a brighter day than expected and lifting everyone's spirits.

'Hey.... you're smiling to yourself... HEY!' An exuberant Esther brought me back from the fascinating sky.

'Thinking about the wedding night, are we?' Esther nudged me; Emily chuckled while Sam and Walter feigned disinterest and shook their heads.

'Tell me, is Abel Isgrove's brother, Noah coming?' Esther's eyes, a darker blue than mine, twinkled, full of mischievous demons; I feigned severity.

103

'He is - and you keep away from him, he has a reputation for being only interested in one thing.'

'Aye, well I shall be pinning a favour to him on the way out and if he's lucky he might get the chance to do *me* a favour after the reception!' Esther roared with laughter causing a bewhiskered and patriarchal figure walking into town to look with disdain at the passing carriage.

Uncle Michael, Aunt Mary, Eliza, Harriet and Richard were waiting outside the Chapel. Esther ran to meet her cousin Eliza and the pair of seventeen-year-olds were soon giggling and deep in a conversation that in all likelihood concerned lads. They could have passed as twins.

Harriet was a delight; at nine she had a beautiful combination of Granny Sabina's Iberian darkness and the bright blue Bullingham eyes. She was destined to break many a boy's heart. Aunt Mary was pale, she rarely ventured far from home even though she suffered no physical ailment and the strain of being amongst a crowd in the centre of town showed in her face. She gripped Uncle Michael's arm for support but her smile of seeing me approach on Walter's arm was heartfelt and seemed to lift her apprehension.

Uncle Michael tapped his pipe on the chapel wall to empty it, displaying at once both his nonchalance and his atheism. It mattered not to him which place of worship he entered; none of them meant a hoot. He swallowed me in a huge hug, lifting me off the ground before Eliza remonstrated with him for crumpling my wedding clothes.

The End of the Sky

'Your fellow is in there awaiting, best we get indoors.' Uncle Michael led the family in with Walter and I holding back for our 'Grand Entrance.'

No music, just a sudden hush. Cooler inside, attention drawn upwards by a brief trill from a thrush perched on one of the high beams darkened by years of tallow smoke. Two great candles, the biggest I had ever seen, were placed either side of a plain altar, their smoking yellow flames leaning slightly and flickering from the breeze that passed across the front of the chapel from a high open side window.

My family slipped off into pews leaving just Walter and I to walk the down the aisle. Before the altar, Enoch, in a fine black suit, his hair combed back and with the bulk of Abel Isgrove straining the seams of a tweed jacket at his side turned to witness my approach. I offered him a shy smile which was meagre in comparison to the one he returned.

I am told there are great abbey and cathedral weddings among the well-to-do that are months in the planning, but nothing could be grander than this magnificent simplicity, with all the fineries stripped away so that the real jewels - the love and bonding of two souls - could be displayed in all their glory.

Someone muttered 'Beautiful' and I almost cried at the thought they might be referring to me. My family, who had made a farthing do a penny's work every day for as long as I could remember had come together to make me feel special. Mother and Esther had shopped for cotton and linen for the repair and replacement of clothes, Father had gone without his tobacco all last week to contribute to the shoes and stockings on my feet and Uncle Michael had paid for my wedding reception. Emily and Samuel had provided my carriage and I had arrived as fine as any queen with passers-by 'Aww-ing' and 'Ahh-ing' as we descended. It was a debt I could never repay - and would never be asked to.

I do not recall reaching Enoch's side; it seemed I was just suddenly there. He looked down at me and his face told a story without words. His love was a fierce thing, elemental, disdainful of the need for ceremony; older than this building and everything it represented. But he had responded to the kindness of Pastor Scorey and so allowed his benefactor's God to bless our union.

'Lass o' the Land,' he whispered.

Pastor Scorey had eyes that looked as if they had witnessed a lifetime of sin and suffering, but they contained no judgement. He had spent many of his working days ministering to broken hearts among the crushed and punished - the clothed beasts beloved of no one but Jesus. His voice reflected this clemency, it was a voice that sought out the frailties of people and administered balm instead of brimstone. A bishop had once visited Mary Magdalene's Church and trumpeted forth as if full of bellows-wind right over the heads of the congregation without once meeting their eyes or touching their souls. Pastor Scorey spoke gently and was all the stronger for it.

He was not much taller than me but broad in the shoulder; his hands were broad too - and rough like the hands of a working man. He wore a gold ring on the little finger of his left hand. He smiled, offered me a wink and took a deep breath...

'We are gathered here today....'

His words were like rolling hills, immovable, permanent and comforting. One could go to sleep in the knowledge that they would hold true the next morning - and for all mornings; the contours unchanged as they had been for countless years. Enoch looked full of thought, did the boy he used to be once dream of a wedding day like this? Was it all he had anticipated? And was I the image of the ghost-bride who had occupied his daydreams?

I had dreamed of all manner of weddings on my long walks to and from school and on errands, from the grand to the mean and from church altar to foreign battlefield. My husband would be anything from a prince to a parson and from a plumed captain to a corsair. But one constant strand had my chosen partner filling my life with romance and adventure; seeking out the path untrod but protecting me securely as we walked together along it. I had not the slightest doubt as I stood by his side; Enoch would live up to my dream.

'...Enoch Edward Johnsey... Wilt thou take this woman, Ellen, to be thy lawful wedded wife? Wilt thou love her, comfort and keep her, for richer or poorer, in sickness and health and forsaking all others remain true to her as long as you both shall live?'

The candles flickered roughly as if from a sudden gust and the one in front of Enoch went out. Without pausing in his speech, Pastor Scorey took a spill from the altar and transferred a light from the surviving candle to its companion.

There was no pause or hesitation; in fact, the final syllable of Pastor Scorey's question was cut off by Enoch's unwavering reply.

'I will.'

Then for the last time in my life I was called the name I had held since my first day.

'Ellen Bullingham, Wilt thou take this man, Enoch to be thy lawful wedded husband? Wilt thou love him, honour and obey him, comfort and keep him, for richer or poorer, in sickness and health and forsaking all others remain true to him as long as you both shall live?'

'I will'

The ring was tiny between Enoch's thumb and forefinger as he slipped in onto mine; a thin band of braided silver, the only adornment my hands had ever enjoyed. Then the thrush sang in the upper beams, its lively tune causing everyone to look up. Even Pastor Scorey paused in his blessing and smiled before finally telling Enoch he could kiss his wife. And, forgoing decorum, Mrs Ellen Johnsey reached up, threw her arms around her husband's neck and gave him a kiss that would have stopped a grandfather clock! I heard a big gulping sob from Esther closely followed by a snotty sniff that brought a chuckle from Walter and William; there was a harsh whisper from Emily telling Mother I had kissed the groom, then everyone stood and the bell high above rang out over Cheltenham, drawing the sun's attention and sending the thrush who had watched our union flying off to tell the world the good news.

'I've got something to tell you.'

I had wanted to tell him the moment he came through the door, the whites of his eyes alabaster among the coal dust covering the rest of his face, but I forced myself to wait until he splashed himself under the outhouse pump. He passed into the living room, sweeping back wet hair and sinking into his fireside chair, a ritual he had carried out six days a week throughout the seven weeks of our marriage. I always covered the chair with an old sheet at this time of day to protect it from his work clothes.

'It's a girl.'

Enoch spoke while taking off his boots, looking critically at the sole of the left one.

After several seconds in which I had just stared at him with my mouth open, he looked up, sweeping his hair back again, grinning – and, for a second, there was the boy who had called 'Lass o' the Land' over the fence at Andoversford Racecourse.

'But I didn't even...'

He stood, braces dangling, he hugged me and then, holding me at arm's length...

'You're... we're... going to have a daughter, Lass.'

And so, we did.

Sarah Ann Johnsey was born in the middle of a cold, moonless night to the screech of an owl and a rumble of distant thunder. She came into the world by the flickering light of an oil lamp with my Mother's hands supporting her head and her Auntie Esther swearing and blaspheming, hands dripping with hot water and vinegar as she held ready a freshly boiled and dried swaddling sheet. Throughout the whole business I could hear

Father's bootsteps just beyond the bedroom door, floorboards creaking.

Father had seen many humans and countless other members of God's kingdom entering the world and the process held no mystery, even so, his anxiety manifested itself in the clouds of smoke from his frantically puffed pipe seeping in above the door and creeping along the ceiling like an incoming bank of Spring fog.

Cocooned in her blanket, this person who had yet to hear a bird sing or feel the warmth of the sun on her skin rested in my arms. Tiny fingers gripped and grabbed, knuckling a face that I would see in my dreams. This little part of Enoch and I...

I recalled a poem I had read in the book Mrs Brooke had presented me with on leaving her schoolroom all those years ago, Dicken's Household Words, Volume Five. I had committed it to memory as an exercise during my time before sleep in the Noah's Ark.

The first born is a fairy child,
A wondrous emanation!
A tameless creature, fond and wild
A moving exultation.
Beside the hearth, upon the stair,
Its footstep laughs with lightness,
And cradled, all its features fair,
And touched with mystic brightness.
So much of those that gave it birth,
Of Father and of Mother,
So much of this world built on Earth,
And so much of another!

There seemed little of me or Enoch in Sarah Ann's face in the darkness of those small hours - her first hours on Earth. But I slept before the dawn and when I woke it was Mother who held her, sat by the side of the bed.

They say at christenings that babies are a gift from God, however, we all know that often God is just as likely to want his gifts returned and so it does not do to become too attached to them. I prefer to think of babies as trees or flowers; the trees will grow big and strong and will be around long after those who planted the seed are gone, the flowers, by contrast, will bloom, beautiful, a delight; but all too soon will fade and wither in a world where tomorrow is a prayer and not a promise.

I hoped and prayed that Sarah Ann was going to be a tree. My big sister, Emily had grown two flowers, William and Charles, but her third son, Thomas, was beginning to walk on strong little legs and thankfully had all the makings of a tree as sturdy and steadfast as his father, Samuel, now Deerhurst's finest blacksmith. My thoughts, as thoughts often do, wandered unchecked into worlds where I had followed a different path.

Had I married Robin Berry (Not that he had ever proposed of course) I should probably have given birth in a room full of light with a doctor or at least a crisp nurse at the bedside and all manner of medicines at the ready should they be needed. He would have studied the baby with a clinical eye and said something like, 'Yes, jolly good, well done old girl, all the parts seem to be there, splendid.'

Sarah Ann's father, in contrast, said nothing. He was not there. Instead, he was in Gloucester Prison, two months into a six-month sentence of hard labour, handed down for stealing nineteen shillings in takings while delivering for Ezra Crook the coal merchant.

His entreaty in court, explaining he was desperate for the money with a new baby on the way and furniture to buy and medicine for his ailing mother was dismissed. Our landlord had spoken for him, stating he paid his rent on time and was always helpful and friendly, but this was likewise ignored. Nineteen shillings... six months, a hundred and eighty-two days, about a penny a day, that's how much a common man's life was worth to them! But there was no time for anger or bitterness. He shouldn't have done it, we would have managed and now there is a dependence on the charity of my parents, my sister and brother-in-law and a most generous landlord who is a Baptist like my husband and who has waived the rent until Enoch's release.

My life became one of routine; rise, light the fire, feed Sarah Ann, make tea and porridge, go shopping and try to maintain that elusive balance between what is needed and what the budget will allow; then it's prepare dinner, wash up and finally sit by the fire, perhaps read, go to bed with the sun and get up with it and start all over again.

Then he came home.

He held us and we all cried and he promised we would never be apart again. It appeared that even six months of incarceration among the desperate and hardened had not stolen the human decency from Enoch's soul.

But to say he had not changed would be a lie. Of course, he was the principal architect of his own misfortune; had he not taken the money he would not have been jailed - but does not a disproportionate sentence convert the perpetrator into the victim? Disregarding the fact that the punishment was meant to be a deterrent to others considering stealing from their masters, it was harsh beyond reason and all it taught my husband was that that society, his employers and even his country, considered him and his family valueless. And there was now a flame of restlessness within him that had not been there before.

9.
Cheltenham, England
Friday, September 23rd, 1870

'Do you know what this is?' Enoch frowned turning the black irregular shape this way and that in the light of the oil lamp as if seeking some undiscovered property of the thing. I guessed the obvious answer was not what he was seeking.

'Yes.' I answered. I had once been lectured by Robin Berry over the true age and nature of what he called 'fossil fuel'. I doubted whether Enoch saw things so dispassionately, he endowed everything with a soul and a sentience.

'This - he pointed to the all too obvious lump of coal, is made of the same type of stuff as what diamonds are made of. There's a cove on Montpellier Grove, wears a fez, he's a professor and he says coal and diamonds are both made from carbon but that coal is made of dead forests and stuff while diamonds is made from more pure carbon - but it goes to show, don't it?'

'Goes to show what?'

He had lost me somewhere but had also surprised me - as he did most days, by knowing far more that I gave him credit for.

'Well, this stuff is used everywhere, it keeps us warm, it keeps them big railway trains going, it powers all manner of engines in all type of factories and yet it's so cheap we sells it by the ton. Then there's diamonds which cost a fortune and they're not really good for anything other than decorations. Men and women and children goes underground and risks their lives to bring this black stuff up in the Dean and in Wales for starvation money.'

'Pity there's no diamond mines or gold mines about here,' my reply brought a strange look from Enoch and I wondered what he had read into what had been, for me, an innocuous comment. He reached across to the little home-made table next to the hearth and handed me a copy of the 'Looker-On' pointing with a black fingernail to an advertisement headlined, 'Calling All Fit and Industrious Men and Women,' beneath which was an illustration of a 'Fit and Industrious' man and woman seemingly hale and hearty outside a rather grand house with a balcony and a horse and carriage waiting in the substantial grounds.

I read on...

'Queensland, that is.' Enoch tapped the paper. The whole place is built on goldfields and you can claim land, free - and fill your pockets with so much gold you'll struggle to hold your trousers up!'

I frowned, 'It can't be that easy though, can it? Everybody would be out there if it was that easy.'

'Oh, it ain't easy my love; you've got to dig for it, under a hot sun, and before that you have to buy tools and have a place to stay which means working for somebody else for a while - but it's possible. I could go

115

out there and be back in five years with enough money to…'

'Oh no you won't!'

I jumped to my feet and raised myself to my full height - which admittedly is not much.

'You ain't going nowhere Enoch Johnsey unless I go too. I waited six long months for you and I'll be damned if I'd wait five years!'

He smiled his smile, gold tooth flickering in the dancing light of the lamp, 'It says men and women lass. I loves you so much I miss you when I go to sleep; I wouldn't go to Gloucester without you, so I'm buggered if I'd go to Queensland.'

'Where?'

Father, when confronted with anything beyond the boundaries of his own world, had a habit of looking out through the window. He rubbed a pane and squinted into the low-hanging morning mist that hovered over the fields, the smoke from his pipe creating a further fog for his eyes to negotiate.

'Queensland', I repeated, I was tempted to add, 'You can't see it from here!' I was not sure if he had even heard of it.

From the yard I could hear the squeak of the mangle as Mother turned the cast iron wheel.

'Queensland,' he spoke the word in a deep rumble with just a hint of sarcasm, 'Bet no queen has ever set foot on it and bet none ever does. It may be a place for fit young men and women, but is it a place for babbies?'

'Well Enoch sent for papers and it says…'

'Aye', he interrupted, 'Oh aye, it'll promise all sorts in papers. Tell me lass, if you found a chest of gold in your garden, would you invite every Tom, Dick and Harry to come and dig for more? I'll tell you what - there'll be gold in Queensland right enough - but it'll already belong to some other beggars and they'll be wanting the likes of you and Enoch to come along and dig it up for them and mend their tools, weave their clothes, grow their food, put the shoes on their horses, brew their ale and wait on their tables - all the things the likes of us is already doing here. Only difference is, you'll be far from home among folk who believes God knows what.'

I must have frowned because Father's tone softened, he dragged his chair next to mine and sat. I felt his arm around my shoulder.

'Thing is see Ellen, there's them as say the only trouble with the rest of the world is, it's full of foreigners - but it ain't. It's full of people who is where they're meant to be and it's them as goes and finds 'em as is the foreigners. You and Enoch, you'll be the foreigners in a land of folk who don't want you there. And no good will come of it, I'm telling you.

'Look at the Yankies and what they are doing to the savages who's been living there since long afore Christian men arrived; it'll come back to haunt 'em you mark my words. Same will be happening in Queensland lass, sooner or later. You'll be shooting them, or they'll be skinning you alive.'

I looked at the floor, noticing scuffed bare flagstones, worn into depressions by generations of feet I could not put a name to; 'Enoch says you can dig and dig in England, but all you'll grow is old. There was a man in the Looker-On who went to Queensland and now he's got a big grand house overlooking Montpellier Gardens and it's got a fountain and peacocks and he was only over there for seven years.'

Father just shook his head.

I was not accustomed to disagreeing with Father and even less telling him so, but a lot of Enoch had rubbed off on me since I became mistress of my own house. And even now, as I sat in the home of my parents, I felt justified in speaking as I saw.

'Grandfather always told me that your home was something you carried inside and wherever you went it went with you.'

Father looked about to respond when Mother entered drying her hands.

'This un's set on going to Queensland, what do you think of that?' Father looked at me as he spoke to her. Mother, although her eyes had all but given up, still moved effortlessly around her little home, picking out plates, bowls and cutlery and placing them accurately on the table.

'Aye? Constance Burrow's lad wrote to her, he's out there. He's lost an eye, but he's made a pile and he's coming home next summer, so he says.'

Before Father could respond, I edged into the tiny silence, 'See Father? Just think of all the good we could do if we came home with a decent amount of money. We could make sure you and Mother were secure in your old age and we could send Sarah Ann to a good school and James could go to college like Robin Berry, he's a bright boy and could make something of himself and...'

Father raised a hand. 'Where's the farthest you been lass?'

I frowned again, 'I've been all over, I've been to Andoversford as you know, I've been to Colesbourne and Kempsford to visit Granddad and Gammer Dubber... I've even been to Cirencester and that's nearly in Wiltshire!' Father's attempt to look severe was ruined by laughing eyes.

'Hear that mother? Woman of the world she is.'

I had to smile too. The thought of leaving my parents and brothers and sisters had tormented me, adding to my indecision over a plan Enoch seemed only too happy to steam ahead with. Then there were the well-known trials and dangers of a long sea voyage; the hardships, the storms, and the diseases that spread on board a ship in such close quarters - and all the time accompanied by a helpless baby.

Enoch, however, with his seemingly bottomless well of optimism, had seen only success, fortune and promise. We were both 'Fit and industrious' and the new world awaited.

Father got up, still smiling, and made his way out of the house to fetch coal for the cooking range. Mother took the opportunity to sit in his still warm chair. She took my hand in hers - it felt cold and I looked up to meet her clouded eyes.

It had been a long time since I had looked, proper looked, at Mother's face and in it I saw the weariness of a thousand hardships, but also zeal - a passion for the welfare of her children and a determination, even though they be adults, to put herself between them and danger.

'Now you listen to me girl - have I ever told you wrong?'

I shook my head, almost immediately realising that she may not be able to see it, so I added a 'No.'

'Right then, I never wanted you to marry Enoch, you know that - I thought you should have put what you wanted behind what you needed, and you might very well have ended up a doctor's wife. But there's no denying your Lad of the Lanes loves you and your babby too; and he's proved himself a provider, he don't drink too much and he ain't laid a harmful hand on you. So, if you wants to go off and see the world and come back with your fortune then you do it, c'os I don't doubt for a minute you've got a man there who'll do his utmost to make it all happen.'

And so, Enoch worked hard, we saved, we cut corners to put a penny away here and a shilling there. I read and studied all I could find in newspapers and magazines about the place we had set our sights and our hearts on. And as I stood on our doorstep every crisp and crunchy morning throughout the harsh winter of 1871 breathing in the raw and ragged air of Gloucestershire, I wondered when I would see a season of frosts again...

10.
Cheltenham, England
Thursday, September 19th, 1872

Right up until his last day Grandfather weeded and tended his crops. He died on the first fine day in weeks after going out, much against Mother's advice, to pull bare sprout plants and gone-to-seed cabbage to feed the pig in the churchyard. He had just sat down under the chestnut where the hedge divides us from the lane; and there he simply drifted away. I had gone out to call him in for dinner and found him with his pipe in his hand and his eyes open as if he were looking out across the field.

Father and William carried Grandfather into the house and laid him on his cot next to the range and I ran into town for Mr Turze the undertaker. He was buried in Mary Magdalene's churchyard with his beloved Sabina. Mrs Brooke the schoolmistress consoled us by remarking on Grandfather's longevity; stating that eighty-eight was eighteen more years than the Bible promised and that he had enjoyed good health almost to the end. Esther sang, 'O'er the Hills and Far Away' which Grandfather had loved and had made up rude words to - but they had to do so in the churchyard as it is not a religious song.

The light caught it as it spun in the air, dancing yellow in reflection from the oil lamp's smoky flame. The coin appeared to stop at its apex before beginning a falcon dive back toward Enoch's outstretched hand. He caught it and closed his fist over it, flipped his wrist, reopened his fingers and brought it down on to the top of his other hand. And there it sat, sandwiched, invisible, implacable and final, awaiting only our sight to make sense of blind fate.

Enoch's lucky shilling had been given to him on the occasion of his release from prison. Despite hardships we had never thought of spending it. According to Enoch it was invested with special powers because his mother had held it tightly in her hand, whispered a prayer in the tongue of her own mother and made it so. Now, the spirit of his ancestors, old Irish and Romany, as wild and free as the wind, lived within that little round piece of silver and as long as we owned it, we would never, ever find ourselves in a place we could not freely leave.

The nurse had told us that Charles, our second child, would not live. He was a blue baby; his heart was not strong. She had given him forty-eight hours and we had given her half-a-crown for her services. A late summer storm had lashed against the tiny bedroom window as I held him against my body for warmth while at the end of the bed Enoch had sat in the rocking chair brought up from the living room with Sarah Ann asleep in his arms. We had spoken little.

'Do you think they'll let us bury him with Grandfather?' I had asked.

'Not until he's dead they won't - and that's going to be a damn sight longer than forty-eight hours lass.'

Enoch's reply had been little more than a whisper, but it was shot through with a conviction that carried me through the fraught and ragged weeks that followed as slowly, baby Charles became the colour he was meant to be, and his little heart began to beat regularly and strongly.

That was eleven months ago and now, on the verge of toddling himself, he was a sturdy young sapling, the delight of his father and a never-ending source of love and attention from his older sister. They were inseparable - but that was about to cruelly change.

Enoch lifted his hand from the coin.

Tails.

I felt the tears well up, deep breaths stifled the sobs, but the anguish was impossible to hide. It would not have mattered which side the coin had chosen to fall; the pain would have been the same. I saw it too in Enoch's face. It was as if a great weight had suddenly been placed on his back. He slumped forward, dark eyes mirroring an inner storm of emotions. It was difficult to tell whether heartbreak or relief was uppermost, but I knew it would not have been a choice we could have made rationally and so we had left it to fate.

Father lit his pipe with a twig from his garden bonfire, Enoch did likewise and the pair of them, like bookends, looked out across the flat fields to where the mackerel sky joined the land.

'Not long dry.' Father squinted up at the elusive sun.

Enoch nodded, 'Rain 'fore tomorrow - Welsh rain too - mountain tears.'

Then the silence returned. Two days before, we had asked Father for a favour which went way beyond the bounds of reason and he had said he would take a day or two to speak with Mother and ponder on it. He must have known we were waiting eagerly for a reply, but he had never been a man to rush anything. Finally, still maintaining his vigil on the horizon he spoke.

'Is there not a chance of you changing your minds?'

Enoch spoke for us; 'We think this is our best chance of a good future - for us all.'

Father nodded slightly, 'And what of you lass?'

If Enoch had felt umbrage at any perceived undermining of his authority to speak as the head of his house, he did not show it. He knew my father well enough to realise that no offence had been intended and that it was simply the way the Bullinghams had always been - if you are an adult, you have a voice.

'It's a hard decision for hard times - Enoch is right. We could be back here in our early thirties with enough money to set ourselves up in a business and provide for all those we love. We would be independent Father, beholden to no one.'

Enoch added, 'It's not a situation we would have chosen Charles, but the rules says one child to a couple for our class.'

'She's seen so much more of the Bullinghams Father, she would be happy here.' I added for emphasis.

There was a silence then, filled only by the sound of a nearby wood pigeon and the neighing of a distant horse. Then Father turned to face us, removing his pipe and tapping on the raised heel of his boot.

'Sarah Ann will stay with us, we will share her with Emily and Esther, she will be loved and cared for as if she were our own - which of course, she is.'

Esther and I could have been twins and were often mistaken for such. On Sunday, September 8th we walked arm in arm down the lane toward Mary Magdalene's for the morning service. I usually went to Philip Scorey's chapel with Enoch but occasionally I still felt the need for the old ways of my childhood; the familiar old building, the knotted elm with the overhanging branches and the little mouse carved into one of the wall stones by a long-gone hand whose name no one remembers.

Enoch, for his part, had always made it clear that as far as he was concerned, God was everywhere so it mattered not a jot where you went to speak to him. And now, with such a momentous change imminent, I wanted to spend as much time as possible with those who had never been more than a long walk away.

'I'd be buggered if I went all that way, can't you just go to London?'

It had become just about impossible for Esther to speak a full sentence without every other word being 'bugger' or 'bloody', it was surprising she hardly ever forgot herself and let them out in Mother's earshot.

I shook my head and frowned my frown, 'London's the same as Cheltenham, only bigger. Rich or poor - whatever you are when you go there, that's what you'll stay; and there's a whole lot more dirt and disease too.'

I had of course never been to London, but that would change in a few weeks when we travelled to catch the ship to Queensland. I was frightened and excited, but the overriding emotion on the day of departure, as now, would surely be the terrible pain of letting a part of me go, not knowing when I would see my beautiful first born again.

Despite Esther's reassurances that she would take care of her niece as if she were her own and the certainty of knowing that, in Father and Mother, Sarah Ann would have the kindest and most loving surroundings possible, it still hurt - and I knew Enoch, for all his bravado, felt it as strongly as I.

The service was as it had always been. The Rev Byron took Luke 9:62 as the theme of his sermon, 'No one who puts his hand to the plough and looks back is fit for service in the kingdom of God.' But I would, I knew, look back. I would look back at every dawn and every sunset, even when I did not know in which direction to look, I would look. I would look upwards at the moon and recite one of Grandfather's old sayings that soldiers said to their sweethearts as they marched away to fight for King George.

> *'There's no ocean so wide that my love cannot cross it,*
> *No sky so vast that my eyes cannot see,*
> *No distance so far that I can't hear your heartbeat,*
> *The moon over you is the moon over me.'*

Sarah Ann cried, and I held her, convulsed with sobs of my own. She had asked why I was putting my clothes and keepsakes in a trunk and I sat with her on the bed and told her that Father and I were going away for a little while and that she was going to stay with Grandfather, Grandmother and Auntie Esther.

Her voice, normally full of confidence and on the verge of laughter, was tiny and hesitant, a mouse in a cathedral.

'Is Charlie going with you?'

I defy the coldest soul, the most battle-hardened soldier or ruthless pirate chief to have looked into those eyes, cornflower blue Bullingham eyes, and not felt their heart collapse into a puddle like a candle placed too close to the hearth.

Sarah Ann left to live with Father, Mother and Esther three weeks before our departure so that she could get used to it. During the first week, Myself, Enoch or both of us visited her daily; for the second week, it was every other day and for the third week it was just twice in seven days. And on Sunday, September 29th, 1872 she held my hand as we walked as a family to Mary Magdalene's Church in Elmstone Hardwicke. Enoch carried Charlie and all around us on an unseasonably warm autumn day my family chatted and laughed as if it were just another Sabbath.

Behind us, as handsome a quartet as you would find anywhere in their Sunday best, a heavily pregnant Emily with husband, Samuel; Esther and her new young man, Henry - a fine singer who, according to Esther, was a 'Bloody sight better that some of the buggers who get paid for it!' Father and Mother brought up the rear with my 'little' brothers, William and Walter, both now taller than me and eyeing up anything unattached and in a Sunday frock.

Rev Byron mentioned me in his address and wished Enoch and I God speed, safe passage and good fortune

127

in our new lives. There would be no long goodbyes to prolong the pain and so at the end of the service we left the church and climbed aboard a waiting trap in which everything we were allowed to take with us was boxed and secured. We had said our farewells to Enoch's family the day before and now, one by one, I hugged those who would be waiting for our return.

'It could be as little as eighteen months,' I whispered to Mother as she held me tightly, she did not reply, just fixed me with a myopic stare that frightened me with its implicit contradiction.

'I won't be in Queensland for the rest of my life, I promise,' I added with a forced laugh.

She smiled sadly and whispered, 'No my lovely, you won't.'

And I did look back, at the dwindling figures standing under the boughs of the old yew. Sarah Ann was skipping with Auntie Esther holding her hands. No-one waved, but I felt them watching long after the trap turned the corner at the bottom of Murder Meadow and headed for the main Tewkesbury Road and the journey to the railway station.

Railway carriages smell of smoke, steam and whoever sits close to you. The seats in Third Class are hard and for the first few moments after the train got up to full speed, I had to close my eyes against the blur of trees, hedges and fields flashing by on the other side of the scratched and grimy glass. Enoch had been on a train before, travelling to Gloucester with his father and sister, but he conceded this was an altogether different beast with a bigger heart and sturdier fetlocks.

Mother had packed some food for us in greaseproof paper; bread and butter, cheese and a few of her little sponge cakes infused with blobs of jam. But between the unfamiliar and disorientating motion of the train and the sure knowledge that the sight of those little cakes would cause the tears to well up again, they remained in my basket.

At some point the train slowed with a series of jolts and shudders as we approached Swindon and I realised I had left Gloucestershire for the first time in my life. I was further from home than I had ever been and although the people I observed on the platform coming and going looked no different to those who had thronged on the station in Cheltenham, there was an unshakeable feeling of alienness about the whole pageant. Those people... that man in uniform, those children being chastened by their harassed mother, the young man standing indolently with his hands in his pockets... they would never have heard of the little village I called home - the place I had been that very morning. The familiarity of well-trod lanes had gone, and I felt their loss like a stolen blanket on a winter's night.

We finally opened the basket somewhere in Berkshire. It was mid-afternoon and the sky, blue in Cheltenham, was overcast here. The train appeared to be going slower now, either that or I had become accustomed to the speed.

Opposite us, A fat man in a dirty waistcoat who had got on in Bristol grunted and opened one eye, his head rocking gently back and forth with the motion of the train. He wrinkled up his nose and nodded off again. Puffs of steam still flew past the carriage window and once a wood pigeon flew alongside us, keeping pace with the iron beast, ducking and dodging in and out of the smoke and steam until it veered off and away as we passed under a bridge.

Less than an hour later and we were puffing through the outskirts of London, tall houses with tiny yards built almost on top of one another and then a small park, then finer houses with large lawns then factories and then yet more smoky streets where children played amid lines of washing that must surely go back into the house smelling worse than when it went out, such was the taint in the air that even found its way into the railway carriage.

There had been a comfort break in Reading and both Enoch and I would soon be needing one again, so it was with some degree of relief that we pulled into London's cavernous and intimidating Paddington Station shortly after 5.00pm.

Outside the station the full cacophony of a big city was overwhelming, but Enoch's confident smile and unerring sense of direction gave me hope that this metropolis would not swallow us up.

An already leaden sky was darkened further by flocks of crows and pigeons, with here and there the odd seagull swooping and rising to and from the chaotic and congested streets where they competed with clever-eyed thin dogs for any scraps which humanity might spare them. And humanity itself seemed in such a hurry, rushing on foot or by carriage in every available direction.

The five miles or so from Paddington to our accommodation, with all our baggage as well as an exhausted and grizzly infant, plus our own fatigue, would be simply too much and so, at the third attempt, we managed to find an omnibus heading close to our destination - an inn called The Globe on Moorgate Street.

With a number of 'I'm sorrys' and 'Excuse me's' Enoch managed to get Charlie and I into the omnibus where we had to pay for an extra seat to accommodate our luggage. Two other ladies were inside, one of whom, with jet black hair and Asiatic eyes, smiled sweetly at Charlie while the other prodded tobacco into a clay pipe with dirty fingers. Her stare, as hard and humourless as the impersonal streets, remained fixed on the world beyond the window. Enoch had climbed on to the crowded roof after getting an assurance from the driver that he would tell us we were at our destination.

At little more than walking pace we rumbled and shook along wide and crowded thoroughfares. The brooding evening clouds confined themselves to releasing just a few large spots to the relief of those 'Upstairs' while we stopped and started and stuttered across the seemingly endless city. After around twenty minutes, Pipe-Smoking Lady alighted, her place was taken by a plump man in a tweed suit too heavy for such an unseasonably oppressive day. He took off his hat and mopped his brow with a handkerchief, grinning mirthlessly like a frog glistening on a muddy pondside.

After almost an hour the driver indicated to Enoch that he was as close to our destination as the omnibus went. My husband climbed down and opened the door to help us and our luggage out. It was getting quite dark as we followed the driver's outstretched arm and pointing finger down a side road to the Inn.

Our room was on the second floor. The bed was clean and comfortable and as I fell back on to it, I conceded it wouldn't have mattered if it had been covered in spikes like the bed of the Fakir that Emily and I had once watched in Pittville Park. I could have slept anywhere. Enoch lay next to me on his side, fully dressed and - like I surely was, reeking of the smoke and the hundred other smells of this vast place. He rested an arm across me.

'We're on our way Lass of the Land,' he rumbled - sounding as exhausted as me.

I should have got undressed, washed and prepared properly for bed but the thought of standing up again was exhausting in itself and so I closed my eyes and my mind drifted back down the long, long railway track to Cheltenham and then along the road out of town, into the lanes and up a set of narrow stairs where part of me slept. I could feel her and smell her as in my mind's eye I bent and kissed her forehead. And I said my prayer - the prayer I had been teaching her:

> *Lord keep us safe this night*
> *Secure from all our fears,*
> *May angels guard us while we sleep,*
> *'til morning light appears,*
> *Amen.*

London on a Monday morning. Imagine all the people you have ever seen, all in one place and all rushing to be somewhere else; now add to this all the horses you have ever seen - and all the carriages and carts. Anything capable of making a noise was making one and the air was so thick you could have cut it in slices, as if everybody had decided to have a bonfire on the same day. The smell of cooking food wafted from countless windows in the tall buildings surrounding us as we stood on a crossroads, our belongings resting at our feet.

Outside the Bank of England, a man with no legs was propped up on an equally legless wooden chair as he played a flute.

'Penny a tune mate,' he called out to Enoch as we passed. Enoch dropped his bags and fished in his pocket, dropping a threepence in to the battered tin cup at the man's side.

'Do you know The Raggle Taggle Gypsy?' Enoch asked him - and to his surprise, the man did, playing it so well he got another threepence for his trouble.

We were heading for Wapping and the London Docks where our ship was waiting and due to leave tomorrow. We had been advised by the landlord at the Globe to arrive a day early in order to get more of a choice of a decent berth in our steerage class quarters. It was good advice and rather kind as he could have chosen to advise us otherwise and got paid for a second night of stay.

Street after street we trudged, we had been told it was less than a mile to the dock and so had decided against another omnibus ride and the cost of a cab. Each terrace was as noisy and crowded as the rest. A naked boy of around nine or ten was thrown bodily out of a house into the mud and manure of the road; he ran back to the slammed door, banging and yelling for re-entry while a drunk, using a lamp post for support, sang tonelessly nearby, seemingly oblivious to both the plight of the boy and the heavy carts missing him by inches. This was not the London of the gentry, the neighing, braying 'Hoorahs'. It was the London of those who worked to eat and of those who either sought to work - or couldn't. It was Cheltenham's Rookery on a much grander scale. The flotsam and jetsam of Empire, the overbred and underfed, trying to make sense of a world they shared but had no stake in.

'You know what makes you poor?' Enoch, as he often did, read my thoughts; 'It ain't a lack of money, there's plenty of coves who ain't got vonga and no way to get none, but they ain't poor. It's lack of hope as makes a man poor. You got hope, then you got tomorrow - and it's not having a tomorrow that makes today as useless as tits on a bull.'

'We've got a tomorrow, haven't we?' I looked up at him as he strode along at my side, vigilant and wary of everyone. I felt well protected.

Enoch grinned and took Charlie from me, exchanging him for one of the lighter cases. 'We have - and a bright and sunny one too.' He nodded his head toward the end of the latest teeming road where, peeping between the tenements, the tall masts of ships could just about be seen.

'Johnsey... Enoch and Ellen Johnsey and our son, Charles Johnsey.' The embarkation office was so small we had to leave our luggage outside.

'Here you are,' the officious little man in the peaked cap handed Enoch a sheet of paper, 'You must hand this to the deck clerk, he will stamp it, I have to tell you that once this has been done, if you leave the ship you will not be allowed back on, so please make sure you have everything you need for the voyage. There will be an opportunity to purchase further supplies from an onboard shop before you leave port.'

Enoch thanked the man, we left the office to stand, disorientated in the organised chaos of the dockside. Passing a tar-coated vessel alive with the calls of workmen and a smaller steam tug we came alongside a ship tied to the capstans with a rope thicker than any I had ever seen.

'Here we go then,' Enoch announced and with no further ceremony we stepped off English soil and on to the damp and dancing gangplank of the Royal Dane.

11.
London Docks, England
Thursday, October 3rd, 1872

Throughout my earliest years, I shared my tiny room with three sisters and apart from the time I worked in the Noah's Ark and at Andoversford in Dolly Doplin's tea rooms I have never enjoyed the luxury of privacy. On the Royal Dane, however, the noise and bustle of my childhood bedroom is brought back to me tenfold.

Married quarters in steerage consists of a large open area the width of the ship where benches and long tables for communal eating take up the middle sections while two tiers of curtained sleeping bunks are positioned around the edges. We are below the water line here and a low wooden ceiling with no natural light makes the whole space feel stuffy - even before most of the passengers have come aboard. One was going to have to learn a degree of social circumspection and tolerance to survive such close neighbours.

Throughout the day more and more people joined us, but Enoch and I have already acquired a berth close enough to the entrance to provide a breeze - but not so close that people moving in and out of the area will be brushing past us at all hours of the day and night. We are

136

determined to make the utmost of our deck times and get as much fresh air as we can over the course of the journey.

Liver, potatoes and white bread was served up for dinner today - the official first day of the voyage; however, the Royal Dane is yet to move an inch and the cheerless, prison-like buildings of London's Dockside still crowd the grey autumn sky. Yesterday we ate only what we had brought on board and I went to sleep rather hungry. Enoch said if no breakfast was forthcoming, he would try to go ashore under some pretext of medical urgency and get us something but fortunately this was made unnecessary by the very early provision of oatmeal, coffee (not very hot and rather bitter) and some bread and butter. Charlie made short work of his oatmeal and I spent the next half hour acquainting myself with the washing facilities.

The berth above ours is occupied by a man and woman a little older than us. The woman seems nice; small, quiet and polite, I have not heard her husband speak yet, he points at where he wants his brood to go and they go there. Enoch says he is courteous enough and probably Welsh, judging by his accent. The next berth to us on the lower level contains a couple with a child the same age as Charlie. The mother is called Martha and appears to be around my age with her husband somewhat older, she has a baby daughter called Flora. She appears quiet and a little intimidated by her new surroundings but that goes for most of us. We are due to get a visit from the Captain this evening after dinner and have been asked to make ourselves available to hear what he has to say.

Our circumstances on board are likely to be more of a trial for Enoch than for me. For all his bluff and bravado, he is a solitary man and at his happiest when walking or riding far from crowded streets (Although as a lad he was not averse to an evening in the Ark with his chums). For me, three years as a serving maid in a busy and often over-boisterous inn has left me tolerant of crowds, strangers and the chorus of unfamiliar voices and accents.

What we do not have here in steerage, thankfully, are the nobs and dandies, neighing and holding handkerchiefs to their noses when they pass too close to common folk. Those who could afford to pay in full for their voyages are called Cabin Class and have their own rooms and their own part of the deck where they can take the air without fear of bumping into the peasantry. Enoch says that if we capsize, they will sink just as fast as the rest.

To begin our quest to make our fortune we have three changes of clothing plus extra bits of underwear, socks and necessaries. We decided to allow ourselves one keepsake each; Enoch has a knobkerry walking stick that once belonged to his grandfather, carved from hazel it has been polished to an impressive smoothness over the generations. I have Grandfather William's medal in a tin. It brought him safe and sound back from Spain with a treasure greater than gold and I am praying it will bring luck to us. Even before leaving England I am dreaming of our quick return, praying that we strike gold early and that it will be me who walks Sarah Ann down that lovely old lane on her first day at school.

We also have seven pounds, fourteen shillings and sixpence upon which to live until we are earning more. Our money is divided into smaller amounts and concealed about our persons. While we are assured our property is safe (Because the penalties for stealing on board are ruthless), we are taking no chances; wherever we go, our money goes with us.

Mid-morning, we go up on to the main deck to take in some air - if you can call the clinging damp and grey murk of London Docks 'air'. It is thick with the unfamiliar smells of water and exotic cargoes, rotting fish guts and boiling tar. The deep brown Thames laps against ragged, time-seasoned timber. Even on the rank mud a kind of life struggles for a foothold; green, slimy moss spreads in and out of worn rocks and half-submerged rubbish. Large and pugnacious gulls cry overhead, the pigeons who rule the streets just minutes away would get little luck here; a pair of dogs chase each other along the near dockside while men, dark swarthy men and slight orientals, shout to each other in many languages.

Dinner was a much noisier affair than breakfast. We now had the full complement of passengers and crew on board and the Royal Dane had become a disturbed ant nest as people scurried here and there to get a place at the long tables. Enoch and I, with Charlie on my lap, got a bench spot near to our berth which we planned to make our own as far as possible for the duration of the voyage.

Our bunk neighbours, the Notts, sat alongside us while opposite an older couple, probably in their fifties told us during the course of the meal that they were heading out to join their two sons and their wives who now lived in Brisbane and ran a successful ironmongery business.

'Nowt in England for t'likes of us,' the man said between mouthfuls of a decent stew that would have stood alongside Mrs Bolt's Noah's Ark masterpiece. 'Since I got the arthur-itis I can't shovel air let alone coal, so t'lads said "Come on out to us Dad, no winters here to speak of and they brew a fair ale!" A hand like a shovel extended across the table towards Enoch, 'Barnfield's the name - Barnfield of Barnsley,' he nodded to his smiling wife - 'And t'other half is Faith.' Enoch shook his hand, 'Johnsey, Gloucestershire,' and, nodding in my direction, 'Ellen.'

'Ellen of Troy!' the man offered me his hand and I shook it, smiling, Faith then did the same and after we had all exchanged pleasantries, the meal continued, punctuated with small talk and anticipation of the voyage ahead.

There was even a steam pudding for dessert and while coffee was passed along the table someone out of my line of vision tapped on a metal pot to call for silence. It was then I noticed the man in the blue uniform, cap under his arm flanked by two crewmen. He took in the gathering as the silence spread out until only an infrequent cough or sniffle was left to compete with the creaking of the timbers and the shriek of passing gulls whose call could penetrate the thickest of hulls.

He took a breath, 'Good evening ladies and gentlemen; as is customary, I am touring the ship in order to meet you all and to tell you a little about the days and weeks ahead. We are likely to be at sea for anything from ninety to a hundred and thirty days, depending mainly on the weather and how well you can all row when the water is flat calm.' A chuckle passed among those gifted with a sense of humour although many a face displayed a brief shadow of consternation.

'My name is Captain James Cooper, this ship is the Royal Dane, she is fourteen years old and as fit and fair a maiden as one could wish to meet. She weighs one thousand, six hundred and fifteen tons and carries a crew of fifty-eight. In all there are four hundred and thirty-seven adult passengers plus two children under twelve aboard - both of them babes I'm led to understand...'

Charlie chose that moment to make his presence felt with one of his louder squeals, bringing a chuckle from the assembly plus a smile and a, 'There we have it,' from Captain Cooper, who continued:

'You will all be pleased to hear that winter has been cancelled this year and you will find January in Queensland a very different prospect to January in England - but not without its own discomforts, I'm afraid. Now, while you are in your bunks tonight, two steamers, the Sussex and the City of London, who are attaching themselves as I speak, will begin the task of towing us off the dock here and out to Gravesend at the mouth of the Thames. This will take us a few days. When we reach there, they will detach, we will make sail and the journey proper will begin.

'Now then, please try not to beard the busy crew with too many questions, we will make sure you know all that you need to know and for those who have not yet acquainted themselves with the layout of the ship, the crew have been instructed to ensure you all restrict yourselves to the permitted areas. Doctor Miller will make regular rounds and can be found in his surgery in emergencies. I'll bid you all a good evening, please feel free to address a duty deck officer but only if you have any matter of urgency. Otherwise, we shall hopefully speak again at Sunday morning service.

He took out his pocket watch and consulted it, 'Finally, it is now approaching six 'o clock, if anyone, for whatever reason, has any doubts or misgivings about the journey ahead or the decision to travel, you have until nine o'clock - that's three hours, to freely leave the ship.'

It was only the slightest of jolts but the realisation of what it represented made my stomach flip. The die was cast! Enoch was snoring by my side in the curtained darkness of our berth. Charlie wriggled in his sleep between us. Tiny shudders caused the timbers to groan and creak. Peering around the curtain, I saw the lamps in the main married quarters area swing gently as the Royal Dane began to move. From an indeterminate berth a male voice muttered, 'We're off!' I could hear the dim chugging of the two steamers which, having coaxed the great ship out of its inertia, were now pulling her along the Thames towards the beckoning sea.

Sunday morning and the Royal Dane trailed at a walking pace behind the two tugs. In the murk of yet another overcast day I could not clearly make out the sparse dwellings on the shoreline. We had passed by the villages of West Ham and Woolwich and were by all accounts close to Purfleet on the north bank. Looking south reminded me of home, dotted farmsteads with here and there the smoke of an autumn bonfire or cottage chimney.

It is remarkable how quickly people adapt to their circumstances. After a bit of pushing and shoving on the first two days, a routine soon developed, unspoken but observed nonetheless, determining where people eat, do their washing, attend to their ablutions and all the little things we did at home without any fuss.

On Monday morning, I awoke with a frown and took a moment to figure out what was missing before realising it was the deep chugging of the tugs. Leaving Enoch and Charlie asleep, I went up on deck to an altogether different morning. A pale autumn sun was rising, we were anchored at Gravesend and looking to the stern I could just make out the two tiny specks of our temporary, smoky companions, Sussex and City of London, heading back upriver towards the grey pall that hung permanently over the distant metropolis. And then, accompanied by those shouts between seamen that mean nothing to landlubbers, we really were on our way.

The sails filled, and the Thames widened until I could no longer make out individual people or buildings on either bank. Passing between distant Southend and the flat and featureless marshes of north Kent we ventured out around England's eastern outcrop and down into the English Channel - and into our first experience of the mercurial moods of the sea.

There was a swing in Grandfather William's garden which he had made from sisal rope and a split wooden branch seat hung over the bough of a sycamore. Granny Sabina had told him off for climbing the tree to attach it because he had been drinking cider. We all loved that swing, Mary Ann, Emily, and me – and even Esther who was only a toddler. I dreamed I was on it, adult now but somehow Grandfather was still there, pushing me higher and higher and me half-scared and half wishing for more. Then I woke, it was pitch dark in our berth - but I was still swinging.

I half-climbed over Enoch to pull back the curtain, as I did the world lurched again and I almost fell out of the berth. The lamps were not lit, but in the deep gloom I could see them swinging from side to side, almost crashing against the beam above with each arc. With another swing I fell back, my elbow digging into Enoch's ribs which woke him with a growl.

'What the…,' he tried to sit up against the inertia of the swing, grabbing the wooden bar above the bed for support. Charlie was awake now as well and - by the sound of it, so were most of the others in our quarters.

'Fair old storm out there,' a man shouted, probably waking those lucky few still in the arms of Morpheus. We could hear crewmen now, shouting out in the strange language of those to whom the sea is a familiar mistress whose moods cannot be pacified. There was no chance of returning to sleep under such conditions and so I took Charlie in my arms and wedged us into the corner of the berth while Enoch sat alongside, his legs and feet pushing against the opposite partition to give us a sense of stability.

A jolt and a crescendo of cries from the deck above alerted us to some mishap. A sailor, cap tied on with twine and his sealskin dripping with spray burst unceremoniously into our quarters.

144

'Ain't nothing to be alarmed about ladies and gents; we've hit another vessel in the sea fog, cracked the foreyard - should have given us a wide berth. Still, she ain't sunk and we ain't neither. Hold tight and all's well!' He disappeared, back to the waiting fury of the storm and we, taking his advice, held tight.

By morning the storm and the fog had cleared but the sea was still restless. I must have eventually dropped off to sleep and when I woke Enoch was not beside me. Gathering a half-awake Charlie, I went up on deck to discover more than a few befuddled passengers looking up at crew members who were trying to detach the broken foreyard in order to drop it for repair. A large canvas hung listlessly from one end of the beam, being tossed carelessly in the remnants of last night's tempest.

Enoch gripped a rail, staring out over a grey-green sea whose complexion matched his own. He looked grim and preoccupied. I moved to stand next to him, addressing Charlie as I did.

'Father's not a Jolly Jack Tar this morning, is he?'

Enoch's eyes remained on the horizon. 'See that? He nodded out across the waves and now I saw it too, a darker strip of distant land.

'France, that is', he wiped his face with his sleeve, 'I'm going to offer the Captain five pounds to drop me off there.'

Prior to embarkation, I had no idea how Enoch or myself would take to sea travel, it was a novel experience for us both. For myself however, apart from being a little tired and in need of my breakfast, I was fine. Enoch, by contrast, was clearly not a 'Salty Dog', affirmed by his response to my suggestion of a morning meal.

'Bugger Breakfast,' he growled, greening a little more at the thought of eggs and oatmeal.

I teased him, 'You can't go to France - you don't speak French.'

He took a deep and medicinal breath of sea air, 'I can play the accordion a bit though, and a Frenchie told me once in Andoversford that I was a 'Bon Cavalier' - that means good horseman. I'll get me a job in a racing stable and marry a can-can girl.' An arm wrapped itself around my shoulder and, green as he was, he forced a smile full of lanes and mischief. A passing crewman patted him on the back, 'It'll pass matey - at least until we get to Biscay!'

The infamous Biscay proved to be in a better mood than the English Channel however and as we sailed further south over the ensuing days, it seemed as though we were leaving autumn behind and returning to summer. It got notably warmer, the skies clearer and, best of all, Enoch discovered his sea legs and began to eat heartily again.

QUEENSLAND

Land of plenty or land of want, where the grey Companions dance,
Feast or famine, or hope or fear, and in all things land of chance,
Where Nature pampers or Nature slays, in her ruthless, red, romance.
(Banjo Paterson)

12.
November 4th, 1872
The Atlantic Ocean

A month into the voyage saw us both becoming acclimatised to the increasing heat, but this was by no means true for all passengers - at least in married quarters. A generously proportioned woman whose acquaintance Enoch and I had not made, but whom we secretly referred to as Mrs Chubby Whitecap, fainted during Sunday service on November 4th and had to be carried below decks to where Doctor Miller revived her with water and smelling salts. He advised her to wear fewer layers of clothing and to 'Get into the tropical habit of seeing the sun as a wolf and not a spring rabbit.'

We should have been at the equator by this time, but the delay caused by the broken foreyard meant we had not been able to make full sail until a few weeks into the voyage. However, we crossed on November 8th - a time of chill mornings, mist and ragged spider webs back home, but here the sky was white hot and us poor partridges were roasted as if on a spit.

Nocturnal walks on deck were discouraged but if one was discreet it was possible to sit undetected between the aft lifeboats and quietly stargaze.

'They're all different, higgledy-piggledy - where's the Plough?' I frowned into the night as countless stars blazed down in unfamiliar patterns. Enoch swept back his hair, 'Can't see that from here - I was talking to Mr Nott night before last - see that up there?' I followed his pointing finger, 'Them four stars, join 'em up and it would be a cross?'

'I see them,' I replied. Charlie wriggled in his sleep wrapped in a thin shawl.

'That's the Southern Cross, that is; they're all going to look a bit different, but it's the same moon, that's all that matters.'

I felt his arm wrap around me. The same moon, here in the middle of this watery desert and also peeping in through the window of a tiny bedroom far behind us.

'Over all of us,' I said.

'All of us, Lass o' the Land, now and always.'

The ship that had seemed so large and indomitable when docked in London among smaller boats and tugs - a Gulliver among the Lilliputians, now danced like a discarded cork between mountains of water. Soaring forward, sails straining and stretched by furious gusts, it seemed as though she were skimming the surface of the ocean like a pondskipper instead of cutting through it. The bowsprit dipped toward the foam before rising up to point accusingly at a belligerent sky where clouds tumbled over each other in a race to the horizon.

Yet still sailors walked the brine-washed deck, many barefoot and swaying like meandering drunks but somehow remaining upright, born to this tempest and unperturbed by the majesty of Neptune's rage. I returned to a married quarter that starkly illustrated all I had ever heard from Grandfather William, Mr Wells and Adder Drew regarding the nature of military field hospitals.

As the deck was awash with the sea, so here it was puke. Men and women who, unlike their brethren above, had not perfected the art of dancing with the swell, slipped, slid and fell, bumping, bruising, cutting and coughing in a stale half-light, their clothes soaked in vomit, blood and floods of piddle and excrement from upended buckets. Enoch was wedged in the corner of our berth, Charlie was safe in his arms, but each had been sick over the other and also on their clothes and our bedclothes.

A trouserless man desperately clutching a bible rolled helplessly under a table where his progress was stopped by Mr Barnfield from Barnsley who was praying loudly.

'Oh Lord who tamed t'tempest, come and tame this 'un!'

But the Lord must have been busy elsewhere that day as the implacable storm raged well into the night, easing only in the strange grey-white pallor of a southern morning, leaving us all to clear up as best we could the detritus of the one-sided battle.

While the below quarters 'aired' Captain Cooper allowed those of us able to face food to dine on deck. Enoch ate little but seemed to benefit from the fresh air.

Even lying on top of the bedclothes in vest and drawers, it was still insufferably hot in our berth. It would be easy for those not acquainted with the ways of ships to trip and fall over ropes, tools and obstacles on deck at night and so all but a few - those who had sailed before and knew the do's and don'ts - were requested to remain below. It is likely that a good many of us boilers and swelterers would be sleeping under the stars given a chance but then a deck strewn with snoring passengers would make the sailors' jobs that much more perilous.

Apart from expected sneezes, sniffles and a broken nose sustained in the storm, Doctor Miller had had little to test him on the voyage and the crew were also saying what an easy passage it had been. I had been unwell the last few mornings but put that down to a disagreeable piece of salted bacon that had given me an unquenchable thirst after which I had drunk lots and lots of water that tasted of rusty tin.

Enoch had once again gone absent in the night. He was good at that, he could sneak about like a cat, unnoticed. It was only when he gently nudged my shoulder that I opened my eyes in the near pitch darkness.

'What?'

'Ssshh! Come on, come on...'

'Charlie...'

'Leave Charlie a mo, he'll be alright - I want to show you something.'

It wasn't until we reached the deck that I discovered by the light of a low moon that Enoch did not have a stitch of clothing on. I pulled him to a stop.

'You've got nothing on!'

'Too hot - look, he led me to the rail where we crouched down behind the rear port cupboard, out of sight of any passing crewmen.

'What am I looking at?' I squinted into the deep maroon.

'There... look, just on the horizon, wait for the bow to rise up a bit... there, see it?'

'That low star? Right over there?'

'Aye, only it ain't a star - that's Moreton Bay Lighthouse.'

'A lighthouse?'

Yes, a lighthouse, Moreton Bay - that's Queensland!

The deck was a sea of people even before breakfast. Captain Cooper had allowed a thirty-minute 'Observation parade' and hundreds of hands shielded eyes as they looked landwards to where a brown-black ridge rose above the waves from horizon to horizon. Behind the ship, the sun threw a curtain of flame across the sea turning it orange and threatening to make our day of destiny a blistering experience.

Throughout our final hours on board, married quarters became a hive of activity. Possessions were packed, pictures taken down from berths, trunks and cases tied and secured. There had been two children in our quarters when we left London, now there were four with one of them bearing the name of our illustrious captain, the doctor and the ship itself, Henry Cooper Miller Dane!

The Royal Dane anchored at Moreton Bay Lighthouse on January 15th, 1873 and we had a frustrating wait of twenty-four hours while the ship was lightened enough for us to proceed to Moreton Bay itself so that we could disembark.

We spent our last night aboard planning the first stages of our adventure. Enoch, being the practical one, was thinking about our immediate needs, accommodation, work and the means to secure all we would need to follow the trails to wherever the gold was. I was leaping ahead, to filling our pockets and standing once more on the harbourside - this time waiting to board for the journey to England, to Sarah Ann and to our fine, comfortable and secure house overlooking Pittville Park and the swans on the lake.

Next day, under a withering heat we watched men toing and froing along the harbourside carrying supplies and equipment down the gangplanks and on to the antipodean soil we were all so eager to tread.

We shook hands with the Captain who had shaken a lot of hands that day and smiled a lot of smiles, nevertheless, ours was as personal and warm as if we had been the only ones.

'Very best of luck to you in your new lives', he said, and we thanked him for his kindness and professionalism. Then we walked carefully down the wooden steps. Enoch stopped on the last step, put down the baggage and, turning to me, gently lifted Charlie from my arms. Turning back, he kneeled and put him down, feet first on to the quayside. Then he followed, still holding Charlie's hands, then I did likewise. Land, dry, solid land stretching to unimaginable horizons - and our son was the first Johnsey to touch the soil of Queensland.

I saw my first dead man before an hour was out. We had been handed a card directing us to a lodging station for those among the new arrivals who had landed without arranged accommodation. We were about to cross a road dividing the dock from a guarded and forbidding compound when two men came past on horses at a walking pace and we were forced to give way to them. They were men unlike any I had seen before, Aboriginal Natives.

The leader wore a blue jacket over a red shirt and a peaked military-style hat; his legs were bare; he had a rifle slung over his shoulder. Following him, a boy of the same race who I would have estimated at no more than thirteen, dressed similarly but armed with a scabbarded cutlass, the belt slung crossways over a shoulder, the horse saddleless. Both looked down and directly at us as they passed, their copper-coloured faces reflecting a wild inscrutability; glinting eyes like bullets, dark and metallic, faces framed by black curly hair. On the third horse, another native needed neither clothes or saddle, he was slung over the animal and tied on underneath, clearly dead, unblinking eyes clogged with the dust and dirt of a journey. I looked to Enoch who grinned mirthlessly.

'Welcome to Queensland,' he said, turning Charlie's face from the passing tableau.

The card in the window said 'Room, two shillings, no Chinamen!' We were led along a narrow, bare brick corridor and out into a yard at the back of a boarded-up shop. The landlord swayed from side to side as he walked, breathing heavily in the afternoon heat. He opened a door that required a kick to help it on its way.

'You can sleep in here, we ain't supposed to have blokes and women in the same room but seen as you're married and strapped for somewhere to drop, nobody'll mind.'

He was a twin of Constable Mossley from Cheltenham, well-rounded with ill-fitting trousers tucked into riding boots. A leather waistcoat covered a homespun yellow shirt stretched over his ample girth. He was burned almost as brown as the natives we had seen earlier. His beard was grey and grizzled, a leather wide-brimmed hat rested on his eyebrows.

Enoch squeezed past him, Charlie and I followed into a room containing two bunk-style beds, a wooden table and two chairs. The floor was bare stone, the small window offered a view on to a busy alley beyond - at least it did for Enoch, being too high up the wall for me.

'The water pump's in the yard and the tub's on the outside wall of the dunny. Make sure you bang the bloody thing before getting in if you want to bathe alone, know what I mean? There's a shop next door but don't use it, she's a bloody rob-dog; go to Chan's down on the crossroads, he's a Chink but he won't sell you short.'

We pushed the two bunks together and Charlie slept at the foot of mine. Our supper was provisions we had brought from the ship and we had tea, sugar, bread and cheese for the morning. I never thought I would have missed the Royal Dane but at least there was a night there. Here, all through the sweltering hours of darkness it may as well have been the middle of the day. Carts trundled up and down with drivers yelling and whips cracking. Drunkards sang and fought and swore, then sang again;

women screamed, cried and laughed coarsely and finally, after an age of fitful dozing, light shone through the small window and my first words to Enoch were, 'That was my first and last night here!' Unsurprisingly, for I knew he had also slept little, there was no argument. We packed and strapped up our belongings, had our breakfast, paid the grizzly man two shillings and headed out to the city of Brisbane.

Albert Ambrose ran a delivery business. If you had something you couldn't carry and you wanted it moved from one place to another, he was the man to do it! It said as much on notice boards throughout the parts of the city we had so far seen, and also in the Brisbane Courier, a copy of which Enoch had bought in order to scour the advertisements for job vacancies offering accommodation.

We met Mr Ambrose outside the Post Office Hotel at the time appointed for a hiring fair. There were a number of other jobseekers milling around, immigrants being conspicuous, as we surely were, by their luggage and pale faces.

'Chelt'nam? Well, I'm a Bristol chap so I s'pose that's close enough. An' you can ride and drive, can you?'

'I can - and well.' Enoch gave a potted and only slightly embellished summary of his equestrian prowess and experience to the man who nodded, smiled and seemingly made up his mind there and then.

Albie - as he insisted we address him, seemed quite taken with Enoch. At stake was a job that payed a generous three pounds, seventeen and six a month with a little house on the premises thrown in. We would have searched for a long time before a chance like that came to pass in England. Enoch beamed and shook Albie's hand and so, with providence clearly smiling on us - and within just over a day on Australian soil we had our first home, and money coming in.

We sat in the back of our new employer's cart, Charlie wide awake all the way and taking notice of the new world around him, while Albie told us his story on the journey to our new home. He had been in Queensland fourteen years. His first wife had died on the voyage and he had landed alone and distraught, bewildered and with his dreams crushed. He had stood on the dockside, surrounded by her cases and keepsakes and had it not been for a man from the local Quaker meeting house who took him in and cared for him those first weeks, he said he might well have thrown himself off the quay.

His new land had been kind to him however, he had found himself a Greek widow who owned a stable yard out of town and he had turned it into a profitable business.

Cabbage Tree Haulage amounted to a big house surrounded by stabling and outbuildings - and a second, smaller house which, when I stepped inside, immediately reminded me of Little Bayshill Terrace where I had made my first home with Enoch. Through the window of the living room, I looked out into the yard, at the horses in their stables and at the tiny figure of Mrs Ambrose - Sophia, hanging out the washing. I loved the place on sight.

'All you got to remember is this...' A man called Frank Eighteen-Months who had worked for Albie for

156

more than three years, was addressing Enoch and I, plus another man called Kincaid who had also just arrived in Queensland and had been hired for his horsemanship. '… If it's got more than two legs it'll bloody kill ya, if it's got less than two legs, it'll bloody kill ya - and if it's GOT two legs, it'll rob ya - and then it'll bloody kill ya! Any questions?' Wisely, I thought, there were none.

Cabbage Tree Creek is on the edge of town with views out over the bushland. Albie says it was where many natives lived until they were cleared off for farming. Most of Enoch's work involves deliveries of supplies and tools from merchants in Brisbane out into the surrounding farms. Usually, it means carting but if it's mail and smaller items he gets to ride which I know he loves and has missed. He is clearly enjoying the work, laughing a lot more than he had during the voyage and currently repairing an old banjo which he found in a shed and that Albie said he could keep.

As weeks passed, while not fully acclimatised, I was finding the heat less of a torment. Sophia was lovely, reminding me a bit of Dolly Doplin from Andoversford. She and her husband had come to Queensland just as the Rockhampton gold rush took off and they immediately headed for the diggings, thoroughly unprepared and with little knowledge of the bush and its dangers.

Her husband had been a fiery and impulsive man who had actually challenged the captain of their emigrant ship to a duel over a rations dispute. A noisy and belligerent hard-drinking scoundrel, he didn't last long among the seasoned bushmen and diggers, accidentally falling down a sink hole in the middle of the night.

For all their hard edges, Sophia found the diggers a kindly and sympathetic bunch and they ensured she was well cared for and protected. She became unofficial cook and laundress, eventually returning to Brisbane with enough to buy Cabbage Tree Stables and employ a certain Albie Ambrose whose equestrian expertise and endless supply of smiles and jokes led them to become more than boss and worker.

Enoch and his fellow drivers were kept fully employed travelling far and near. Sometimes this involved spending a few nights away to take goods from Brisbane Docks to stations far inland at places like Dalby, Bowenville and Leyburn.

We were managing to save twenty to thirty shillings a month and still live well, often sharing meals with Albie and Sofia who had become friends as well as employers. Enoch heard rumours of digs in the north from his fellow drivers but there were rumours every day and it was a brave man who would head out into such wild country with all its pitfalls and dangers without the real and concrete promise of some reward.

'It just goes on and on, that's the thing about it,' Enoch paused to light his pipe, a few sparks rising into the night. We were sat on a swinging seat in our small front garden, built by the previous tenant who had left for the Gympie goldfields and never returned. 'On and on and on,' he added, 'D'you know, even if they built a railroad from one side of Australia to the other and the train never stopped, I reckon it would take a week to get across it.'

Silence then.

'I'm halfway through a letter to Father, is there anything you would like to say?'

He did not immediately reply. Putting his arm around me, he took out his pipe, pointing the stem at the stars. See, there, them two bright stars? Well, the one on the left, that's Rigil Kent that is, sailors navigate by it; Frank Eighteen-Months has been teaching me the stars in these parts.'

I brushed away a curious and persistent buzzing creature, 'I shall tell him we're well and that Charlie is beginning to take a real interest in his surroundings. We are all over the trials of the voyage and that we have a job on a sort of ranch - then I'll tell him what a ranch is out here. Do you think we should write a simple letter to Sarah Ann, with all little words in it?'

The sudden tears came from nowhere and there was no stopping them.

Enoch squeezed me tighter and kissed the top of my head, 'We'll both write, a letter each - I only knows short words anyhow. We'll tell her we're working to get the money to get a mule and a tent and picks and shovels and pots and pans and red shirts and stout boots to catch a ship to go to the North and dig for gold to bring home and go into the best dress shop in Cheltenham... no - the best in London, and we'll buy her the prettiest frock in the shop and parade her all around the park so everyone can see just how well-to-do she is - all of us are!'

I smiled through the tears, reassured now that Enoch's plans had not changed and that this was only a temporary expedition. I chuckled, 'Yes, all four of us, and everyone will doff their hats as we pass and comment, "What a fine family, the Johnseys."

Enoch's gold tooth glittered in the clear night as he smiled, putting his lips close to my ear, he whispered, 'Five - and counting!'

13.
Brisbane, Queensland,
Thursday, July 10ᵗʰ, 1873

We grew a flower that bloomed and faded as our English bodies steeled themselves for a winter that never came. Mary Johnsey was with us for three short weeks. She cried, slept, woke and fed as fathomless, ocean-blue eyes took in the strange world, her mother, father, and curious brother.

She was perfect, although smaller than Sarah Ann and Charlie. Tiny hands gripped my fingers strongly and her legs kicked as she danced to some inner rhythm. Then, one night, she slept, never to wake again. Did she not like what she had seen? She would have been loved beyond words; a daughter, here in this topsy-turvy place, conceived in faraway Gloucestershire and carried, growing, across great oceans. I thought I had known pain and sorrow, but until that morning they had been strangers to me.

We buried Mary on the edge of Cabbage Tree Creek where a piece of land formed a small scrub-covered plateau before dropping away to allow a view of distant horizons. Albie gave Enoch a couple of days off work to be with me, but if I am honest, I was not good company.

In the end, Enoch retired to the garden and worked on his banjo repairs while I wrote a long letter to Father and Mother.

I am careful in my letters not to allow too much sentimentality to creep in between the words. It would not do for my family to think I was sad and regretful. As the days passed, the melancholy - while not disappearing - became no more than a subdued chorus to my everyday song and thanks to Sophia and newly hired kitchen girl, Theresa, I was never alone long enough to become maudlin, especially now that Charlie was running here there and everywhere in and out of any trouble he could find.

Charlie was at his happiest when sat astride a saddle in front of his father, holding on for dear life and laughing uproariously the faster they went and it was clear Enoch equally enjoyed the experiences, spending as much time as possible with his son.

The longer trips were becoming more regular however and so Charlie and I seemed to be seeing less and less of our man. Deliveries deep inland or to the north grew as more and more settlers made their way from the city and into the endless bush as far as Moraby, Auburn and Hawkwood and even beyond to the frontiers of settlement.

'Don't worry Missus, we'll bring him back in one piece,' Frank Eighteen-Months pulled his reins this way and that to bring an unfamiliar mount under control as he waited for Enoch to saddle up. The pair were accompanying a cartload of tools and supplies to the site of a new logging station in the Bunya Mountains. Iain

162

Kincaid, driving the wagon along with his blackfella boy, Tuesday, would have been a prime target between here and there for any marauding bushrangers on the lookout for an easy payday.

Enoch and Frank were carrying Martini Henry rifles while Mr Kincaid had a holstered pistol. Frank's reassurance did little to allay my concerns for Enoch although I could not show him how worried I was in front of his mates. Instead, I painted on a smile and said, 'Bring back something for the pot.' Enoch understood my concerns however and flashed me a smile as he patted the stock of his gun. 'I'll bring us a fat one,' he grinned, not specifying the species but at least signalling his intentions to take care of himself.

'We'll be dandy missus - your fella looks more like a bloody bushranger than any we'll meet out there'; Frank's laugh was taken up by the rest of the party and with a creak of the cartwheels, a shout and a crack of the whip they were off. I watched them all the way down the dusty red track until they disappeared over the horizon. This was not the first time Enoch had gone off on a job, so why did I feel such a sense of foreboding on this occasion?

The windows were opened to allow in a bit of fresh night air and the curtains waltzed to the silent music of a lazy breeze. The light of a full moon played through them, illuminating the timber walls of the bedroom. Charlie's cot sat below a crucifix which Enoch had carved from the dry branch of a red gum. Hanging from the cross was a crudely fashioned medallion on a leather thong that had once dropped on to a table in front of me in the Noah's Ark. *'For he shall give his angels charge over thee to keep thee in all thy ways'.* I wished I'd had the foresight to give it to Enoch to carry before he departed. Charlie chattered in his sleep, 'Dadda come soon,' and I echoed his prayer.

There was something about Theresa I didn't like. It sounds terrible to say for she had never given me real cause to dislike her; nevertheless, there was something in her manner, a hint of confrontation, challenge, a worldliness that did not sit easy in a seventeen-year-old. She appeared somehow predatory and I never really relaxed while in her company. Sophia, however, appeared not to notice anything untoward in the demeanour of her new hired help and the pair seemed happy in their own relationship.

Theresa was very pretty with bright auburn hair, green eyes, freckles across her nose, a ready smile and a way of walking that was provocative but managed to stop just this side of wantonness.

She was singing as she scrubbed away at pots and pans over the outside sink, a pretty Irish song called Mantle of Green. Noticing me heading for the washing line she smiled and waved, and I forced a smile and waved back. Perhaps it was me, insecurities preying on my disorientation. Here I was, not a year out of England, in a strange land living a life unforeseen. We were bred for the rain, the frost and the chills of February mornings, damp hedgerows and branches bowed under the weight of ice and snow - all those things I would never see again if we failed to make this land pay.

'Is yer man away for long?'

I had been so preoccupied I hadn't heard her approach. She smiled - even white teeth, like Enoch's, she probably chews 'Spanish' - the liquorice root sticks that Enoch bought in the market back home. They may well grow wild here.

'They've gone on a delivery, could be a few days.' I didn't make eye contact but could feel hers on me. As children we had always been taught it was the height of bad manners to stare at people, even those who dress themselves up hoping to be stared at.

'I'm off to the city this afternoon for shopping with Sophia, why don't you come with us? Bring the wee man; sure, we can have a girl's afternoon.'

I didn't really want to spend any time with anyone, being so preoccupied; however, it might serve to take me out of myself.

For a woman of four feet eleven, Sophia was a formidable cart driver and we thundered down the curling, steep sided road which joined on to the main highway into the centre of Brisbane. Clouds of dust rose behind us, forcing a following cart to drop back. We slowed as the road became busier. All along one side of the wide thoroughfare on the city side of Breakfast Creek, a hotchpotch of market stalls had been set up selling all manner of foods and kitchenware, clothes, tools and even livestock tied to hastily assembled hitching poles.

Occasionally, we had to pull up sharply as some other road user chose to stop without warning to study some article that had caught their eye, this usually brought about a chorus of yells and swearing from those waiting behind them. When a carter behind us shouted at Sophie to 'Get a bloody move on!' Theresa stood up and turned to face him, hands on hips, retorting with, 'Do ye want me to come and entertain ye while yer waitin'?' Which brought a roar of laughter and cleverly cooled an irate situation. I began to think she was a much better engineer of human emotion than her youthfulness would have one believe.

Despite my initial reluctance to socialise, it turned out to be a lovely afternoon. I bought a leather belt for Enoch to replace the one he had come out of prison with and also a pair of boots for Charlie a size too big so he could wear them now with paper stuffed up the toes and the growing room would give them a long and useful life. Then the three of us and Charlie had coffee and a cake in a coffee shop from where we could watch water birds taking off and landing all along the river.

Theresa had been given the job of replacing a number of worn kitchen utensils and impressed Sophia with her bargaining skills. I would never have had the confidence or the impudence to cross swords with astute and artful market traders, but here was a young woman fully aware of her attributes and how to open doors with them. To my shock, when a market trader suggested, 'Show us an ankle and save a shilling,' she showed him a good deal more and saved half a crown!

It was early on a Sunday morning; the red light of dawn was halfway down the crucifix on the wall and the first of the chooks was calling for the others to shake a feather. They were distant sounds at first, then closer and then unmistakable - the creaking of wagon wheels, men's voices and the snap of reins. The party were back.

The End of the Sky

I pulled on a dress over my nightclothes and ran out into the yard. Enoch was dismounting. Frank Eighteen-Months was already removing the saddle from his horse and Iain Kincaid was lowering himself slowly from the seat of the wagon as if in pain. I reached Enoch who turned and looked down at me, his face a portrait of exhaustion, pain and something unfamiliar - as if a part of him had been stolen and the rest had flowed into the space left behind, making the whole appear somewhat watered down. He held me tight, breathing heavily.

'Pour a bath Lass, I'll be there directly.' He turned away and began to unsaddle his mount which I now realised looked as exhausted as her rider.

Scrubbing his back showed up the beginnings of angry bruises on his ribs and shoulders. He had said little since groaning while easing himself into the cool water. I knew him well enough not to prompt him until he was ready to speak but was fully aware that there was a story to tell. His exhaustion dripped from every word as he spoke.

'Did you look in the cart?'

I hadn't.

'No? Should I have?'

He breathed out, rubbing his face; water dripped from his beard and he let his head droop forward.

'Tuesday's in there, he's dead.'

The scrubbing paused, 'Oh my god...'

'Aye, Tuesday's dead, Kincaid took a bullet in his arse... and I'm going to Hell.'

There were a thousand questions, but it was clear my husband was in no state to answer them. He needed food and rest, in whichever order he felt like them.

It was rest first, he had almost dropped off in the bath and so I got him out, dried him and led him to bed where he was asleep before he hit the pillow. He woke mid-afternoon, rose and ate two plates of lamb stew with most of a loaf of bread.

Afterwards, he lit his pipe and we sat out on the porch where we took it in turns to continually call Charlie back from the edge of the scrub where Theresa had been startled by a snake only the day before. When he spoke, Enoch still sounded hoarse from the dust of the road.

'It was early morning, we were on the track that circles east around the Crow's Nest, not much of a road to be fair but when it's dry it can cut a chunk out of the journey according to Frank. We came across two coves kicking a campfire out and they stopped us and asked us where we were heading. When we told them up the north end of the Bunyas, they asked if they could join us for the ride, bit of company and safety in numbers so Frank agreed.

'They seemed a bit rum to me but then I don't know all the types around this part of the world, nevertheless, I told Frank I had a feeling. He just laughed and said it was normal to ask for a tagalong in wild country. Anyway, all was well for a few hours, we chatted about the goods we were carrying and the outlook for logging jobs up in the mountains. They said they'd been working on a station out west, but the place was burned out twice by blackfellas and the owner finally gave up and headed south to Sydney where he had relatives.

'Frank called a halt not long after noon in this place with an overhanging rock and a nearby stream which was out of the sun. I was kneeling over the fire setting the billys up and this bugger calls 'Bail up ya bastards!' Me and Kincaid turned at the same time and the pair of mongrels had guns trained on us.

'We both put our hands up, but they were obviously not very skilled highwaymen; they'd made the stupid mistake of not checking where everyone was before pouncing. Frank had said he was off on a dunny run and Tuesday, being Tuesday never missed an opportunity to do a bit of hunting for the pot.

'Now in that country when a bloke goes on a dunny run, he takes his gun and Frank, coming out of the bush saw what was up and called out 'Drop 'em you bastards!' If it had been me, I would have shot one of 'em or both of 'em before they even knew I was watching, but Frank's father was a Quaker and they must have brought him up not to take life as a first option or something.

'Anyway, they turned and one of them took a shot at Frank who ducked down; at the very same time a big rock whacked the other one on the side of the head chucked down by Tuesday from the overhang where he had been looking for bush tucker. The bloke went down, his mate turned and sent off a couple of shots up at the lad. It was all Kincaid and me needed. I ran and jumped on the bloke and fell backwards with my arm around his neck. Meanwhile Kincaid had picked up the rock and given the other bugger a few hard whacks with it in case he had any ideas of getting back up.

'While he was doing that though, the mongrel I had hold of managed to get a shot off in Kincaid's direction, catching him in the arse. Kincaid yelled and Frank came running now, up out of the bushes with his rifle. The bloke I was holding could see the game was up and stopped struggling. He dropped his gun, Frank kicked it away, I let go of him and we both stood up.

'We were about to tie his hands when poor Tuesday fell out of the trees and slid down over the shale - dropped right across from us. One of the shots had got him in the neck. Of course, the murdering swine knew he was heading for the noose now, so he made a dash for it on foot, he knew he wouldn't have had time to unhitch his horse, which was behind us anyway. Frank fired a shot in the air and was all for letting him go, Kincaid was on the ground with his hand on his arse and then... from where the rage came, I don't know, but I was across to my horse in two bounds, got my rifle, took aim and shot the bloke in the back. He kept running but I knew I had hit him as he spun with the force of the bullet. He staggered on for a bit, then dropped.

'Kincaid had done for the other one by bashing his head in and we chucked them in the cart along with poor Tuesday. We dropped the two crooks off at a police post in the Bunyas where a medic got the bullet out of Kincaid's rear end and patched him up enough to get him home. We delivered our goods and brought Tuesday home. We're going to bury him out in the bush.'

Neither of us spoke for a few minutes and then Enoch stood and looked out over the countryside to the north.

'I've killed a bloke Ellen; I killed a man - I pointed a gun at a man who was running away from me and shot him dead.'

I stood and wrapped my arms around his waist, sharing his stare at the far horizon where dark blue hills blended into a yellow sky.

'You killed a killer. He was going to hang for what he did - all you did was give him a quicker send-off. Poor little Tuesday.'

'I know…. But…'

'No buts - if Pastor Scorey was here now he would tell you the same, you know he would. He would say that God works in ways we can't always fathom. You shot an evil man. He was escaping and might have lived to do evil to other travellers, women and children, perhaps. Who knows who you saved by doing what you did?'

He put an arm around me, we called Charlie, and we all went inside. There would be police and questions, but Enoch had the well-liked and respected Frank Eighteen-Months as a witness, and it was likely the two would-be Dick Turpins were already known to the law.

It developed that, not only were they known to the law, but the one shot by Enoch, Bart Nelson, had a hundred pounds reward on him, so we had a thirty-pound share coming. We used part of the ten pounds left over for a funeral for Tuesday with a parson to say some words and a proper cross and the rest went to the mission in Wickham that takes care of sick and injured blackfellas in memory of the little lad who never stopped smiling, worked as hard as any grown man and showed us nothing but friendliness.

Frank was back in the saddle and out on a job the very next morning, but Enoch had been given a day of home duties; there was tack to repair and most of the animals needed time to recover from their trek. We visited Kincaid who we found lying on his side in his nightshirt outside the barrack block reading the Courier. He grinned at our arrival, passing the paper to Enoch.

'Here - have a decko at this; fancy a bit of digging?'

Enoch took the paper from him and frowned with concentration as he read the story. He would have deciphered it all splendidly given time, but his impatience often saw him passing things to me in order to read for him. On this occasion the paragraph had clearly piqued his interest and he handed me the paper to read aloud.

'Payable gold found in the north.'

'That's the one, read it out lass.'

Right, it says, 'A report has reached the news desk of The Courier stating that prospectors Mulligan, Brown, Dowdell, A Watson and D Robertson got a hundred and two ounces on the Palmer River which they prospected for twenty miles. They saw nothing of the country outside the river.'

'Kincaid eased himself up on one elbow, grimacing as he did so, 'What d'ya think Nockie? Worth a go?'

'Aye,' Enoch took out his pipe, 'Certainly worth thinking about. How much d'you suppose they got for a hundred and two ounces? Does it say lass?'

'It doesn't say,' I replied. There was little further information beyond speculating on the likelihood of a rush to the new diggings. Was Enoch really thinking of heading north? We needed to have a chat; he could see I was concerned as the frown had appeared. He stood.

'Take care of that arse Kincaid - you won't ride far standing up.'

'Nah, I could get used to all this lying down mate, Theresa'll be along directly with my tucker; don't work too hard.'

We emptied the cocoa tin, took the little wooden box down from behind the clothes in the second drawer of the cupboard, pulled the rolled up notes out from the hollowed space in the leg of Charlie's cot and laid out our combined fortune on the table.

'Twenty-one pounds, seventeen shillings and fivepence.' I announced.

'And thirty quid to come, remember?' Enoch added, 'Right - good God, more than fifty quid!'

I realised it would take my father the best part of two years to earn what we could now lay our hands on. Yes, Queensland had been good to us so far. We had no fear of hunger or homelessness, we were far from the workhouse, Charlie was well clothed and fed. Should any of us need a doctor we could afford to send for one. We were young and healthy, however and had so much to be thankful for.

'I've been doing some sums…', Enoch announced, '…and I reckon it would cost about twenty or twenty-five quid to get us up north and fully equipped to go prospecting. That would then leave us a good twenty-five to live on until we weighed our gold in.'

I shook my head, 'It can't be that easy Enoch, surely; you can't just turn up, lift a load of gold as if you are raising some potatoes for Sunday dinner and then walk off rich. It just can't be that easy; if it was, everybody would do it and there'd be no need for anybody to do anything else.'

'That's the whole point', he stood and began pacing, just like Father used to when he became animated, 'Everyone IS doing it - that's what a gold rush is. Look -

all we've seen of this country in nine months is just one tiny corner of it. It's huge Ellen, there's enough room - and apparently plenty of gold - for everybody. We go up, two to three months, get as much as we can carry on a donkey and get out. And we go home with enough to make sure we never go short again.'

He sat again and took my hand in his, 'I've been thinking about it, we set up a carting business like this one of Albie's, meeting trains and delivering anything and everything out into the villages and farms; we'll employ drivers and riders so I don't have to go out as much and you can have a maid so we can spend our time doing the things we want to do. I might even take up painting.'

I laughed at the thought of Enoch wearing a French beret, sitting at an easel in the park, but then, he was unique, as an artist has to be, and ploughed his own furrow. All of art, great paintings, music, books and plays are the work of lone wolves - never sheep or those who follow the herd. It brought to mind something Grandmother Sabina had told me on more than one occasion, 'All you will learn from a sheep is how to be a sheep, listen to the wolves who live in a world without fences.'

Unlike her, I never laid in my bed at night as a child and heard the cry of wolves, but I had surely married one; and I knew, as comfortable and safe as our life was in Cabbage Tree Stables, there was a call as irresistible to Enoch as the scent of water to a thirsty fox.

And for better or worse we were destined to answer it.

14.
Cabbage Tree Creek, Queensland
Wednesday, November 5th, 1873

Enoch tapped his pipe out against the rock seat we shared. Despite being eager to acquire the gold for our return and our future life in England, I had been less than content with the lack of consultation; I was determined to make my feelings clear.

'So - having decided we're going, have you decided when?'

He shrugged; the sarcasm lost on him.

'Soon as we can get all our supplies together. Best to get as much as we can here because they'll have your purse and your kidneys up North, so I've been told. I reckon a cart, good moke or a bullock, kit, tent, supplies, guns and ammo and we'll be independent.'

His inner fires were burning, and the demons danced in his eyes. He had often told me I saw destinations before journeys, but that was the pot calling the kettle black! When he gave life to a dream it sometimes became more real than the world around him. As far as I could make out, he didn't even know how to pan for gold or what to do with it afterwards.

And I had heard tales of the North.

175

'…No place for a decent lady - or any sane bloke come to that…'

'…Cannibals…'

'…Bloody awful weather, heat like you wouldn't believe…'

'…Anything that can bite ya is going to...!'

'…Drunkenness… murder… gunfights…'

All to which Enoch had the same one-word answer - 'Gold.'

He stood, stretching and patting his backside to bring the circulation back, 'Of course, the obvious answer - and I would hate this as much as you by the way - would be for me to go and for you and Charlie to remain here; but that can't happen even if we both wanted it to. Albie is a great bloke, best master I've ever had, but the home goes with the job and if I ain't hauling goods then he'll have to get somebody who will.'

It was not exactly love, not in the way I had loved Little Bayshill Terrace, but our home in Cabbage Tree Creek had become a place I was very fond of, a sanctuary in a wild and unfamiliar land decorated with mementoes of a distant somewhere that still tugged at my dreams.

We had made it our own in the short time we had spent in it - the little house on the end of the stable block wherein Enoch had built a cot for Charlie and on the wall, a cross-stitch of the Bullingham's Cottage, done from memory and with a decideldly crooked roof, sewn in the half-light of the Royal Dane's married quarters.

We now had more money in our pockets than we ever had at home, we ate meat when we wanted it. Enoch had a secure, well-paid job and even the heat was proving less onerous as our bodies adapted. Amusingly, thanks to the influence of the hands and in particular native-born Frank Eighteen Months, Charlie's accent was becoming less and less like that of his Gloucestershire parents and more like that of the land in which he had taken his first steps.

But every day or so it seemed there were new reports of fortunes being panned from the Palmer River and its tributaries - tempered with news of hostile natives, swarms of Chinamen intent on taking every last speck of gold and a breakdown of law and order in the new towns and camps springing up out of the virgin bush.

'We can't just up and go, Enoch, we've got to plan this - make certain it's a safe place for Charlie... and me - not to mention you.' I frowned; I knew I was frowning because Enoch mimicked it, forcing me to smile.

He sat on the rock again, putting an arm around my shoulder and using the other one to pull a protesting Charlie close.

'What did I say to you on the twentieth day of June in the year of our Lord 1869?'

'You said, "I do?"'

'As well as that - I said I'd look after you, protect you and keep you - and God hisself heard me say that, so he ain't going to let me do anything that would put you in danger now is he?'

'I suppose not, but...'

'Never mind the buts - we'll do it and do it proper, make plans, take advice, get up there, get the job done and get back out.'

Frank Eighteen Months bit off a plug of tobacco, chewed, spat and looked my husband in the eye. 'If you was to say to me you was going up north for the gold I'd say you were a hopeless optimist, but if you was to then say to me you was taking your missus and a nipper, I'd reckon you were bloody insane mate!'

Enoch smiled flatly and nodded, patting his mate on the arm. Frank was Australian born, as burnt as the dry bush and as knowledgeable as a white man can be concerning the home his Scots parents had crossed oceans to find. He had blue eyes that seemed out of place in a face so brown, they were almost permanently narrowed against the elements, but softened by laughter lines. Short, stocky and carrying not an ounce of fat, his bandy-legged gait told of a life in the saddle beneath an unforgiving sun. He never touched alcohol but occasionally smoked the sweet-smelling 'Cigares de Joy' which are said to calm the nerves, lift the spirits and cure a cough.

He had once been married, but his wife died in childbirth ten years back taking their new-born son with her. According to Enoch, Frank was the best horseman he had ever met - and that was praise indeed coming from someone whose own prowess had been highly regarded by those whose business it was to know how to get the best out of a mount.

Frank had once been bitten on the ear by a snake while sleeping on the ground and his mate, hearing the cry of pain, had leapt into immediate action, biting off the top part of the ear, sucking out any poison and dousing the wound with whisky. It had possibly saved Frank's life, but also earned him his new name - having, as he now did, a 'Yur-and-a-half'.

'Listen mate...' Frank was a foot shorter than Enoch and had to reach up to put a brotherly arm around his shoulder, '...you and your folks have got it bloody good here, do you really want to chuck it all in on a gamble? There's a reason why white folk ain't settled the north, hell, even the bloody Chows don't stay a second longer than they have to; and another thing...'

Enoch's laugh interrupted him, 'I know Frank, I know, but I've got a lucky shilling and a whole lot of belief which has always seen us through.'

Frank shook his head, 'You're a bloody idiot Nockie, but I wish you all the best; come back with your pockets full, ya mongrel!'

'Half of me thinks you're as daft as a bezom and the other half wishes I was young enough to be going with you.' Albie's Bristol accent always made me feel that home was closer, and I was genuinely going to miss him. Sophia too had been a good friend, showing me how to adapt local ingredients to make the best bread and how to prepare ointments for the inevitable sunburns, rashes and bites.

Enoch shuffled his feet, always a sign of his awkwardness when it came to formal speaking. 'I'll never know unless I give it a try - but I've said this to Ellen and I'll say it to you, you're the best master I've ever had, and I want to thank you for taking us in and for the work and the home.'

Albie grinned, 'Aye, well since we're being honest, I'll tell you; my first thought was "Aye aye, he's a rum 'un" - you looked a bit too much like Frank the Darkie and I had visions of you bailing me up at the first chance then heading out into the bush - but your missus is a gentle-looking little thing and then there's the nipper of course - and when I got a-talking to you, I thought, "He's got a good old Gloucestershire voice, he can't be a bad 'un," - and you're not, you're a nice bloke Mr Enoch Johnsey, a bit noisy with a drop of rum in you but that ain't a bad thing in moderation - and you're a damn good banjo player, although you can't sing a bloody note to save your life!'

The more we got down to the actual logistics of the adventure the more it became clear that we were attempting a challenge even bigger than the one that had taken us from Cheltenham to Brisbane. We could take nothing with us to the North, no luggage but for a change of clothes, none of the things we had accumulated in our time at Cabbage Tree Creek, just the personal mementoes that had crossed the oceans with us and items of necessity.

Unlike our arrival in Brisbane, there would not be the convenience of ready accommodation, established shops, or even proper medical help. Where would we sleep? In a tent out in the wilds - with Charlie? What would we eat? How would we cook in the rain? I trusted Enoch and knew he would lay down his life for us, but should he do so, who would then stand between us and the countless unholy dangers of the wild country and those who called it home? It was foolish, I decided and for the first time since the earliest days of our friendship in long-gone Andoversford, my husband and I found ourselves with daggers drawn.

'Here's the situation…'

Enoch was pacing our room, passing back and forth through the speckles of relentless dust illuminated by a setting sun glancing through the small oblong window. He would pause at one wall and then the other before repeating the pattern.

'…We could have stayed in Cheltenham and been poor and miserable…'

'I wasn't miserable.'

'Oh, I see…' he raised his arms as if struck by a revelation, '…So I forced you at gunpoint to come out here when all the time you were perfectly happy making hambone and cabbage soup and darning holes and…'

I stood and spoke as if he were fifty feet away instead of five, 'I came here because you wanted to, and because I bloody loved you - and I still do, but that don't mean I'd follow you over a cliff Enoch - at least not while I was carrying your son in my arms!'

Interrupting my husband would have been alien to the old me, but Australia and its women must have rubbed off. I couldn't imagine Theresa or Sophia being 'told off' by anyone. I had endured the same hardships as Enoch, therefore, as far as I was concerned, my opinion was now as worthwhile as his. Father would definitely not have approved but I could imagine Esther, away on the other side of the world, applauding and shouting, 'That's bloody well telling the bugger!'

Enoch looked as if he had been shot and stuffed. He stopped pacing and stared at a space somewhere between himself and the facing wall, mouth half hanging open and hands by his sides. His frown was not one of anger, but incomprehension as if his ears were fighting to convince his brain of what they had heard. After a few seconds he turned to look at me.

This was the neutral stare, intimidating enough on its own, but it was the one he used when he was at a fork in the road. It would either turn one way - and explode into laughter, or the other and burst into a flaming rage - a state that I had never been the target for, but even experiencing it as a third party had been disconcerting enough.

The reaction, when it came, however, was completely unexpected; his gaze never left me as he walked to the door and passed through closing it silently behind him. I assumed he would sit on his rock, puff his pipe for a while and then return, affronted and bringing with him a silence so profound it froze the air around it. Instead, after a few minutes of waiting I heard the stable door swing shut then milling hoofbeats settling into a rhythm before vanished eastward toward the darkening city.

Without sleep, Charlie would be a challenge in the morning, but it was going to be hard to get off without knowing where Enoch was - and what he was up to. He was perfectly capable of taking care of himself in the lanes and inns of Gloucestershire, but this land threw up a new surprise every day and, as Frank had told us on arrival, the most dangerous of all the creatures here were the ones who walked on their hind legs!

I must have dozed and was woke by Rover - Albie's cockerel, just as the light was returning; Charlie was still asleep. Outside, the rooftops of the distant city were turning from basso profundo to tenor as the sun climbed slowly out of the South Pacific. For a brief moment it reminded me of the sun rising over the frosty fields of Uckington but there was little else here to compare with home.

The buzzing of flies and the anxious call of a Noisy Miner bird were competing with Rover for attention; but there was another noise too. Distant at first but now, backlit by the sun the source became clear. The deep lowing of a reluctant bullock interspersed with the shouts and cajoling of a rider steering his mount this way and that in an attempt to keep the beast on the road and travelling in the right direction...

'Bought him off a bullocky in town, his name's Dacker - the bullock not the bloke...' Enoch was unsaddling his horse while the bullock stood in the shade of the stable block bridled with stout rope and seemingly docile, the creature looking as tired as I felt. So far there had not been a word of explanation and Enoch was still using the flat tone of the affronted and injured party.

I spoke to his back as he worked; 'I was worried about you and couldn't sleep much - do you think it was kind to disappear all night, knowing somebody who loved you would be so worried?'

183

He paused, then let the saddle he was holding drop to the ground. Enoch was many things - a lot of which God might not wholly approve of, but he was not unkind; my words seemed to have found a way through the armour because he turned to me and the coldness had gone.

It was probably the tiredness, but I cried as he held me, there was exhaustion in his voice too, but still determination, 'You're right Ellen…' he turned my face up to look at his, '…I been thinking and you're right; the North ain't no place for a woman and a little boy and I ain't taking you up there. I been talking to some blokes in town, friends of Frank, and they reckon the best way to go about it is in a small group of men, sticking together, prospecting as a team and sharing the loot.'

'Are you suggesting…'

'Come on, indoors, breakfast first, then a rest, then we'll talk - and I'll need to speak with Albie again.'

It was happening again; decisions were being made for me. Theresa had offered to take care of Charlie for a few hours while Enoch and I made up for the lack of sleep then, before discussing anything with me, he had gone to see Albie. On his return I made it quite clear that nothing more was to be done until I knew what was going on.

'Right then. Here's the bare bones of it. I'm going north to prospect the Palmer River with four other blokes - one of them's from Charlton Kings, says he's had more than one or two drinks in the Noah's Ark, how about that? You are going to stay right here in Albie's place. He's got a job for you, bit of tidying, stable work, helping Sophia and Theresa…'

'Wait a minute, I don't…'

'Hang on, let me finish; you know Albie, he's a straight-dealing bloke, he'll see you get a pound a week, a roof over your heads and all the tucker you can eat - and while I'm away I'll sleep at nights knowing you and Charlie Boy are safe and sound.'

'And just how long are you planning on being away?' I tried to pack as much disapproval into the question as I could, but Enoch, being a man, heard the words but not the music.

'We reckon about three months at the most.'

Noticing that I was about to fire a full broadside into his plans, he quickly continued.

'Three months Ellen, then back here with our fortune, another three months on the ship, that's six months from now… May - next May, just as the blossom is coming out all along Lansdown and in Montpellier Gardens - and who will be parading there in all their finery? You, me, Sarah Ann and Charlie, that's who. I'm going to get a topper and you can have a parasol and a hat with a big wide brim. Six months, Lass o' the Land - and we could be home.'

I was thoroughly unhappy about Enoch and I being apart for three months. I hated it when he was away for three days on a delivery and although much had happened in the past four years, there remained in a bleak and rarely visited corner of my memory, the place where the cold ache of longing still lurked, the six months of emptiness that stalked the days and nights during my love's incarceration - a chill so profound and indelible it had left behind an abiding anxiety whenever Enoch was away from me.

I was even less enthusiastic about the enterprise when it developed that Theresa's room would be going to Enoch's replacement and that she would be moving in with us!

'Ach think of all the fun we'll have - and it'll be nice to have someone to talk to.'

Theresa clearly viewed our impending house share with more enthusiasm that I did. In addition to all her other infuriating ways, it was clear Charlie really liked her, and somehow that annoyed me more than anything.

I managed a half-hearted smile while pumping away to fill the water bucket. It was not yet seven and already too hot for me. We had endured the first few months in what was apparently a pretty moderate Queensland summer before winter arrived, bringing temperatures that would have passed for a rather fine summer in Gloucestershire. But now they were on the rise again. Nights offered little respite and dawn brought that orb from hell up out of the bay to throw down volcanic heat on all those it caught in the open.

I recalled all those mornings of queuing for the Noah's Ark bread order as January Jack whipped around the corners of Cheltenham's streets breathing shramming cold straight into the bones. I used to dread the frost and snow, now I longed for it.

'It's going to be another warm one,' Theresa raised a hand and looked out across the shimmering bush, 'Yer feller still in bed, is he?'

There it was - something about the way she said the word 'bed' in the same sentence as my 'Feller.' I forced a smile.

'No, he's been up since five, away to the dock with a shopping list for Albie.'

'Ah, he'll be off up North soon then - and back with a fortune 'fore ye know it. Hey, perhaps he'll employ me as your housekeeper?' She knelt, ruffling Charlie's hair, 'What about that then Cathal, eh? Sure, we'd charm the pants off em so we would.'

Charlie laughed. Theresa, for all her annoying traits, was a natural with children and had such a disarming smile - at once both guileless yet full of devilment, that I never truly knew how to feel about her. One minute I'd be wishing her to the other side or the world, then laughing along with something that would have seen Father's eyebrows disappearing under his hat. She reminded me more than a little of Esther.

I had a letter from home. I had written twice since arriving and had been concerned that my letters had made it safely to the other side of the world but now here, in my hand, after ten months, was a letter from my family.

The address on the envelope was written in lovely copper plate swirls and had probably been done by someone like The Rev Byron or Mrs Brooke. The handwriting on the letter itself however was unmistakably Father's to begin with.

'My Dear Ellen,

I hope this letter finds you and your family well and in good spirits. As I write this it is the second half of July and the weather is quite warm this summer, although likely not as warm as that which you experience in your climes.

We are prospering to a reasonable degree; I have work fencing and hedging for a man called Balcombe whose farm is close to Deerbrook Forge. He is known to Samuel who does his smithying. He is a fair employer who pays wages on time and also mutton when he has it to spare.

You will be interested I am sure, to learn that your friend from the Noah's Ark, John Drew was sentenced in his absence to be hanged for robbery in which a man died. He ran before the constabulary could arrest him. They combed the fields and lanes with dogs and troopers, but he was not found. He then sent a letter to the Chronicle saying as how he didn't do it. The letter was posted in Bristol but there has been neither hide nor hair of him since.

Mrs Brooke asked about you and I showed her your letters which pleased her, she sends her best wishes to you.

This next bit is from your Mother, I am writing this for her. She is well but sees very little now of what is in front of her.

'Dearest Ellen.

My Darling, I hope you are well, and that Charles and Enoch are well too. Sarah Ann is thriving; she is a curious and pleasant little girl whose smile reminds me

188

so much of yours. She told a lady in the market that, 'My Mama is in Bristol,' I had to correct her, but it was so endearing.

'Your sister Emily is fine and well, she had a fever earlier in spring but recovered, Samuel is a fine husband who never left her side. He is a good provider and their family seem to be secure and happy. Walter does not much care for work, he had a job with the coal merchant that Enoch once worked for and on one occasion he left home to attend work but did not get there, spending the day instead skulking around the town with a number of young ne're-do-wells. I am afraid to say Father administered suitable correction and he has not repeated the offence.

'William is working at Andoversford for a veterinary surgeon and loving his employment. He is learning much of horse diseases and is said to be an expert rider and budding trainer.

'I pray for you every night and know that there is no distance so great that the Lord cannot watch over you. Keep safe my dearest, write again to us soon. God bless you.

'This is Father again writing now. I shall now pass this paper to your sister, Esther, who is sitting at the table holding the inkwell. We have not yet lit the lamp because the low sun is lighting the room splendidly.

'The writing changed from Father's laboriously crafted letters to Esther's rushed hand with so many undotted 'i' s and uncrossed 't's that would have brought an admonishment from Mrs Brooke.

'Hello Sister, Esther here; dearest darling Ellen, I miss you so much. Father says that this letter will take months to get to you and so by the time you read this I may likely be a married woman. Henry and I have set the date for Saturday, November 7th and are praying that the weather will be as clement as it was for you and for Emily.

'I was going to write something about what Constable Mossley caught Noah Isgrove and Ruth Morrison doing behind Stockwell's grain store, but if I did Father would only make me cross it out and so it will have to wait until we meet again. When will that be? Have you struck gold yet?

'Do you remember Edward Little from school? He was the one with a funny eye. Well, he is heading for Queensland too. There are stories in the paper here about gold in a place called Gympie, is that close to you?

'Please take care over there in that strange land, tell Enoch that he had better take good care of you or he will have me to answer to - and you know I'd tell the b***** straight. (Father made me put those dots there). I love you and think of you every day. Write soon - and come home soon too, with a fortune - or even without one, I will still love you.

Your devoted Esther.'

It took three read-throughs before I could see the letter without having to constantly wipe away tears. I would use the time without having Enoch's company to write a long letter telling them all about this place in detail, about the land, the heat, the people, our hopes for a swift return and even perhaps a photographic likeness should money allow.

Bristol. Not Brisbane. The familiar sting of tears, my heart in my eyes.

If only.

15.
Cabbage Tree Creek, Queensland
Friday February 6th, 1874

I had thought a year in Australia would acclimatise me to the summer but the one of 'Seventy-four was an inferno. The sky became an implacable sheet of white hell, the earth shimmered and everything that could move retreated into the shade. Stick an arm out of the window and it would become a rabbit over a campfire, walk across the yard to the pump and you would swear the sun was just a few feet above your head.

At night, as soon as the furious red ball sank below the lands to the west we would emerge and take it in turns to put our heads under the pump while someone worked the handle. It was a moment of paradise one dreamed of all through the torment of the day. Charlie, as naked as the day he was born, would run in and out of the water while I and 'Auntie' Theresa pumped away.

Sharing a home with Theresa was not as bad as anticipated. I believe she had given up trying to shock me and the pair of us settled down into a routine of our work around the stables, cooking, cleaning the home, washing, eating together and telling each other stories of who we once were and who we dreamed of being.

192

Theresa was born into an impoverished family in Tipperary, the second eldest of four children, although her baby brother died along with her mother. After her mother passed away and her father fell to drink, the convent took her in with her elder sister before they ran away and travelled to Dublin, walking most of the way and either begging or borrowing to eat.

They worked in a kind of guest house that entertained in a very unusual and special way which she promised to tell me more about when we knew each other better. Her sister then
married a man whose parents owned an inn and, with no other family, she embarked on a journey across the world to seek out relations who had left for Australia a generation before.

As she explained it, 'Because I was a young healthy woman travelling alone, I was awarded assisted immigration to Queensland where such creatures were in short supply. I read the document carefully to ensure there was no legal obligation to breed when I got here, but thankfully this was left to the individual.'

Her relatives were in Victoria and, like many from the British Isles, she had greatly underestimated the scale of things here, not fully realising until she landed in Brisbane that Melbourne was more than eight hundred miles away.

With no more than a few shillings to her name, she sought work and was taken on by Alby. Her revised plan was to go north when it had 'Civilised a bit', dig some gold then head south to seek out her long-lost kin.

We would do our washing together in the yard, both taking it in turns to sing. It appeared I did not know any of her songs nor she mine, however, after several renditions of 'Her Mantle So Green' I had picked up most of the lyrics and as for the rest we hummed along with Sophia occasionally making up a trio.

Charlie was becoming more and more adventurous; he would chase the new native hand, Tomtom, around the yard with the pair of them yelling and whooping. Tomtom was teaching him a dance of his people which was supposed to bring luck while hunting and already Charlie knew more blackfella words than anyone else in the stables.

As February turned into March and summer turned from a hot-flushed youth into a livid and angry old man the storms became more frequent and furious. A thunderhead had been brewing since afternoon and had begun its first rumblings as we went to bed. I had not expected it to amount to much, but as the heat built and kept on building it was clear that when it broke it would do so with a belligerence to wake the dead.

A sudden bang shattered the night and set the sleeping animals squealing and the birds screeching. It sounded as if God himself had furiously grabbed the sky and slammed it into the ground to gain respite from the heat. The flash lit up the room as if the curtains were not there, cupboard doors shook, and dust fell from the roof beams.

That first bang also woke Theresa and she cried out in shock. Charlie, needless to say, slept through it, having as he did his father's utter disregard for the weather whatever its moods. In the dim light of the room, I saw Theresa get up off her bed covered only in a sheet and, dropping that, she scurried across to my bed and, to my shock, got in without so much as a by your leave. I am no stranger to sharing my bed, I have done so for much of my life with either Emily, Esther or Mary Ann - but they were flesh and blood - and they had nightclothes on! Although, to be fair, it is a lot cooler in Gloucestershire.

I had already been uncomfortably hot and another hot body hugging mine did nothing to cool me down.

'Sure, I hate it I do,' Theresa shivered despite the heat. I hugged her back instinctively, praying for the sound of rain to bring a cooler to the night. A few more bangs followed before rain began to fall and the rumbles grew distant.

'I think it's safe for you to go back now.' I told her, but she appeared to be half asleep and just mumbled something incoherent.

She was still there when I woke in the morning. I couldn't remember dropping off, but I got up without disturbing her and went out into the yard to fill the bucket for the wash basin. It seemed so out of character for someone like Theresa, outwardly fearless and full of the confidence of youth, to be afraid of thunder, but I suppose we all have our frailties. I have always disliked worms - odd for a country girl... a 'Lass o' the Land', but I used to shudder when Grandfather William offered a particularly fat and juicy specimen to the chickens.

The sound of the water being poured from the bucket into the wash basin woke Theresa who sat up yawning, fiery hair tumbling over her face. She parted the locks as if she were opening curtains and gave me a silly smile.

'That was a storm and a half'. She got out of bed and stood, rubbing her eyes, caring nothing for her state of undress.

'Will I be starting breakfast while you wash the wee man?... What?'

I hadn't realised I was staring at her, I shook my head, 'Nothing... yes, if you could get the porridge on that would be good.'

She beamed an engaging smile to compliment the first rays of light coming in under the door and began pouring oatmeal into the pan.

'Are you going to put some clothes on?' I asked as I picked a reluctant Charlie out of his bed.

'No, I thought I'd go into Brisbane and do the shopping like this, see if I can give that miserable auld bugger in the grocers something to hang his onions on eh?'

How could I have ever not liked her?

Frank Eighteen Months and Tomtom were heading out towards Ipswich with a cart of tools and offered to take Charlie for a ride. They would be away for the day and I knew he would be eager to go, but at two and a half I thought it might be a little early to expose him to the dangers of the trail - even a well-travelled one like the road to Ipswich. However, seeing him sat on the driving seat between the pair, a too-large wide-brimmed hat shielding his eyes and tiny clay pipe in his mouth, bought especially for him by Frank, it would have been a hard mother indeed who would have lifted him down and send him indoors when adventure beckoned. Also, I trusted Frank more than anyone with his safety and was reassured by his promise that his 'apprentice' would return safe and sound.

The End of the Sky

A stable hand had left and a new one was due to move into quarters the next day and so Sophia and I spent most of the morning cleaning out the room, putting the mattress out to air and doing an inventory of crockery and cutlery. Theresa meanwhile had been sent into Brisbane with Kincaid and a shopping list, mercifully, she had dressed first.

I tried not to worry too much about Charlie, but it was his first excursion without Enoch and myself; however, he was his father's son with that streak of independence and what Mother used to refer to as 'Something of the lanes' about him. And then there was Theresa, it was probably just a cultural difference and what she had done during the storm was likely a natural thing for her. I also reminded myself she was only seventeen. When I was that age, during Enoch's incarceration, I was often confused about who I was and where life was leading. Now, at twenty-five and with so much already behind me, I had to confess that, dreams aside, I still had little idea of which road would turn out to be most travelled.

All the concerns about Charlie going off on his adventure were unfounded. He turned up with his teammates at dusk, tired, dusty and wearing a bandana with a wide smile on his face. Before bed, I washed him while Theresa scrubbed his clothes and he told me about his day, observing that, 'There's some stupid bastards on the roads y'know.'

'… and you know that snooty mare of a woman who works for the ironmonger, the one that always pronounces the 'g' on the end of shilling, well if you ask me, she does more than work for him - anyhow, I went in there for two billys and some leather needles and she says to me '...Do you think bare shoulders are "Happroptiate" for shopping in the daylight?' I said to her - in her own silly posh voice, 'Does Madam open in the night-time?' 'Oh no, certainly not,' she says, 'Well then,' I say, '...You'll just have to put up with them - I take it you've no objection to me money?'

Theresa kept on chattering throughout the dinner preparation, stirring away boisterously, pausing to pull Charlie's trousers up properly as he came in from the dunny. 'Have ye seen the new hand? Sure, he's got a face like a horse, he'll fit right in here, he's from South Wales - the old one not the new one - and his name's Joseph. I think I'll take him a plate of stew if there's any left over, make him feel a bit more welcome, he's only a lad, can't be much older than me.'

New hands were a regular feature at the moment. No sooner did one start than they picked up a newspaper full of tales of the fortunes that men were allegedly making in the far north and they were off again, gold fever driving them on. Pity they did not bother to read the other stories about the dangers, the weather, and the shiploads of disappointed, broke and broken prospectors disembarking every day in Brisbane and farther down in New South Wales. I did not read the stories too closely, worried as I was about Enoch and his new chums.

But what if he did - really did - find gold? Imagine going home with pots of money. Seeing Mother and Father well cared for in a nice house and a doctor for Mother's eyes and Father able to give up work and potter in his garden and Sarah Ann, my darling girl, going to the Ladies College and marrying a gentleman.

Each morning I went out of the corral gate and looked down the road to the distant rooftops of Brisbane for any sight of a man on a horse trailing a bullock.

I woke up gasping as if in shock. I must have cried out as Theresa rose on an elbow, squinting across from her own bed as dawn began to turn the sky red beyond the curtains. Brushing her hair back she croaked, 'Are you alright?'

'Must have been a dream,' I managed to gasp, still breathless but reassured the danger had all been in my head. I had tasted smoke and there had been a bang like thunder, but I knew it could not have been. There had been a scream too. While I was still chasing my thoughts, which seemed intent on running away, Theresa had left her bed and got into mine.

'There ye are, just a dream, there's no real harm in them,' she whispered hugging me. But even then, wide awake, I could still hear the echo of the scream and the thunderous crash. I desperately wished Enoch were home, safe and well, with or without his fortune. Thinking of him, I realised he was in some way linked to the dream.

'I think it was about Enoch, I didn't see him, but I felt he was in trouble.' I whispered into Theresa's hair. She kissed me on the cheek, 'He'll be home soon enough, and all of him in the same place as when he left. Until then, I'll look after ye.'

Across the room, Charlie muttered something in his sleep, I hoped his world of dreams was a happier place than mine, although the closeness of Theresa succeeded in holding the darkest corners away.

16.
Cabbage Tree Creek, Queensland
Thursday, March 26th, 1874

I counted the hours and minutes of separation and was furious with myself for doing so, forcing my wayward thoughts into order as a sheepdog herds a flock; driving them in the correct +direction; concentrating on the work in hand and the tasks before my eyes. I had meals to cook for Charlie and me as well as young Joseph who seems to have adopted me as a surrogate parent.

He is a personable and kind young lad whose accent reminds me of tragic Richard Price who would have seen so much right - and so much wrong - in this distant world. But, as I pump for a bucket of water and carry it back to the cottage, I find myself looking down the long red road that leads into Brisbane where, even this late in the summer, the air shimmers and the dust devils dance in a hot wind.

What is wrong with me? My husband was, at this very moment, probably risking his life to gain us the better future we have talked and dreamed about. A ticket home and prosperity, reuniting with our darling Sarah Ann, good schools for her and Charlie, a lovely house, security for our families.

I had not seen or heard from Enoch in almost three months, his voice, his smile, his reassuring presence and self-composure in whatever circumstance... And yet, as I stop again and look once more down the road before disappearing into the comparative cool of the cottage, it is not his outline against the lowering sun that I seek, but that of an Irish girl sent to the city for a week's employment to help out a friend of Albie - and due back today.

'Stupid.'

I didn't realise I was speaking aloud until Charlie piped up with, 'Who's stupid Ma?'

Closing the cottage door, I topped up the pan to prepare boiling water for the small red potatoes that still surprised me with their alien texture.

I chuckled, 'I am, my little chicken, just stupid thoughts...Your great Granddad would have had something to say about these potatoes - "Ain't a lot of Gloucestershire in 'em" he would have said.'

I felt better for simply invoking the memory of Grandfather William - who left and went abroad and came home again. Loneliness - loneliness and the disorientation of a strange land. It would never happen in Cheltenham, in the bosom of my family and the sure and certain return of my husband every evening. It's just friendship, close friendship born out of loneliness.

It was getting dark now, where was she?

She came home after dark. Charlie was asleep but on hearing her subdued, 'T'is only me' and the clicking of the door catch, a tired voice came from the direction of his bed, 'Aunt Theresa?'

I saw her shadow-shape walk softly over to his bed.

'That's right my little bush fella,' she bent down to hug him, he giggled.

'You wait 'till the morning, see what I've got for ya.'

She called across to me in a whisper that reached me as a shout, 'Are you awake over there?'

'I was asleep,' I said in a hastily concocted semi-conscious voice.

She chuckled and it trickled over me like the warm waters of a summer stream, washing away cares and all thoughts of anything that lay the other side of our door.

'Liar,' she giggled.

The newspaper of Friday, March 27th carried a story with the headline, 'All that glitters' and it told the story of the many who had risked all in the pursuit of northern gold and were now returning dejected, destitute - or not at all.

According to the report, hundreds, if not thousands, were trapped in the far north, not having the fare to catch a boat back to where they came from. I couldn't help wondering whether Enoch was one of the poor souls wandering, as the paper put it, 'Like ghosts along the muddy and murderous roads between the Palmer River and Cook's Town, assailed on all sides by hostile tribes, disease and, increasingly, by those they would have regarded as chums and compatriots on the journey of hope just short weeks before.'

Needless to say, I had not heard a word from him, nor did I expect to from such an untamed wilderness. My thoughts swung wildly most days between the tragedies that could have befallen one so untutored in the ways of the land he was wandering and conversely, the knowledge that he was himself a born wanderer, trained from the time he could walk to fend for himself and live by his wits. If anyone could make it home - and in style - it was Enoch Edward Johnsey who could light a room with his smile, leap expertly on to the bare back of a cantering horse as it passed by and see tomorrow as clearly as those more domesticated saw today.

He would return, surely, and all would be well. If his expedition was successful, then we would be heading into the city and the dockside and booking a passage on the next boat to England. I would write to my family and tell them to expect us. If he returned without gold then we would leave Cabbage Tree Creek and head south, through New South Wales to Victoria and we would make our fortune from the land, establish ourselves and then send for Sarah Ann and build a future in the new world where free men, green fields and the bleating of healthy sheep would paint the background to the portrait of our lives. And I would have more children and grow old surrounded by the offspring of Charlie and Sarah Ann. Enoch would smoke his pipe on a verandah and I would sew.

And I would forget all about Theresa who would marry Joseph and raise a brood of unruly but happy children who would grow to ride bareback, sing and chase Noisy Miner birds in the lands around the Creek.

And I knew even as my thoughts painted this picture that it was a fantasy.

I told myself that I had created a surrogate sister out of Theresa to replace far away Esther, Emily and poor Mary Ann - but I had never felt this way about my sisters.

It suddenly occurred to me that I hadn't been in a place of worship since goodness knows when. Maybe there would be an answer in a house of God, guidance - a light to lead me back to the path of righteousness. I would go into Brisbane on Sunday and find a church or chapel, any church or chapel would do - and the man of God would, by his words, open my eyes and the road ahead would be clear.

But I didn't get to the church, because, on Saturday, March 28th - a restless and mischievous day full of gust-tossed gulls, dust devils and dancing lines of laundry, Enoch came home.

Thinner - and with a beard he could almost have tucked into his waistcoat, he dismounted in the yard, patting the rump of a horse I had not been acquainted with. He took off the saddlebags, throwing them over a shoulder and led the creature to a hitching post and only then turned to look around. Spotting me he stopped, tilted back his battered hat and spread his arms wide. Dropping my peg bag, I ran, crying into his arms.

As he had done on the occasion of our first kiss so many years ago and oceans away, he lifted me clean off the ground. He smelled like a horse but at that moment I wouldn't have cared if he smelled of the brimstone of Hell itself. I squeezed him so tight he had to finally lift me clear and put me down, laughing, patting the dust from his clothes, his black eyebrows light red from the trail, his voice dry.

'Coffee I'm thinking...' He rummaged in a saddleback, pulling out a kid leather drawstring bag, '... there should be enough in here to pay for it.'

He dropped the heavy bag into my hand and, arm around my shoulder, walked us to our door.

'Dadaaa!'

Caught up in the moment, I hadn't even thought of how Charlie was going to react to the return of his father, changed so much as he was from the comparatively groomed man who had left at the height of summer. I need not have worried. Our little bushman almost left the floor, springing up from a prone position where he had been reading, he ran straight into Enoch's arms.

'Good God, look at the size of you, Mother must have been feeding you well,'

'And Auntie Theresa too… 'Charlie laughed, '…did you bring me back a present?'

'Did I ever, 'Enoch's laugh filled the room, '…but you'll have to wait until Dad's had coffee, tucker and a good old chinwag with Mother, alright?'

Charlie's mention of Theresa brought two worlds crashing together. I thought that when Enoch returned all would be as before but… no - I mustn't expect everything to change in a heartbeat. These were early moments, and I was, beyond any doubt, as full of joy as I could have been at the return of the cornerstone of my life.

Theresa seemed happy for me when she came back from shopping - and why shouldn't she be? I told myself. She hugged me and planted a big kiss on my cheek that seemed… sisterly but I had always been guilty of leading myself up the garden path and it was clear that this is what had happened over the past six weeks or so. But… could I have got things that wrong?

The End of the Sky

I have to admit I was slightly hurt and just a little annoyed at her reaction as she joined us for our evening meal. We sat at the table while she bustled about stirring things and singing as if she had not a care in the world. But the presence of Enoch, especially now that he had taken a bath, was a balm to all my worries. He had not fallen foul of ambush, disease or accident; he was back, all in one piece among his loved ones and, so it seemed, with some fruits of his labours.

There were two leather bags, Enoch tipped the first out gently on to a newspaper spread on the table. Dinner had been a noisy affair and rather that badger him with questions, I had waited until he had finished what he said was the 'Best tucker in months!'

Spreading out, tiny grains glittered in the flame of the lamp with here and there larger nuggets although all smaller than a new-born baby's little fingernail.

'This is my share of the gold our little gang got out. What I've got, all together and all in, is a tiny fraction over two pounds in weight which, in real terms is worth, so I've been told, 'bout a hundred-and twenty-one-pound sterling.'

He must have seen my look of amazement and couldn't have failed to hear Theresa's 'Bloody hellfire.' He smiled and shook his head at the same time.

'Now, Lass o' the Land, this is certainly enough to get us back to England but - and this is a very big but - it ain't going to do us a lot of good when we get there, which is why I'm going to have to go back up North.

The tears sprang involuntarily from some well that had been dripping inside me, dank and lonely, 'I'm going

207

to say this once Enoch Johnsey, I will not wait here again, helpless and hopeless. I will not, and that's final. Now I don't know much about gold and finances - or the cost of things in this place, but a hundred and twenty-one pound is more than I've ever seen in one place in my whole life. Even in the Noah's Ark on Gold Cup day when I once saw 'bout a hundred pound on a table when some Hee-Haws were playing cards. You ain't going and that's that!'

Theresa stood, 'Come on little bushfella, we're going for a long walk.'

Charlie jumped down off his chair, 'But Dad's got a present for me Aunt Theresa.'

'Yes - and it'll still be here when we get back. Come on.'

She reached out a hand and half-reluctantly, Charlie took it and, with a smile across to me full of butterflies and lavender, she led Charlie out, leaving Enoch and myself facing each other over the table, an irresistible force and an immovable object. I stared at the tabletop in the silence that followed her departure. How was she feeling about this? The prospect of Enoch returning to the north leaving her and I... Or the prospect of me going back to England...? Enoch dragged me back to the there and then.

'The point is this Ellen; we have about a hundred and twenty pounds. Getting you and I and Charlie back to London will cost around fifty. So, there we are in England with about seventy pounds. A house in Cheltenham - even a modest one, is going to cost four or five times that, so... say we rent a place for me and you and Charlie and Sarah Ann, now we're down to about fifty pounds. Fifty pounds may be enough to start a modest business, buy a horse and cart or something but the truth is, with things the way they are over there, I'd be out working for someone else within a year and probably, so would you and it would be as if we had never left. All those miles, the journeys, the struggles and separations would have been for nothing.

'But I have something now Lass o' the Land, something I didn't have when I left here to go north.' He tapped his forehead before taking both my hands in his. I could not look up at him because I know I would have just folded, given in and agreed to anything he said. The slow tick of the wall clock and a noisy miner bird somewhere out in the surrounding bush were the only things breaking the silence until he spoke again.

'Ellen, look at me...'

I did, and a sorry sight I must have been. The tears of joy from just a few short hours ago had been replaced by tears of fear and confusion. For the briefest of times, I had felt myself standing on solid ground but now the sands were shifting again.

He stroked the side of my face, 'That's the face I have been dreaming about for endless nights, only I dreamed it smiling.'

I forced a weak and unconvincing smile, 'I don't want you to go again, this is not what we came here for. If you must go back up north, then I'm coming too - and Charlie's coming...'

'But...'

'I cut off his interruption with one of my own, '...and Theresa's coming.'

'Theresa?'

'She will help us, look after Charlie and help to support us with chores - even help with the digging if necessary, she's a good one Enoch.' I spoke with such conviction that I almost convinced myself that the reasons I wanted her to travel with us were purely functional.

Enoch, having won the victory of heading north again raised little objection and, to be truthful, I think he was buoyed at the thought of having his family close at hand. Surely, he would not have agreed to it if he didn't think he could care for us and keep us safe in that wild place?

I hugged Sofia and Albie, I hugged Frank Eighteen Months, even after he had called my husband a 'Bloody mad mongrel'; I hugged young Joseph who was set to take over as head drayman and I hugged Tomtom who cried to see us go. We left Cabbage Tree Creek on a bright and beautiful autumn morning in a cart loaned by Albie who would send someone to the dock compound for it later.

Charlie sat beside his father on the driving seat while Theresa and I sat on suitcases in the back.

I had said, as casually as I could while she and I were bustling about the washtub.

'Would you like to come with us?'

The sound of rinsing and wringing had stopped, and it was, I knew, one of those moments a journey reaches a fork in the road. I had experienced others; there had been the pastry shop in Cheltenham when Robin Berry had sat studying the menu, then when Enoch had proposed in the shade of a horse chestnut tree - and then when that fateful coin had spun in the air condemning

Sarah Ann to year and more so far without her parents to hold her.

It had been a significant moment for Theresa too, I could tell. She would never be short of admirers at Cabbage Tree Creek and would undoubtedly land a husband who would devote himself to her. But did she feel... whatever it was, as I did? Then the rinsing and wringing had begun again.

'Alright then,' she had replied in a voice as soft as Irish linen.

She had not looked in my direction, but she had smiled, and I had felt light.

It was not as wild in the North as people made out according to Enoch who, admittedly, had a different interpretation of 'Wild' to most people. He spent the trip to the dock talking over his shoulder to us.

'There are families doing alright up there. Cook's Town is a lively place to be sure, but we'll not be stopping, we're off upriver. It'll be a bit of a trek but there'll be plenty of company and... there's even a school planned so I heard before we left - not that we're staying like I said, but it just goes to show...'

This was Enoch, as he had always been, his thoughts and his will as dry leaves to the wind, here and there and everywhere at once. I had no doubt that most of what he had said was true - or at least he believed it to be, but it all came coloured by the lens of his imagination. He thought something - therefore it was.

I was about to get on a boat with the three people who filled my world. We were going to a place I knew nothing about beyond what Enoch and the newspapers had told me. I didn't fully understand what alluvial gold was but apparently there was tons and tons of it ready just to pick up where we were going.

As we alighted from the cart in a cloud of gulls and gust-driven straw from a nearby carter loading hay, the smell of the sea reminded me of the day, just fifteen months before, when we had stood not a stone's throw from this spot, cases at our feet and Charlie in Enoch's arms, looking out at this bewildering new land we had crossed the world to find, far from the familiar pastures and fields of Gloucestershire. I had been excited, but not afraid. I was with a man who would be the better of any danger or mishap that befell us. And now that I stood here again, I remembered that this was what he had promised, he would make us rich and then take us home. And I told myself, as our little party climbed the gangway on to the straw-covered deck of the Rigil Kent, that was exactly what he was doing.

Millions of tiny living things making up one enormous living thing! If someone had told Uckington Ellen that such an entity could even exist, she would have scoffed behind her hand - unless or course it had been Robin Berry and even then, she would have wondered if his source was trustworthy.

But there it was, stretched across and below a sea of so many shades of blue it could have been a reflection of Heaven itself. It was probably the most beautiful natural thing I had ever seen.

'D'you know what it's called?' Enoch asked.

I shook my head.

'Great Barrier Reef.' Theresa chipped in looking out to sea, hair the colour of this great island's heart billowing in the warm wind. She turned to us, glittering emerald eyes half-closed against sun, grinning, 'We got religion, geography and little else in the school I went to.'

There were a few making their first journey north who appeared equally enraptured by the view of the reef and those that weren't seemed to more enamoured by Theresa who, to her credit, had dressed more modestly than everyone at Cabbage Tree Creek had become accustomed to and toned down her brazen smile.

She was not unaware of the attention, whispering to me in a voice full of devilment, 'I'm not sure I'd feel safe with all these lusty miners if I didn't have you to protect me.' Subtly reaching for my hand she gave it a squeeze and the sensation made my whole body glow.

The Rigil Kent was nothing like the Royal Dane. This was a working ship and made no pretence to be otherwise. It was designed to carry goods with a small crew and the ablutions were completely overwhelmed by the two hundred or so humans and animals crowded on the deck. Enoch, as a returning prospector, had the wherewithal and wisdom to secure us a little privacy in a small damp room with a half door. It looked and smelled as if generally served as a holding pen for livestock.

We spent the nights on the floor of this room with coats below and over us as the ship groaned and creaked and the passengers and crew yelled and swore around the clock.

Tide being no sympathiser with the needs of man or beast, we arrived in the mouth of the Endeavour River just as a watery dawn was breaking over the Pacific, all of us in an exhausted and disgruntled condition, in need of a wash and a good meal.

'Give him here,' Theresa took Charlie and trudged down the gangplank into a shallow sea of ankle-deep mud and manure with me following. Enoch led Bucephalus carefully down the gangplank. Theresa had renamed him after hearing his previous owner had called him 'Bad Tempered Bastard.' There was nothing regal about the creature, he had one blue eye and one brown, his head looked too big for his body and, irrespective of what he ate, he would fart furiously with every few steps. But, according to Enoch who knew about these things, this was a very good sign.

'A farting horse will never tire!' he had stated.

Cook's Town - some people are trying to change the name to Cooktown but there's much more than the name that needs changing! Brisbane was rough and ready - a big noisy place that had little in common with Cheltenham, but there was a real desire to give it an air of permanence; buildings constructed to last, a place of the future planning to serve not only those who had crossed the world to find it, but also their children and grandchildren.

Cooktown had not been here when Charlie was born and would, in all probability, not be here when he died. This was not a place to put down roots, it was a sandcastle place, a town of playhouses and disposable people, destined to be adored for the moment before falling once more into the arms of nature and sleeping, dreaming of its brief brush with fame.

I remembered Grandfather William talking about some place in Spain that was insufferably hot; he had said,

'There's places as belong to Mother Nature and she be choosy 'bout whom she wants there - some parts of this Earth just ain't meant for people.' And yet here they were. People like I had never encountered. All languages and shapes and sizes, Chinamen in blue tunics with huge conical hats, unspeaking, walking in a line like ducks to the pond. Music and laughter coming from makeshift inns… there were even gunshots; and above and around us, invisible but all-encompassing - the heat, like a wash house on a hot summer's day, roiling and boiling.

My clothes were already damp, sweat trickled down my back, Theresa's hair stuck to her flushed face. Enoch took off his hat, wiping his forehead with a sleeve. He took the lead and we walked behind the shops and the milling throng on the main street to a small and comparatively well-build store where a selection of pots, pans and tools hung from hooks all along a wooden verandah. Enoch tied Bucephalus to the rail. A painted sign announced 'General Hardware Supplies' and a sleeping yellow dog opened one bloodshot eye as we entered before returning to his slumber. The inside was sheltered from the direct sun but no less warm.

'Upriver kit?' The storekeeper spoke to Enoch over the shoulder of a Chinaman who was already at the counter. The little man raised a finger, 'Excuse… want…'

'I'll tell you what you bloody want - and I'll tell you when you can bloody have it!' the storekeeper snapped, pushing the man aside with an arm almost as thick as the Chinaman's body.

'Now then…' he turned his attention back to Enoch, 'Upriver kit?'

'That's what we're after,' Enoch confirmed.

The storekeeper spread his arms wide across the counter, further marginalising the Chinaman who had been effectively herded into a corner.

'Right-o, well let's start with what you've got and then we'll have an idea of what you're gonna need.'

'I've got a horse and tack, two women and a small boy,' Enoch took off his hat again to give the storekeeper the full benefit of a no-nonsense stare. To his credit, the man remained straight-faced.

'Fair enough - I assume you've got what it'll take to pay for all this?' Enoch nodded and within a few short minutes the counter was piled with all sorts of accoutrements, most of which I would never have thought of; the largest item was a bundled tent.

'Now then, no delicate way of saying this mate… are you lucky enough to be sleeping with both these young ladies - or will you be wanting another tent?'

'The ladies and the nipper can have the tent; I'll have a sleeping bag and… is that a Henry Repeater?' Enoch pointed to the rifle chained to a rear shelf. Theresa and I shared a surprised glance which she followed up with a wink that sent a shiver through me.

The shopkeeper unlocked the chain securing the rifle and cast an eye over the pile of merchandise spreading across his counter. 'Well, you'll be wanting more hooves that's for sure. Now you might not like what I'm going to say but there's this Chink… Charlotte Street, behind the Empire about a quarter of a mile up the track. Him and his boys - and girls for that matter, they got a bit of a paddock. They buy neddies off blokes returning from the diggings with the arses out of their trousers, lots of good beasts. He'll charge you a fair price, not like some of the

216

bloody mongrels here. Leave your goods here, go get your horses, donkeys, whatever you want and then come back. Stop at the Empire, you're passing it anyway, you'll get a bath and some half-decent tucker if he ain't full up.'

The Chinaman had smiled shyly at me and I had smiled back, Enoch was shaking the storekeeper's hand after agreeing a price for what looked like half his stock. Theresa was in the doorway looking out on to the street, still with an almost-asleep Charlie in her arms.

I was standing in a strange store in a strange town in a strange world. I had no home and no-one outside the shop door knew or cared about me. It required a great leap of imagination to carry me from there to Pittville Park on a summer Sunday afternoon, promenading on Enoch's arm with the children skipping happily ahead.

What it would take to make the dream a reality lay somewhere out there beyond the town, in the hostile Badlands, alive with toxicity and terrifying natives with a taste for human flesh. Somewhere beyond the laws of man it lay sleeping in the ground, awaiting the pick and shovel, the pan and the swirling water. The glittering key that would unlock the door to tomorrow.

17.
Cooktown, Northern Queensland
Friday, May 1st, 1874

I didn't think it was much of an eighteenth birthday present, a little gold Chinese dragon on a chain, but Theresa said adored it. Beneath the dragon was a Chinese character that I had been told by the merchant represented 'Love'.

'Shall I tell you the two reasons I love it so much?' She was drying her hair with a towel which had once carried the legend, 'Empire Hotel' but had since had most of the colour boiled out of it. I was trying to get an over-excited Charlie to eat breakfast while Enoch had gone out to saddle and prepare our animals in the secure stable. We were now owners, in addition to Bucephalus, of a pair of donkeys who according to their seller had no names but were now called Chin and Chan.

'Go on then, tell me,' I smiled up at her. She was wearing only her drawers as she stood before the yellowing mirror doing up the clasp of the necklace, but Charlie and I had long since become accustomed to seeing far more of Theresa than any priest would approve of.

'Well, first of all I adore it because it's lovely, it's Queensland gold and wherever life takes me I will take a part of all this with me. Secondly, it's the only birthday present I have ever been given - apart from a chicken when I was six which we ate the next day - and a squeeze of the arse and a sixpence from Father Kenny when I was ten. Oh, and thirdly… and thirdly because it came from you,' she stooped forward and kissed me on the cheek.

'And that's the second birthday present of the morning,' she whispered in my ear - a moment of tenderness brought to an abrupt end by Charlie's shout of, 'Bloody hell - there's a naked bloke running up the street!' His yell caused us both to run to the window where in the street beyond a man wearing only the skin God gave him was indeed tearing through the mud of the track that passed for a major road while behind him another man aimed and fired several shots from a pistol, sending onlookers scattering for cover.

Fortunately for the running naturist, the man with the pistol was staggering drunk and could not have hit a barn door at ten paces. It was only several minutes later it suddenly struck me that my three-year-old had come out with a succinct cursing sentence his Auntie Esther would have been proud of.

At the sound of footsteps approaching our door Theresa ducked behind her sheet screen and began to hastily dress.

'Only me!' Enoch rapped on the door and I unbolted it. He entered and with him came the more than welcome smell of freshly cooked bacon and coffee. Putting the large tray on the bed he took off his hat and fanned himself with it.

'I can't eat it for you!' he called out, but Charlie had not waited for an invitation, tucking into a dripping-soaked chunk of bread.

To our surprise, Theresa emerged from behind the screen dressed in red flannel trail shirt and trousers, hair tucked under a bush hat and a pair of no-nonsense, almost new boots.

'Makes sense for the trail don't you think? I ended up paying half what the feller in the store was asking. He said if I changed in the back of the shop I could have even more knocked off, I politely declined. Well? Will I pass for a digger?'

I laughed, Enoch grinned and shook his head while Charlie looked confused until Theresa picked him up and planted a big kiss on his forehead.

The plan was for me, Theresa and Enoch to take turns on the back of Bucephalus although we were only going to be travelling in short hops. Even now, at the end of the wet season, it was still considered early - too early according to many seasoned diggers - to be heading up the Endeavour into the wild country beyond.

But it was clear we were not the only early birds planning on getting the fattest worms. The trail was a busy one with diggers and their animals heading in both directions. Many of those heading back into Cook's Town were doing so with an air of defeat and dejection but, as Enoch pointed out, this was in many cases simply due to the rigours of the trail.

'Also…' he tapped his temple as yet another pair of dead-eyed diggers stumbled down the track, '… it don't pay to look too prosperous, there's them who wants the gold but ain't got the inclination to go and dig for it.'

Charlie spent just about all of his waking time riding Bucephalus as one or the other of us led the lead animal. No one wanted to carry him in a climate that made each step seem like two and anyway, someone had to lead Chan who was harnessed in tandem with Chin, who in turn appeared content to go anywhere his twin went.

Once clear of Cooktown and its outlying tent villages, the countryside would have been pleasant if not for the afternoon heat. We took regular stops which I'm sure Enoch travelling alone would not have needed but his eagerness to get to the diggings was tempered by a realism that a litter is only as strong as the runt and if the aim is to bring everyone through in one piece then sacrifices must be made.

Despite the rush, there were many daily instances on the trail when we were alone, and it was at these times Enoch seemed at his most wary. He may have played down the tales of murderous encounters with the natives of these parts, but I had read the newspapers and over the last few days had heard first-hand stories of those who had had recent run-ins with tribesmen.

Enoch had told me of deadly attacks on his first expedition up this trail but had reassured me things were settling down as the natives had begun to understand they were hopelessly outgunned. I shared my concerns with Theresa who, far from reassuring me, stated; 'I can only speak for my own tribe, but once, in Dublin, there was a man in a cafe with only one leg - the man not the cafe, ye know what I mean - and I spent an hour with him because he bought me and my sister a plate of stew and asked nothing in return but a little bit of company. Well, he said, "You can defeat a man who fights for money, you can defeat a man who fights for a woman, you can even defeat a man who fights for his God - but ye'll never ever defeat a man who fights for the ground he stands on."

For the first few days there had not been a breath of air, but on a Sunday morning in late May a strong breeze picked up, pushing dark clouds in our direction and the sky went from dazzling blue to almost black as a storm burst overhead.

'I thought you said the rainy season was over,' I yelled as I dragged on Chan's harness in an attempt to pull the pack animals under a rock overhang. Theresa, Bucephalus and Charlie, still on the horse's back, were already tucked as tight into the rock face as they could get. Enoch joined me in pulling the stubborn donkeys whose instincts were telling them to stand still, cover the spot below you so there would be somewhere dry to rest when the sun came back.

We were still there, waiting out the last dregs of the storm when group of Chinese prospectors passed us. They briefly looked in our direction then carried on, heads down, trudging, drenched, along the path and around the bend.

When the sun returned it did so lower in the sky, dazzling in contrast to the retreating darkness.

'Not much point in setting off again now, it'll be dark in an hour.' Enoch lifted Charlie off the back of Bucephalus and began unsaddling the animal ready for a rub down. Where she found them, I don't know, but

Theresa produced some dry kindling and thicker sticks and we soon had a fire going.

'You carry a fistful of tiny kindling along with you,' she explained, '...all tucked into a pocket and then if it rains you light a little fire and use it to dry out bigger sticks and then when they catch you dry out even bigger ones. She smiled, blowing the steam from the billy and tucking even more kindling beneath it.

'That was a late one,' Enoch pronounced as we sat in the dancing light of our campfire after a supper of thin sliced beef and beans. Next to the fire a line of boots stood, steaming in the warmth as they dried, Enoch's mine, Theresa's and Charlie's. I rested my head on Enoch's shoulder and felt the exhaustion of the day creeping in to claim me. Theresa, with Charlie on her lap, rested her head on me, tucking her arm around my waist. Enoch's rifle lay in his lap. I mentioned I had seen no other women on the trail. 'Wait 'till we get to Edwardstown - you'll see a few there,' Enoch said.

I did not fear guns, but I was wary of them. Although they had no minds of their own, they were, like the guard dogs of the gentry, utterly without conscience and would kill on command. They were an extension of a man, an executor of his will. I had learned from Grandfather William that it's not just hatred or evil that make men kill. When it comes to creating killers, hatred has always played second fiddle to fear. In fact, hatred is probably in third place, right behind pleasure.

'Now then, hold the butt, finger around now, over the trigger - don't squeeze yet; other hand over the first to help you steady it...'

223

Try as I might, the weight of the pistol meant the end of the barrel was still wavering all about and it would be pure luck if I hit the bully tin wedged in a tree branch no more than ten paces away.

'And... fire!'

I squeezed the trigger, and bang! The kick from the weapon brought home to me for the first time the power and venom of a bullet... the smell of cordite... I took a step backward, my wrists shook, I became suddenly aware through the ringing in my ears that Enoch was talking to me and Theresa was laughing. The tin had gone.

After several more shots in which I did not repeat my marksmanship, I liked guns no better than I had before, but I was a little more confident in handling a pistol. Just as well because Enoch produced a pair of gun belts, one for me and one for Theresa who strapped hers on and instantly looked completely at home with it, swaggering with all the panache of a bushranger in her trail trousers, red flannel shirt and boots. She could shoot too, showing no fear of weapons.

My gun felt heavy strapped around my waist, so I took it off and wore the belt over my shoulder, causing Enoch to remark, 'That's the Spanish in you, that is'. What would Adder Drew think of me now, as armed and dangerous as he had once been? Would he have been an equal to this place? I suspected not. This was no country for the loner, a bloke needed his mates here and there was definitely safety in numbers.

There is a place on the trail called Hell's Gate, it's approached by a steep climb which Chin and Chan took one look at and immediately rooted themselves to the

224

ground; sometimes donkeys are so much cleverer than horses - or people! We lost an hour of daylight simply coaxing them to go forward at all. There is a winding path through massive rocks which appears impassable but then there is an opening leading into what old diggers call The Gates.

Huge rocks towered above us on both sides of the narrow trail and no sooner were we through than we came upon what Enoch called 'The Devil's Staircase'.

Passing through these obstacles Enoch commented on how lucky we were not to meet anyone coming the other way as there was no room to pass safely. Either side of the trail were the carcases and skeletons of animals who had fallen, or been pushed, from the path. Around us, in various stages of decomposition, lay horses and bullocks, some with loads and saddlebags still attached. Such a waste of good livestock; the suffering of faithful beasts would have brought tears to the eyes of Father or Grandfather William. How the skeletal waifs of The Rookery would have made use of such creatures!

The relief of passing through this dangerous place soon melted away at the sight of the country beyond. We were faced by a gloomy and sandy plain criss-crossed with gorges and broken rocks. If we thought the sight of the animal skeletons in the Gates was bleak enough, they were joined here by the remains of dead Chinamen who had lain unburied and unlamented as their comrades had trudged wearily on.

'A lot of them get eaten by the Blackfellas - they prefer Chinamen to white men as they're less salty,' Enoch stated.

Fortunately, the rigours of the Gates had taken their toll on Charlie who slept throughout much of the rest of the day.

We had seen neither hide nor hair of the natives since leaving and Enoch, who sensed these things, assured us there were none around at present.

We camped within a day of Edwardstown and as usual Theresa got a good fire going to prepare supper and boil the billys. There was little conversation as we ate, we had learned to be economical with sound on the trail and it was this that may well have saved our lives that night.

In the deepening gloom of the tropical evening, where night drops like a hunting peregrine, Enoch suddenly froze, spoon halfway between plate and mouth. Putting down his plate he whispered.

'Boots on, quick and quiet...'

Theresa and I were rapidly into our trail boots then we grabbed Charlie and did a foot each while Enoch scooped up handfuls of earth and sand to throw over the fire. Some travellers would pour the contents of a billy over the flames to put it out in a hurry but apparently this causes the smell to travel further and give your position away to anyone tracking you.

The moon-facing side of a great rock the shape of an elephant's head was cast in a stark and ghostly white as we crept into the shadows. We huddled together while Enoch got Bucephalus to lie down. He could do this to horses faster than anyone I had ever known, faster even than Emily's Samuel - a man who had lived alongside horses since birth. Chin and Chan, however, were not so compliant and, disgruntled on being woke, complained about being herded, shoved and manhandled into a bunch of rough scrub out of sight of the trail.

At this point, none of us were fully aware of what it was we were hiding from, whispering to Enoch brought just a finger to the lips and an urgent pointing to something out of sight down the moonlit trail. Theresa hugged me, I hugged her and we both hugged Charlie and then we hear the first of the footsteps.

They were either the footsteps of white men or Chinamen far away or of tribesmen much closer, such was the Merkin tribesman's deftness at passing wraith-like through the night. Then they were around us. Many passed by on the trail just an arm's reach away while others were travelling through the bush behind us, all seemed to be carrying spears. They must have gone right by Chin and Chan and it seemed impossible that they were completely unaware of our presence.

This suspicion was confirmed when one of their number slowed, stooped and looked straight at us. He tapped a compatriot on the arm and pointed straight at our little group. I heard the click of Enoch's pistol being cocked causing my heart to thump madly. Both tribesmen now stared at us for what seemed forever then the one pushed the other forward and they walked on after their band.

We stayed in the shadows for several minutes, long after the footsteps faded up the trail. There must have been more than a hundred of them - and they were just the ones we could see. Who knows how many more padded silently by in the dark and the cover of the brush, the moonlight serving to make them no more than a fluid part of the night?

'They're a raiding party and they're after bigger fish - see how many of them there were?' Enoch's half whisper prompted the rest of us to break our silence.

He patted Bucephalus who got to his feet, snorting before ducking into the bushes to lead out Chin and Chan who, in that way donkeys have, went unbidden to the spot they had been resting in before their disturbance.

'There's a fine little fella you are for being so quiet,' Theresa hugged Charlie, subtly holstering her pistol. I had not even drawn mine but promised myself I would behave with more alacrity if such an episode were repeated.

'You lot sleep...' Enoch stated, 'I'll keep an eye out for a while in case...'

His speech was interrupted by the distant screaming of black cockatoos, but it was not birds but tribesmen who had adopted the call as a war cry. Then came the first of the shots; faint shouting followed, then more shots, then a fusillade of rifle and pistol fire from somewhere not too far away up the trail. The firing became more organised, volleys one after the other and then silence.

It was hard to get even a little sleep and I'm sure Enoch had enjoyed none when he gently woke us in the young daylight of the new morning where a low and slanting sun cut through a world of malevolent shadow with blades of dazzling silver.

A quick scout of the area showed no sign of the visitors who had disturbed our night and soon breakfast was cooking and a billy boiling for coffee.

'They ambushed the gold escort, but it was a bloody sight better protected than they thought,' A trio of diggers heading out of Edwardstown crossed our path and brought us up to date with the events of the previous night. 'None of the escorts was hurt but they reckon they bagged a couple of Merkin as they made their getaway.' The leader of the small band, a long-bearded bandy-legged man wearing an eye-patch, stopped to light an old briar from our campfire before the group made their farewells.

Edwardstown was every bit as rough and ready as Cooktown but, speaking for myself, it appeared a safer place somehow; there was an air of adversity overcome, trials and risks shared and the stoicism inherent in those who have walked a hard path and learned how to bounce when they hit the ground.

There certainly seemed to be many more women, a few of whom were clearly intent on doing their gold digging in more comfortable and intimate surroundings than in the ravines and riverbeds of the Palmer and its tributaries. Others were as fearsome as any pugilist. But for the most they were like Theresa and I, there to dig, wash and make the best of it along with their menfolk.

It was a place of work where leisure was almost unknown, an afterthought, something to be dreamed of once a fortune had been taken from this remote ground and carried back to somewhere with stone buildings, parasols and china teapots. And our first day on the diggings, in an overgrown ravine where hanging boughs and bushes offered the double-edged sword of shade and spiders, gave us cause for real optimism.

We would never have found it if Charlie had not wandered off into the bushes and had to be brought back by Theresa who was the first to notice the hidden stream with the wide flat banks almost obscured by the overhanging growth. Enoch wandered in and came back out grinning, 'This'll do!' he announced and so within earshot of other diggers who had inexplicably overlooked this place we went in an began to pan.

To be more accurate, Enoch and I went in and panned, Theresa took one look at a couple of huge spiders clinging to a branch and stated quite emphatically that she 'Wouldn't go in there if the Pope and Saint Peter themselves were handing out gold bars.'

We agreed on a system. Enoch and I would dig and pan while Theresa and Charlie stayed in the communal camp about a mile down the track closer to town where there was fresh water and it was easier to cook, wash and clean. These jobs were essential to our small group and so we entered into a verbal contract. Theresa, as an equal partner, would get a full third of all we found.

And find we did. With no previous experience of prospecting, I assumed this was the natural order of the job, we dug, panned and there was the gold! I had no conception of how lucky a find Spider Creek - as we called it - really was. There were diggers who went months, often until their supplies and subsistence money ran out, without seeing a single glitter in the dirt. They dreamed of it, they could almost taste it, but, as elusive as a poltergeist, it tugged at their sleeve and vanished, leaving just another rude dawn, a head full of dreams and an empty belly.

Enoch's assertion that most of the Chinese diggers didn't bother with such formalities as a claim was tempered by the knowledge that, without one, anyone could follow us to Spider Creek and crowd us out and so he said he would go into town and lodge a claim. however, it was unlikely anyone would follow in our footsteps.

What a loss to the theatre stage it was when Enoch decided to go prospecting rather than treading the boards. He would return each day from our diggings as dejected as a winter's day with his own personal raincloud hovering above him having washed and bagged a good day's haul of gold which he would unload from Chin or Chan's pack and add to the growing haul in our tent.

Enoch slept just inside the entrance to our tent and often I would lie next to him while Theresa and Charlie were next to the small cooking area nearer to the back although almost all of our cooking had been done outside. Our gold was divided into three packs, two of which came everywhere with us while the third was buried beneath our tent as we slept and ate above it.

The days blended into each other and consisted of digging, panning and returning home to eat and share news of our day with Theresa and Charlie. There was no time for much else in the way of socialising and this was true for everyone in our part of the world.

There were plenty of diversions on offer in the town for those who were not too fussy about hanging on to their gold. Popular entertainments included women who, apparently, would take off their clothes, one garment at a time, charging a small nugget for each one. One close evening a woman had put on so many garments to maximise her earnings she fainted, and the two diggers being entertained took the opportunity to recover their gold.

On another occasion we returned home to find a man trying to pull Theresa into our tent. She was yelled at him to clear off, but he was taking no notice.

'Hoy - are you deaf?' Enoch shouted, immediately getting the lout's attention. It was only then we both realised just how big a creature he was, closer to seven feet than six and with arms as thick as my waist.

'Piss off and mind your own bloody business,' the giant growled in what, under different circumstances, would have been a lovely Devonshire accent.

'I won't ask again,' Enoch said flatly; I was amazed at his coolness, he stood, legs apart and thumbs tucked into his belt, he was even smiling.

The huge man released Theresa from his grip, she hustled Charlie into the tent before returning armed with a hammer. The giant took a few steps toward Enoch, stretching out his arms before punching one fist into the palm of the other.

'Right then Gyppo…'

Enoch did not move or give any indication that he was preparing for defence or attack. Before the hulk reached him, another man, equal in size, appeared at a run and felled our tormentor with a flying blow that would have killed anyone of average stature. The man dropped, stone cold and the second giant turned to Enoch.

'Sorry 'bout my brother, he's a damn nuisance with a drink in him.'

Grabbing the unconscious man by a boot he dragged him down the hill, pausing to retrieve his hat. I ran to Theresa and hugged her, she smiled but I could feel her shaking.

'I'm alright, at least I am now.' She whispered hugging me in return.

Enoch tilted back his hat and tied Bucephalus to a nearby tree we had adopted for the purpose.

'A brave fella you are and no mistake,' Theresa told him as he passed by, ducking to go into the tent.

'What would you have done if he had hit you?' It must have sounded like a chastisement, but I was so relieved it had not come to a fight.

'I'd have died probably, but he wasn't going to hit me,' Enoch grinned, planting a kiss on my cheek before disappearing inside.

No further explanation was forthcoming but knowing Enoch he would likely have ducked the blow, or ran, or shot him; that was the thing, there was never a pattern, he was as unpredictable as an October day - and English October that is - and I could read him no better now than when he had winked, doffed his battered hat and wished me a good morning while leaning on the rail of a long-lost racecourse.

On August 28th, 1874 we had gold worth almost three thousand pounds sterling - a fortune. The daily hauls from Spider Creek were dwindling, however and for the last week there had been little to show for the long hours of digging and panning. And so, at the end of a long and dusty Friday as we all sat outside the tent enjoying a very agreeable Irish stew, which Theresa claimed her grandmother invented, Enoch announced that we would be packing up and heading back to Cooktown, then Brisbane, then London, then Cheltenham.

The End of the Sky

We had taken our gold and paid a man to weigh it into three parts and then take the first two parts and divide them into three. The plan was to give Theresa her share then split ours for the journey between Chin, Chan and Bucephalus. Theresa had decided to store her gold in the safe of McCann's Hotel which she said was a Catholic establishment run by a man trusted by both Europeans and Chinese, it would be safer there, she said, than in the turbulence of the tent town and that she would collect it when we embarked.

On a dazzling blue Sunday morning, I asked Theresa if she would like to share a walk with me, across a footpath that ran along the east bank of Oaky Creek into the meadow. Enoch and Charlie were busy cleaning and packing kit, carefully stashing the well-concealed gold and checking over our livestock in preparation for the long trek back to Cooktown.

It was clear from Theresa's demeanour that she knew there was a motive for our walk. Her smile to me was subdued, her eyes a darker shade of green and her mouth pursed. She blinked a lot which always meant she was thinking thoughts too heavy to carry.

I took her hand in mine and my gentle squeeze was returned in a way that made my steps lighter. The far mountains looked like a child's painting in the spring light as we walked away from the creek path, heading for the silence of the nearby meadow.

18.
Oaky Creek, Northern Queensland
Sunday, August 30th, 1874

In terms of temperature, there appears little to choose between a late August day in Uckington or in Oaky Creek. It was winter here, but in name only. The tribes who have called this land home for millennia before the coming of the Europeans and Chinese were strangers to January Jack and had no concept of a season where Mother Nature slept.

A gentle, ambient breeze fell off the far hills carrying scents of flowers I had no names for and somewhere hidden in the trees that lined the nearby creek a laughing jackass yelled out his song in defiance of the solemnity of the Sabbath.

A patchwork blanket that had once witnessed the soul departing from my sister Mary Ann and had then found employment as a curtain to our tiny world on the Royal Dane was spread over the grass of the meadow where the bullocks and mounts of diggers were taken to graze - always with an armed guard patrolling the perimeter. We sat in the loneliest corner of the meadow in the shade of a tree so old it offered little true shade at all; stooped and arthritic, it stood isolated from a nearby copse as if it had been sent away to die.

'I hadn't planned to be up here for a year or so, but I'm glad I came,' she smiled, half closing her eyes and looking into the distance to the hazy hills.

'I'm glad you came too...' I replied, trying to think of something profound or clever to continue with. Nothing came, I raised my knees, putting my arms around them, smiling first across the meadow and then at her.

'I think...'

'Shall we...'

We both started speaking at once then laughed awkwardly, we had never been awkward together, even at the beginning when I had been less than warm to her and, if truth be told, a little scared of that lack of inhibition. I watched the guard take off his hat and use it to shade his eyes for a better view across the meadow. Brushing an errant wisp of hair behind an ear, I felt the tension build in me born of a rapturous and terrifying imminence impossible to avoid.

'I was going to ask...what?'

My voice faded away as she moved closer, our bodies together now, pressing, side by side. She smelled of lavender water and wood ash from the breakfast cooking fire. Gently touching my cheek, she turned my face to hers and everything I wanted and feared was there. Eyes that could be as mischievous as a Spring sunrise when glittering with devilment were now bottomless dark green pools and I knew that if I were to fall into them, I would be lost.

They moved... little darts, as she seemed to be taking in all of my face and I realised I was doing the same. There was a transparent want and ferocity in her, passions battling for supremacy, the freckles across her nose a reminder of the child not long gone. My heart went from trot to gallop without passing through canter and I shivered despite the warmth of the morning. A line was about to be crossed and all the impulsiveness, tossing coins and boiling seas, blazing heat and bags of gold... all of it came down to this moment and, just as I was wondering if this was the real reason God had sent me across the world, she kissed me in a most unsisterly way.

It began gently, a brushing of the lips, nervously, lingering, increasing in urgency, a rising tide from deep within. Her arms were around me, and almost unbidden mine were around her, she shivered and sighed softly, and we held each other tighter. Was this how sin felt? Was she a demon sent to test me? That which had hitherto gone unsaid, subject to misunderstanding, confusion and doubt, was unspoken no more.

Whoever it was that declared, "Love is a friendship set afire" must surely have experienced the inferno. I don't know how long the kiss lasted, it could have been seconds, or the sun could have set and risen again but, heaven forgive me, I knew I didn't want it to stop.

Our lips parted and she held my head between her hands. Her eyes, made even larger by a film of tears, were now the whole world and she spoke with an urgency that threw out a challenge to the forces that would drag us oceans apart.

'I love you Ellie, I love you - and those are words I have said to no man, woman or god before. I swear I don't know where it came from and I didn't invite it but here it is - and you feel the same, sure I know you do - the big sweeping tumbly airy feeling in the belly, the way all the colours go bright and how you smile at strangers and sing to yourself. You've felt it too, isn't that so?'

'Yes... yes, it... it just happened...' My voice was shaking, '...It happened while you were away in Brisbane and every day, then every hour, then every minute until you came back became more and more painful.'

I knew it sounded naïve and silly. There were tears on my cheeks, I was shaking all over and felt that trying to stand would be a mistake. Taking both her hands in mine, I squeezed them; they were working hands although small and delicate - perfect for embroidery but for an accident of birth.

'You have to come back with us, tell me you will, I couldn't bear it if you didn't.'

She nodded, 'I will, I will - but... if I do, it's you I'll go back with - you! I will give myself to you, body heart and soul and I'll love you more than you ever have been or ever will be loved...'

'I...' But she hadn't finished.

'But I can't share you Ellie - you don't share me, nor would you ever - and I know I wouldn't be able to bear the thought of you lying in the arms of another while I slept alone, burning for you in a cold room with a tall ceiling and the English rain beating the windows.

'I will come back to England with you, or I'll stay here with you, there's nowhere I call home. We have money now and we need no help from anyone - and there will never be day in your life when you will feel unwanted or unloved. I will never leave you.'

I don't know whether my tears were from the joy of our love released or from the desperate and inexorable choice I now faced. At that moment there was nothing I would not have sacrificed in order for Theresa and I and that tired old tree to become an eternal island, a fortress where pendulums hung motionless and our embrace endured until the stars went out.

But others were in that world too.

'What about Charlie and Sarah Ann?'

'Welcome with us - anywhere and always. I'll love them as you love them.'

She stroked the side of my face, gently brushing away a tear. Her eyes were full too, her fierce need apparent, and I understood this was not a defence she would have lowered unthinkingly. The world had given Theresa no reason to expect unconditional love and every cause to believe kindness came at a price and passion brought consequence.

I nodded, taking her hands once again in mine, '…and Enoch?'

She frowned, looking down at our hands, squeezing my fingers, 'Well, I was thinking he could sleep with you Monday to Friday and give me a good seeing-to on the weekends.'

I pulled my hands away and when she looked up the demons were once again dancing in her eyes. She smiled and poked me playfully in the shoulder.

'Wouldn't like that now, would ye?'

I was catching up, realising she had only been teasing, but my emotions were all over the place and it had been a calculated blow.

'D'you see Ellie? That's what being the gooseberry feels like. I couldn't bear that pain and I would never ask you to. That's why, my beloved, you have to decide what you want the most. You're going to hurt someone and you're so kind my darling that whatever you decide, it's you who will be hurt the more keenly.

'The truth is, we have all become different people now and it's going to take a little time to see who we are in our new skin. We have money, and money - whatever anyone tells you, changes people. You don't know wealthy Enoch Johnsey, you may not even know wealthy Ellen Johnsey.'

The armed guard passed across the meadow, shouting to someone who was trying to rope a bullock. I took a deep breath, but the butterflies were here to stay it seemed. A part of me wanted to get up and run round and round the meadow just laughing and singing out loud. Instead, Theresa and I kissed again, and we held each other tightly so that not even the smallest thought could come between us to drive us apart.

A newly declared love is like a bonfire, roaring and dazzling. Sometimes this love will settle like a glow in the grate banked up before bedtime with damped-down coal dust to carry the lovers through all the chill nights to come - or it may burn hot and white like a smith's forge, dying away to nothing when the last iron is quenched. How did I know what winds would gust to make these flames dance, or what storms could blow them out leaving us shivering in their loss? For all her wild passion she was eighteen and her will could be the wind's will. Would she wake up one morning in the near future, look at me as I really was and wonder what was over the next hill?

'I'm going to go into Edwardstown now,' Theresa took one of my hands in both of hers, 'I'm going to book myself into McCann's wee hotel...'

'No - don't go, stay here, stay with me!'

I held her then, clutching the rough, baggy arm of her red trail shirt.

'It's alright, listen to me now; I'll be at McCann's and you have to see Enoch and you have a decision to make. It would be a sin to just leave and say not a thing. You have to tell him that you're going with me - or you have to tell him nothing at all. I'll be there until sunrise tomorrow, if you don't come, well, that'll be my answer - but come to me Ellie, come to me before morning because if you don't each of us will be hollow 'till the day we die - no matter how cleverly we learn to hide it.'

She stood and looked down, tangled red hair roughly pushed under a bush hat, shirt half in and half out of her trousers. She smiled, backlit by the sun, I rose hastily and hugged her again, kissing her. She stepped back until only our fingertips touched and then our arms fell away. She was breathless when she spoke.

'Sure, I don't know how love works but if I did, I'd bottle and sell it and we'd be richer than all the diggers in all the fields in Queensland. Do what you must, but please come to me Ellie - bring nothing but the clothes you stand up in if you like - and not even them if you dare. Come to me before the sun rises and I swear by all the saints it will never set on you again.'

Enoch was telling a digger in a nearby tent about us packing it in and pulling out for Cooktown. I didn't catch much of the exchange beyond, '... not worth the bloody effort mate.' Then he noticed my approach.

'Ah, here she comes now the donkey work's done eh mate? He ruffled Charlie's hair, standing and smiling as our son ran to meet me. Our tent had been folded and packed along with all the bits and pieces that had made it a kind of home in this surprisingly kindly place.

'Where's Auntie Theresa?' Charlie asked, looking behind me back down the trail.

'Yes, where is she?' Enoch pushed back the wide brim of his hat.

I had hoped for time to collect my thoughts but now here I was, right on the spot.

'She's...' I took a breath and prayed for strength, 'She's... she...'

It was beyond my power. I turned from them to spare Charlie the tears and melted. Losing the fight for silence, my shoulders shook and gulping sobs escaped through clenched teeth; then Enoch's hands were on my shoulders. He turned me to him and held me tight. There was the familiar smell of his pipe, the strong arms, his coarse beard against my cheek.

The euphoria of less than an hour before floundered in a sea of impossible choices. The thought of not seeing Theresa again was simply unbearable and to lose this man who had kept every promise he had made to me and with whom I shared such history was equally bleak.

I had waited for him for months, turned down others and followed him to the ends of the Earth and now he was ready to take me home, to Sarah Ann and a secure, safe future where we would bow and curtsey to no one; and I did not for a second doubt him when he had said that, in all his travels, he had remained true to me. Then this terrible, beautiful fire had been lit while he was away, no doubt fanned by loneliness - and now it was all-encompassing, blind and furious and utterly beyond my power to control.

I knew that if I asked him, he would go to McCann's Hotel and talk to Theresa, try to persuade her to return and become a part of our family - but I'm pretty sure that neither he nor she would be agreeable about the roles I wanted them to play. She was right. I could not be so unkind as to drag her back to England where she would give all of herself only to be rewarded with half of me.

The tears subsided and with effort I pulled myself together, wiping my face and regaining control of my breath. Enoch released me from his embrace.

'Staying here is she?' His voice slow and deep.

I nodded, 'Yes… no, I don't know…I tried to persuade her to come with us but… I don't know.'

Enoch took out his pipe and began plugging tobacco into the bowl, squinting into the high sun. Putting the pipe between his teeth he lifted Charlie on to the back of Bucephalus.

'What about you?' He struck a match to light his pipe.

He had spoken softly, unchallenging but still the question rocked me back on my heels; my shock must have been only too apparent.

'You alright Ma?' Charlie called from the horse's back.

How could I have possibly imagined that Enoch, of all people would not have noticed something as hard to hide as my distraction? He had lived and travelled with us and he would not have missed a single shared glance, nuance, sisterly hug or word of affection. We were all open books to him. This was a man who could tell what animals were thinking and knew when people were nearby before anyone else had sight or sound.

I could read nothing in Enoch's stare. No anger, judgment or pain; it was flat, illegible and patient. The weight of heaven bore down on me, not only the souls of those I had loved and said goodbye to, but of those yet unborn. Grandfather William would have known what to say, but he was not here.

If I had the time I could have sat and considered how valuable my desires were when weighed on the scales against the love of others. What could I say or do that would cause the least pain? I had no time to measure these things and, if truth be told, I could not have done so given a week to ponder them.

Some poor souls go through life and never feel love, it seems that others are cursed with a surplus of it. Before me I had the proven, slow-burning flame of Enoch's devotion. Flashing through my memories came the feeling of his presence in Dolly's Diner at Andoversford when I saw him as the centre of the world. He had made my heart sing then as Theresa did now.

Yet he could now leave me for months on end, years, probably, if he had to - and I was supposed to bear the loneliness.

Oh Theresa, my Theresa!

19.
Laura River, Northern Queensland
Thursday, September 3rd, 1874

There was anger tinged with urgency in his whisper.

'In here, quick... see those rocks, get Charlie behind 'em and tell him to keep his head down and to keep quiet whatever he hears - no matter how scary it is.'

Enoch pushed me firmly into the small cave, following behind me dragging Bucephalus by the reins. Chin and Chan, for once, needed little encouragement to follow and Enoch was quick to herd them towards the rear where I was busy tucking Charlie into a small space behind a jagged rock that, from the front appeared to offer a false rear wall.

'What's up Ma?' He asked and I had no answer beyond urging him to keep as quiet as he could. Enoch beckoned to me to remain tucked into the wall on the opposite side of the entrance to where he was now crouched, rifle in hand.

It occurred to me that this was the most Enoch had spoken to me since we had left Edwardstown on Sunday but to be fair I had not cared, wrapped up as I was in my own black and hopeless cloud following the crushing loss of my beloved Theresa and the hurt I had surely caused

245

her. But there was no time to think of anything now but our safety.

Outside the cave all was silent, but if Enoch had sensed danger, then danger there was. He turned to me; eyes full of savagery, miming the drawing of a gun. I pulled my pistol clear of the holster, he mimed cocking it, clearly impatient with me now. I did so and he turned his attention back to whatever lurked beyond the entrance.

I didn't see the spear that flew in from somewhere in the trees on the opposite side of the track but Enoch's yell as it hit him in the thigh seemed to set the world alight. Another spear bounced off the rock to the side of my head, two more smashed into the opposite wall and would surely have killed Enoch had he not dropped to a knee to pull the first missile out. Then they were on us. Appearing in the entrance to the cave they came in a bunch. Enoch fired once... twice, three times in rapid succession, the reports of the Henry painful to the ears as it rang around the cave.

I had no time to think and that is probably what saved my life. Acting on instinct and the urge to protect Charlie I pointed the pistol and fired. I must have hit the closest tribesman; he could have been no more than six feet from me. He looked surprised then staggered backwards, falling into the path of a comrade intent on getting to us. I screamed but I did not hear it, what I heard instead, inexplicably, was the congregation of Mary Magdalene's Church singing, 'Love Divine All Loves Excelling' roaring through my thoughts, filling my ears and my mind; it drowned out even the guns. How could such a thing be? Was Grandfather William – a soldier, watching over me? Comforting me?

Enoch had retreated a few paces but was still firing into the mob of tribesmen who appeared undeterred by the sight of several of their comrades now lying in the cave entrance. My wrist buckled painfully each time I cocked and pulled the trigger, screaming into the faces of our assailants. Bucephalus whinnied in pain as a spear struck his flank and his cry startled Chin and Chan who stampeded, unstoppable out of the cave, across the trail and away into the bush as fast as they could run. They knocked over two tribesmen in their escape, one of whom Enoch dispatched before the yelling figure could regain his feet.

Then from outside the cave, drowning out all other sound, came the crash of several rifles, screams and yells. The tribesmen in the entrance to our cave so far unhurt turned to run, some fell fatally injured by the fusillade while others limped into the trees. Then the cave entrance was filled with many more tribesmen - and they had rifles.

Enoch and I pulled our triggers together and were rewarded by the clicks of empty chambers. He limped across the cave and placed himself in front of me. We had no words. Images of Theresa, Sarah Ann, little Charlie and a youthful, grinning Enoch leaning on a fence flashed across my mind. I prayed our end would be quick and I felt... really felt, Grandfather William, Granny Sabina and dear sister Mary Ann close by, close enough to touch - and suddenly I was no longer afraid.

The tribesmen's eyes glittered in the subdued light. Then in the entrance to the cave a European appeared.

'It's alright, these blokes are with me.'

'Lucky for you we were in the vicinity chums.'

The man looked down at Enoch's leg. Now that the immediate crisis was over Enoch was feeling the pain for the first time, his face was screwed up, but he was trying not to make a sound as a white-faced Charlie was nearby, shocked but safe in my arms now. The man turned to a nearby tribesman dressed in white shirt and tartan trousers.

'Medic bag!'

The tribesman left the cave, the man turned his attention to us. He knelt, taking out a knife he cut Enoch's trouser leg and long-johns beneath revealing the wound.

'The name's Palmerston, Christie Palmerston.'

He was a wild-looking man of a similar stamp to Enoch. Black curly hair, a generous beard and dark, Mediterranean eyes. He wore a felt hat with goggles on the front of it, a shirt that appeared far too expensive to be wasted on the trail and a hand-stitched gun belt of pale leather. The exotically dressed tribesman reappeared dropping a pack by Palmerston's side.

'Who might you folks be then?'

'Johnsey,' Enoch replied, grimacing as Palmerston poured whiskey from a small flask and began washing the spear wound. 'Enoch Johnsey, my missus, Ellen and young Charlie.'

'Well Mr Johnsey, I think this is a clean wound, lucky for you. Some of the bastards dip the spearpoints in their own shit or in putrid carcasses and then you've got a big problem. I'm gonna bandage you up and keep watch over this place tonight then you can get on your road tomorrow. They ain't going to come back this way for a day or two after such a beating so you should make it safe into Laura.'

'Any sign of our mokes out there?' Enoch asked.

Palmerston called to a tribesman outside, rattling off a request in the man's own tongue while he continued to patch up Enoch. I began to build a fire with what I thought in my muddled state were sticks until realising they were bones. I was still shaking but forced myself out of the cave to collect kindling. A tribesman passed me heading purposefully into the cave, calling to Palmerston who was lighting a cigar while Enoch filled his pipe.

'Your neddies have scarpered sorry to say mate, they're probably halfway to God knows where by now, y'know what they're like, spook 'em and they'll run for hours. Gonna end up as Merkin tucker more than likely.'

We got £3 for Bucephalus in Cooktown from the Chinaman who had sold us Chin and Chan. He was not a young horse and although Enoch, with the help of Christie Palmerston had treated his injury, we had walked much of the way back and the loyal old man had carried Charlie only. We would have completed the whole journey this way but for a kindly returning digger with a small cart who had spared our legs for a huge stretch of the trip. Enoch in particular had been grateful for the help with his own thigh wound, which he insisted on dressing himself, spurning my offer of help.

We got a further eleven pounds and six shillings reselling our used upriver kit back to the store we had bought it from and as we sat in a small room in what was described as a hotel but was in reality a large partitioned barn, we had time to rest and take stock of what we had – and what was lost. Enoch had suggested the Empire Hotel but the ghosts would have shredded what was left of my broken heart and so I made up an excuse about damp bedsheets and bugs which he undoubtedly saw through.

'Six hundred and eleven pounds, seven shillings and eightpence.'

Enoch had been to the exchange and now dropped the bank draft, bills and coins on the bed cover. Taking off his hat he threw it across to our unpacked bags resting on a rough wood cupboard.

'Forty quid to Brisbane, twenty for food and provisions and clothes for a voyage, sixty to London, ten to Cheltenham, four hundred for a home – what does that leave?'

He already knew the answer and the exhausted bitterness in his voice suggested any reply would be the wrong one, so I closed my eyes. Charlie was already asleep and all I wanted to do was join him in the blissful escape into a world where all stories had happy endings and no problems were irresolvable. But Enoch was clearly ready to fight his own tiredness.

'Eighty-one pounds.' He sighed, 'Eighty-one bloody pounds.' He slumped back against the wall and closed his eyes. This was the first time in weeks we had been in a room, simple as it was, a room with a bed in it but it appeared that even though our bodies were here, our hearts and minds were elsewhere.

But we did not go back to Brisbane, instead we boarded a boat for Townsville, just down the coast, from where Enoch planned to go inland to a place called Charters Towers because a young native boy called Jupiter had discovered a gold deposit leading to a rush which my husband saw as a chance for financial redemption.

The closer our boat got to Townsville, the more my doubts grew about us going back to England. Enoch had been wounded - not just by the spear of a tribesman which the passing days, the ministrations of Mr Palmerston and serendipity had all but vanquished. But by the loss of the hard-won gold - well over a thousand pounds sterling worth of it which had galloped off into the trackless bush along with Chin and Chan - and with it any chance of a triumphal return with enough to start our own business and be independent. Enoch's pride would not allow him to go home with anything less.

We had looked for the donkeys of course, much against the advice of Mr Palmerston who had told us our best bet was to get back to a safe town as soon as we could. We had veered from the path, cutting across fathomless countryside before returning to the trail, but the animals were nowhere to be found.

Every half hour or so I had looked back up the trail throughout the journey. It could have been for sight of Chin and Chan, or for evidence that the tribesmen were still tracking us, but that was not the reason and we both knew it. And that was the other wound Enoch had sustained.

I kept playing over and over again in my head the image of Theresa arriving at the campsite at dawn - I knew she would go there; she would have to - and the emptiness would have lain before her like an open grave. She would have paced out the flattened rectangle, recognising in it the crushing confirmation that I had made my choice. Would she have realised how much it hurt, or would she have imagined I had simply cast her aside?

I had tried to engage with Enoch, bring things out into the open several times but it was incredibly difficult. How could I frame such a thing? I would say, 'I'd like to talk to you,' and he would reply, 'Bout what?' And although we both knew 'Bout what' he would offer no opening and I would say something like, 'Anything you might be uncertain about.' And then he would say, sarcastically, 'Ain't nothing I'm uncertain about, rest assured', and I would be confused and worried over all its possible meanings.'

After the loss of the gold and a fight for our lives, I felt it was not the time to bring up any other matters and I resolved to have this out in clear and plain speaking as soon as we got to our destination.

It was only in the Queens Hotel, Townsville, where our room was a cut above any others I had slept in, that I finally managed to sit down with Enoch for a proper clear-the-air talk.

I began with, 'This trip... this endeavour has not been kind to us, and you have cause to be disappointed. But please Enoch, we still have one another and Charlie and if I have hurt you, I am truly sorry. Theresa...'

'Theresa...' he cut in, '...Yes, let's talk about Theresa, shall we? Tell me Ellen, what if I had fallen for her? What if I had mooned and dreamed all around her and... and kissed her passionately in a meadow? What then? Would you have had anything to say about it?'

My mouth must have been moving but nothing came out, once again it seemed he knew more than I imagined.

He shook his head, 'The guard... the bloody guard. His name was Ernie Jackson - he came and told me you was kissing a bloke - bloody keenly too, under the lonely oak. "What bloke?" I had asked him, and he said, "Cove in a red shirt, long ginger hair" and I knew straight away who he meant. 'Course he was at a distance and fair play to him, it would have to have been bloke, wouldn't it?'

I took a deep breath; the silence in the little room was broken only by Charlie attempting to assemble a painted wooden puzzle I had bought him from the sell-everything shop next door to the hotel. My voice sounded older, my throat dry.

'Right, well here you are. I have hugged and kissed my mother and sisters, and your sister, and your mother, and Mrs Bolt in the Noah's Ark and probably others - but if I was to tell you this was the same as the kiss I shared with Theresa I would be lying. I loved her Enoch, I still do - not in quite the way I love you, but real love all the same. And she asked me to make a choice and I made it. From the time I first kissed you I have been true to you - and that includes the times of my life when you were not around and when a young woman's thoughts turn readily to matters of love.

'I made you a promise and I have kept it because I couldn't bear the thought of losing you - but it hurt

Enoch, it hurt more than anything ever has, more even than saying goodbye to Sarah Ann because I always expected to see her again. But doesn't that tell you something? That I was ready to bear that hurt because losing you would have hurt even more? And it's not only my hurt I'm talking about, it's your hurt and Theresa's. The thought that I have caused pain to people so dear to me is the biggest agony of all.

'She kissed me and told me she loved me, and I told her I loved her too, maybe it happened because I was lonely or maybe we were just two young people with no solid ground beneath us - I don't know where it came from. But I am here, now, with you - because I choose to be. You have my love and my loyalty. I promised you that I would be yours as long as we both shall live and that promise remains unbroken Enoch Edward Johnsey. So where do we go now husband? What do we do from here?'

We just looked at each other, his midnight eyes giving nothing away, I prayed he could sense the genuine love in me and that he would soften. Then Charlie broke the silence.

'I wish Aunt Theresa was here - she'd know how to do this bloody thing.'

The sun came out, the ice melted, the dam burst, and we laughed and cried together at the blindness of Cupid, the madness of mules and the sure and certain damnation that awaited killers.

It was on Christmas Eve, 1874, almost two years since setting foot on Queensland soil, that I finally understood I would probably never see my parents again. It was going

254

to be years at best before I once more walked a Gloucestershire lane. We bought supplies, new kit, outfits a medical bag and a horse and a cart with a cover over it at Woodstock Yard on a day far too hot to stand and haggle.

The horse was huge and black with a white streak on his nose and the stoic, gentle face of a chum accustomed to hard work and a kind hand. I judged, as did Enoch, that he probably had more than a little Clydesdale in him; he was young and would not tire easily. Charlie named him Tomtom after his old friend from Cabbage Tree Creek.

We stabled him and our cart at the Hotel, spent a sweltering and impersonal Christmas there and in early January headed inland to once again seek our fortune.

I still wasn't sure exactly what our plans were beyond accumulating three thousand pounds - the amount Enoch said he would be content to go home to England with. I wondered if she had been right, that if I made the wrong decision, we would both feel hollow forever? There was certainly an emptiness inside me. Perhaps born of the agony of her absence coupled with the pain of the loss of our hard-won fortune and the enduring maternal ache for Sarah Ann.

My daughter would be starting school soon, trotting off down Lowdilow Lane into Mrs Brooke's classroom, making friends and coming home each afternoon with a dozen stories about what she learned and who did what - and all with her mother on the other side of the world following dreams that were becoming more and more elusive. I determined that in my next letter home I would send the money to have her sit for a photograph they could then post to me.

In the meantime, our journey home would be interrupted by a detour to the gold town of Charters Towers where we would throw the dice once more.

20.
Charters Towers, Queensland
Monday, January 11th, 1875

There are thirty thousand people in Charters Towers, that's more than any town in Queensland except for Brisbane of course, and from the appearance and the activity we encountered on arrival it seemed as if they had all got there just the day before.

Imagine a disturbed ant's nest; swarms of people bustling in random directions, many carrying things - and they all seemed to know where they were going.

It's a fact that, unlike lizards and snakes, the hotter it gets the slower humans move, Brisbane is certainly a quicker place than Cooktown, but here, halfway or so between the two, the mode seems to be to scurry for a short period, then stop for a rest, then scurry again.

Like Cooktown, this is a gold town but there the similarity ends. Cooktown was wild, riotous and lawless but Charters Towers appears a place of work, of construction and ambition, where gold is scooped from the ground on an industrial scale by great machines and the power of collective effort.

Enoch seemed delighted at this hive of industry, but the presence of so many new chums made the search for accommodation a challenge.

'Pity we sold the tent,' he muttered as we passed yet another 'no vacancies' sign in a hotel window. Eventually, a local who said he had been in the town all of six months pointed us in the direction of the town cemetery where he said a trio of Greek blokes had done the bunk from a house the previous night owing a month's rent and the owner had not yet posted a to-let notice.

The house was on a track called Cemetery Road and seemed to be listing precariously, but its progress had been arrested by two huge wooden beams placed against the weak wall.

'It's got a good roof,' Enoch the optimist pointed out.

'As long as it stays up there,' I frowned.

The mood of the place was in keeping with its proximity to the graveyard, Enoch ascribes souls not only to humans and other animals but also to inanimate objects and he told me he felt the soul of this house crying, but that we could make it smile again. It cast a grey shadow over a small, neglected garden, the windows looked as if they had never been cleaned, the front door had a head-sized hole in it and a yellow dog in need of a good feed lay stretched across the doorstep. It raised its head and opened a coppery brown eye as Enoch approached. He knelt and scratched the creature's ear, earning a wan wag in return.

'It's eight quid a month which if you ask me is a bargain,' The house's owner who appeared as neglected as his property scratched a vest that looked capable of walking unaided and squinted at Enoch, a half grin revealing orange teeth - a bite from which would probably be more toxic than an Eastern Brown.

'Does that include the dingo?' Enoch enquired.

'Last blokes left that behind, do what you like with the bast... blighter,' he corrected himself in midstream remembering there was lady and child present.

The owner, Mr McLeish and Enoch shook hands, we gave him eight pounds as he insisted on payment in advance and our promise we wouldn't sublet to any Greeks.

The interior was better than I had dared to imagine, it all needed a good scrubbing and a lick of paint, but it was liveable. Tonight, we would sleep on our camp beds from the trailer and tomorrow we would go shopping for new - or at least clean, furniture. The water pump in the back garden worked after a few vigorous pumps to clear the rust and staleness but I still planned to boil everything before drinking for the first week.

'Come on Christie!' Enoch had opened a tin of bully beef and was feeding his new friend from his own plate.

'Christie?' Charlie had to ask.

'After Christie Palmerston, the bloke who saved our lives on the trail, remember? Now I'm going to save this mongrel's life,' Enoch patted Christie as he enthusiastically ate his first square meal in who knows how long; the dog wagged with increased vigour in return.

The ground floor of the house consisted of a parlour, sitting room, kitchen and scullery and a big room with large double doors offering direct access to the yard and rear walled garden. This, we agreed, would be Tomtom's quarters - safe, sheltered. Upstairs were four bedrooms and an ablutions room with a tin bath in it containing a dead possum and the biggest huntsman spider I had ever seen - and it was definitely alive. Even though I knew they were mostly harmless I couldn't bring myself to touch it and so I called for help.

'Enoch... huntsman!'

I heard the sound of mannish and more youthful chuckling from downstairs before Charlie entered the ablutions room and, gently brushing me aside, leaned into the bath and picked up the interloper, placing it on his arm, smiling as it crawled toward his shoulder.

'Looking up at me with Enoch's devilment shining out of his eyes he asked, 'You OK with the possum?'

We had been in the property for just over a month, in which time we had scouted the town and its environs before Enoch and I sat down after the evening meal and held a council to determine our future direction and, as was usual with Enoch, it was not a direction any of us could have foreseen.

'Right... the plan is this...'

'Be a bushranger Dad, bail the bastards up!'

A stare from Enoch was a solid object and Charlie did not have to look up from his illustrated book to know he was the target of one. He shrank down a little behind the pages and Enoch continued.

'I'm going to stop you reading those novels if you're not careful. Look it's a simple matter of supplying what is currently not available - that's the secret. There'd be no point in opening a grog shop here, there are hundreds of them - same with tools and hardware or... a blacksmith, we passed half a dozen on the way in. No, tell me - when you walk about around here, what is it you can't see?'

'The sea?' Charlie offered, chuckling.

I couldn't help it, I simply had to join in, adding to the endless number of things that could not be readily encountered on the streets of Charters Towers. Enoch's bemused expression only added to the hilarity.

'Hot air balloons?... Bathing machines?... Stroud Town Hall? ...Sharks?'

'Aha!' Enoch pointed to Charlie, getting closer Son, getting closer. Now then, take a look at this.' He crossed to his jacket hanging on the door and took out a newspaper, handing it to me. 'Have a look… this page, third column, about three quarters of the way down… read it out, go on.'

I frowned, scanning the page.

'There look, Fruit Trees…' He pointed out the relevant item. 'Go on… read it.'

I read aloud, the bemusement in my voice reflected in Charlie's face.

'Fruit Trees - Mr E Johnsey announces that he is prepared to supply fruit trees, shade trees, and flowers of all descriptions on the shortest notice. He also informed us that if is his intention to get a daily supply of fish from Townsville, and his arrangements for that object are now nearly complete. Mr. Johnsey is also going to supply cabbages and vegetables of all descriptions which are grown only by white men. If Mr. Johnsey carries out his ideas he should make a pile in no time.'

'Fish?' I read the announcement through a second time. How are you going to..?'

'Train,' he interrupted, '…comes in every day from Townsville, it serves the mining outfits mostly, but I met with a bloke from Townsville who has a fishing business, two boats, and he was looking around here to find an outlet. I told him of my experience in the fish trade and he offered me the chance to be a partner here. I buy fish off him, telegraph him every day to tell him what I want; he sticks it on the train in ice boxes and I sell it here. Fresh fish, these blokes about here would kill for a bit of fresh fish.'

I stood, holding my forehead in an attempt to keep all my thoughts in the right order.

'You said... you told him... about your experience in the trade?'

'Yeah, that's right... before I met you that was.' He looked furtive. Standing, he went to the window and peered out across the cemetery, 'Blimey - look at the size of that bat!'

But I wasn't letting go.

'Enoch, I've known you since you were seventeen and you've never mentioned your experience of fish trading... I've never seen you catch a fish... in fact - I've never even seen you *eat* a...'

He broke in, 'I was only a lad, me and a pal caught a trout in the River Churn and sold it to the old boy who repaired oil lamps. Well... I say sold, we swapped it for two apples and a goose egg. The point is, no-one is selling fish around here and that's an opportunity, same with the trees and vegetables. People round here ain't got time to garden, they spend every waking minute looking for gold - we know what that's like. We're providing a necessity.'

I tried to sound supportive, 'So, when are you launching your campaign to feed the five... thirty thousand then?'

He smiled a smile from his disarming and youthful repertoire, 'First load of fish comes in tomorrow and the two gardeners arrive at eight in the morning. Now, there's a thing, one of them is Greek, Nico - I'll have to warn him that if a man in a dirty vest asks him who he is, he has to say he's Italian.'

'Where are they going to garden?' I thought it a reasonable question, but Enoch looked at me as if I'd grown a second head, 'Well in the bloody garden of course!' Charlie laughed but I persevered, '...and who is going to keep an eye on them while you're out selling your fish?'

Now the smile was almost pitying; walking over he put an arm around me, kissing the top of my head, 'I'll be keeping an eye on them, and helping them dig... *you* will be in the food market - on the fish stall.'

I got the second two-man smile of the day. I looked at them from one to the other. Charlie grinned, 'You'll be great at it Ma, you've just got to shout out the names of the fish - or just "Fresh Fish!" will do.'

Enoch nodded, 'Yep, just like he said. I'll bet you're in there for less than fifteen minutes and all the fish'll be gone. They'll fly out.'

'Flying fish,' Charlie gave me the thumbs-up and they both laughed again.

I should have been angry, but what good would that have served? Enoch had spent two pounds - a week's rent - on fish which he assured me would bring in twice that much. I left the railway station platform at first light the following day pushing a trolley with a crate of fish balanced on the frame. It was a pleasant enough summer morning, but that would not last. It would be searing before very long, cooking the fish and anyone else foolhardy enough to be challenging the sun to a test of strength. I was in no mood for a two mile walk to market at a time when I should have been serving breakfast before starting on the hundred and one other things a woman has to do in the home - all of which would still need to be done after I had sold our wares.

And what kind of fish were they? The label on the steel crate simply said 'Fish - The East Coast Prawn Trawl and Fish Company.' The crate was also supposed to be waterproof as the fish were packed in ice but there was a small drip from one corner.

On reaching the market, I discovered a bare wooden table had been reserved for me between a butcher and a cheese and butter purveyor. Scrawled writing on a piece of paper said 'E. Johnsey - fishmonger.' The lid of the crate was helpfully detachable and folded out further into a fair-sized 'counter' on which to display the wares.

One of the reasons I have never seen Enoch eating fish is that I do not give him any. I just don't like the feel of them, the smell of them or the taste of them. I was happy to serve up many a fish dinner in the Noah's Ark which had been prepared and cooked by someone else but handling the cold dead slippery things here was not a pleasant experience.

Having laid them out, all forty of them - a shilling a fish - I waited for customers. The dairyman on the next stall screwed up his nose and frowned at me, but the butcher was friendly and took pity on what was obviously my first day as a marketeer.

'Give 'em a yell out Love, like this…' he bellowed, "Legs 'o lamb… lovely legs 'o lamb, fresh prime beef…"

I have always been uncomfortable drawing attention to myself, it goes against my every instinct. 'A good servant is invisible,' Mr Wells used to say, and this was also my Father's sentiment as he sought peace in a crowded home. However, it seemed to be acceptable in this place to announce your wares and so I began… tentatively with a cheery call of…

'Fish!'

I repeated it a few times. The butcher grinned, 'Put a bit of poke behind it Blossom, go on, fill the lungs, imagine you're calling the kids in for supper and they're half a bloody mile away…'

I took his advice.'

'FISSHHH!'

The butcher nodded as several people close to my little table turned in shock.

'Better…', he said scratching the side of his nose, '…but you've got to sound friendly at the same time - you want these galahs to buy your fish - you're not threatening to slap 'em with one.'

I was standing there for just over an hour, I took the last two fish, plus three pounds and eighteen shillings, home - along with the announcement that this arrangement was going to be very short term and if Enoch wanted a fish business, he could find himself another fishmonger!

For a short time, he employed a Portuguese woman called Mariana whose shouts of 'Feeeesh-ah' rang around the market hall each morning but there was little profit in return for the effort and that arm of our enterprise passed into history. The trees, however, did rather better and along with the vegetable garden, we made enough to live on.

Our adopted town - now a city, was booming. People referred to it as 'The World' because it was claimed there was nothing that couldn't be got in 'The Towers'. There were plans for a proper hospital and even a stock exchange. Charters Towers. for all its roar and bluster, was a tenuous place however, utterly dependent for survival on the lure of the gold and its continued supply. Being a service industry, we managed to weather the peaks and troughs but as the decade rolled on, we became, like so many, victims of this success.

The trains from Townsville could bring in vegetables and fruit from the more fertile coastal gardens and sell them cheaper that we could produce them. There were more fresh produce shops than ever before and at least two substantial planters were bringing in fruit and shade trees by the trainload to turn our dusty city green.

But we survived by diversifying. Enoch took a job at the Venus State Battery gold processing plant which, although he was just an employee and not a partner, brought in enough to supplement the dwindling market garden takings and Charlie, got a part time job with a cartwright.

'Have I failed us Ellen?'

The pale light of the moon flooded across the bedspread and illuminated the small cross above the dressing table. I rose on one elbow and looked down on his silhouette.

'What? What do you mean?'

'I promised to make us rich and then take us home and I have done neither. I've got the fare home for all of us - not that I would like to do that to Charlie, he's a Queenslander through and through - but I've got little else. We would go home no better off than when we came out here... how long ago now? Six years? So... I have failed us.'

I had been just on the point of dozing off, but this deserved a wide-awake response. I rose, lit the lamp, lit a fire and put the kettle on for a pot of tea. He lit his pipe and I put his hand between mine and looked him square in the face as he puffed away, squinting in the smoke.

'If we had stayed in Cheltenham, we would have had less money that we have now, and every day we would have seen those with unearned wealth parading and strutting and braying and hee-hawing and looking down their ugly long noses at us. We have a healthy, free-living boy growing up with chances he would never get in England. He'll judged on his merits here - he can be somebody. You have loved us and taken care of us and led us on adventures that a young man I once knew would have given his right arm for.

'I have seen the world Enoch, I'm a shepherd's daughter from Uckington and I have seen... the green coast of Africa, the southern oceans and this huge and sometimes awful frightening land we all now call home. I'm glad I married you and if it was that day again and I knew all I know now, I would - in my sister's words - bloody well wed you again in a heartbeat you big fazey bugger!'

But Enoch had been a worried man for weeks; there was talk of lay-offs at the plant and we were in need of an urgent plan. We still had close to a hundred pounds, but that would not last long with no more coming in.

When the inevitable happened and he came home from the plant stating he would not be going back, we weighed up our options. If you are mining gold - and getting it, Charters Towers is a good place to be. But if you are not, then the inflated prices for everything in the shops puts you at a disadvantage.

We could, of course, have moved on but this was the longest we had stayed in one place since crossing the ocean and we had put down some kind of roots - dry and struggling though they may be. Enoch walked the town and rode to every outlying claim and farm looking for work as the last of our money seeped away.

And finally, he resorted to stealing what he couldn't earn.

I knew, the moment the leather drawstring bag hit the tabletop with a sound indicating coins within, that Enoch had not come by it honestly. We had nothing to sell and my husband looked both ashamed and furtive. He knew what getting caught stealing meant in Queensland and must surely have realised, if he had thought it through, what it would do to all of us.

However, what he lacked in book-taught knowledge, he more than made up for in natural worldliness and downright cunning. Besides, he had been caught and punished once and had sworn never to make such a mistake again.

The bag contained sixty-five sovereigns which he said he had found on the hard red dust out at the racetrack. A subsequent explanation revealed it had contained seventy sovereigns when he found it, but he had wagered five on a horse with odds of fifteen to one. Had the animal won, his plan, he said, would have been to replace the five sovereigns and then hand the bag over to the police, pocketing seventy sovereigns in winnings.

'No doubt the owner would have given me a couple as a reward,' he added with a humorless grin. But the horse had not won or been placed, so he had brought the rest home.

Two weeks passed, Enoch still sought work and I had made him swear to keep away from the track. But while he has always been willing to listen to advice, he rarely follows it. He is like a stream after a tempest, the path of least resistance will always prevail even though it offers nothing but temporary solace.

Emboldened, perhaps by his success, he found another pile of money, this time in the back room of a crowded bar, where he had no right being - and this time Lady Luck was looking the other way. He had turned to run and found himself staring down the bores of several guns and very shortly afterwards, at cell walls.

Four days later and our world fell about our ears as Enoch was sentenced to a year's hard labour on the other side of the continent which the judge told him was a chance to redeem himself.

He kissed Charlie and then me before climbing into the back of the black wagon that would take him and another man to the station. He was actually smiling, was it bravado, or did we really mean so little to him by now?

The parting kiss, however, was heartfelt and although his eyes remained dry, there was a world of broken dreams in them. There is nothing so painful as a last embrace; the scent and feel of someone you never want to release, how many of these are we designed to bear?

I wanted to remember everything, hold on to this image which would be all I had of my beloved for twelve long months. I recall the scuffed heels of his riding boots, a paper package stuffed in his jacket pocket containing bread and cheese. A broad and strong hand gently stroking the side of my face. His eyes, devil's eyes that could still shine with more goodness than those of a saint, the stem of his pipe just visible in the pocket of his green leather waistcoat.

'I love you, Lass of the Land...'

My smile was a mask, serving only to divert the course of tears, and it was not until the black van turned around the corner and disappeared from view that I replied.

'You leave us with sixteen pounds and seven shillings - rent to pay and food to buy and your son to raise...

...and yet, for some reason, I love you too.'

21.
Charters Towers, Queensland
Wednesday, December 17th, 1875

Enoch would be home in a month. It said so in his letter posted a week before, which made it just three weeks - and he would be here.

He had been working at a timber mill near Perth and had apparently impressed them with his industriousness to such a degree they had offered him a charge hand's position on completion of his sentence with a good monthly wage and a cabin for Charlie and I to join him out west where, he said, the air was drier and healthier.

The money we had been left with had gone, Tomtom had been sold, but our fresh provisions market stall earned enough to feed us and I obtained a license to collect firewood which I bundled and sold for little more than pennies. Mr McLeish agreed to accept food in payment for rent, realising, as Enoch had repeatedly pointed out, it is the only real currency.

It was hard, especially in the heat of summer. Charlie and I would tend the garden beginning in that blessed time when the sun lights the sky but has not yet peered above the horizon in all its lividity. After two hours or so we would retire indoors for breakfast and then head to market with our wares; vegetables, plants both medicinal and decorative and eggs when we had them to spare.

We made very little money, not being able to compete with the coastal growers, but we bartered a lot and frequently came home with as many goods as we took, notably cloth, meat, second-hand shoes and chinaware.

I signed for a letter on Christmas Eve, sent from Perth. Sitting on a wooden chair as tired as myself next to the front door and with Christie's head on my lap, I anticipated the contents. It was going to contain travel warrants. Enoch had sent for us and I wasn't sure how I felt about it.

My son and I had survived a year in a harsh and unforgiving land without our man; I had a daughter on the other side of the world, a mother and father, sisters and brothers I would likely never see again. And now he wanted me to live in a cabin, the wife of a timber man until I grew old and died - which I would have been happy to do in Uckington, but it was not what I crossed oceans for, not what he had promised. I would make our cabin a home and then he would get the wanderlust again, or 'find' some valuables. I was sure I no longer needed him, but... did I want him? Did I love him?

'Yes,' I told myself aloud. 'Yes, I do.' And despite all it had cost me, I knew it to be true.

I opened the telegram...

...Mrs Johnsey... Why would he call me...? The fool...

I read on and then read it through again - and then looked up from the paper at a different world - a new world where I didn't know the rules. Meaningless sounds came and went; everything, everywhere, had sharp and unfamiliar edges. I tried to speak; my mouth formed the words, but no sound came out. My heart raced and ice settled in my stomach, each sensation feeding off the other.

Tunnel vision, I gripped the door frame, but my hands were shaking so much I found it difficult to hang on. I knew that trying to stand would bring on a full faint and so I leaned forward and squeezed my eyes shut, teeth gritted, I began to shake. And then from a place so deep inside the light never reaches it, came the howl.

I felt Charlie's hands grip my shoulders, his voice strange... echoing.

'Ma... MA!'

I screamed and it withered away into convulsive sobs, Charlie was holding me tightly and I realised he was now crying too. I gripped his arm.

'Oh... my precious darling...'

'It's alright Ma, it's alright, I've got you... I've got you, come on, come on indoors...'

Had Charlie not been holding my hand I would have fallen in a heap. I somehow made it to the bedroom and a fell on my bed close to the open window. He brought me a glass of water and an orange. I held him tight, sobbing great gulps into his hair.

And the house we had found crying... and taught to laugh, wept again.

I neither ate nor hardly slept those next two dreadful days. My dear Charlie, his own heart surely as shattered as mine, never left my side. Mr McLeish sent around his housekeeper who cooked and cleaned and cared for the chooks and Christie. On the third day, necessity and relentless coaxing forced me to eat a bowl of vegetable soup with some bread and on the sixth day a small package arrived from Perth. Charlie offered to open it, but I could not bear to put him through that.

Within was a letter, typewritten, along with two smaller envelopes which I decided to open first. One contained twenty-one pounds and six shillings, a sum explained as overtime wages and a collection by workmates. The second envelope contained a small linen drawstring bag within which was Enoch's wedding ring and his lucky shilling. I had thought myself drained of tears but from somewhere an untapped reservoir found an outlet and it was several minutes and a washed face before I could read the letter.

> *Dear Mrs Johnsey,*
>
> *It is with deep regret that I am compelled to write to you regarding the tragic accident which claimed the life of your husband, Enoch. Mr Johnsey had become a well-respected worker at the Mill during his time here and was popular with his comrades and his superiors.*
>
> *The unfortunate incident occurred mid-morning on Monday, December 20th when, during the unloading of a wagon, a large piece of timber measuring eighteen inches by eighteen inches and weighing a considerable amount fell upon Enoch who had*

slipped and temporarily lost his footing.

He sustained serious injuries as a result of this and was immediately transferred to the Colonial Hospital in Perth where staff determined that he could not be saved. It may comfort you to know, however, that after the administration of morphine, he was not in pain and left this world peacefully at around seven o' clock that evening with a nurse and a Baptist minister at his side.

The Mill is, without prejudice, willing to cover the full cost of Enoch's treatment and funeral expenses.

Once again, I am most dreadfully sorry for your loss; my sympathies, along with all of those who knew Enoch, are extended to you and your family.

Sincerely yours.
Lionel White, General Manager.
Canning Jarrah Timber Mill.
Perth. Western Australia.

The next morning, Christmas Day, the postman delivered a Christmas card from Enoch. It showed a woman and child in a sleigh, waving and smiling. On the reverse it said…

'Dearest LOTL, I can't wait to see you.'

To reprise the past is a pale substitute for a stolen future, but in the absence of tomorrow then yesterday must again be asked to don its stage clothes and repeat the performance, speak the lines once more, this time overlaid with the poignancy of a known finale.

I recall his hands first, restless, spinning a coin on the table under the window in the Noah's Ark before picking it up and flipping it hypnotically in and out of his fingers; not looking at it but beyond, into some distance that others were not privileged to view. Then, as brave Richard Price introduced me to his Merry Men, Enoch had looked up and into me with those fathomless black eyes and I wondered, right there and then, how it would feel to be the subject of his undivided attention.

He leaned on a fence at Andoversford Racecourse, grinning lazily as I passed by, long black hair tossing in a wind he had probably whipped up just for the occasion.

'Lass o' the Land...'

He had appeared, hat in hand, gold tooth and earring glittering in the lamplight of our cottage after delivering five pounds which meant the salvation of our family, smiling guilelessly at my parents and winking at Esther. I never discovered how he had come by such an amount in so short a time and I had never asked him.

He had taken my hand and led me up the creaking stairs of his parent's home to a room where a home-made patchwork quilt covered a feather mattress on a wooden bed. I had been nervous but not afraid because I had already decided this was a man who would never, ever hurt me.

I had seen examples of his explosive rage, but only when confronted with injustice or cruelty. It was a righteous fury directed solely at the enemies of the only god he truly worshipped - Mother Nature.

He had knelt beneath a lonely horse chestnut and offered me forever and I had accepted gladly.

He had stood impassionate in the dock while a bewigged citizen, who had never known hunger or want, stole six precious months of his young life - and his first thought had been for me.

'I'm worth waiting for!'

I would have waited fifty years at that moment for as he entered the forbidding stone cold cell, my heart followed him, comforting him as the door slammed.

He sang our babies to sleep, he sang to them in English, Romani and Old Irish. He nurtured our trees and buried our flowers, held me as we were thrown madly through ocean canyons - and, defying death, he had stood squarely between his loved ones and those who would do them harm.

I had asked myself how I was supposed to carry on without him and Grandfather William's deep and reassuring rumble, distant Gloucestershire thunder, had come back.

'We ain't without 'em, they're of us and in us and we are in all o' them. They sees the world through our eyes, our hearts beat for 'em. When a branch falls, our leaves is more important to the tree than ever.'

The ensuing weeks dulled the raw edges but still left me incapable or unwilling to do more than the bare minimum and throughout the insipid Queensland autumn all I wanted to do was hibernate, close the curtains and shut out the pitiless world beyond my door.

I went through the motions of tending the market garden, feeding and caring for the chooks and collecting the eggs but I cared little or nothing for my own appearance or welfare.

The evenings brought the company of my dear boy, but we were not a contented cocoon of chatter and industriousness, more a brood of carefully chosen words, yawns and sighs punctuated by the turning of pages and the clicking of needles while lamps flickered in defiance of blood red skies, lowering suns and the hissing of a neglected kettle.

And so, as autumn turned to a winter in name only, and then to spring, we emulated nature in waking from a slumber. Slowly I began to look forward again, but always with that voice in my thoughts; hypnotic, rustic and petrichor… dawn birdsong along an Uckington lane with just a hint of the devil whispering in the frost. He would live within me until my last breath.

> *'Dark-winged angel with the golden smile,*
> *How will I travel without your light?*
> *For you have shone so long for me,*
> *And I'm so frightened of the night.'*

22.
Charters Towers. Queensland
Friday, April 10th, 1883

A boy will always grow to be taller than his mother and so it was with Charlie, not that I set a difficult target! Halfway between his eleventh and twelfth birthdays, if I stood in stockinged feet and he stood on tiptoe, we were the same height; he was going to follow Grandfather William. He grew in wisdom and knowledge too and excelled in his part time job at the wheelwright's workshop in between schooling and home chores.

When he smiled, or turned to catch someone's eye, I plainly saw my own mother in him. He had the kindest eyes, his glance was going to melt hearts, not stop them like his dear Dad. And he was not an Englishman. He was a Queenslander from top to toe, bronzed by sub-tropical sunshine and the great outdoors. He no more belonged in frost-carpeted Gloucestershire fields than Tomtom or poor Tuesday. He had never expressed any interest in the land of his ancestors although he often added a 'Hello, hope you are all well,' to the grandparents and sister he didn't remember when I wrote home.

I did not grow, either physically or financially over the same period, but I grew in wisdom and in a wealth of friendships. Mr Gordon McLeish attempted for a while to spark our association into something more that I could ever feel. He eventually gave up, but our friendship remained and became a deeper and much valued part of my life. I was happy to wash and iron his clothes, sit with him of an evening as he played the old out-of-tune piano and we would promenade the neighbourhood when the heat permitted. In return, he insisted I live rent-free, touchingly stating my company and friendship were beyond price.

As the town's fortunes waxed and waned, it had long become obvious I could not compete with the big growers and suppliers of vegetables and so I turned my attention to flowers and decorative shrubs in pots which I either bought wholesale and resold or grew myself.

Plants and people have much in common - many varieties of both from Europe thrived here in the warmth, flowering longer and bigger than at home. I found a good market for these pretty patches of nostalgia among those older residents and even people of the next generation who had never seen the lands of their ancestors.

Gordon and I made a movable pen for the chooks and while they fertilised a patch of garden, we planted the rest, rotating regularly to enrich the soil and our little enterprise proved better than I had hoped. I took out an advertisement in the Northern Miner which read:

The End of the Sky

*Flowers from Europe and
Queensland of all descriptions
supplied on the shortest notice by
E JOHNSEY
Elizabeth Street*

Gordon was a bit of a hand with clay and kiln. A Glaswegian, he had come to Queensland via New South Wales as a teenager. His father, a minister, had dreamed of bringing the gospels to the natives but had lost his own faith after his wife died of fever.

He had not followed his father into the church, instead finding employment in a Brisbane pottery, rising to the rank of deputy works manager before striking north in search of gold, prospecting on the Palmer and the Laura but with limited success and spending what he accumulated on two tired but still habitable properties here in The Towers, one of which I lived in.

We expanded into selling flowerpots and reasonably well-produced garden ornaments and since I had begun laundering for him his appearance had greatly improved, making him a useful meeter-and-greeter to our customers. I had to restrain my laughter and surprise on the morning he turned up sporting pristine new teeth which reminded me of an over enthusiastic stallion.

Any hope or ambition I had ever entertained about returning to England had died with Enoch. I knew with certainty I would never see my parents or Sarah Ann again. Our little flower business earned enough to pay bills, buy the essentials and sometimes put a few shillings aside for luxuries such as clothing materials. But it would never get me home.

A steep downturn in Queensland's economy caused the newspapers to predict lots of people losing their jobs. Already many had left Charters Towers for the new strikes far away in the West while others headed south to Brisbane, Sydney and Melbourne, but things were apparently little better there.

The prime minister of Queensland, Sir Thomas McIlwraith, visited Charters Towers on St David's Day to see for himself the effects of the downturn and of all places he was going to pass our house. Gordon put on his best and only suit and to our surprise we were approached by a member of the Premier's staff to ask if I would be happy to pin one of my flowers on the great man's lapel for a photograph.

He was very gracious and shook my hand and I pinned one of my yellow roses, of which I was particularly proud, to his lapel, apologising for it not being a Scottish thistle or a bluebell. He thanked me for being so thoughtful and asked about my life in Gloucestershire, and commiserated sincerely on the death of my husband, citing the 'Priceless seeds settlers have sown which will be reaped by generations of healthy and wealthy native-born Australians in the decades to come.' He also spoke at great length to fellow Scot, Gordon about Glasgow and mutual places familiar to them. When he left, he said farewell in both English and Gaelic. A photograph appeared in the newspapers with the caption:

The End of the Sky

"Widow and florist, Mrs Ellen Johnsey, pins a flower in the buttonhole of Queensland Premier, Sir Thomas McIlwraith during his visit to Charters Towers on March the First."

An increasing percentage of my customers were Chinese, which may have indicated an overall shift in the make-up of The Towers' population or maybe the different values of the orientals who are said to believe that if a man has two pennies, he should spend one on bread and one on a flower. Either way, their trade was welcome and helped sustain us.

Mr and Mrs Chou, Sam and Susan, took up residence in a tiny cottage with the disconcerting name of Judgement Day Lodge which sat at the entrance to the cemetery. Susan nevertheless made it a delightful little home surrounded by brightly coloured flowers and bushes, many bought from me or propagated from plants relatives had left on graves.

Mr Chou worked in the office of the Barabbas Crushing Mill. He had lost a foot after being bitten by a snake but got about remarkably well on a wooden one. Susan, about a decade his junior was, she thought, around forty but where she came from girl's births were not recorded and were regarded as unfortunate.

Sometimes they would visit and we would share tales of our childhoods with Mr Chou often remarking that 'Goss-tasha sounds a very strange place.'

It wasn't until I heard a passing man calling out to a friend that it was the April the tenth, I realised it was my birthday, my thirty-fourth! I had long since stopped celebrating them and while Charlie almost always remembered a card or at least a well-wish I had never bothered telling anyone else in my life when my anniversary was. Some years I would get a card from Father, Esther or Emily but more often than not their own lives were of greater significance than a relative who had all but fallen over the edge of the world and disappeared.

Correspondence from home had become sporadic and stilted. Father's news was always sad so it seemed; Mother's eyesight continued to deteriorate and he relied more and more on the charity of Emily and Samuel. Esther lived somewhere in London with Henry and their children. Walter worked as a shepherd like his father and grandfather before him while William was now in Grouse Creek, Utah which, from his description, had a lot in common with Queensland.

But birthday or not, the work could not stop. I had fashioned a shade by adding a longer handle to a parasol and embedding it into a wooden block, keeping the sun off my back while potting and repotting plants in the open garden at the front of the house - which now also served as my shop window.

It was not uncommon for people to stop and browse so, as yet another shadow fell across me, elongated by the morning sun, I didn't bother turning around or getting up from my kneeling position where I was trying to break a particularly stubborn Snake Plant into three smaller ones.

Dawn is always noisy, full of birdsquabble and mill sirens. Across the road, I noticed Susan Chou cleaning her windows. I called over my shoulder.

'Is there anything special you're looking for?'

There was a short pause before a contralto voice replied, 'Actually, I'm looking for an English rose.'

'Any type in particular?' I responded, trying to recall which were currently ready.

There was the barest hint of a chuckle.

'Oh yes - very particular - sure it wouldn't surprise me if it was one of a kind...'

23.
Charters Towers. Queensland
Friday, April 10th, 1883

As long as I did not look around… as long as nothing contrary intruded into this moment, then every possible world could exist beyond my senses. But loneliness is a deceitful ringmaster who makes hearts dance to songs no-one else can hear. I concentrated on the half-potted plant before me while absently rubbing soil-covered hands on my apron. Then, straightening my back, I forced down the ridiculous delusion; having nursed a broken heart it was repaying me with a cruel lie.

How many with that accent? How many from that ill-used island had sought sanctuary on this one? Tens… hundreds of thousands? But… English Rose? My heart already knew - and my head, with only baseless denial as a weapon, was losing the battle.

Turning my head showed little other than my parasol shielding me from the glare of the golden dawn. Brushing hair from my face - streaking my cheek with soil, I stood, squinting, my feet in the shadow of the visitor who, seeing me rise, paced around clockwise so that I was not staring into the sun.

But I ended up dazzled all the same.

Her smile was a sword slashing the shroud that had draped my soul. She wore a dress of deep emerald with a high collar and a brooch of amber at her neck. Atop elegantly bound auburn hair sat a teardrop hat with what looked like a spray of edelweiss embedded in it. Craftsman-made verdigris leather boots complimented fingerless gloves of spring green lace. She looked prosperous, a supposition emphasised by a fine waiting carriage behind a sleek black horse, harness in the hands of a bowler-hatted driver waiting on the roadside.

Stupid, stupid tears, could they not have waited? I tore my eyes from her, wiping my face with the edge of my apron. Hair bedraggled and half-tied in a strip of rag, I stood in my tired and grubby work dress and scuffed boots. Whatever my first words were, they would be wholly insufficient to illustrate the wave of emotion I was failing to hold at bay.

'I'm sorry… I wasn't expecting… I've got soil all over my…my…'

And then a big gulp and, at thirty-four, I stood sobbing like a silly child. Then her arms were around me, squeezing so tight, kissing my head and the side of my face over and over. I hugged her and clung to the back of her dress, knowing I was probably covering it in potting soil, but I couldn't help myself. She was crying too; I could feel her tears falling on my cheek, mingling with my own. She smelled of lavender.

'My Ellen…'

'Oh Theresa… it really is you, isn't it…?'

'It is, it is, my dear darling Ellen.'

She pulled back, holding me at arm's length and smiling through the tears, 'Well, would you look at the pair of us!'

I was laughing now through my own sobs, finally daring to believe my eyes. She had filled out and presented a shapely figure. A beautiful woman had usurped the lost youth on the cusp of adulthood who had danced uninvited but irrepressible through my dreams for so many years. But maturity had not chased the child from her laughter as she gently brushed a strand of wayward harvest mouse hair back behind my ear.

All I had said was… 'Would you like a cup of tea?' And it had set her off, she took my face in her hands…

'Well, isn't that the most English thing I've ever heard.'

Inside, she took in my surroundings, smiling as she spotted the embroidery of Bullingham Cottage. I put the kettle on the hob and lit a fire beneath it.

'I remember this from Cabbage Tree Creek.'

I rinsed the soil off my hands, wiping my face as I dried them, 'I didn't know you were in Charters Towers, but then I don't get out and…'

'I live in Brisbane,' she picked up a photograph of a smiling girl standing in the shade of a Gloucestershire yew.

'Sarah Ann?'

'Yes, her ninth birthday likeness. My father sent it to me.'

Theresa smiled sadly, 'She looks like you - and I can see Enoch in her too.'

'Would your… husband, like to come in for tea?'

She recognised the big question within the little one and chuckled.

'He might if I had one. The feller outside is Oswald, or so he tells me, he's a hire driver from the hotel I stayed at last night. I arrived on yesterday evening's train and thought about coming around then but I didn't want to wake you and I wanted to surprise you on your birthday. I saw your photograph with the Prime Minister in The Courier. I had to go out and buy another copy because I cried so much over the first one it went wrinkly and when I waved it out of the window to dry, the wind caught it and it blew away.'

The kettle was singing, she came closer and took my hands in hers, 'I had to come Ellen, I just had to. If... if you don't want to see me for whatever reason...I mean, I don't know how you're situated now... I'll make myself scarce.'

I squeezed her hands before pulling her close and hugging her again fiercely.

'Don't you dare! - are you listening to me?'

She was crying again; I could feel her shuddering and that set me off.

We looked into each other's eyes, reading there the scratches and scrapes left by the years we had spent walking separate paths, but the very sight of her face blew away the ages like cobwebs in a storm.

'Oh Ellen,' she whispered.

'The kettle's boiling,' I whispered back, causing her to laugh out loud through her tears.

We sent Oswald back to the hotel with orders to return mid-afternoon. I cooked for us.

And then we talked...

I felt that as Theresa had sought me out and we were now sitting in my parlour, I should be the one to hang the washing out and let the air get to it.

'I am so very, very sorry I left you in Edwardstown...'

She tried to interrupt, but I held up a hand, determined to exorcise that which I had waited so long to purge.

'...It hurt as much as any bereavement to know I had been the cause of such pain. There has been an empty space in me I have found impossible to fill - just like you said there would be. I made the choice I made, and I have to tell you that, even knowing the pain I would feel and sorrow I must have brought to you, I would make the same choice again. Because I had made a promise, I had said the words - "As long as we both shall live."'

'All down the years I have carried you inside Theresa, wondering how things would have turned out if I had come to you... where you were now and what you were doing and who you were doing it with. I hoped and prayed you would find happiness. Every May the First I sent up a special prayer to Jesus, asking him, 'Please don't let her hate me. I love her ever so much and I expect I always will.'

She looked out of the window at the big lavender, her eyes red from tears and her face a mask of beautiful sadness. She put down her cup and locked her fingers.

'I'm the one with the apology to make...'

Now it was my turn to try and interrupt but she, like me, was determined to have her say.

'...I'm sorry for forcing such an impossible choice on you. I was young, thinking only of what I wanted. Of course, you were going to choose Enoch, you had to, he was your man, your soulmate and I was the intruder.

'Now here's my confession. You were a good friend, and I should have been content with that, but I wasn't. I wanted to play a game, get closer, see where it went, the devilment was in me, mixing up all my feelings in a big pot. I would sing to baby Charlie, but I knew you were just the other side of the door, out in the yard, listening - and I was singing as much to you as to the wee man.

'But then, when I was scared by the thunder, which I still am by the way, I got into your bed and you hugged me... it was like seeing a lamp glowing in a window after a long journey through dark woods and I knew I never wanted to be anywhere else. When ... what was his name... Albie sent me to Brisbane for a week, it was almost unbearable being away from you and I realised I had been caught in my own trap. And then when I came back and you pretended so badly to be asleep, my heart sang Ellen, because I knew then that you felt it too. Then you asked me if I wanted to come with you to the goldfields - and I knew exactly why you had asked, and it was like a million blackbirds singing inside of me.

'The road from there to the shade of that lonely tree on the Laura was one I was compelled to travel. I was no longer in control. That moment we first kissed... if you had pushed me away, I would have died. It wasn't a game anymore; it was the most real thing there had ever been in my whole life.

'I'm a well-off woman now and there have been proposals. I have had the cards and flowers and the old "I will love you more than you have ever known" but I could no more love another than a bonfire could outshine the sun. You are, Ellen, the only sun that has ever shone my sky. And I know I am not the only sun that has ever shone in yours, nor would I ever seek to replace dear kind Enoch. But I promised myself on coming here that if you were pleased to see me, I would offer you all of me and all that I have now and forever. I would beg you to forgive that youthful Theresa for the pain she caused and ask you to promise with me that we would never be apart or hurt each other ever again. And... so, that's what I'm doing...'

I took a breath to reply, but she stalled me with a hand on mine.

'Be careful now, you've got my heart in your hands and it's made of the thinnest glass ever blown; no one else has ever held it and no one ever will.'

I held her hand between mine, her skin was soft, mine, like mother's, bore the battle scars of a family raised. I had told her what was in my heart, now I had to let my head have its way.

Charlie frowned, face smudged with oil and with bicycle spanner in hand, staring at the cold cooking range then at the dead fireplace beneath it. He had my frown and he turned it on me with a question in his eyes that eventually reached his mouth.

'You were singing to yourself, are you feeling crook Mother?'

I smiled, 'Thank you for your concern, but no, I am not feeling crook. Now get your hands and face washed and find your clean shirt for me to run an iron over it.'

He frowned, shook his head and departed, muttering something about being 'Bloody starving.' I lit the big fire in what used to be Tomtom's quarters and placed two water churns over it on the grill, they had begun to steam when Charlie returned. He frowned, studying the rising steam.

'You havin' a bath on a Friday Ma?'

'I grinned, I am, strangely enough, yes. And, hungry as you are, you will be delighted to know we're going out to dinner this evening at the Royal Private Hotel because there's someone special we will be meeting.'

He raised an eyebrow in the way my sister, Emily had been able to, 'I hope Mr Someone Special is paying for it, they charge a half a dollar just for looking at the bloody menu in there according to Stumpy Hall. His old man took a woman there for dinner and he ended up having to sell his neddy to pay the bill.'

Charlie was even more perplexed when, just over an hour later, a carriage arrived and we were helped aboard by a top-hatted coachman.

We passed through the hotel's lobby where Charlie gave a whistle of approval.

'Don't tell me… Horsesteeth McLeish has proposed again and you've finally given in, yeah?'

I responded with a smile and a finger to the lips as a concierge approached. 'We're expected by Miss Kelly,' my smile was returned, the man gestured us to follow. I smiled even wider at Charlie's puzzlement which turned to awe at the splendour of the dining room, taking in the pristine tablecloths, shining silver cutlery, flowers on every table and a pair of waiters waltzing between obstacles with plates and glasses much as I once did in the smaller and less salubrious Noah's Ark.

And then there was Theresa. While every other female in the room had worn their hair for a formal dinner, pinned and bound; hers was the fire in the forest, ready for a summer picnic, like its owner, free and unbridled - a crown and cascade of flame draped over shoulders and almost reaching her waist. She was breathtaking.

She wore a high collared double-breasted jacket in what was clearly her favourite shade of green, but the shock came when she stood to greet us, causing Charlie's eyebrows to almost vanish above his hairline. She was wearing trousers - a common sight on the goldfields and, according to newspapers, in the more bohemian quarters of Sydney and Melbourne, but surely a first for The Towers. She kissed me twice on the cheek and once on the lips.

Then she turned to my son, hands on hips, 'Hello my little bushfella, sure you've sprouted like bamboo, so you have!'

His lips were moving soundlessly, his whisper when it came was barely audible.

'Aunt Theresa?'

Her eyes filled and her lip wobbled, I was about to hug her myself, but Charlie beat me to it.

If there's one thing other diners present on that evening will recall, it will probably be the screams of unbridled laughter - and the occasion when Theresa, clearly tired of the scowls and 'harumphs' from a nearby table went over to the party and said, 'I'm awfully sorry for the noise - I'm a missionary and these poor lunatics are refugees from the goldfield, how about I stand your table a case of wine by way of an apology?'

The End of the Sky

We were still there long after bedtime and the anecdotes were seemingly endless, never was there a more prolific raconteur with an audience so eager. It was only when the concierge yawned and almost fell over from tiredness that we called it a night agreeing that Theresa would meet me for lunch the very next day. We had hugged and she had whispered, 'I'll be watching the rail station and all the roads out of town, don't try to escape.' I had kissed her and promised nothing was further from my thoughts.

The next morning was a struggle having retired so late and with so much laughter, wine and excitement, not to mention delicious and normally unattainable food. Neither Charlie or I were inclined to eat a lot of breakfast and so we sat at the table with tea, toast and a woodpecker in my head.

He cleared his throat in the manner of his father; an announcement was approaching.

'It was nice to see you laughing Ma,' he stated.

'I think we all laughed most of our devils out last night,' I smiled back, 'It did us good.'

To my surprise, he stood and moved to my side. He put his hands on my shoulders and kissed the top of my head. When he looked at me it could have been Enoch - that same all-knowing gaze that saw not just the present, but all the roads that had led to it and all the paths yet to take. He had inherited many of his father's mannerisms and, having been called upon to become the man of the house years before his time, I sometimes imagined my husband spoke through him.

'You've got my blessing Ma.'

There were occasions when I had to remind myself he was still short of his teens; It was almost as if he recalled previous lives and had retained all the wisdom from them.

I half-frowned, knowing it was unconvincing, 'For what?'

'You know what.' He kissed me on the cheek.

We met in a delightful hotel room with a verandah overlooking busy Mossman Street. It smelled of beeswax, lavender and lemon myrtle. A polished wooden bed was adorned with crisp white sheets, and on the small oak table sat a vase of fresh flowers and a beautiful ornamental oil lamp made by Falk Stadelmann of London. I sat on the bed, she knelt in front of me and took my hands in hers...

And for the second time in my life I said, 'Yes.'

She smiled and closed her eyes, but the tears still escaped, squeezed out, falling from her chin to her dress. She rested her head on my knees, I leaned forward and kissed her.

We promised to be together forever - and to never hurt each other again.

I was not surprised to discover Charlie did not want to come with us to Brisbane, he had plans of his own. I could have forced him of course, influenced as I was by my attachment to him; and having left one child behind I could not countenance the thought of abandoning another.

But Charlie had made his feelings clear. While he loved his mother dearly and was glad she had found a love too, he wanted to try his luck as an apprentice wheelwright in Townsville in the employ of a friend of Gordon, Ted Parker who had a lad of the same age and would give Charlie a roof and decent tucker. And, as Charlie pointed out, if it all went crook, he could still join us.

We all travelled to Townsville together and met his employer. We discussed Charlie's work and what he would earn and learn and were reassured by the openness and jollity of Ted and his lovely wife. We left knowing it was a trustworthy and happy home full of laughter. There were no tears or waving hands, we boarded the boat for Brisbane and Charlie simply said, 'You look after each other, right?' Before turning his back and walking off, hands in pockets, whistling.

24.
Brisbane. Queensland
Friday, May 26th, 1883

Two laughing men left the gentlemen's lounge chased by wraiths of tobacco smoke clinging to their retreating forms, raucous baritone laughter from within was subdued as someone pulled the door closed.

'This way,'

An animated Theresa took my hand and tugged me along the busy corridor. I would have liked a slower progress through this wonderland, taking time to admire the playbills on the walls interspersed with sputtering gas lights, but she was insistent. I followed, clutching her hand tighter as we moved closer to open double doors from behind which came the sound of a band.

'We'll miss the start, come on!' It was her childhood again with every moment an undiscovered land.

The music sounded military; rhythmic, made for marching and to stir the blood, but I was excited, as I have always been, simply by the prospect of enjoying a group of musicians in performance.

The recollection of my first such experience was still vivid. So captivated had we been by the sight of the marching men, resplendent in red coats and bright white helmets that the music had seemed almost a secondary consideration. But of course, it was not, it was the great wave upon which the whole vessel had sailed through the centre of town. We had been entranced by the formation marching, the glittering instruments and the thudding of the bass drum played by the tall mutton-chopped man with a leopard skin over his uniform.

We had followed the parade as far as we were allowed; laughing as young local boys swung their arms and shouldered sticks cut from hedgerows in the manner of Enfield rifles, marching off to put down the Indian Rebellion and reassert Victoria's power before going home for their dinners.

Sometimes too, bands would play in Pitville Park or Montpellier Gardens, but music under a roof, in a more formal setting, had always been beyond our means. If I were to discount the occasional fiddlers or concertina players in the Noah's Ark or the Mary Magdalene Church organ, I had never, in all my years, heard musicians playing indoors.

We could not see much of the band as they were in a pit, but the sound filled the theatre, the deep notes of the tuba reminiscent of the imagined call of one of Robin Berry's ancient giants who he claimed walked the earth before the time of man. We could have sat in a box, affording us a better view, but Theresa said she wanted to experience the show from the point of view of the average theatregoer in terms of comfort, visibility and general ambience.

'If we're to invest in this enterprise, I want to get a good idea of what the customers get for their money,' she shouted over the increasing cacophony as more and more filed into to find their seats.

It was what she now did. She invested. First, she had invested in a gold expedition to the Palmer River on behalf of a mission station in Laura which had repaid her outlay many times over. She now owned a small guest house where she also lived. But what she really enthused about was the place we now found ourselves - Brisbane's Bay Theatre and their resident troup of actors, The Warrigal Players.

The main lamps in the auditorium were turned down low, making those illuminating the stage appear all the brighter. The Radetzky March, according to the programme, played through a curtain of smoke and a group of actors in the uniforms of British soldiers from a century before ran onstage, adopted crouching positions, rifles at the ready, their shouts of command replacing the music. The drama had begun.

The only previous time I had been to a theatrical performance was to watch As You Like It by Shakespeare in Pittville Park on a warm Cheltenham evening in the summer of 1861. I had been given a Wednesday off by Mr Wells for having worked the previous Sunday and had accompanied Robin Berry and his family.

We had sat on rugs between the trees although some had brought chairs. I remember laughing a lot although at what I wasn't sure. Most of the speeches I did not understand, I couldn't decide whether people were laughing at the wit of the writer or the fact that they all found it as confusing as I did. But there were pastries and raspberry cordial and at the end the cast all did a jig.

But 'All the world's a stage' returned to me as, from somewhere in the wings, came the sound of distant cannon and the shouts of the wounded while a snare

300

drummer in the pit played a subdued drill underlining the nature of the action.

'Well?'

We walked along the riverside promenade, a winter breeze - not angry but argumentative, blew the scent of the ocean through our clothes and hair driving out the tobacco smoke and the last of the paint, polish and perspiration of the theatre. A policeman standing in the doorway of the haberdashers gave us a smile as we passed.

'Well, I enjoyed it.' I replied to her prompt.

'Will we invest in them then?'

I was still surprised at being consulted. Theresa had made it clear on our way from Charters Towers to Brisbane two weeks or so ago that as far as she was concerned, we were now... wife and wife, and that all we decided, we decided together.

However, despite my little flower business making enough to feed Charlie and I for the last seven years, I readily admit that when it came to finance and investment, I didn't know a duck from a donkey's backside - as Grandfather would have had it! However, it was clear Theresa was captivated by the world of theatre and for that reason I suggested a hard-headed approach. I had once witnessed Enoch buying a saddle and the first thing you have to do is convince the seller that you don't really want it.

'Perhaps you should tell them you'll seriously consider it, but you want your bank manager to look over the books and then ask for a plan of how they see the next five years going if you invest.'

She looked at me in the deepening evening, smiling, a stray wisp of wild copper dancing across her brow; she kissed the end of my nose.

'I'm glad I've got you to look after me now, so I am,' she squeezed my hand, leaving me to decide whether to take her response at face value or to read a layer of gentle retort into it.

'Full pockets, empty heart - and for all of my short life it had been the other way around. It was like I was in a permanent daze, neither knowing nor caring what was what. Sure, if someone had come up and said, "Give me all your gold!", I probably would have, I just didn't want to look ahead.'

It was the morning after my first experience of indoor theatre, I let the music of her lovely contralto flow over me as I sat back in a beautiful cream ceramic bathtub with a pattern of weaved pink cherry blossom around the edge, revelling in the softness and warmth of bubbles and scent. It was certainly a step up from the tin tub of a few weeks ago and several steps up from the second-hand Belfast sink with the crack in it that had sat under grey skies in the muddy vegetable patch of the Bullingham's Cottage.

She was combing out my wet hair and began humming an unfamiliar tune. There was a melancholy in Theresa that had not been there in our first flush, it was no match for her exuberance, but remained an outer sign that, in our years apart, her sky had not always been blue. I gently took her hand in mine.

'I… you do know, don't you, with absolute certainty, that I have no interest in money, yours or anyone's. I have a shambly old house and we make enough to…'

Her green eyes suddenly filled with anxiety, 'Ellie… oh Ellie, I never thought for a single second you would… listen… no, listen to me, if it was money you were after, then first thing tomorrow, I'd march you to the bank, take out every single penny plus the deeds to everything I own and give it all to you because if it wasn't me you wanted - then everything else I have wouldn't be worth a snapped whistle.'

She stroked my cheek, 'I know you better than that, you loved a kitchen girl with two pairs of drawers to her name - one pair on and the other on the washing line, remember?'

I smiled and squeezed her hand.

We were both now determined that wherever the future road led, we would travel it together, but from where should it begin? I had told Gordon McLeish I would be away for a month or two and said little more. Experience has taught me, as I suspect it teaches everyone, that nothing brings tears more readily to the eyes than the smoke from burning bridges.

The Kelly Marine Guest House is a bright and cheerful building close to the corner of Queen Street and Albert Street with sea-green pillars supporting a white painted verandah. There are eight bedrooms, a dining room and lounge, a cold cellar and some land to the rear enclosed by the buildings and grounds of the neighbours.

Staff at the Kelly Marine are happy and irreverent, sharing banter and jokes with their boss which told me all I needed to know about Theresa the businesswoman.

It was not, she said, a great money-making enterprise, but it 'paid its way' and kept a roof above us and four people in employment. In addition to her commercial activities, Theresa also contributed food and medicine supplies to Moreton Bay Quarantine Station, supported a local treatment centre for alcoholics run by Catholic Church and funded a school for aboriginal children near Enoggera.

'Shall we go riding? Our baker has couple of horses he is happy to lend to me.'

It was the first time I had enjoyed two baths in a week since I fell over in the stables in Andoversford long, long ago. Just soaking unhurriedly in warm water was such a luxury. I was still becoming familiar with the place and the surroundings and after so long inland at Charters Towers, it was a joy to smell the ocean and wake to the cries of great gulls on the morning breeze.

'I can't ride,' I confessed, 'I mean, I can sit on a horse and make it go forwards in a walk or a trot, but I must admit I would have difficulty getting it to change direction or go any faster.'

She laughed, 'Sure you'd be surprised how quick you'll pick it up; horses know how experienced their riders are and the kind ones will compensate for it. Both these handsome boys are very kind, I promise you'll be safe - and you won't fall off.'

She unfolded a large towel and rolled up the sleeves of her dress, sitting, watching me. I smiled at her lazily, 'I've never seen you ride a horse; you took your turn on Bucephalus on the trail but even that was rare and only when Enoch or I held the reins.'

'Ah - that was then, I've learned from an expert since. My cousin was one of the best horsemen Australia has ever seen. Of course, that's not what he was famous for, but even so, he could have made a horse talk.'

She had surprised me.

'So, you found your long-lost relations on this side of the world?'

Theresa chuckled, 'That was my reason for coming over here, I must have told you... or perhaps I didn't. With Mother gone to the angels, Father lost in the mountains - and also in the bottle - and my big sister Clare married off to a man whose first loves would always be Guinness and gunpowder, I thought I'd come out and track down the only family I had left - apart from Uncle John who doesn't say much; oh... and my wee brother Edward who likes kites.

'I had a rough idea of where they were thanks to Uncle John back home, so I headed to Victoria and found a friend of a relative who got word to my Auntie, and we had a bit of a get-together. My cousin and his clan made a big fuss of me, talking about his parents and mine and Caishel and the old country he had never seen for himself and all the deeds he had done and was aiming to do.'

'I spent a while there and he taught me to ride - and to shoot, and when one of his larrikins got a bit too familiar, he taught me where to kick him.' She stood, 'Right... out of there with you, before the water gets cold!'

I smiled and stood reluctantly, 'It never gets cold here - when were you last cold?'

305

'I've seen snow here,' she draped the towel over my shoulders, '… down Victoria way, in the hills; snow and frosty mornings.'

I stepped out of the bath, 'Perhaps we can go sometime, in the winter? I haven't seen snow for so long - we could visit your cousin.'

She put her hands on my shoulders and turned me to face her, a whimsical smile, a shake of the head. 'Do you not read the papers? They hung him!'

In truth, I had never read newspapers papers regularly apart from the local ones back home. As a result, a lot of what was shaping the globe and the land I lived in had gone unnoticed. My family had been my world, my news had been that which touched our lives.

Theresa, in contrast, was well abreast of current affairs and had some strong views about what was right and what was not. She and Enoch would have been kindred spirits when it came to injustice, its causes and remedies.

She was a supporter of the Australian Labour Party which had just branched out into Queensland, a local group met at the Kelly Marine. She once had a sugar cane planter called Aladice thrown out of the Hotel because he was a 'Blackbirder' said to ill-treat his bonded workers, who were in many cases no more than slaves, tricked and coerced from their homes in the South Sea Islands to work under the whip in plantations. She had laughed as she told me of their confrontation.

'Do you know who I am?' He had puffed himself up, towering over Theresa who is only a few inches taller than me.

'I know what you are,' she had replied before waving to the fearsome Leo Brannigan, the ex-pugilist porter who can allegedly bend six-inch nails. The planter was ejected into the street by collar and belt to a round applause from all who witnessed it. He complained to a passing policeman only to be told in the broadest of brogues that if he couldn't behave himself in hotels, he should stay out of them.

Mr Trewellard, Theresa's bank manager, had light brown, intelligent eyes and the most magnificent white moustache which appeared to contain all the hair that had once been on his head. He also had a Cornish accent that would not have been out of place on the poop deck of a pirate ship. I could not help but call to mind Long John Silver and was a little disappointed when he rose from his seat and walked around the desk to greet us on two perfectly good legs.

His office too could easily have been a captain's cabin with its wood panelled walls, a painting depicting a sea battle and an ornamental anchor coiled with stout white rope. He frowned into the bowl of his pipe as he filled it, nodding occasionally, while Theresa outlined her desire to invest in the Warrigal Players theatre group. Finally, between puffs, he offered his verdict.

'Yes, well as a gift, or a donation if you will, your idea would be most welcome to them, I am sure; but as an investment... I would be failing in my duty if I did not advise you against it. I have it on good authority from a theatrical friend of mine - well, of my good lady's anyway - that there is only one way to make a small fortune out of the world of theatre - and that is to invest a larger fortune.'

Theresa looked crestfallen; I patted her hand. She had introduced me as 'The most dear and beloved person in my life,' which, given her fondness for superlatives, retained enough ambiguity to have drawn an affectionate nod from the banker and a smile that said, 'Ah the fairer sex - bless them.'

'Of course, it's your money, but... well, if you'll permit me to sound paternal for a moment, you are a young woman with decades ahead of you and one day you might wish to marry.' Theresa coughed, gave me the briefest of glances before smiling sweetly across the desk.

'Hmm... married, yes,' The buccaneer voice continued, unconsciously taking its rhythm from the deep tock of a wall clock with a plate-sized face. 'Now, if it's an investment opportunity you are seeking, you have come at the most propitious moment...'

The Rope Walk Inn has two entrances, both leading into the same big tap room, it is set down a narrow side street which makes the bar appear all the larger when you pass through the door.

Theresa and I entered to a distinct lull in the level of conversation; voices dropped, eyes peered at us from below caps pulled down over foreheads, a pall of smoke clung to the ceiling, reluctant to leave despite the open doors. I would have been quite happy to have turned and left. There was a presence here, a hostility; we were not welcome despite an invitation. The Noah's Ark had hosted its own 'characters' but there the threat was safely within the genie's lamp - don't rub them up the wrong way and you would remain unharmed. But here, the menace was palpable, these people were, as we discovered, soldiers guarding the hive - and their Queen.

A man approached and introduced himself as Conway.

'Kelly sisters?'

'Kellys yes, sisters no.' Theresa returned his curtness.

It would be impossible to look at Conway and not think of a rat. His hair, black and oiled, was swept back behind small but fleshy ears, his nose twitched as he talked and he had little black eyes, restless and wary. When he looked at you it was easy to imagine several motivations, and none of them wholesome.

He shrugged, 'Follow me' and headed for the corner of the huge room to a door set into the wall which he struck in a clearly coded knock. It opened and we followed him into the shadows at the base of a staircase, aware a man behind us was closing and locking the door. Up the narrow stairs we went as I mentally compared the brightness and welcome of the Kelly Marine to what we saw here.

'Watch this stair, it's not there,' Conway stated, pointing down to a gap through which a cellar storeroom was visible. At the top we passed along a landing to yet another locked door where Conway rapped and waited.

The first word that came to mind as we passed into the room beyond was feral. It might once have been a pleasant first floor parlour but now, faded furniture and a threadbare carpet, disconcerting, cobwebbed corners and wallpaper spotted like the hands of a crone suggested years if not decades of neglect. A grimy window garbed in sad and ragged drapes added to the gloom.

On a deep green leather Chesterfield chair, with the window at her back and a small table at her side containing a bottle and glass, sat an old woman who at first glance looked as threadbare and neglected as the room itself until one noticed fingers and wrists glittering with gold and a red walking cane embossed with silver stars along its length. She appeared thin and sparse, but with an alacritous and vital sense of movement suggesting a fitness creditable for her apparent age. Either side of the woman, young, big men, clearly brothers if not identical twins, stood like royal footmen. They were bowler-hatted and almost identically dressed, bringing to mind an oversized cruet set.

The tip of the cane lifted and pointed at Theresa who, unlike me, had paid little attention to her surroundings, concentrating instead on the room's inhabitants. The old woman's voice was piano soft and yet penetrating; you felt that even in a cathedral it would reach every corner. Each word was brought forth with a clear Irish lilt as if it were delicate linen being lifted from a drawer. It was a voice that reminded me of Enoch's mother.

'Was he as handsome as they say, your cousin? Could he shoot and ride like they claimed he could?"

'He was - and he could,' Theresa, blank-faced, looked around the room now, her reaction to the surroundings giving nothing away.

The old woman smiled, 'Can I offer you some tea, or would you care for something stronger to remind you of home? Oh, and please, ladies, take a seat. I'm sorry, I was only expecting one of you.'

She turned to the man on her right, *'Cathaoir eile'*.

He left and I sat on the plain wooden chair at Theresa's insistence as the man returned with a second chair for her.

'Tea would be fine; I don't touch alcohol.' It was not meant to be judgemental or an admonishment, but the old woman raised an eyebrow, nonetheless.

'Well, I suppose that's wise for a serious businesswoman... and it's a serious business we're engaged in Miss Kelly.'

'Mrs.' Theresa's smile held no warmth.

'My goodness, I am getting it all wrong with you, aren't I? Anyway, I take it Edgar Trewellard has briefed you on what I do and what I am planning to do?'

'He has.'

Theresa was not her conversational, gregarious self. Mr Trewellard had painted a promising picture to us of the fortunes to be made in the logging and the timber trade - Red Gold, as those who harvested this bounty of nature liked to call it. He had told of an investment opportunity with another of his customers where returns were potentially quite substantial and then, with a hint of caution, he had told us who the other customer was.

The old woman leaned forward, her face falling into a shaft of sunlight reflecting from a yellowing mirror, making it clear for the first time. Eyes as black as those of a shark and teeth, when she smiled, yellow, worn and lupine. I felt that had she been Red Riding Hood's grandmother, the Big Bad Wolf would not have had so easy a time if it.

'I am Gráinne Clancy, these are my sons, Fiach and Fergal, and you are Theresa Kelly, yes?'

She reached out a hand, Theresa rose from her chair and stepped across the gap to take it.

'Let me guess, from the few words you've graced us with so far, Limerick? Tipperary?'

Theresa gave her one more word, 'Caiseal'.

Gráinne nodded, 'Caiseal, yes, never been there. I'm from Drogheda and my husband, may the Devil forever pile coals upon him, brought me out here forty years past. Well, the truth is, I brought myself out here of my own free will, following after himself who came out here much against his wishes and, on rare and silent mornings, I sometimes remember what foolish love felt like. She reached out an arm to me.

'And you my dear?'

'Ellen... Ellen Kelly.' I rose and took the hand, surprised at its chill despite the warmth of the room.

I sat and her eyes went from one of us to the other and back again. I awaited the usual question, but it was not forthcoming. She raised a sceptical eyebrow before taking a sheet of paper from the table and unfolding it.

'Let me read to you from a letter penned not by myself, although I fully endorse its content...

"To the legislators of our State. Travel over the whole wide surface of Australia, and everywhere you will behold the handiwork of the bush worker in house, shed, stockyard and mine.

"The Australian may live in a wooden house, in a wooden town, walk on a wood paved street, travel in a wooden carriage over wooden sleepers and wooden bridges; ship his goods from wooden wharves, shear, refine and manufacture in wooden sheds, enclose his land in wooden fences, and look forward to making his exit in

312

a wooden coffin, and yet remain blind to the tremendous significance of it all because he has not read it in print. The man of letters ignores the man of timber. Prose and verse know him not."

'Now then, *Cailín*, it's your investment I'm after, not your soul - so what is it that you have heard, or been told about me that makes you so wary, eh?'

'It is said - and with some justification, she's the most dangerous woman in Queensland,' Theresa was frowning in concentration as she studied once again the proposal set out by Mr Trewellard by which we would become partners in a new enterprise, The Prior Creek Timber Company, whose activities would be in the Atherton Tableland far to the north.

It was a relief to be back in the Kelly Marine, in the light and the fresh colours, rather like leaving a cold church on a warm morning and seeing flowers dancing among the graves; but it was clear our visit to Gráinne Clancy had unsettled Theresa.

'Well, I thought you conducted yourself very well.'

I meant it but, quite out of nature for my Shamrock, she had done so from behind a barricade. Enoch had been able to weigh up another soul within a minute of meeting them and it seemed Theresa was the same. Nor did I doubt her judgement. Gráinne Clancy carried the same aura of menace as Adder Drew, but I doubted that, unlike Adder, a soft centre lay beneath a hard shell.

It had turned very warm for a spring evening, we had agreed to dine in our room, windows open to the eastward breeze off the river which also carried the scent of livestock from one of the market wharves. Theresa frowned as she read the partnership proposal.

'I am really not certain about us entering into a partnership with her, even though, according to these figures, we could be looking at quite substantial... good God, it says here that investments in successful timber operations are realising returns of up to... holy saints, we could be looking at making a hundred thousand pounds, well... half of that anyway. I think we should sign - but we should keep our eyes and ears open and watch we don't step on any tails - what do you think Country Mouse?'

On a good day of wood collecting in Charters Towers, I earned up to five shillings and here we were talking in fortunes for harvesting wood on an enormous scale. This was the trade upon which everything else rested, the industry set to build the foundations of Queensland. And it was also the industry that had cost my husband his life.

'It would make a lot of other things possible.'

I felt she had already made up her mind, but I also knew she would abandon it if I were to say I had concerns. And I did have concerns. Even making allowances for the fact that that this was not England, and it took a special breed to succeed here, both Theresa and I came from the ranks of the exploited. Having felt the whip, could we ever be happy cracking it? The Kelly Marine, Albie's Haulage Yard and the Noah's Ark had all shown me it was possible to run an operation based on respect and compassion. I feared these attributes did not rank highly on Gráinne Clancy's list of priorities.

We signed the partnership agreement in Mr Trewellard's bank, and The Prior Creek Timber Company came into existence on Thursday, June 29th, 1883 with five directors; Miss Theresa Kelly and Mrs Ellen Johnsey - because the State of Queensland would not have recognised our union, Mrs Gráinne Clancy (Managing), Mr Fiach Clancy, her eldest twin son by twenty minutes and Mr Fergal Clancy.

Within weeks a small army of labourers and loggers, cooks and caterers, smiths and surveyors would descend on Prior Creek in the Atherton Tableland where those who called it home saw nothing in the wide and empty sky to indicate an approaching storm.

That night, in the half-asleep world where the people of dreamland dance to the music of the awakened, I thought of Grandfather William and of his simple life. He had seen for himself on the battlefields of Europe the depths to which humanity could sink and the evil they could do.

I also called to mind the cold, painful, empty-bellied and brutishly short lives of the wraiths in the Rookery Slums, jaws moving in their sleep as they dreamed of a next meal that would come from God knows where, while at the same time fat judges threw the broken and ragged into cold stone boxes before dining on venison and Severn salmon.

'There is nothing either good or bad but thinking makes it so.'

Mrs Brook had quoted to us from Shakespeare but qualified it by stating the laws of the land were there for good reason. I had thought about this and by the time I arrived home from school I had decided she was only half right. The laws were there for a reason, certainly - but whether it was a good reason and whether they were applied equally to all was another matter. I had asked Grandfather and he had told me the only purpose of courts and constabulary was to protect the rich from the poor, and then he had said something which came unbidden to mind as I watched my beautiful Shamrock lying next to me, crowned with fire, breathing gently, eyes closed...

'Everybody have got a right to be happy, if you be kind and harm no one, then you are a good soul.'

Dawn was breaking to the chorus of great gulls, clattering hooves and the rumbling of cartwheels. A Pacific breeze tossed the lace curtains and rattled the bamboo room divider decorated with the image of a south sea island girl.

I had not soiled my hands in six weeks, they were already softening. To the north was my little world of ramshackle walls and ill-fitting doors where I had made patches of flowers grow in a sea of red dust. This morning, like all the others, Gordon would be tending the plants and feeding the chooks - and waiting for news from me about my return.

Over the seven years of my separation from Theresa, the white heat had cooled but a small candle remained, timid, outshone by my feelings for Enoch and our mutual battles - first for prosperity, then simply for survival. It is true to say that in the year following his death I bitterly regretted ever agreeing to cross the world with him. We might have struggled, but there would have been four of us, and likely others, and with our families at our sides we would have prevailed.

Even after I had reconciled myself to my lot, a perpetual stranger in a strange land, I knew that should the opportunity have presented itself, I would have gone home… home, to sweet Gloucestershire with its grey skies and rain, cold winters and hee-haws. And I would have carried inside me that little candle as a memento of someone who, uninvited, had lit a fire in me, terrifying and all-consuming.

Then I would have trudged to Cheltenham Market, shopping basket and children in tow, making my few pennies work as hard as they could. I would have scrubbed here and waited on tables there, laundered and ironed to keep our bellies full.

And in the rain battered nights, the candle inside would have flickered like a magic lantern showing images of a lost Kingdom of the Sun, red dirt… and her hair dancing in a hot wind…holding me tight against the majesty of the storm, the scent of her, and her lips on mine… thousands of miles away.

I leaned forward and kissed her gently on the forehead, her eyes half-opened.

'I love you,' I said, and she hugged me close and sighed.

25.
Enoggera, Queensland
Monday, June 26th, 1883

There was surprisingly little smoke from the big wood fire. We sat, cross-legged in vests and bloomers while a man in nothing but a pair of baggy grey shorts who could have been anything from fifty to a hundred judging by his one blue eye and one brown, wild grey hair and straggly beard, poked the logs with a long stick while chanting in a low monotone.

I understood not a word but the rhythm, the rising and falling, presumably blessings and prayers, seemed comfortable in their surroundings having been wedded to this place for thousands of years.

A young woman, a teacher in the school Theresa supported, had knelt before us, squinting in the twilight as she finger painted our faces with white pigment. Theresa and I smiled at each other, her face decorated with a pattern as old as this country itself and mine surely the same.

The old man rose and walked around the fire to us. Taking my hand and Theresa's, he bound them together loosely with a strip of hide before placing his hands, one on her head and the other on mine; the chanting grew louder.

He then waved a burning stick beneath our noses and above our heads before clapping his hands together several times, simultaneously shouting the same sound. The young teacher then approached again, bidding us to stand and bow to the old man who also rose, took the strip of hide from our wrists, bowed back and handed each of us a small human shaped wooden figure before turning and walking away.

'That's it,' the young woman smiled, 'Your two spirits are joined not only in this life but beyond it. You will dream the same dream for all of time.'

'Did you believe it?'

The carriage was taking us back to our tiny guest house where we planned to spend the night before returning to Brisbane. We had washed away our ceremonial paint - although Theresa had missed a spot on her eyebrow which I wiped off with the corner of my handkerchief. She smiled out at the gathering dusk as I turned the tactile wooden doll over and over.

'Makes as much sense as any other religion,' she replied, 'More than a lot of them. The church I was born into would not have blessed us and probably neither would yours. But these people have no holy books, they see the natural world and understand it in ways we've forgotten. They see love for what it really is - a wind that doesn't ask which way it should blow.'

She turned my face to hers, eyes twinkling, emeralds against the orange swansong of a memorable day, 'So… should I be Theresa Johnsey, or will you be Ellie Kelly?'

319

We laughed together, agreeing that as far as the rest of the absurd world was concerned, we would play the parts we had always played, but in the true spirit of this ancient and uncomplicated world, we were now new people with no further need of masks.

'Good Lord!' Theresa declared, 'I can't believe I'm finally a married woman at twenty-eight... twenty-eight! Sure, I'll soon have one of those warty witches' long noses and all my teeth will be gone.'

'You're just a slip of a girl, 'I laughed, 'Here's me thirty-five next time around.'

She smiled, took my hand and squeezed it.

'Ellie Kelly... mine forever.'

Brisbane laughs in the mornings. Cheltenham coughs, but Brisbane laughs. The sun had barely risen on what passed for a winter's day and already a pair of men had chosen the walkway directly outside the Kelly Marine to stop and have a chinwag and a good chuckle. I missed most of the conversation but the phrase, 'I wouldn't bloody put it past him!' set them both off again. I was tempted to stick my head out of the window and tell them to bugger off down the road, but they were only guilty of being happy and careless.

Theresa had skirted over the aftermath of our parting in Oaky Creek, but I understood that her pain had been the equal to mine - surpassing it in all probability, because I had left with Enoch and Charlie.

She poured me another cup of tea in a pretty cup and saucer with a pattern of bluebells. Frowning, she must have felt the time was right to fill in the gaps in my knowledge of her.

'Let me tell you about Laura, the little place on the river of the same name. I arrived there early September, I was carried into the mission hospital with typhus and I didn't leave there until January - and I remember clearly the weak and wobbly walk to the river on my first day out.

'I went before dawn, before the heat and the buzzing, biting clouds. I splashed my face with the cool, welcoming water, soaking and flattening my short-ragged hair. I cut it all off after you left and travelled as a boy for safety. I looked at my reflection in the water and straight away wished I hadn't. What a scarecrow I was - thin as a stick, dull-eyed and dead-skinned, ravaged by fever, wrung out and left so weak it had taken me more than three months of building my strength to walk just the half mile.

'I recalled little of the weeks that had passed - except talking to my father, who I found inexplicably sat by the side of my bed in the hospital ward of the Mission - the St Vincent Catholic Mission it was. He told me how he had walked to Cork City and then, because the sea is really shallow if you know where the underwater paths are, he carried on walking all the way to Queensland to find me. He said Mother was around somewhere, but he couldn't say exactly where and that she was probably asleep. He also said I was not to worry, that it wasn't yet time for me to join them and that there was much for me to do here and that I would one day be strong and happy again.

'Father Marlec, by contrast, told me if I wanted to survive, I would have to eat - even when my stomach revolted at the thought; and I would need time to regain my strength because typhus is a bitter enemy when it has a death grip, and by resting, it is possible to fool it into assuming victory and letting go. And thirdly, I had to pray. He taught me The Lord's Prayer in French and I taught him the same in Irish and we laughed together at our efforts.

'He never seemed to rest from the time he rose at dawn to sunset and beyond. He must have been well over six feet, but so skeletal he must have scarcely weighed more than me - the old me... before the fever came. He moved like a swaying tree, slow and graceful; with black eyes that remained sad even when he smiled, as if the weight of all the sin in that hellish place was on his shoulders. He said he was forty when I asked, but he looked older with black hair greying at the temples and as in need of the attention of a good hairdresser as my own.

When it became clear I was not going to die, the darkness returned. Yes, I was going to live, but it would be in a cold, lonely, impersonal world without my Ellen...'

I felt my eyes fill and reached for a handkerchief from my sleeve; I had not heard the whole story of Laura and agonised at what she must have endured while I had been busy making a home for Enoch, Charlie and myself in booming Charters Towers.

'It's alright, my love,' Theresa's eyes had come out in sympathy and we were both dabbing away as Sara arrived and took our orders. She looked from one of us to the other, 'You alright Mrs Kellys?'

We both smiled and nodded; reassured, Sara headed for the kitchen.

'It was the strangest thing, the delirium, vivid dreams. You came to me, sometimes in the form of a light brown rabbit with sapphire eyes and other times as yourself, but frozen, naked and shivering. I would reach for you, to thaw you with my burning body, but when I held you, you would melt away until only tears were left.

'I had gold; hundreds of pounds locked in a small safe hidden beneath a stone slab under the bed of Father Marlec. He had not asked for a penny towards my keep or for the ministrations of a medically qualified nun, Sister Philomena - she spoke only in one-word answers but had the most expressive face to make up for it. Even so, I knew I owed his Mission a debt that gratitude alone would not pay and so I gave him most of my gold - which he had not asked for - to finance an expedition by the Mission, led by an experienced guide, to see if, with God's help, they could strike payload for themselves. He cried when I gave it to him, bless him. I remember him saying... forgive the accent, 'If we were to unearth a fortune, we could establish schools and a proper hospital in these parts! Mon Dieu Therése - if St Vincent intercedes and The Gracious Lord approves of our enterprise, I will reward you twentyfold for this.'

'Anyhow, as I got my strength back, I worked in the hospital alongside Sister Philomena and Angelique - a native nurse converted to the faith - and we treated everything from gunshot wounds, fevers and rashes to septic scratches and spider bites on the magairlí - which one poor man suffered on three separate occasions.

'A man called Burrowes showed me his impressive haul of gold and proposed on the spot, offering to take me to Derbyshire in England where I would live in a grand house with servants and greyhounds. I don't

323

suppose laughter was what he expected. He left the settlement the same afternoon taking his gold with him.

'I remember looking at myself in the mirror and I could not for the life of me see a reason for Burrowes to have made such a proposal. The hair was growing again but it was like an orange besom. I looked like my Mother. My face was gaunt, cheekboned and hollow; teeth a pale yellow for want of attention; only my eyes, emeralds against the ashes of a dead fire, were left of the old me.

'I had this faded green dress, given to me by the Mission, it hung on me like the ragged mast of a castaway's raft, stopping just short of skinny ankles and my feet in flat brown shoes.

'I don't recall it, but I'm told that when I stumbled down the trail and collapsed on the Mission steps, Father Marlec himself carried me in and undressed me, getting quite a shock on discovering I was not the feller he had imagined. He had hastily called in Sister Philomena and rushed out to care for Kenny the donkey - who had fared better than me at the Mission - he found himself a girlfriend called Maud who belonged to the storekeeper's daughter, Hilda, a pretty wee thing a year or so younger than me who smiled a lot and spoke to both animals in Dutch.

'But I slowly began to fill out again as my appetite returned, I chewed liquorice root until my teeth were white, and Angelique washed my hair every other day with soap and bay rum. A great bruiser of a man called Mulligan with the biggest haul of gold I had ever seen offered me a wedding ring and a grand home in County Meath, but I declined as he had hard eyes and the hairiest arse I had ever seen on a human being - upon which I had to lance a boil!

'I had decided to go back to Brisbane where there was at least an illusion of familiarity. Sickness and strangers had lit in me an urge to commune with the past before I could once again face the future; although I knew that in some form or other you were always going to be with me, a ghost of what should have been.

'I had enough for passage, new clothes and the renting of rooms. I would be a burden on no one and might consider some modest business enterprise to sustain me while I waited for what Father Marlec assured me would surely come - a reason for being and a love that lay waiting.

'And then the expedition returned, and all our plans were turned on their heads. Father Marlec prayed solidly for twenty-four hours, giving thanks not only for the safe return of his parishioners but for the bounty they brought with them.

'It was a Sunday of relentless rain that pummeled the tin roof of the Mission like a brigade of drummers, he called me to his office; he didn't say a word and he pushed this large wooden box with metal corners across the desk to me, eyes full of tears. 'Twentyfold… twentyfold my dear, dear Thérèse.'

She paused to take a sip of her tea, 'So, there we are, I left with an escort for Cooktown. The boat from Cooktown to Brisbane stopped overnight in Townsville, which allowed me to transfer my gold into the safe keeping of the Australian Joint Stock Bank and enjoy a meal on dry land.

'Brisbane brought with it familiarity and torment. I could have paid a visit to Cabbage Tree Creek, walked where you and I walked, caressed the walls of the cottage in which we shared a bed, feeling your arms and hands around my naked body, pulling me to you - and me on fire inside despite my fear of the storm, trying desperately not to get carried away. But I stayed away, afraid of the pain.

'The harbour looked busier than ever, ambitious, full of boats from all over the world. I could have spent a few days sightseeing and then headed for California or Ireland or even London. I could have travelled to England a wealthy woman, bought a grand house in Cheltenham and...watched you pass by, as far away as if I had stayed in Queensland, and it would have torn my heart like communion bread - The Body of the Saviour.

'I went into a church to pray, I don't know why, perhaps because I had seen a kindness in Father Marlec I had never encountered in Ireland. I knelt and said, "Dear Mother of God who made me what I am, why fill me with music then forbid me to sing?"

'When I finally returned here, Brisbane felt cooler; it was not winter cool, not Tipperary cool, but neither was the air full of steam and it had a growing sense of permanence - a vast sprawl, as if someone had built Dublin or Liverpool in a hurry. Somewhere among the maze of bricks that grew by the day were people who had walked the streets of Caishel and though we may never have met, we would look at the world through the same eyes, using the same yardsticks, grafting this belligerent land on to the broken-hearted one that shaped us.

'And I determined to make a real go of it. I bought this place as a going concern. It was run down but I could afford renovations and I kept Mrs Shepherd the cook on and… and well here we are - and the important thing - the very important thing, is that none of this would have come about if you hadn't made me a shareholder in your little prospecting enterprise. You deserve to share all this Ellie Kelly, and please say you will and never worry about it again. You are my whole world and everything I have is yours.

'Father Marlec had heard my confession as I lay incapable of even raising my head from a sweat-soaked pillow. I had told him of my love for you and he had said all love was good love, but then I had told him of our kisses and how it had made me feel. I asked him if I was going to Hell and he had responded, "There is no love in Hell Therése, forbidden or otherwise."

I shook my head, 'Do you realise how much I adore you?' I squeezed her hand. She smiled back:

'My Country Mouse… my Ellie…'

26.
Brisbane, Queensland
Sunday, August 19th, 1883

'Deep regret stop Mother dead stop all others well, letter following stop'.

I bought a black dress for the occasion and we sat in a church at eight o' clock on a stuffy spring evening having paid the priest and an organist to remain behind after evensong. Simultaneously, at eleven o' clock in the morning in autumnal Elmstone Hardwicke, my family would be congregating in Mary Magdalene's Church to say farewell to my dear Mother.

I am a rural girl, a 'Country Mouse' as my beloved calls me, and like my Grandfather and Father before me, I know more than any city dweller about the turning of the seasons and the impermanence of all we hold dear. As the Bible says, there is a time for everything, and a season for every activity under the heavens: a time to be born and a time to die, a time to plant and a time to uproot, a time to kill and a time to heal, a time to tear down and a time to build, a time to weep and a time to laugh, a time to mourn and a time to dance…

Like any flower or tree, Mother grew, bloomed and withered. And later, in her increasingly shrinking view of

328

the world, she would have turned inward to the only things she would always see clearly - her memories. I prayed I had been among them.

I chose, 'Love Divine All Loves Excelling', a reading from Romans and the Lord's Prayer. Meanwhile, Charlie, eight hundred miles to the north, would be reading some words he had written himself about how even though he did not remember her, she would always be part of him.

I sat with Theresa amid rows of empty pews and prayed there were more people in the cold little church on the green that I had not been in for a decade. I tried to recall faces, voices and felt wounded that so few could be brought to mind. How many of them would remember me? Would my mother's spirit, freed from its broken cage, fly across the world to say farewell? Tonight, as an Englishwoman far from home, I would mourn; tomorrow, as a daughter of Queensland, I would go on - as Mother would surely have wished.

Father's letter was notable not only for the inclusion of a small likeness of a young lady in the uniform of a chambermaid, but for its unaccustomed brevity. I saw Charlie in her face, the eyes were those of someone for whom smiles were frequent visitors, although on this occasion circumspection was taking centre stage.

The picture told me little of my daughter beyond her occupation, but perhaps I asked too much of a mere photograph. Enoch had consistently refused to have his picture taken, insisting all photographs, unlike portraits, were of the dead, a timeless image where no heart was beating, no blood flowed through veins, not even time to formulate a single thought.

Then there was the single sheet of paper where once there had been several. And not even that solitary sheet was filled.

'Dearest Ellen, I hope this letter finds you well. It was pneumonia that saw your Mother off, she had a high fever which broke, I thought she might recover but she was too weak and went in the night. Ann came up from Kempsford for the funeral. Mrs Brooke paid for flowers and they were very nice. Emily and family were present although Esther could not make it from London as one of her children also had a high fever.

'I note in your telegram that you and Charles paid your tributes in churches over there for which I am thankful. I am still able to work although not every day and I am grateful to Sam and Emily for their assistance, one of the children visits every day to see that I am well. I hope that you and your friend Theresa are in good health. It is very cold here, winter has come early, the old master pays me a few pence to walk the fields breaking the ice on the water sinks for the animals, but a few hours later they are frozen again.

'Sarah Ann is a Godsend, she a good worker and nothing is too much trouble for her. She works as a maid in the Queens Hotel but has a day off every week which she spends with me, mending my clothes and cleaning and washing. She is highly thought of there and sometimes brings me pastries or pies which were left over.

'May God bless and keep you dear Ellen.

'Your loving Father.'

And there it was - a brief insight into a world that was no longer mine. With the passing of a decade the bonds, although unbroken, were now tenuous things, cotton that had once been hemp. Father had accepted I would never return, I had seen too many false dawns to make concrete plans, despite Theresa's optimism. As I accepted the passing of my Mother, I also had to concede Gloucestershire was now irretrievably a foreign land.

Despite not wearing the collar of his office, I knew the identity of the man sitting with Theresa in our day room as I returned from the shops. She looked up as I entered, haunted and distant. The man stood, offering a smile clearly tired from swimming upstream to reach his face.

'Ellen, this is Father Marlec.'

I took the offered hand; my curiosity must have been evident. The usually cheerful room of lemon light and sea breeze was leaden, burdened and bleak.

'There's tea on the way,' Theresa said, her voice flat.

I sat, 'It's very nice to meet you Father, Theresa has told me of your kindness while she was ill, and I would like to add my thanks and gratitude for that.'

He smiled sadly again, a knock on the door announced the arrival of refreshments. I had been expecting a quiet hour to write back to Father before lunch.

'Right so, Father, here we are, two out of the four directors of Prior Creek Timber, now then, tell us what you have to say.'

He sat again and told us why he had travelled almost a thousand miles to speak to Theresa and I face to face, having discovered to his shock the girl he had rescued almost a decade before, and who had been his Mission's benefactor, was one of the owners of the Prior Creek Timber Company.

He told us how they came with axe and saw, bullocks, mules and guns. Some ran from them, ran and ran, away from the land they had always known into the lands of other peoples who did not welcome them and drove them back, back toward the black muzzles. And the invaders cut down trees and people, burning them and all they owned like lightning upon grass. They spread out from the initial wound like a poisoned rash sparing only those who outran their weapons. The less agile, the lame, the old, children, babies... all were slaughtered.

And it was continuing, he told us, even as we sat, sipping tea. The rising smoke and the stink of their campfires, the crack of rifles and shouts and yells are ceaseless. Trees that had stood before the time of any living man are falling, rolling to the river and lying there rotting because they cannot find a way to move them further.

Their labourers, many of them slaves, kidnapped from the South Sea Islands, are treated little better than the indigenous people. Some lie dead and unburied in the shallows of the creeks along with the corpses of natives and pack animals. And still the masters and overseers drive them on.

Father Marlec had tried a number of times to speak with them, with those in charge, only to be laughed at and on one occasion punched to the ground, a gun barrel pushed in his face with a warning to leave and never return.

'I feel I already know by your reaction the answer to this question, but forgive me Therése, I have to hear you say it. Please tell me you knew nothing of this barbarism… this inhumanity, and you, Madame Ellen, tell me you are equally unaware?'

Theresa knelt in front of him and took his hands, as she did with me when she wished to communicate something completely free of ambiguity.

'Father, I swear by all the Saints, by St Patrick, St Denis and by the Holy Mother, I did not know of this, I utterly condemn it and I will do everything in my power to stop it. Neither Ellen or I would ever support any activity that used humans or animals so cruelly.

His smile was as bleak as a winter sun, 'You understand, do you not Therése and Ellen, why I cannot simply go back having achieved nothing?'

We discussed the Prior Creek Timber Company and the implications of what they appeared to be doing well into the night. On the advice of a well-respected and well-liked financier we had invested everything that was not tied up in the Kelly Marine. We would in all probability make a sizeable profit on our investment - but at a tremendous moral cost.

'Every time we spend a shilling on a luxury it would be at the cost of a slave whipped to exhaustion, children murdered, and faithful beasts worked to death. I cannot do it Ellen; I cannot do it.' Theresa screwed up a damp handkerchief in her lap, I sat next to her, pulling her to me. 'Nor can I my Shamrock, nor can I.'

We were faced with two choices. We could meet again with Gráinne Clancy and Father Marlec could appeal to her to join us in condemning the current activities of the company and follow a more humane path - or we could act ourselves, we were directors who between us owned half the company. Appealing to Gráinne's better nature would be trying to paint the wind. I took Theresa's hand.

'We could telegraph the site manager and order an immediate change of operations; we could outline the rules and...'

Theresa cut me off, '...and he would immediately telegraph Gráinne who would order him to ignore us before sending some men around to smash our windows.'

'Come back Therése, come back with me, both of you, they cannot defy you if you stand before them. They would not dare disobey the people who pay them.'

Motivated in part by the opportunity of visiting Charlie in Townsville on the way to the Tablelands, I nodded, 'He's right my Shamrock, perhaps it's the only way to stop this.'

I suddenly felt Enoch in the room as sure and certain as if he had been standing beside my chair. The scent of him, country lane, frost, strong tobacco and damp leather, his warm breath in my hair. I looked up and to the left, fully expecting to see him, or even a fading shadow as he returned to the realm he now called home. Suddenly, I knew two things. I was destined to look directly into the hollow and timeless face of Death, he would raise his scythe, the blade would swish through the air, and my soul would hover between this world and the next.

I also realised with a chill this was an unavoidable fate. The die had been cast and I was once again set for the wild north.

27.
Townsville, Queensland
Tuesday, November 6th,
1883

Had he been walking away from me on a crowded street, in poor light - and even with my less than perfect sight, I would have picked him out in a heartbeat. It was his father's swagger. And as he approached me, tilting back a battered hat, it was his father's smile. No matter he was covered in sawdust and wood shavings and smelling like a horse, he was the handsomest man in Australia! And just to allay any final doubt about his parentage, he lifted me clear off the ground to kiss me.

We had sent a telegram advising Charlie's boss, Ted Parker of our impending visit and he had messaged back insisting there was no need to book a hotel as we could shack up at his place for a couple of nights before heading even further north into the Tableland.

Father Marlec had not travelled with us, he was petitioning the Government in Brisbane and trying to raise support from various religious organisations from the Holy sisters to the Quakers to raise the profile of the people of the Tablelands and their suffering. But we knew where to find them. As directors we had been furnished with maps and schedules and we could afford guides this time.

The boat from Brisbane had encountered unseasonal seas, deep green valleys and boiling whitecaps grabbing our vessel and leading it in a wild gavotte, sending Theresa and a handful of other landlubbers to the rails. We were so relieved to reach port and to be back on the hard-packed dirt of the foreshore with Magnetic Island playing hide and seek through a sulky bank of cloud. But the overcast sky did little to alleviate the heat of late morning, if anything, it seemed to serve as a lid, trapping us inside a pot boiler and even before heading up into logging country I was beginning to dread the trip forward.

By evening, the sensation of perpetual movement had left our stomachs and legs and we looked forward to Eve Parker's 'Special visitor spread' - a treat for the nose even before it made an appearance. We dined in a room overlooking Ted's yard and workshops, a better view, he maintained, than the Pacific Ocean, visible from the front of the house.

'Gone into timber eh? Good move!'

Ted grinned. Charlie took his place across from us and I couldn't help feeling both proud and a little annoyed by the way my son fitted so seamlessly into this family.

'Hat!'

Three voices, Ted's, Theresa's and my own all spoke at once and a laughing Charlie took off his battered work hat and flung it over his shoulder where it landed on a big yellow dog who had wandered hopefully into the dining room enticed, as we all were, by the aroma of roast lamb.

'We certainly hope so, but it's not a happy reason that brings us up here.' Theresa proceeded to give an abridged account of Father Marlec's visit and the reasons for it.

Ted Parker shook his head as a bull shakes off blowflies before lowering it as if getting ready to charge. His almost ever-present smile had gone, and the frown made him a stranger.

The arrival of well filled plates and the order to 'Don't be shy, dig in' was enough to temporarily forestall any attempt at conversation but it wasn't long before Ted offered his viewpoint.

'For me it's a communication problem. They don't understand why we're there and there's no way to explain to them. They can't understand English, Chinese or anything else but their own babble. No doubt the brightest of 'em could be taught but you'd have to catch a few and tame the beggars first. I know there's native police blackfellas trained and clothed and all sorts, but these Tableland blacks are cannibals, wild as bloody wolves they are. Well, I don't need to tell you Mrs J, Charlie tells me you've had the pleasure of meeting some of 'em close up. To be fair, we can't fathom their lingo either, it ain't a real language see - no writing or reading, just pictures.

'Now, if they're killing bullocks and the like - attacking blokes with spears... good God, it's a dangerous enough caper as it is; I mean, take Charlie's old man - your husband God rest his soul... but to have these heathens chucking poison spears at you on top of it, well, it's no wonder the crews are sending 'em packing with a few rounds. They got no choice.'

Theresa made to speak but Ted continued, emphasising his points by tapping the table noisily with the hilt of his fork.

'We had a bloke in here, comes from just out of Town, big tough bloke he is too, Morgan Reid, you know him Charlie, floods of bloody tears - they speared his bullock... Tex?' He looked over at Charlie.

'Max' Charlie offered.

'Aye, that's the bloke, Max... Maxie. Well, Morgan had owned him since he was no more than a calf, six years or more, trained him and cared for him. He could muster him as a lead with Stew Holmfirth's Puck or stick him right back as a poler, didn't matter where you put him, he got on with it. Like a son to Morgan, he was, and then he had to watch him frothing and foaming and bellowing in pain - shot the poor bugger in the end. So, can you honestly blame him for wanting to go up there and send a few of the bloody savages to whatever they have for a hell?'

Theresa paused in her meal - and for Theresa that was noteworthy. This was a woman who would finish her dinner in a burning house or on a sinking ship.

'I cannot bear the thought of any living thing suffering, in pain, and I have no respect for anyone who would inflict suffering on any servant of man. But these people are desperate. They are facing an enemy unlike any they have encountered in all the thousands of years they have lived here. Just imagine the sheer terror they must feel when faced by guns - which can kill from farther away than the best among them can throw a spear. They encounter these strangers with the skin of ghosts and eyes

339

the colour of the morning skies who seem intent on killing them, their women... babies.

'Now I know all about how important timber is, by all the saints, Australia couldn't go forward without it, but what we need to be doing is courting, not ravishing. Take gifts, not death, earn their trust, learn to communicate. It might take six months; it might take a year. But if we show them how they could profit... give them food security, safety from their neighbours...'

Ted gave a mirthless smile which managed to encapsulate his own entrenched opinion and also what he thought of Theresa's perceived naivety.

'I don't think Gráinne understands the concept of patience.' I felt I had to point out the obvious, 'We might be two directors, but we would still not get any proposal to suspend operations through a vote - Three against two,' I added for emphasis. She fell silent, frowning at her plate. Of course, she was right, it could all have been so different. If the Prior Creek Timber Company had embarked on a diplomatic mission, won the natives over with gifts and tokens of friendship; had we sent teachers and ambassadors, skilled negotiators who spoke the universally understood languages of kindness and generosity, we might have made our fortunes without bloodshed.

But bibles whisper while money screams and Gráinne might argue, and with some grounds, that in the scramble to harvest that which takes generations to grow, it's the quick that take the trunks.

My Shamrock's mood was no better the following morning. After breakfast, we saw Charlie off the workshop before heading into town with the intention of seeking a boat to Cairns to haul us and our bags, such as they were, on the first part of our journey to the operations site. We were seasoned prospectors, albeit a decade distant, and had little illusion concerning the kind of country we would be entering or what we could expect from all that crept and slithered, walked, wandered and called it home.

The more I thought about the potential dangers and hardships of our trip, the more I began to wonder if what we were proposing would have any effect at all. If anything, it would be likely to infuriate Gráinne with repercussions I did not want to contemplate. Theresa was a creature of passion, led by her heart - and a wonderfully kind heart it was, but the more I thought about Ted Parker's diatribe, the more I came to believe it was the popular view among all but church groups and a minority of politicians and that two women with little influence or connections would find themselves at best mocked and patronised and at worst...

We had left Leo in charge and told staff at the Kelly Marine we were heading to Townsville to stay with friends. Walking along The Strand towards the harbour we passed a bench, I suddenly let go of her arm and sat, my eyes fixed on the horizon. The low morning sun looked broken; dissected by a cutlass of cloud that made it appear as if the bottom half no longer joined up precisely to the top. And it bled, lemon curds over the deceptive flatness of the Pacific. She sat beside me; I did not have to look to my right to know I was the centre of her attention.

'What?'

It was her pillow voice; I closed my eyes for just a second to thank God she was in my world. Sighing, I put an arm around her.

'You know, don't you, that I find what is going on up there in the wilderness just as distasteful and cruel as you do?'

'Go on...' This was her non-committal voice, flat, expectant.

'What will happen Theresa? When we get there and tell them to stop work, call them all together, me and you, two small women confronting a logging manager, foremen, others, fifty... a hundred working men... working for pay. Telling them to stop and listen to us?'

She sat up, took my hand, squeezed it. 'We are NOT two small women - we are their bosses, directors, investors who pay their wages, and we're not trying to halt the logging, just the killings, the brutality - to the natives and their own poor south sea islanders. They have to listen to us Ellie, we tell them to stop and they have to stop.'

'Yes, yes... but only as long as it takes the manager to telegraph the Clancys who will order him directly to ignore us and get back on with it!' Then the trip will have been for nothing. All that effort for no purpose. I think we should...'

'Yes? What is it that you think we should...?' Theresa had never raised her voice to me in anger - ever! The shock of it must have been apparent. It hurt, it hurt, and it made me uncertain of what I was doing and where I was - and with whom. Whenever there had been a careless word between us and the hurt has been apparent, there had always come an immediate retraction, an eagerness to balm the wound. But her gaze was still there, twin green fires. She had let go of my hand as well.

I floundered, 'Well... I... Let's talk to the local politicians, see what they make of it.'

She stood now, pacing up and down in front of the bench between me and the ocean, hair dancing in a warm zephyr. She stopped and snapped at me.

'What connects policemen, politicians and potatoes?'

I shook my head, this was not turning out the way I had hoped, I had clearly underestimated Theresa's determination to fight her good fight.

'I'll tell ye, shall I? All three can be bought, but there only one you can't live without! You can bet a pound to a plate of pig shit that all the politicians who have any interest at all in the Atherton Tablelands are already in Gráinne's pocket - and so, therefore, is the law. The only... ONLY way to halt this evil is to go there, be there, watching and supervising.'

'For how long my Shamrock? And before you say, "As long as it takes" I don't want us to spend the next five years in the back of beyond, risking life and limb, waiting for a convenient accident to happen - and you know as well as I do that Gráinne would not be above such a game.'

She turned her back to me and looked out to sea. I stood and moved to her side. 'Let's go home, tell the Clancys we want nothing to do with their wickedness.'

Her attention snapped back to me, 'We can't - can we? Because we - you and I, helped to make the wickedness possible with our money. We sent the men and their guns into the forest... we PAID for their guns and bullets. If we walk away now the damage is already done - and it will go on. The Clancys will get richer, invest in other logging sites and the blood and sap will flow ever faster until there are no natives left except the cowed and enslaved. Is that something you can live with Ellen Johnsey? Because may the Divil take me, I can't!'

Johnsey? Where had Kelly gone all of a sudden? I felt my own sap rising now, my family were good and gentle souls who knew a thing or two about hardship and never hurt anyone. How dare she assume she was somehow holier? I tugged her arm, forcing her to spin and face me. It was her turn to look shocked. Charlie always said his Father's angry face was terrifying - but his Mother's wasn't far behind.

'You bloody well listen to me you sanctimonious bugger. Don't you dare tell me I'm cruel in any way or that I don't care. I care about you, about us - and I care about Charlie...'

'Oh yes...' she paced away and returned, '...well you've seen Charlie now, so you've done what you came up here for.'

I don't know which of us was the most shocked then, her by the slap or me by the fact I had actually done it. Mouth open, she raised a hand to her cheek. The fire in her eyes remained, in fact, it focused more, her pupils now pinpoints of fury, amplified by a film of tears. Breathing in, she stood taller, her voice a hiss as if she were the only snake Saint Patrick had failed to banish.

'Well, there ye have it - the English answer to everything. Beat them... shoot them... STARVE them! Holy Mary, I've been a bloody fool.'

I grabbed her arm as she turned to leave, she shook and tugged but the devil himself could not have made me let her go.

'Is that really what you think of me Theresa Kelly?'

My anger faded as quickly as it had risen to be replaced by shame and fear. She squeezed her eyes shut, causing tears to cascade down her cheeks to her chin before opening them again. She sniffed and swallowed.

'Well?' I asked her again, 'Do you really think I'm a devious and cruel person? Do you?'

She shook her head, shoulders shaking with sobs.

'I love you Theresa, and the thought of you falling into danger, being killed by natives or Gráinne's henchmen... Yes, I'm selfish for wanting to keep those I love safe and I'm sorry for putting my feelings ahead of the needs of those poor people somewhere up there. And... and...' Now it was my turn to cry, '... I'm so sorry I hit you, please give me one back if you want, I'll still love you as much.'

She took my arms and pulled them around her waist before putting her own around mine, sniffing loudly in my ear, 'Ellie Kelly...'

'That's better my Shamrock', and then, holding her shoulders at arm's length as she wiped her nose on her sleeve, 'And it ain't the English way - it's the English ruling class way - they don't treat my people no better than they treat yours. The squire with ten thousand pheasants on his land will have a starving man flogged and thrown in jail for taking just one of 'em to feed his family. I ain't nothing like them, and I'm proud of that.'

She stroked my face, just a minute after I had slapped hers, 'I know you're not Country Mouse. It's just...

they're not savages up there, they're innocents, women and wains… we have to try my Ellie, or we'll never sleep peacefully again.

28.
Allumbah Pocket, Queensland
Monday, December 25th, 1883

No Herald Angels sang in the steaming green world of dripping fronds and bleeding cedars. Laughing jackasses, whipbirds, the lowing of bullocks and the coarse yelling of loggers calling out to familiar faces formed the only fanfare for the virgin birth which, until the coming of the European, had been unknown to this wilderness.

There would be no gathering of the faithful, King Wenceslas would look out, but would not see us so far over the horizon and all around, in the deep and brooding forests, were those to whom snow and sleighbells would be inconceivable.

Here was the all-encompassing smell of life, living things, trees, plants, bushes and briars - a language we experience but choose not to understand. Flowers had fed us, Charlie and I, in the lonely years; blooms and brightly coloured leaves tamed and exhibited in pots, thriving still, thanks to the indomitable will to live. Flowers, Mother Nature's laughter - but in these badlands she must surely be crying.

Giants stood here when Shakespeare laboured over his plays. They were now great stumps, each sat in a sorrowful sea of sawdust, chippings and chunks of its butchered body; golden blood seeping into the earth that had sustained and nurtured it while ten thousand storms lashed its limbs. But I reminded myself, I could afford my sentimentality - I was not hungry.

Christmas Day. Theresa and I said a prayer in the small living room of a log cabin in the company of the dwelling's tenant, Mr Kenneth Law, site manager of the Pine Creek Timber Company's Atherton Camp. He was, he had been eager to inform us, a lay preacher who saw all employees as his flock and the indigenous people as 'Stray sheep, staggering blindly through the wilderness bereft of the Saviour's guidance and grace.'

A beard and moustache, unkempt and fully in keeping with the hostility of his surroundings was turning from red to white, conspiring with a bowler hat when outdoors to hide most of a weather-beaten face lit by the bluest of eyes - miniature icebergs refusing to melt despite the all-pervading heat. He did not smile in our presence but when he grimaced, he showed teeth quite separate from one another - like a child's drawing and while the loggers, Europeans and South Sea Islanders, generally worked in thin shirts, Mr Law always appeared in waistcoat and thick jacket, collar and tie, shining shoes and gaiters.

When our small party of horses, pack animals and guides had turned up at his door midday on Christmas Eve he had reacted with surprise, then something approaching annoyance before we introduced ourselves. Aware of our status he adopted grudging deference and curt politeness and this shield had remained since. So far, we had only informed him of our desire to see our investment in operation with our own eyes and had concealed any misgivings we might have about method.

348

The revelation of his religious leanings led us to a short-lived hope that he would be as concerned as us when confronted with Father Marlec's reports of atrocities. But Mr Law's compassion, we discovered, was a hidebound thing, scriptural and intransigent, burnt by heavenly fire into tablets with each commandment subsequently qualified by appending the word 'Unless…'

'I won't bore you ladies with the logistics we face here. The challenges of logging are best left to those whose business it is to overcome them, but I will say that we have a fine team, a fine team indeed.'

His voice, the resonance impaired by a persistent cough and a blocked nose, reminded me of Gordon's. 'Further north, Highlands probably' Theresa had suggested. He was currently using a sleeping bag in his living room, having apologised to Theresa and I over the necessity of us sharing the only bed. All hands were being mustered for a Christmas
Morning service and as upwards of a hundred men gathered in the clearing, on the only level patch of ground we had seen, there was a palpable curiosity over our presence as well as speculative comments, some muted and some brazen. Particularly confusing to some of them was the sight of females embracing practicality and wearing shirts and trousers.

We halted, facing the semi-circle of men. One of their number approached.

'All here boss apart from seven crook and injured.'

The newcomer, short, but as broad as he was tall, took off a battered hat and swept back shaggy black hair before replacing it. A spade beard framed his face where eyes, dark as Enoch's, narrowed as he tucked his thumbs into a wide belt and gave us a thorough staring at.

'Thank you, Mr Moon. Ladies, this is my site foreman, Mr Moon who will show you around the immediate vicinity after this short service. Mr Moon, these... ladies are directors of the company and I will now leave them in your capable charge.'

Perhaps half a dozen of those present joined in the singing of 'O Come All Ye Faithful' and the 'Amen' at the end of Mr Law's brief lesson was barely audible. However, Mr Moon's bellowed, 'Alright, get back to it ya bastards!' was missed by no-one. Christmas was clearly over.

A precarious platform of narrow poles supported by thin wooden legs and a rough ladder is placed ten feet up or so against the trunk of the mighty red cedar. A man scales this while his partner supports the rickety construction and hands him tools as required. While so balanced the man swings his axe, biting chunks out of a trunk several feet wide, over and over, metronomically, seemingly never tiring, until they switch roles. This goes on until the men decide enough has been cut out to drive in the wedges which are hammered into the cut until the weakened giant emits a loud 'crack'; the men jump clear and the colossus falls, branches ripping off against neighbours throwing clouds of moisture and debris into the air. Birds scream and anyone unfortunate enough to be caught below has little chance which, according to Mr Moon, has happened more than once. I thought of Enoch and shuddered.

'Mr Moon tells us there are many native peoples in the vicinity. Have you encountered them?' Theresa's question was matter of fact and thrown casually into the dinner conversation while a kanaka boy of around eleven or twelve removed the dinner plates and a girl of the same race and around the same age quietly brought out dessert dishes. Mr Law nodded, pouring himself another cup of ale and offering the same to me, Theresa already having told him she did not imbibe.

'The Idindyi live in this neck of the woods, there are others, but these are our main bugbear. Just when we think we've scared them off, back they come, doing their best to disrupt operations - but you can rest assured, quotas will be met, production will not be impaired. We have doubled the guard on the bullock compounds and main trails and, I'm both relieved and delighted to report, a detachment of police and native trackers are on their way so we should be able to mitigate this threat once and for all.'

'Were you aware of the recent troubles north of here, along the Laura River?' Theresa enquired.

'Aye, there was an operation just south of there, finished now, difficulty transporting timber to the river, so I'm told. I have men here who worked for that outfit. They lost some good hands there, bullocks too. In my opinion, they took too long, way too long to get to grips with the savages... interfering papists, deputations, peace offerings - and a great lot of good it did them. They lost more men and bullocks in seven weeks than I have in the same number of months - and they left thousands of feet of good, prime timber to rot on riverbanks and muddy slopes in the process.'

Theresa had sat up straight and closed her eyes, her deep breathing was an indication of a storm front approaching and I hoped she had taken to heart my lecture on the way here. 'A calm voice is a strong voice.' I had told her.

'Anyway...' Mr Law had decided enough had been said about business and began to rise, 'If you'll excuse me, ladies...'

'It's said they killed more than a hundred men, women and children there?' Theresa made eye contact with our host for the first time during the meal. Mr Law frowned and shook his head in obvious puzzlement.

'Shouldn't think so, shouldn't think so at all. They lost about a dozen men to my knowledge, to savages, accidents and fever. They lost a handful of good bullocks too but as far as women and children are concerned... I don't believe there were any there. Not the place for families - these camps, mine are in Toowoomba.'

'No, I mean... native men, women and children.' She persisted.

'Indigenous people,' I added superfluously.

Mr Law's puzzlement was evident, he put on his jacket and bowler while he talked, 'I really have no idea, but if they did then it underlines what I said, they exacerbated the problem by trying to appease these creatures. You don't get rid of foxes by feeding them lamb - unless you poison it of course. If they had sent them firmly on their way at the first sign of trouble, there would have been a lot less bloodshed - both human and animal. Now then, good evening ladies, I must do my rounds.'

There were things screeching in the night that I could not put a name to, but I felt safe. As directors of the company Mr Law had deemed it important that Theresa and I survive our visit and go home intact. To that end two men armed with Henry Repeaters were patrolling around the cabin, reassuring us of their wakefulness by whistling, chatting and farting throughout the hot tropical night. Theresa whispered in my ear, 'When he said, "Both human and animal", which side of the line do you think he was putting the natives?'

'He's a cold fish, that's for sure,' I agreed.

'Well, he'll likely get a lot colder tomorrow when we lay down the law.'

Mr Law shook his head, took a few paces away from us, returned and shook his head again, this time punching his palm for emphasis.

'No - not under any circumstances. It has been more than a week since we even saw a blackfella so if you think I'm going to halt a smooth-running operation - which YOU are set to benefit financially from, then I invite you to think again ladies.'

'Do I have to remind you who we are?' Theresa wasn't shouting yet, but the pressure was building.

'We're not here to disrupt your operation Mr Law...' I began.

'...Well, it seems like it from where I'm standing!' Was the disrespectful retort.

Where we were standing, on a Boxing Day morning of hot mist and half-light, was halfway to the bullock enclosure with a view of musterers coaxing stoic beasts into harness.

'Well, we'll soon...' Theresa's response was once again rudely interrupted '...Mr Moon!' Mr Law called out to his foreman who had been striding off in a direction ninety degrees to us. The man turned and raised is hat in acknowledgement, now heading for us. He arrived yawning and wiped the ever-present perspiration from his eyes.

'Boss?'

'Mr Moon, would you kindly tell these ladies about our encounters with the savages over the last few weeks?'

The foreman looked puzzled, but for only a second. 'Well, it's been quiet the last week or so but that's because we gave the fuckers a bloody good... begging your pardon ladies... we gave the fuckers a damn good broadside, must have got half a dozen by most reckonings but we only found four bodies, three bucks and a ginn. They got two bullocks though, poisoned spears, bloody evil bastards - beg pardon again ladies.'

Before either Theresa or I could respond, Mr Law cut in, '... and do you Mr Moon, or indeed any of the white men, think that halting production - with all that means to your bonuses - whilst we attempt to appease these creatures would be a good plan?'

'Hell, no Boss, we've got that copse on the stream bank to tackle this week and the Wet's only going to get bloody worse. Christ knows... sorry Boss, ...goodness knows how it's held off this long. It's usually pis... pouring down by Christmas. If we can get them and what we've got stacked down to Cairns, we can sit the worst of it out and still hit target. Anyway, the traps and their darkies will be here directly, they'll sort 'em out once and for all.'

Theresa frowned, 'There's something I've been wanting to ask you, Mr Moon, tell me, why do you carry a whip? Don't you think those poor bullocks have a hard enough life without inflicting of even more pain?'

He looked down at the ground and gave the faintest of chuckles before tilting back his hat and taking a step toward Theresa, unhitching the whip from his belt.

'I ain't never struck a bullock with this in all my days, bullocks know their job and they do it. Kanakas... well, there's a different matter.'

Mr Law nodded, 'Thank you Mr Moon, please go about your business.'

Touching his battered hat respectfully, the foreman turned on a heel and made for the invisible shouts of loggers among the trees. Mr Law spoke to the sky's many shades of grey as if willing the clouds to part.

'Of course, as directors, you can order production to stop, irrational as that would be - but I have to tell you that if you did, I would immediately telegraph Mrs Clancy with the information and await her inevitable response. She ordered a sovereign bonus for each man involved in the last blackfella attack and there were ten sovereigns each for the families of the men lost at Laura and here. When this camp was set up, Mr Fiach and Mr Fergal Clancy ordered every man to get a week's pay in advance to buy tucker, new clothes and personal tools. The Clancys ask a lot, but they give a lot too and the men respect them.'

Theresa paced away, she was stamping her work-booted feet, fists clenching and unclenching. Mr Law seemed unconcerned,

'I have to say, Mr Law,' I began, 'I find you ill-mannered and more than a little above yourself. I know masters who would have you horsewhipped for speaking to them in that tone.'

He looked down at me.

'Oh aye? In England, are they? Well, that's why I'm here Madam, in a land where men are judged by backbones not bloodlines. And I'll remind you that I'm your employee whose duty it is to help make you rich and I will not allow anything to get in the way of that. Now I won't expect understanding, that's not the way of bosses, but you can either relieve me of my duties or stay out of my way and let me perform them.'

We left for Priors Creek township, booking ourselves into the only hotel worthy of the name, planning to head back down to Cairns and from there, home. Mr Law was quite correct, as I had feared. One word to Gráinne and she would immediately order him to ignore us and everything we said. All that was left was to concede we had tried, admit defeat, pull out of the profoundly distressing enterprise, lick our wounds and move on.

Defeat, however, was a foreign concept to Theresa and she was hell bent on returning Mr Kenneth Law's fusillade with a forty-gun broadside.

29.
Priors Creek, Queensland
Thursday, April 10th, 1884

And then it rained.

Nothing in our Palmer River adventures of a decade
before prepared us for the full elemental fury of 'The
Wet'. There is little an Englishwoman does not know
about rain; fog and flood are her siblings, and she grows
to tolerate them - but here, on this tropical plateau of
forests and torrents it rains in a way my homeland has
never known.

Impenetrable, relentless, it batters everything beneath
it, smashing fronds, flattening and flooding every
clearing, saturating fallen timber, mingling with fluid
earth to drive rivulets down every channelled gradient. It
drives human and animal into hiding, thwarting those
who hunt meat and those who harvest trees.

During The Wet, timber-getting comes to a standstill.
Hunkering in tents the white men made themselves as
comfortable as possible while the South Sea Islanders
created what shelter they could from the materials
available. Mr Kenneth Law provided some canvas, and
the rest was hacked, weaved and fashioned from the
forest itself. The small army of bullocks, mules and
horses were corralled close to town on the property of a

group of Dutch farmers already beginning to work the cleared ground.

The Wet closes roads and tracks. No one, unless driven by urgent need, goes abroad or attempts the trails and this year even the desperate would think twice. Locals who had witnessed many a Wet said this season was a record beater. Our hotelier, Larry Duggan, was content for us to stay until the trails reopened on the promise of payment from the company's account.

Standing less than five feet, Mr Duggan was dwarfed by his muscular and ferocious-looking Tongan wife. She did the lion's share of the work around the tiny four-bedroom house and bar. With his long white beard, liquid blue eyes and almost permanent grin it was hard not to think of an elf. He also whistled almost constantly which was useful as there was no lock on the shared ablutions room.

Our world confined, we had come to know the outline of every tree and shrub in the immediate vicinity as well as many of the tiny town's inhabitants. We had also read the only two books on the premises - A Tale of Two Cities and The Whale several times each. It therefore came as a welcome break in the monotony when my thirty-fifth birthday dawned in sunshine, allowing us to venture out past the limits of the town and along a forest path, followed at a discreet distance by a man with a rifle. There had been no problems with the natives so close to the town, but Larry Duggan touchingly insisted we take along a guard as he had grown so fond of us, stating 'It's nice to have female faces about the place!' which drew a murderous look from Mrs Duggan, who preferred to be called Loa - which apparently means 'Storm Cloud.'

The End of the Sky

We took ourselves just out of town as far as a spot where a little creek had been turned into a rushing fury, barging and battering its way down a steep incline, pushing aside plants and shrubbery.

'Probably far enough ladies,' our escort called, raising a hand to shade his eyes as a sudden shaft of sunlight found a gap between browbeaten branches far above. A breeze sprang up tossing Theresa's wild and unpinned hair like a dancing fire. I remarked how it almost reached her waist.

She laughed when I asked her to keep our guard occupied for a second while I answered a call of nature. Disappearing into the bushes, I skidded on what I took for a slick patch of turf. At first, I thought the blow on the side of my foot was a fallen stick but then came a strong and frantic pulling. I looked down and screamed as a snake threshed to dislodge itself from my boot where its fangs had become embedded in the leather. It must have been six feet or more, olive and livid, twisting and whipping.

Alerted by my scream, Theresa burst through the bushes and flew across the gap between us, landing feet first on the snake which was ripped from my boot by the impact. Whipping its head around it struck her waist, once… twice before lunging away into the foaming water to be washed downstream.

She appeared unaffected, dropping to her knees, taking my boot in her hands, tugged frantically at the laces and pulled it off followed by my sock. Our guard appeared then, alert for an assailant.

'Snakebite,' Theresa yelled over her shoulder. The man knelt, grabbing my ankle from Theresa and peering closely.

'What'd it look like?'

I described it in gasps. My ankle throbbed; I was breathing far too fast.

'Bloody brownie,' he cursed.

'Right! Sorry 'bout this…'

Unceremoniously, he tore off my underskirt and further tore it into a long strip before winding it tightly around my leg from ankle to halfway up my thigh. Then, picking me up he turned to Theresa.

'Grab my gun, run ahead and tell Duggan to fetch Jack the Quack, go on, scarper!'

Whether my rapid breathing was a result of venom or panic I could not tell but the bottom half of my right leg felt as if it were on fire.

'They only got short fangs Missus and from what I can see there's only one puncture on your ankle, your boot may have saved you getting the full measure.'

He strode off at a brisk pace which turned into a trot as we regained the forest path. I felt dizzy and feverish and closed my eyes against the rising pain. My carrier yelled, 'Hoy - don't you bloody go to sleep or die on me; I'll lose my job. Come on, tell me where you from?'

'Glos… Glos…' I couldn't get the word out.

'Glossop? Well, there's a thing - my granddad was from Nottingham, he weren't no Robin Hood though, he robbed the rich and bloody spent it, that's how he came to be out here.'

Every step my rescuer trotted was like a dagger being driven into my leg. Then he cried out to someone…

'Brownie bite - here on the ankle.'

Then I was carried through a door and laid on a couch, another man's voice was muttering as he loosened the rope around my ankle and poured something on to the site of the bite. It stung and smelled like piddle. Then he filled my field of view, balding, white hair, pale eyes... he was looking into my eyes, producing a small flask.

'I'm Jack Hollins, Here, take a good mouthful of this and swallow, don't spit it out mind...'

I had never tasted brandy before, and it was like drinking fire, but it made me breathe harder and within a couple of minutes I felt the beginnings of the numbness that comes from strong drink taking the edge off my panic.

'Now then,' he said, 'I'm going to take the wrapping off your leg and it's going to be painful, I won't lie to you...'

Mercifully, I didn't have long to take in the implications of what he had said as a wave of nausea and darkness lifted me free of consciousness and when I finally sank back into the real world, I was lying on our hotel bed, Theresa was stretched out next to me fully clothed.

'It bit you too,' my voice was croaky, my throat a dusty track.

'Belt - never underestimate the usefulness of a good leather belt,' Theresa did not open her eyes, but her hand felt its way to mine and I managed a weak squeeze in return for hers.

'Someone up there was watching over us today,' she added, rolling on her side to face me, eyes now open,

'How are you feeling?' She gently stroked damp hair away from my face.

All my joints ached, I half lifted my eyelids but shut them again against the low evening light, red spots crawled and scurried at the back of my eyes like mites in a chook house and with each slow and steady beat of my heart a throbbing rose from ankle to hip.

'I'm still alive,' I replied.

'Jack the Quack says you're going to make it, but you owe St Luke and St Jude a barrel of thanks, so you do, brownies pack more of a wallop than John L Sullivan. I'm to call him out if you feel crook but he thinks the worst is over.'

I felt weak and sore for many days and it was two weeks before I saw the sky again. Theresa had stayed by my side throughout.

I sat at the mirror as she brushed my hair, 'They're nasty old things, Brownies, aren't they? We had adders back home, but I never saw one more than once or twice. I saw Enoch pick one up when it was sunbathing on the side of the lane. He put it in a field so nobody would see it and kill it.

'Ah well, you've seen more than I have then.' She spoke in little more than a whisper.

She sounded tired… no, not tired, tearful.

'Are you alright my Shamrock?' I turned to face her; the brushing had stopped.

Her eyes were full, the bottomless green pools that never failed to turn my heart to water. There was a little girl looking out of them, relieved that something dark and terrible had passed her by. Had I not fully known before,

I realised then just how much this wild and mercurial lady had invested emotionally in me. She took my face gently in her hands, her voice trembling...

'Don't you ever, ever do that to me again - do you hear?'

We discovered the trail was open when we stepped out after breakfast on a bright Sunday to see the square in front of the hotel full of mounted police and native trackers calling out to stragglers, beckoning them into some sort of mustering order. The horses steamed in the harsh light as more and more men dismounted, heading for the livery buildings behind the hotel.

The trackers, partly dressed in ill-fitting uniforms each with a yellow armband, aided in the unsaddling and rubbing down of the mounts. The police were heavily armed, several pack animals carried munition cases with one towing a cart-mounted Gatling Gun.

'Looks like the trail's open.' Larry Duggan had appeared at our side, towel over arm, clearly preparing for a busy day.

'Indeed, we'll be on our way soon,' I smiled, trying to remain positive while Theresa at my side looked anything but.

'We can go home my Shamrock,' I stroked her back, she turned to me, her face a haunted house.

'Here the thing Country Mouse. Did you wave at the soldiers and the police? March along beside them? Did the little boys grow up dreaming of uniforms and guns and medals?'

'Well...'

She didn't give me time to answer.

'We feared them; feared and hated them. We crossed the world to escape them - and here they still are. I'm sorry Ellie, but you don't see what I see - and we both know why they're here.'

'You Mr Duggan?' A uniformed trooper, tall, sun blasted face with high cheekbones, substantial side whiskers and the kind of eyes that never smiled towered over the hotelier.

'I am,' the little man beamed.

'I'm Sergeant Cornthwaite, in charge of a mounted contingent and native trackers up from Wondecla through Herberton. We've got pretty much what we need but if you've coffee and fresh bread, plus stabling for tonight we'll be obliged…. Ladies.'

He touched the brim of his cap. Larry Duggan smiled again and headed inside.

'What brings you to these parts Sergeant?' Theresa forced a smile.

'I might ask you the same,' the sergeant scratched his whiskers - are your husbands about?'

'Mine's deceased and she hasn't got one,' I replied, beating Theresa to it.

He frowned. 'Don't seem the kind of place for unaccompanied white women.'

'Well, we're directors of the Pine Creek Timber Company and we are here appraising our investment,' Theresa enlightened him.

He nodded, 'Yeah? Well, that's convenient then, I've got a letter of authorisation here from… here we are, Mrs Grain… Granny…'

'It's pronounced gron-ya.' Theresa failed to keep a swelling anxiety from her voice.

'Right, well you'll be glad discover we're here to help you with a little bit of pest control. Now then, much to do, so good day ladies.'

He touched the brim of his hat again, turned on a heel and walked off to his men, barking orders and waving arms.

'Suit yourself,' Sergeant Cornthwaite shrugged, tugging his mount's reins until he faced us, '...but if you insist on coming, we can't be responsible for your safety.' He trotted off to muster the column already forming under a dawn sky as a light wind carried the smell of woodsmoke from the smithy across the square. The track from the town to the logging camp was the one we had taken just after Christmas and the Wet had left it in need of some repair. Occasional potholes pitched our cart left and right, up and down as we struggled gamely to keep up with the troop as it followed a trail along Mazlin Creek, named after the logging brothers who worked in the area.

Mr Kenneth Law was manifestly not at all pleased to make our reacquaintance. His look said it all although he must have realised we would still be in his part of the world thanks to the impenetrable Wet. Without dismounting, Sergeant Cornthwaite handed him the letter from Gráinne requesting his cooperation and assistance. The logger boss nodded waving an arm to indicate the troop may rest and recuperate where they pleased.

Rather than impose on a hostile Mr Law for accommodation, we took advantage of some docile weather to sleep in our cart under the canvas cover having shared a meal of cold bully beef, bread and lukewarm stewed tea.

We woke in the night; fires were lit and men who had formed into a column were marching into the bush. There was with it an entirely different atmosphere in the camp. It would be wrong to call it jubilation, but there was tangible excitement and a level of alertness we were unaccustomed to. Undoubtedly, Grandfather William, far off Mr Wells or Adder Drew would have been familiar with what we subsequently discovered were the taut senses of men breaking camp in the expectation of a battle.

It was infectious; both Theresa and I felt as if our stomachs were full of angry bees. Unlike the police and trackers, we had little idea of what specifically lay ahead, but a deep mire of foreboding turned legs to lead and drained the warmth from an otherwise balmy night. Wrapped in thin blankets, we walked over to the remnants of the column which was now heading along paths our cart could not follow. A corporal with a black moustache paused as he passed us, 'It's not a long way ladies, but it's a walk I would advise you not to take.' He strode on followed by a small band of native police.

'Come on, back to the cart,' I pulled Theresa's sleeve and to my surprise, she followed, her eyes large in the waning moonlight. 'There's nothing we can do to stop them now my Shamrock, nothing at all; and if we try, we'll likely get ourselves shot or speared.'

I pulled her along behind me like a reluctant toddler, afraid she would change her mind and vanish into the bush following the last of the straggling column. We reached the cart and I busied and bullied her on to the driving bench before climbing up beside her. From the east, a tropical dawn broke with customary urgency, painting the sky first blue and then deep yellow. Birds woke and drowned out any noise from the last of the men to disappear into the trees

'We can't change the past Theresa… look…. look at me - what we did, we did out of naivety and with the best of intentions. We could have done a lot of good with them big profits and I know you would have too. But we can't stop it on our own. We'll go home, pull out of this, to hell with the money, we'll have our souls. Right… hold tight…' A snap of the reins and the impatient horse who had brought us here from Cairns took the strain and set us on the long trail home.'

And then, from deep in the bush, muffled by the thick air and the trees between us, but still clear and unmistakeable, came gunfire; and on the wind, at the very edge of hearing, there were screams. I turned to Theresa, but she had gone. Having jumped from the cart she was running, heading in the direction of the increasing sound of the barrage. I screamed in vain, then I jumped down too…

30.
Skull Pocket, Queensland
Tuesday, April 29th, 1884

Theresa stumbled, tripping over a root, but any chance of catching her vanished when I did the same, falling flat on my face into the churned-up mud of the path. I sprang to my feet, the snake attack still a raw and tangible presence. I stumbled on, clothes snagged on branches and bushes, tugging hair from clips, scratching hands and cheeks. The sound of gunshots was louder now although there were fewer - but the screams increased, high-pitched, horrified.

'Wait... Theresa, wait!'

She was slowing, staggering with the exhaustion and emotion of her flight until she stopped, breaking out of the trees on the edge of a wide clearing lit by the sun in dramatic contrast to the surrounding shade, like a stage before an audience. She simply stared straight ahead, mouth open, panting, gulping, tears springing, welling and overflowing down scratched and muddied cheeks. She raised a hand to her mouth, her eyes, already wide, grew wider. As I caught up, she turned to me revealing a soul witnessing all the devils and demons of Christendom crawling from between the pages of the holy books and slipping unchained into the world to fall like wolves upon lambs.

The dead were all around. Men women, children who until minutes ago lived and loved, ate and planned. They lay in groups or as solitary bloody outlines in the grass. A campfire still burned with uneaten meat suspended above it. As we watched, a girl of perhaps three or four went running, screaming toward the trees but was caught by a native policeman who snatched her up by her ankles and dashed her head against a rock before dropping the lifeless body and walking on. A woman, clearly badly wounded, was trying to crawl towards another dead child but a policeman pulled back her head by her hair and slit her throat.

I was numbed and beyond tears, part of me refusing to believe that what I was witnessing was anything more than a grotesque play in which all the performers would miraculously come to life to take a bow at the end. Theresa still stared ahead, I tried to turn her away, hold her to me, but she broke free. Her voice, although torn by trauma, was surprisingly strong and clear.

'I will witness this; I will not turn away. I will witness this, and I will tell what I have seen.'

She stayed until all other living souls had gone, most on foot, a few on mounts, disappearing into the bush, and I stood with her, holding her, among the silenced voices. The tears had stopped, there were none left. The birds began to call and sing again, the trees rustled in a quickening breeze, the river of life flowed on. Eventually, muddied, wet through, emotionally exhausted, she turned to me and we hugged each other, finding what little comfort and sanity we could in the midst of Hell on Earth.

Larry Duggan and Loa had welcomed us back into the hotel. Larry downcast, his smile subdued, voice velvet. Teresa sat, silent in the bathtub, allowing me to wash away the detritus of our morning. I bathed myself then knelt, combing out her wet hair. I had witnessed all the seasons of her moods, the exuberance of spring, the passion of summer and the reflective melancholy of autumn, but this, the cold desolation of winter when not a hope stirred, was so unlike her. When she remained in this state the next morning, I feared for her sanity and at my bidding Larry sent out for Jack Hollins.

'She ain't got a fever - I reckon it's shock, seen it before when Lottie Stroop's lad got killed, she was like this. Time's the thing Missus, time and a drop o' brandy if she'll take it, otherwise get her to chew on this.' Jack handed me a small bag of pungent leaves, I sniffed at them, frowning.

'It's alright, they won't kill ya, some blokes smoke it, but she don't look the pipe sort. She'll be fine, time's the thing - time, rest and quiet.'

I thanked Jack for attending and showed him out. The great space at the front of the hotel was deserted now save for a small mob of argumentative black butcher birds and a scavenging white dog. Larry gently took my arm on my way back to our room.

'Listen, just a quick word', he spoke in hardly more than a whisper. 'If you should see a young Kanaka lad creeping about the place, it's OK, we know he's here. He ran away from the logging camp and my Missus speaks the lingo. We're hiding him until we can get him away to

Cairns and on to a boat. His name's Maau and we've told him you and Ginger are good people and won't give him up to Creeping Jesus or Mr Moon - that's right, ain't it?'

I told him it was and then, spontaneously, hugged him. His smile was a sad one.

'Dark times Missus, bloody dark times…'

She slept around the clock, she woke, I fed her broth and then she drifted away again. While she slept, she hardly moved, in complete contrast to her usual tossing and turning. I stroked her hair away from her face, kissed her, held her hand… occasionally she would mutter in Irish, I would just whisper in her ear in my softest Country Mouse voice. 'It's alright my darling, it's alright…'

She slept through her twenty-ninth birthday, I sang 'My Merry Mayday Maiden' to her and she murmured *Mo Anam Cara'* in reply.

My own sleep had been troubled, a place of sharp edges and cold winds where hard men snarled at unseen threats, shards of broken glass lay in puddles of blood and I could hear Mother, somewhere… crying.

The timber camp had moved on. They were now five miles further north leaving destruction in their wake. The forest was a threatening place of poisonous snakes and even more poisonous people, I feared it as though it were the Underworld. When she was well enough, we would leave this place, never to return. But I would not run as a beaten dog runs, cowed with tail between legs…

In an act that had nothing to do with common sense and that would have drawn bitter remonstrations from Theresa were she awake, I stepped out of the hotel and,

371

telling Larry I was simply riding into town for some air, trotted off on his mare, Lulu.

They stood, taller than any man but were still mere parodies of what they once were. Here was death and dismemberment, the desecration of the ancient and innocent. The great stumps of mighty Cedars, in a clearing now, sun beating down on lesser lives accustomed to shade. Unadorned they would have been a tragic enough symbol of man's tyranny. Their majesty had failed to stay the barbarians at the gates; now slaughtered and dragged out of their world, they were robbed of dignity in death like the great whales of the north.

But someone had clearly sought to underline their conquest for upon each stump a human head had been impaled. Lifeless eyes, teeth bared in a final cry for mercy. Scarecrows - a warning to anyone daring to raise a hand against the incoming tide.

Of the many biblical locations learned as a child, only two still invoked images and emotions. There was Bethlehem of course; snow, rosy cheeks, glittering shop windows, log fires and meat on the table; and then Golgotha - the place of skulls and tears where a light left the world so that man need sin no more. And now I understood what Grandfather William had meant when he said his faith died on the battlefields of Spain. There were many things beyond my power, but there was one I could be certain of, my Shamrock would never know of this.

And then, the next morning, during a 'tail-ender' of a violent rainstorm, she woke fully and sat up.

We embarked on our journey to Cairns in the company of a pair of men from the logging camp who had decided to try their luck farther north around the all but worked out Palmer tributaries. Although my Shamrock was clearly still in shock from the events at Skull Pocket, my disbelief was probably the greater.

Queensland was a British colony under the rule, ultimately, of the British Government and with Queen Victoria as its head of state. What we had witnessed, therefore, happened with all their blessings. But should I have been surprised? Richard Price had told me of the massacres at Peterloo and Newport. It appeared all human life, save that of the landed, was of secondary value when compared to profit in the eyes of John Bull.

Our travelling companions were courteous and respectful, saying their prayers morning and evening; one a lowland Scot and the other a German with impeccable English. We told them what we had seen, but I did not bring up the hideous tableau I had subsequently encountered. They were not surprised, but neither did they attempt to justify it, Gerhard in particular espousing the sanctity of all human life.

It was as if the land itself was weeping, rain fell slowly, silently and gently for much of the journey out of the Tableland and down through the mangroves to Cairns and the ocean, clearing only to allow us our first glimpse of the Pacific.

Our first action on reaching the town was to send telegraphs to the Brisbane Courier and, on the recommendation of our travelling companion Andrew, the Manchester Guardian, stating, 'We have witnessed a massacre stop There is much we have to tell you stop. E and T Kelly.' The Courier responded within an hour stating, 'We have a man in Cairns, Elliott Devonshire stop Meet at Riverstone Hotel noon stop.'

'Yes… I don't doubt it… Dear God ladies… that's beyond evil…' Mr Devonshire nodded throughout and punctuated our story with questions, specifically keen to put names to the main protagonists and instigators. He reminded me of Mr Wells from the Noah's Ark, impeccably dressed, wayward dark curly hair refusing to be tamed by oil, eyes alive and inquisitive and what Mother would have called pianist's hands, long slender fingers, holding his pencil as a surgeon might wield a knife, careful and precise, accuracy being paramount.

'Was Mr Kenneth Law present at the massacre?'

'Was Mr Edgar Moon there?'

'Did Sergeant Cornthwaite make any attempt to curb the violence?'

'Were the white troopers involved in the killing of the children and women?'

'You said they had a letter from Mrs Gráinne Clancy…?'

Finally, he thanked us for contacting the Courier, advising us to speak to no one about any impending story until he had finished his research.

A steamship, the Southern Argus, stood at harbour, fussing and grumbling impatiently; a rusting anchor and a hull in need of a coat of paint marked her out as a goods vessel with her best years behind her, overshadowed and

outstripped by more modern crafts, quicker and sleeker -
a battle scarred old matelot watching new recruits at drill.
But she was heading directly for Brisbane. I did not want
to take a port hopper; had we stopped in Townsville
Charlie would have instantly known there was something
wrong and it was not a story I wanted him to hear until
such a time he had to.

The skipper shrugged, took our money and allowed
us use of the room reserved for the vessel's owner on the
rare occasions he took it into his head to travel with the
ship. It was dry, relatively clean, containing a bed just big
enough for the pair of us with a large ginger cat as
motheaten as the vessel itself asleep on it.

Neither of us were in the mood to confront plans for
the future. At that moment, the sea was a good medicine,
away from the land wars of man and a sanctuary from
confrontation. The old ship took us south, passing
Townsville and Mackay tracking the endless green wall of
Queensland's coast. We ate and slept and ate once more,
promising to take stock when we had a familiar roof over
us.

'That was Conway, wasn't it? Gráinne's pet rat?'

Theresa stared at the retreating figure as the man
hunched his shoulders and half walked, half trotted away
while we alighted from a carriage that had carried us,
weary and hungry, from the dock.

I hadn't noticed him. 'Off to tell his mistress of our
return if it was', I stopped and stretched, lifting my small
bag as a beaming Leo appeared, picking up our cases and
welcoming us home.

In the Kelly Marine, housekeeper Jane castigated us for arriving without notice as she could have freshly made the bed. Even though it was early afternoon I could have cheerfully fallen on the feather mattress and drifted off with my hat and boots on. Leo carried our cases to our room telling us he would bring us up to date later with all that had happened in our absence - 'Not that there's a lot to tell' he grinned, 'I told that spailpín, from the Rope Walk to clear off a couple of times.'

I lay on the bed; Theresa lay next to me. We had asked Jane to call us for dinner although any appetite I had at sea seemed to be fading now. My Shamrock felt it too. We were home, but it no longer felt like it. Had we really been that naïve? Was it really, as Ted Parker and Gráinne supposed, 'The way things are done here?' There were many who would agree, so-called churchmen among them and was there anywhere in the world, including the lands of our birth, where such things did not happen?

The knock on the door snatched me out of my reverie. I had been at the point where images from my unbridled mind were playing out prologues to dreams. Theresa as always, had beaten me to it. I shook her gently.

'Hey... Dozy... dinner.'

But it was Leo who opened the door gently and spoke around it.

'Mrs Kellys... Gráinne Clancy is downstairs, in the lounge. Says it won't wait.'

'Who...what...' Theresa reluctantly returned from Nod.

'Gráinne - downstairs,' I told her, causing her to sit upright, blinking, hair tumbling.

The End of the Sky

Leo cleared his throat, his head fully appeared around the door, 'She had two fellers with her, I told them to wait outside. They tried to push in so I shoved them down the steps, one fell on his arse... beg your pardon. Then the Auld Lady told them to stay out and wait.'

It was the first time I had seen her standing and she was surprisingly tall. She coiled herself uninvited into a chair with serpentine grace, curling gold and jewel bedecked fingers around the handle of her equally flamboyant cane. A folded newspaper rested in her lap. All was black, her eyes, her ribboned bonnet and her dress with a brooch of polished jet at her throat. Seemingly unaffected by the warmth of the afternoon, she looked from one of us to the other as if trying to read our hand before playing her own. Theresa conspicuously turned her back on her, absently adjusting ornaments on the large Welsh dresser neither of us were particularly fond of.

'Thus, conscience doth make cowards of us all!'

Her voice, soft and melodic might have been a thing of beauty had it come from another source. She smiled, her eyes did not.

'I'm no coward, neither of us are!'

I was surprised by my own vehemence. I was almost a foot shorter than Gráinne but was made taller by my anger. 'I have shot at least one man dead and looked into the terrible eyes of another who killed dozens. The logging trade took my husband and I have seen horrors you couldn't imagine - or perhaps you can, seeing it was you who unleashed the worst of them.'

Theresa turned then as if to fire a broadside of her own, but Gráinne beat her to it, finally displaying something approaching compassion, but without the depth.

'Well, you do surprise me Mrs Johnsey. And you have my sympathy; my husband too was lost in a felling accident. Do you have children?'

A voice roared in my head, Enoch's voice, yelling the word 'NO'.

'No,' I answered, suddenly buoyed by a certainty I was being watched over.

'I don't suppose you have had a chance to catch up with all the latest yet,' she unfolded the newspaper and tossed it on to the table, 'This is three days old - I haven't been able to bring myself to buy one since. All those poor people... twenty-three to my certain knowledge, dreadful.'

'Take it from a witness', Theresa's voice dripped acid, 'There were more than that - many more.'

'Oh, of course, I don't doubt it', Gráinne's icicle smile faded, 'I'm just referring to the bankrupt investors themselves, you are quite right, there are their families to consider, their employees, lost homes, some have lost all they had, children going into orphanages, one poor feller hung himself. And they have all turned up at my door demanding to know who was responsible for their losses. Of course, I told them you were away up north and that when you got back, I would let them all know.'

Theresa closed the gap between them, looking directly up at our visitor, 'You wicked evil soulless old witch! There is no depth of Hell hot enough for you.'

The new smile was a winter wolf impervious to all warmth, 'Well then, the Divil will have to send out for more timber, won't he?'

She turned to leave, then turned back, appearing to speak to the floor, 'I have nothing further to say to you ladies and anything you have to say to me is of no interest, but I will leave you with this… I've never to this day personally killed anyone; does that surprise you? I'm not saying others have not done so on my behalf out of foolish loyalty.

'I did once kill a horse though - a horse I had trained and cared for since it was born. I raced it, it lost, I raced it again, it lost again. It lost me money, so I took it out into the paddock and killed it with a sledgehammer. Then I personally butchered it and fed it to my dogs.'

I stood in shock and revulsion as she retraced a few steps to look down at me.

'It… lost… me… money - sleep tight'.

She turned and left; a chill remained.'

31.
Brisbane, Queensland
Wednesday, May 28th,
1884

Theresa held up the page so I could see the headline, 'The
Price of Timber - Terror Amongst the Trees as Loggers
Move In', then she read to me as I sat, eyes closed,
listening to the evening traffic and the sounds of the city
to which we had become quite unaccustomed.

'From your reporter, Elliott Devonshire in Cairns...
They moved in at dawn, as silently as foxes. They
observed old women lighting cooking fires and mothers
tenderly feeding their helpless babies. Men, weary from
the endless rain, looked forward to the promise of
sunshine and a bountiful hunt. They awoke as they have
always awakened, since before the Saviour walked upon
the Sea of Galilee and the great stones of Egypt were
placed one upon another. But none of those who
welcomed this sun would see it set.

Imagine if you can how minds who had never
conceived of a weapon such as a gun would have reacted
to the crashing of this strange thunder, hails of white-hot
lead, death suddenly all around and within them.
Witnessing their loved ones slaughtered - and in ways this

380

reporter hesitates to repeat. Suffice to say, none were spared.'

Theresa put down the paper, reached for her handkerchief, drying her eyes and having a good old blow.

'Here, let me…' I picked up the paper, found her place and read on.

'The column of Queensland police and native trackers had fallen on their prey at the request of the Prior Creek Timber Company who had been suffering losses of men, bullocks and equipment as a result of raids by the Ydinydji Tribe. It may be that news of this massacre would never have left the forests of the far north had it not been for the courage of two of the company's directors who witnessed the event and were horrified by it. A forewarning of the impending revelations was received by shareholders and clients last week. As a result, shares in the company have become virtually worthless as customers distance themselves and many investors now face ruin.

'But this, in plain language, is how we deal with the aborigines: On occupying new territory the aboriginal inhabitants are treated exactly in the same way as the wild beasts or birds the settlers may find there. Their lives and their property, the nets, canoes, and weapons which represent as much labour to them as the stock and buildings of the white settler, are held by the invaders as being at their absolute disposal.

'Their goods are taken, their children forcibly stolen, their women carried away, entirely at the caprice of the white men. The least show of resistance is answered by a rifle bullet. Little difference is made between the treatment of blacks at first disposed to be friendly and those who from the very outset assume a hostile attitude.

'As a rule, the blacks have been friendly at first, and the longer they have endured provocation without retaliating the worse they have fared. In regard to these cowardly outrages, the majority of invaders have been apparently influenced by the same sort of feeling as that which guides men in their treatment of the brute creation. Many, perhaps the majority, have stood aside in silent disgust whilst these things were being done, actuated by the same motives that keep humane men from shooting or molesting animals which neither annoy nor are of service to them; and a few have always protested in the name of humanity against such treatment of human beings, however degraded.

'The brutes who fancy the amusement have murdered, ravished, and robbed the blacks without let or hindrance. Not only have they been unchecked, but the Government of
the colony has been always at hand to save them from the consequences of their crime.

'When the blacks, stung to retaliation by outrages committed on their tribe, or hearing the fate of their neighbours, have taken the initiative and shed white blood, the native police have been sent to "disperse" them. What disperse means is well enough known. The word has been adopted into bush slang as a convenient euphuism for wholesale massacre.

'It is a fitful war of extermination waged upon the blacks, something after the fashion in which others wage war upon noxious wild beasts, the process differing only in so far as the victims, being human, are capable of a wider variety of suffering than brutes.

'The savages, hunted from the places where they had been accustomed to find food, driven into barren ranges, shot like wild dogs at sight, retaliate when and how they can. They spear the white man's cattle and horses, and if by chance they succeed in overpowering an unhappy European they exhaust their savage ingenuity in wreaking their vengeance upon him, even mutilating the senseless body out of which they have pounded the last breath of life.

'Murder and counter murder, outrage repaid by violence, theft by robbery, so the dreary tale continues, till at last the blacks, starved, cowed, and broken-hearted, their numbers thinned, their courage overcome, submit to their fate.'

The street had gone silent, as if all the traffic and pedestrians had suddenly stopped, the only noise was the heavy tick of the big clock above a fire grate built by someone in whom old habits prevailed; blindly believing that January Jack would follow them across the world. At that moment I would have given all I had to be in Uckington, safe in Father's cottage, watching Sarah Ann crocheting... the smell of woodsmoke and the crackle of logs.

Almost all I had. In truth, I would rather be here with the threat of danger hanging over me and with Theresa at my side than safe in Gloucestershire without her.

She lit the lamp, I closed my eyes, hoping to hear the guidance of a guardian angel, Enoch or Grandfather who had stood in the path of bullets. But no voices came, just a vision of my Shamrock in fear and pain, her pretty Sunday dress drenched with blood, her eyes closing for the last time as she faded from me. And then, the shock of hot lead, tearing through skin and fat and bone, driving deep… deep through organs, ripping them, fighting for breath… and then the cold and the dark.

Night fell, we went to bed but, at my insistence, fully dressed. Theresa did not argue.

'If all's quiet tonight, we'll have a good long bath in the morning,' I told her and we lay in the dark, holding each other tight.'

A deep thud, then another came from somewhere outside, down on the boardwalk. Then dancing light. In my exhaustion, I had incorporated it into a dream about a churchyard bonfire and an old workman knocking in fence posts with a pole driver. Voices now… then smashing glass and shouting. It was full dark; I could usually tell what time it was when waking at night without recourse to the clock and I estimated it at around two thirty.

Theresa was in a deep sleep, I stood up and crept to the window, surreptitiously peering through a small crack in the curtains. There must have been twenty or more people, all men as far as I could see. The only ones I thought I recognised were Conway from the Rope Walk and Sergeant Madine from Queen Street Police Station who was stood, hands in pockets, under the gas lamp across the road, doing nothing to interfere with the work of the assembly.

More smashing of glass - and then the smell of smoke. I shook her, harsh whispering in her ear.

'Theresa... THERESA! Wake up, come on. Fire... we're on fire Shamrock.'

As fast as she falls asleep, so she can also recover when necessity demands and she was standing by the side of the bed, coughing while I wrapped a coat around her.

'The back way, she croaked...'

'Come on then...'

I led her to the door. Opening it, we faced a wall of flame rapidly climbing the stairs. In a way it worked in our favour, holding back the mob below in the hallway. We were spotted.

'There they are... HEY, ya bloody freaks!'

'Theresa grabbed my arm, leading me to the back stairs, we rushed, almost falling down, reaching the rear door.

'Wait - the cash box... the safe', Theresa turned back.

'Leave it! Come on'. I coaxed her, but she was gone, the smell of smoke stronger now, paint was visibly peeling on the door that led through the main pantry to the kitchen. In seconds she was returning, coughing, eyes streaming, cash box and a bag under her arm, through the smoke-filled corridor, a pair of enraged men were in pursuit, fighting each other to reach her first. One grabbed her shoulder, spinning her and causing her to cry out, the other struck her on the side of the face, she cried out as he raised his hand for another punch when he himself was flattened by a murderous blow as a nightshirted Leo Brannigan appeared from the adjoining passageway, knocking out the other man with a single uppercut before standing squarely in the way of the advancing mob.

385

'Leo, come on!' Theresa, cut lip dripping blood from chin to the front of her dress, grabbed his arm. He shook her off.

'Not now - get going ladies, you leave these bastards to me!' He turned to face them. 'GO!' he yelled over a shoulder, then, arms windmilling, he tore into our attackers.

We half expected more assailants cutting off our retreat, but the back garden was empty. Behind the sheds and my little plot lay a door between the Kelly Marine and the yard of the adjoining St Luke's Presbytery. The bolt was rusty from lack of use. It took almost a minute to open, in which time flames had started to peek between the tiles and smoke billowed out from the front of the building rising over the roof. There was still a lot of shouting from inside and it wouldn't take very long for those in pursuit to determine how we had left.

Creeping through into the dark yard beyond we kept to the wall in the black shadow where the low moon did not reach. We would exit the yard on to the main road hardly a hundred yards from the assailed front of the Kelly Marine. I put my head out first before taking Theresa's hand.

'Stay tight to the wall, single file, we'll turn down Queen Street then run like hell, right?'

She nodded. At the front of the Kelly Marine a window blew out and a huge jet of flame caused the crowd to scatter, distracting them.

'Now' I tugged her arm and hitching up our skirts we ran.

I knew she was capable of running much faster, but she travelled at my speed, not letting go of my hand. She still had the cash box under her arm while I carried the contents of the safe in a bag. Any patrolling policeman could have been forgiven for assuming we were a pair of footpads, unless it was Sergeant Madine who would have seen us on our way for a handful of sovereigns.

A mile and a half from the Kelly Marine our run slowed, first to a trot, then a fast-paced walk and finally a full stop under an archway below a rail bridge. We caught our breath, then walked, senses alert for pursuit or police although we had committed no crime. As the eastern sky turned from black to blue, we reached the docks.

'I don't want to go to Townsville... too risky,' I whispered, although the need to do so was probably over.

'Will ye take two paying passengers?' Theresa called to a uniformed officer who had reached the bottom of a gangplank below an imposing steamship huffing and groaning in captivity, eager to be released from land.

He shrugged his shoulders then inclined his head in an invitation to follow him on board.

'Where...?' I began.

Theresa shrugged, 'Anywhere away from this cursed land, Country Mouse, once and for all, away to safety.'

The Saint Francis steamship was a far cry from the Royal Dane. Just seven years old, she cut through the waters of Moreton Bay and out into the ocean just before dawn with no regard for wind or waves.

The lights of Brisbane peeked through the gaps between Moreton and North Stradbroke Islands. An exhausted, bloodied and blackened Theresa had vanished below, but I remained, alone at the rail. I had to bear witness. A tower of smoke somewhere in the middle of the city curled skywards in the half light. I shook with exhaustion but still stood until the lights blinked out and just one beacon remained, calling out like a siren to the hearts full of hope who still came with their bundles and bags, prayers and promises. Some would thrive and some would be broken. We had dreamed, Enoch and I, of leaving with Charlie, going home, wealthy, successful, having taken on Queensland and won.

I refused myself permission to cry but did so anyway. I whispered into the salty breeze, 'See you soon my darling boy' and then, 'Sleep safe my Dark Angel'. And as I dried my eyes, handkerchief streaked with ash, I took a final look back across the deep orange waves. Moreton Bay Lighthouse had dipped below the horizon.

Australia was gone.

- * -

The End of the Sky

BZ (Bob) Rogers was born in
Wales and attended twenty-eight
schools during his early travelling
years, including William
Shakespeare's alma mater in
Stratford Upon Avon.
His father, from rural North
Wales, spoke no English prior to
army enlistment while his

Anglo/Irish mother had her roots in and around
Cheltenham.

He left school at fourteen, not returning to education
until his mid-thirties when a love of writing led him to
study journalism, leading to a career in newspapers and
broadcasting. A return to university in later life brought
an honours degree and an MA in creative writing.
Drama and comedy commissions from the BBC and
ITV followed. His stage play, Trevor's House, was a
recipient of the London Playmakers Play of the Year
Award and the BBC Radio series, 'Kerr in the
Community' was described by producer Gareth
Gwenlan as one of the all-time funniest he had been
involved with. He also wrote the acclaimed children's
novel, Northwind.

Bob is an active campaigner for animal welfare,
supporting a number of wildlife charities. He shares a
home in South Wales with his London-born partner and
a small menagerie of adopted animals including a deaf
dog, a three-legged cat and a house chicken.

BZ Rogers is represented by Jüri Gabriel Agency of
London.